DANCE WITH ME

Heidi Cullinan

Sometimes life requires a partner.

Ed Maurer has bounced back, more or less, from the neck injury that permanently benched his semipro football career. He hates his soul-killing office job, but he loves volunteering at a local community center. The only fly in his ointment is the dance instructor, Laurie Parker, who can't seem to stay out of his way.

Laurie was once one of the most celebrated ballet dancers in the world, but now he volunteers at Halcyon Center to avoid his society mother's machinations. It would be a perfect escape, except for the oaf of a football player cutting him glares from across the room.

When Laurie has a ballroom dancing emergency and Ed stands in as his partner, their perceptions of each other turn upside down. Dancing leads to friendship, being friends leads to becoming lovers, but most important of all, their partnership shows them how to heal the pain of their pasts. Because with every turn across the floor, Ed and Laurie realize the only escape from their personal demons is to keep dancing—together.

Heidi Cullinan, POB 425, Ames Iowa 50010

Dance With Me
Copyright © 2015 by Heidi Cullinan
ISBN: 978-0-9961203-3-3
Print Edition
Edited by Sasha Knight
Cover by Kanaxa

First publication 2011
First Heidi Cullinan publication 2015
www.heidicullinan.com

*for Susan Danic
and Rebecca Lee*

Acknowledgments

Thanks to Mike Webster for the music, Ricky Jimenez for the football advice and for giving Ed his neck injury, Keith for Minnesota domestic partnership research, and Crystal Thompson for help on navigating the Twin Cities. Thanks to Sue for alpha reading and general cheerleading, Dan, Crystal, Jason, Chris, Cate, Signy and Marie for helping me iron out the kinks in the draft, and Jules for the Hail Mary in act three. Thank you to the Goodreads m/m romance discussion group for the finer points of sex in a hot tub, Marie Sexton for moral support and so much more, and Sean Roberts for translating my football nonsense into something remotely possible. A huge and enduring thanks to the Mary Greeley Medical Center Physical Therapy department for teaching me all the weird ways my body isn't quite doing it right and how to fix that, so I could in turn pass all this on to Ed.

Thanks to Sasha Knight for helping me freshen things up a bit for the second edition, Kanaxa for the *amazing* cover (as usual), and thank you to all the readers who have loved Ed and Laurie as much as I do.

To be fond of dancing was a certain step towards falling in love.
—Jane Austen

Author's Note on the Second Edition

When I wrote this novel, it was 2010, and the world was a very different place for LGBT rights than it is five years later as I publish this second edition. In that time Minnesota has waged two campaigns regarding marriage equality, first one attempting to codify discrimination into their constitution (this measure failed) and then another effort to bring full marriage equality to the state (it succeeded). The United States Supreme Court gave us national marriage equality between the time I sent this second edition to my editor and she returned it to me. LGBT rights have gone from a ripple to a tidal wave. This is to say nothing of the Affordable Care Act, the implementation of which would also have had a huge impact on this story.

This leaves me with a wonderful problem: several of the major plot twists of *Dance With Me* are now technically out of date. The novel is both contemporary and historical, because the aspects of the story focusing on the legal aspects of partnership and logistics of marriage are no longer an issue.

I considered attempting to alter the novel to reflect this shift, but I quickly found it changed too much of the story. *Dance With Me* has become in part an illustration, in a way different than it was when I first drafted it, of why the fight for equality is so important.

OVERTURE

I T WAS THE first game of the summer semipro 2009 football season. The May evening was crisp and cold, but sweat rolled down the back of Ed Maurer's neck as his breath formed in clouds in front of his face guard. The pulse of the crowd burned inside him, the heartbeat of the game beating in time with his own. Ed's body hummed like a piano wire. He'd never been this on, never felt so connected to the game itself. He knew with a certainty he couldn't explain this would be the game of his life.

The ball flew through the air to the wide receiver, who charged the path between Ed and the cornerback. Grinning, Ed headed for the ball as the rush of the game raced like electricity through his veins.

It was the 2005 International Ballroom Championship in Toronto. Only years of training held Laurie Parker together as he waited with Paul in the wings. Tonight he would crack the world like an egg and dance inside it. Tonight he would change the world of dance forever.

The announcer called their names, and Paul led them into the spotlight on the floor. He heard the buzz of the crowd turn to surprise. Beside him, Paul faltered, and Laurie squeezed his arm.

This was how it would start, yes, but it wasn't how it would end. This was their revolution. The music began, Paul took his place, and Laurie gave himself up to the dance.

Ed launched himself at the wide receiver. The impact rattled his bones and sent off a humming inside his ears. For a second he thought the guy might get away, but then his team's cornerback slammed into the receiver and finished what Ed had started. They arced through the air in a strange sideways samba.

Ed tried to roll away, but the shoulder pads didn't make that easy, and all he did was make himself a better obstacle. The wide receiver smashed him flat, his elbow catching the side of Ed's helmet.

That blow wrenched a little, but it didn't hurt. What screwed him was when the receiver rose and rolled off of Ed at the same time as Ed sat up, giving him a face full of cleat and a mouthful of mud. The cleat came down a second time in the corner of his shoulder, caught the base of his helmet, and pushed.

Something grisly cracked in Ed's neck, and when the pain cut through the adrenaline and drilled into his brain, he screamed.

The dance was flawless. They hit every turn, made every leap, executed every step with precision and grace. This was why Laurie had put in months of practice for this routine, why he'd engaged in subterfuge and chicanery to have this chance. He wanted to draw off this last veil, to bring his whole self to the stage.

He didn't want to be Laurence Parker, ballet legend. He didn't want to be the celebrated modern dancer. He didn't want the pinnacle everyone pushed him toward. Not as the Laurie he sometimes felt was not flesh and blood but carved from ivory.

The song ended, and Paul bent Laurie back for the final pose. The pulse of the dance still beat inside him, and he waited for the roar of the crowd.

But the roar didn't come.

The crowd's murmurs were dark and angry, not full of wonder. Frowning, Laurie looked to the judges' table and saw the head of the organizing committee speaking intensely to the panel, glancing occasionally out at the floor.

The pain cut across Ed's neck and shot out in lethal tendrils to explode inside his shoulder, back and head. Somewhere far away a whistle blew, but Ed knew only pain. Pain like he'd never known, pain that scraped at his bones, pain that made it feel as if his teeth were melting.

By the time the paramedics put Ed on a stretcher, the pain was so intense he threw up, but retching made the pain worse. Every movement increased the pain, and he knew by the time they got him into the ambulance he'd pass out.

A shadow appeared beside the stretcher, and a familiar voice sobbed his name. *Mom.* That was his mom. But her voice sounded watery to his ears.

The lights above Ed went out, and darkness descended on a final wave of pain.

Worried and needing reassurance, Laurie reached for Paul's hand. But Paul moved away. The murmur of the crowd grew louder, sending fear down Laurie's spine. The committee head strode toward them, grim and unsmiling.

"I should never have let you talk me into this." Paul's voice trembled with fear and rage.

The committee head stepped forward into their spotlight, and the cold fury in her features doused the last of Laurie's now-very-fragile hope.

She pointed to the doors, where large, gruff security waited to escort them out of the building.

Laurie walked through the crowded hall in a daze. Cameras flashed. Reporters' microphones thrust forward. The press kept up with their every step, wolves waiting for the kill. Waiting for Laurie.

This was Paul's sport, but Laurie was Laurence Parker, the internationally famous ballet star. He'd entered as Laurie, and they'd assumed he was female. Drama. Deceit. Scandal. The story practically wrote itself.

Laurie didn't engage them. He climbed into the waiting car and ordered the driver to take them away from the arena and back to his hotel. He didn't relax against the seat but kept himself rigid as he rode across the city to the safety of his hotel suite.

He unplugged the phone and took the room's portable stereo into the bathroom. With comforting music playing softly in the echoing space, Laurie stepped into the shower, felt the water slide across his face, and let his ivory mask fall.

CHAPTER ONE

*abrazo: the dance hold, or embrace, in the
Argentine tango.*

October 2010

ED MAURER TAPPED his thumb on his steering wheel as he inched through Twin Cities traffic, sloughing off a rough afternoon as he headed to Halcyon Center.

Three more people from his department had cleaned out their desks, the latest victims of corporate downsizing. Ed had been torn between feeling bad for them and feeling fucking relieved he hadn't been one of them. His neck was a little stiffer than it should be, especially since he'd taken four ibuprofen half an hour ago. But that was probably stress.

He did his best to put work out of his mind, because tonight was going to be fantastic. Tonight he was going to be a teacher to some great kids who didn't get enough support and help in life. His volunteer work at the center made him feel good, useful in a way he hadn't in a long, long time.

His mood dimmed as he caught a glimpse of the playing fields off Payne Avenue and saw two guys tossing a football back and forth. His gaze lingered there longer than it should have, both for safety and for the preservation of his fragile optimism. As if it knew his thoughts, his neck sent a sharp twinge down the long, vulnerable cord of muscle.

Ed forced his eyes onto the road. After a few seconds, he reached for the MP3 player hooked up to his stereo. Fumbling through the music between glances at the street, he punched at the machine until he found the song he wanted. He didn't calm until a breathy voice declared, "It's Britney, bitch."

At Halcyon, Ed pulled into a parking spot, grabbed his duffel and his notes, and headed into the building. He winked at the receptionist, grinned at an old buddy and tossed him a cheery, "Heya!" and high-five. As he ducked into the locker room, he sang under his breath.

"Oh, fucking A, somebody's singin' Britney Spears. Look out. Maurer's here."

Ed laughed and waved in the direction of the voice without looking. He saw the young man who had spoken to him out of the corner of his eye, a dark, overly clothed shadow leaning against the line of lockers. "What's up, Duon? You keeping out of trouble?"

"Fuck, no."

Ed glanced at him, making sure he didn't let his gaze linger too long, because Duon got mad when people checked up on him. But a cursory glance revealed a bruised cheek and a cut beneath Duon's right eye. Ed grimaced. "Vicky see that shiner yet?"

Duon snorted. "Yes. Called the fucking cops. Like they're gonna care."

Ed tried for levity. "Need to find yourself a big strapping boyfriend to protect you."

"Fuck you, bitch. *I'm* the big strapping boyfriend." He folded his arms over his chest and glared at Ed.

Fighting a smile, Ed unbuttoned his shirt before hanging it in his locker. "You coming to my class tonight?"

"Maybe." Duon came over to sprawl at the end of the bench. "Damn, man, but I hope I can stay as buff as you when I get old."

Ed turned his head to explain with full eye contact that thirty-four was *not* old—but he winced instead as his neck exploded in pain. For a few terrible seconds, he couldn't see or hear anything at all.

When his vision cleared, Duon stood in front of him, looking at Ed with wide, worried eyes. "Shit, man. You okay?"

Ed rubbed the muscle, careful not to fire it up again. "Fine." He rolled his shoulder, pain easing with each successive rotation, eventually settling into a dull roar. "I'm fine."

"You need to get your ass back to that doctor."

"It's already calming down." He started to nod at Duon then changed the gesture to a wave of his hand instead. "Go on. I gotta get ready. Swing by the copy room and find those waiver forms for me, will you?"

Duon was clearly reluctant to leave Ed, but he did, and once he was gone, Ed sagged briefly against the locker next to his own. Then he squared his shoulders and his resolve, and finished getting dressed.

Ed's whistle was a bit forced as he finally ducked into the hall, his notes tucked under his arm. He tried to get his game back. He was going to go teach a class, and it was going to be fucking great. He turned the corner and headed for the weight room.

Music blared down the hall from the main gym, shitty house music circa 1997 made worse by being pumped through the P.A. system. Over the top of it came a shrill, insistent call of "And one, and two, and three. Work it, ladies!"

The nasal tones hit something primal in Ed's hind-brain, making his neck light up. Wincing, Ed double-timed it to the weight room, muttering under his breath, "*No.* Not again. Not *tonight.*"

But the same ear-splitting cacophony from the hallway blared into the weight room too, and unlike in the hall, here the music wasn't muted. Nobody who wasn't completely deaf could stand to stay in the room for more than five minutes, let alone teach a class.

Ed swore under his breath. Then he headed up the stairs to Vicky's office.

Halcyon Center's director was on the phone when Ed stuck his head through the gap in her door, but she waved him in and motioned toward the chairs on the opposite side of her desk without so much as missing a beat in her conversation. Ed entered, but he didn't sit. He took in the smiling faces of the local gymnastics team's poster and a Minnesota Gophers basketball calendar, but he was mostly using the images as focal points to calm his rage.

Vicky hung up the phone and turned to Ed, but Ed was so agitated he couldn't wait for her to invite him to speak.

"It's happening again." Ed pointed in the general direction of the gymnasium. "He's playing music over the P.A., and it's piping into the weight room. It's even louder than it was the last time."

Vicky pursed her lips and reached for a notepad. "I'll have Bob look into it first thing in the morning."

"But my class starts in ten minutes."

"We'll have to cancel it for tonight. I'll make sure they have it sorted out by next week."

"Why can't *he* get cancelled? He's the one making all the noise."

"Because that class has ninety people in it paying fifty dollars a head for eight weeks to hear him make his noise." Vicky glanced at him over the top of her glasses. "This place is nonprofit, but tell that to the light bill. When your weight class brings in that kind of cash, you'll get that kind of treatment too."

"Vicky, my class is never going to bring in money. Come on, Vic. It's my *first real class* on my own. I've been looking forward to this for a month, and now you're telling me to go home and watch TV?"

"I'll make sure it's fixed for next time. I swear. Even if I have to ask Laurie to cut his class short by a half hour." When Ed perked up, she held up a hand before he could ask. "I can't ask tonight. He's going to need to be finessed after how badly you riled him up the last time. If he even *thinks* this might be coming from you, it's never going to happen at all."

"I still don't see why he can't bring in a sound system of his own."

"Because it's a huge, echoing gym, and nothing portable would work. All we have to offer him is the P.A. You know damn well that anything worth ten bucks around here gets stolen."

"What about that old system in the storeroom off the stage?"

"It shorts out half the time, so it's practically useless. Laurie does this for free as a favor to me, and, once again, he brings in a lot of money for the center. He's also a good friend, has been for years. We still get together every so often to discuss our mutual love of Barbra Streisand. And don't turn up your nose at me, football-player-who-listens-to-Britney-Spears."

"She's just misunderstood," Ed grumbled.

"Be that as it may, I can't prioritize your class over his. I'm sorry, Ed, but this is the way it's got to be."

Ed slumped his shoulders briefly in defeat, then nodded. "Okay."

Vicky eyed him suspiciously. "You never give in that easily. What are you planning?"

Ed held up his hands and shook his head. "Not a thing, I swear."

Which was true. He didn't have a plan.

Yet.

Vicky tapped her pencil on the open ledger on her desk. "Can you promise me I'll still have my extremely lucrative aerobics class after whatever ill-advised thing you're about to do?"

"Oh, yeah." Probably.

"With my exceptionally affordable instructor still at its head?"

"Not a problem." Except boy would that be a lovely thought, no more Laurie.

Her eyes narrowed. "Do you promise I will not be interrupted in the middle of my phone meeting with a coordinator for a potential grant by a harangue about the bumbling Neanderthal who doesn't know his place?"

Ed's eyebrows went up at the "who doesn't know his place" comment, but he nodded. "No calls, Vic. I swear."

Vicky tapped her pencil a few more times before sighing and leaning back in her chair. "All right. But make sure I have plausible deniability."

"Promise." Ed grinned over his shoulder as he exited the room. "Good luck with your meeting."

"Goodbye, Ed," Vicky called without looking up.

Ed saluted, then headed for the gym.

LA BOUCHE PULSED through the gym as Ed pushed his way through, some remix of "Be My Lover". Generally Ed preferred to leave the nineties right where he'd left them, but he had to admit, this song always made his toe tap.

Of course, not once in his memory had the song come with a hyped-up chipmunk with a mic screaming over the top of it.

Laurence Parker was some big-time dance instructor whose family lived in Medina and who used to dance on Broadway or something. He was everything Ed hated in a man: rich, from the suburbs, and a freaking billboard for gay stereotypes. His whole life Ed had fought the "gay is girly" shit, and he was damn sick of it. Gay could also mean a semipro football player. Who listened to Britney, yeah, but he knew a few of the other guys on the team who did too. Really, Ed was a pretty macho guy who happened to be gay.

Not *Laurie*.

He was overly feminine both in his looks and his gestures. He was a dancer and an aerobics instructor. He fussed about getting dirty. He was stylish and graceful.

He listened to Barbra Streisand.

They weren't great reasons to hate somebody, but Ed got his back up every time their paths crossed. So far in the month Ed had been coming to the center, they'd fought over Ed's mess in the locker room, space on the bulletin board, whether or not it was unhygienic of Ed to spit into the drinking fountain, whether or not everyone from the suburbs was a pompous ass, the relative merits of dancing and football, and above all, the volume of the music Laurie used to accompany his classes.

This wasn't the first time the P.A. system had failed to work the way the maintenance people swore it was wired to. On other nights when he was in the weight room with a client, Ed had been content to vent his spleen and make Parker as worked up as he was. Sometimes he'd managed to get the volume turned down, but that was it.

Tonight was different, and so tonight he planned to make his approach differently. To start, he smiled as he wove his way to Laurie through the throng of sweaty, flailing, middle-aged women. But Laurie didn't smile back.

"No." Laurie flipped up the mouthpiece of the mic, still stepping from side to side in time to the music. "No, I will not turn down my music. No, it is not my fault the system keeps screwing up. No, I will not use a CD player, because I can't. And yes, I have to count, because *that's the way we do it in aerobics class.*" He gave Ed a withering look. "Did I miss anything? Or have you thought up some new idiotic objections?"

"I'm teaching a class too." Ed nodded to the hall. "In the weight room. In five minutes. Where right now no one can stand to be for more than ten seconds because it sounds like the aerobics class from hell."

"It's *not my fault—*"

"No, it's not. But you're the only one who can do anything about it right now. I want to know what it takes to get you to use a different sound system for tonight."

Laurie pursed his lips. "There is no other—"

"There is, actually. It's old, and it's fussy, but it would work for one night. This class of mine isn't like training somebody where I can go out to the hall and explain something and then use sign language to communicate in the weight room itself. I need them to hear me."

"Tell them to come back next week when the system is fixed."

"I have as much right to be here as you do. You get your way every time this happens. It's your turn to bend over."

The look Laurie gave Ed could have cut glass.

"I'm sacrificing too," Ed said quickly, because he honestly did not want to piss Laurie off further until he got what he was after. "So I want to know: what is it you need? Something here at the center, something outside of the center, you name it. Your car washed and waxed while you direct me from a lawn chair, your flowerbed dug up, whatever. What do you need?"

Laurie regarded Ed thoughtfully for a few beats. "You *really* want it this time, don't you?"

"I do. Surely you can think of some suitably degrading task you'd love to give the meddling Neanderthal in exchange for one half of one night on a subpar sound system."

Laurie blushed and looked away. "She wasn't supposed to tell you I said that."

"Give me something. Anything. Something embarrassing. I'm never going to give you a better opening than this. Anything, buddy. *Anything.*"

For a minute Laurie seemed haunted and oddly vulnerable. "Anything?"

"*Anything.*"

Laurie's expression became hard again. "What I need is for you to come one night a week and be my assistant at my dance studio."

Ed blinked. Dancing assistant? "What night?"

"Tuesdays. Seven to eight. For five weeks."

Ed grinned. "Consider it done."

"There's more."

Ed rolled his eyes. "Then tell me already. My class is about to start."

"As my assistant, mostly you'll be dancing with me."

Ed shrugged. "Okay. Is that all?"

Laurie regarded him with extreme suspicion. "*You* will dance with *me*. Just like that?"

"Do I have to do it naked or something?"

"I'm serious about this. So if your plan is to agree now, get your way, and then stand me up—"

"If I'm not there, you can go to Vic to get your pound of flesh. You know she'll be good for it. Now, can I get you the damn sound system?"

When Laurie nodded in reluctant approval, Ed hurried to the stage. But before he had half the equipment out, he felt a hand on his arm. Laurie was there, holding out a business card.

"You'll lose your class time. I'll do it. Here, take this, and go."

Ed stopped with one speaker hoisted in midair and raised an eyebrow.

Laurie pressed the card into his hand. "Six forty-five next Tuesday at the address on this card. Wear comfortable clothing and dress shoes with a heel. If you do this for me, it really will be a favor, and I don't mind hauling out the equipment and pausing my class to do it. But if you *don't* show up, I'll collect the pound of flesh myself."

"Fair enough." Ed put the speaker down, pocketed the card and stuck out his hand. "Thanks, buddy."

Laurie put his hand in Ed's, his slim fingers swallowed in Ed's beefy paw. "You're welcome."

"See you at quarter to seven on Tuesday," he called out, breaking into a jog and vaulting off the edge of the stage for his class.

CHAPTER TWO

*fantasia: flamboyant style of tango used
for performance.*

TWO DAYS AFTER giving his card to Ed at aerobics class, Laurie sat in traffic, trying to convince himself he shouldn't get Ed's number and call his favor off.

On a good day it was a thirty-minute drive from Laurie's studio in Eden Prairie to his family's house in Medina, but when it was rush hour, Laurie could plan on adding at least another fifteen minutes as he joined the SUVs and midlife-crisis convertibles on their treks home. Today all the tops were up on the convertibles, however, because an arctic air mass had forced Indian summer to give way to October cold. Laurie turned the heater on full blast, which meant the fan was so loud he could barely hear Robert Siegel's comforting delivery of more bad news about the economy over the airwaves of Minnesota Public Radio.

The cold, traffic and regret over his arrangement

with Ed made an already unpleasant errand so unpalatable he had nearly turned off three times at different exits and gone to his apartment instead of dinner with his parents. If he thought he could come up with an excuse his mother would buy, he might have bailed. But if he did, this dinner party would happen on a different day, and between now and then he would need to deal with increasingly aggressive maneuvers by his mother. Best to get it over with.

He dallied, however, getting off at Shoreline Drive to drive past Lake Minnetonka. The lake was beautiful at sunset, and Laurie slowed down as much as he dared so he could drink it in. He used to take this drive all the time in high school. He'd come here when he was upset, which was admittedly often. While other kids were out getting drunk and getting laid, Laurie had parked alone along the shore, staring out across the water, dreaming of the day he would get out of Minnesota.

Now here he was, back again.

Laurie parked the car where he could look out over the water, leaving the vehicle running, though he did turn down the heater fan so he could hear himself think. In afterthought, he turned off the radio as well. The past was starting to make him feel morose, so he thought about the present instead: about his mother's party and Ed Maurer.

The two made strange bedfellows, and for a moment Laurie smiled. Polished, china-beautiful Caroline

Parker and big, brutish Ed Maurer. He imagined show-ing up at the party, Ed, his workout clothes damp with sweat as he broadcast his crude humor, Laurie's mother in her cream-and-beige pantsuit and pearls, slender hands folded together in front of her as she tried not to show how horrified she was. For a minute, Laurie wished he'd asked Ed to be his date tonight instead of asking him to help with the ballroom dance class.

Which was a flatly ridiculous thought. Why would he bring Ed to his parents' house? To be insulted in front of people he knew for a change? And *why* had he asked Ed to be his assistant in that ballroom class?

Maggie, his co-owner of the studio, had accidentally overbooked herself and asked Laurie to take the group as a favor. A bunch of old couples from her church wanting to be able to dance for a cruise. Laurie had thought after all this time it wouldn't bother him, that teaching ballroom would be the same as teaching anything else.

He'd been wrong. It bothered him a lot. He was a lousy ballroom teacher, and each session brought back so many bad memories he went home and huddled under his comforter in the dark every single time. He was in such a state that sparring with Ed was preferable to going to class.

When Ed had asked if Laurie needed a favor, he'd thought Ed as his ballroom partner would diffuse the situation. Except it was a stupid idea on so many levels. Did he really want Ed Maurer making snide remarks when he was already feeling vulnerable? This was to say nothing of what the Baptist blue-hair brigade would think of Laurie dancing with a man. What the devil had possessed him? How had that ever seemed like a good plan?

Determined to put this fire out before it started, he reached for his phone and scrolled through his address book. Vicky answered on the third ring. "Hey, Laurie. What's up?"

"I'm at Lake Minnetonka on my way to one of my mother's partics."

"Wish I were there with you and not buried in paperwork. Though I can't say I'd want to go visit your mother. You're going? Voluntarily?"

"Command performance. She has something to show me."

"Uh-oh. Well, at least it won't be a blind date."

Laurie rubbed his thumb against the steering wheel, watching the leather dimple under the pressure. "Say, Vicky, would you happen to have a phone number for Ed Maurer you could give me?"

"Shit. What the hell did he do to you now?"

"Nothing. He was going to do something *for* me, but I changed my mind and need to let him know."

"Sure. I don't have his number handy though. Can I text it?"

"That'd be fine." He glanced at the dashboard clock and grimaced. "I need to get going. It's later than I thought. But I'd really appreciate the phone number."

"You got it." She paused. "You sure everything's okay?"

Everything wasn't fine, but he didn't want to get into that now. "Don't worry about it."

"Well, if you need me to kick his cocky ass for you, let me know."

Laurie smiled. "I'll bear that in mind. Thanks, Vicky."

"Anytime, hon."

Laurie lingered a few more minutes with his wrist resting on the wheel as he stared out over the water. A beep on his phone drew him out of his reverie, and he looked down to see the display announce he had a new text. He clicked it, saw Ed's number. Then he turned the radio back on and headed to his parents' house.

Everyone in the area called his family's house and grounds "the Parker estate", which he'd thought was cool until he was fourteen and his mother had taken him to a mansion in Upstate New York to meet a dancing master. Once he came home from seeing a life of real opulence, his family's wealth, while not inconsiderable, suddenly seemed mundane. After all the traveling he had done over the years he'd spent touring, Medina had become shabbier and shabbier, nothing more than a copycat playing at the success of the rest of the world.

To his parents' friends, the Parker home, estate or otherwise, was a crown jewel of the neighborhood. Frequently these little parties turned into champagne-drenched fêtes of fifty people or more. It was only a moderate crowd tonight, judging by the number of expensive cars in the driveway, but once he'd parked his own vehicle and headed for the front door, he got a glimpse of the guests inside and grew as apprehensive as if it had been a crush.

There were a few locals, and Laurie's godfather Oliver and his partner, and almost everyone else were people connected to the local arts scene. Several of them he would swear were dancers. They had The Look about them. And if his mother had invited dancers to her party, this was a gathering Laurie didn't want to be a part of.

Caroline Parker appeared from a crowd in the living room and came forward to embrace Laurie lightly with a cheek pressed to his instead of a kiss. "You're late." Her tone was light, but the tighter-than-necessary grip on his arm made it clear she was not amused by his attempt at delay.

The Parkers did not have servants beyond a housekeeper who came in three times a week, but for events of any importance Laurie's mother always hired staff, and one of those employees hired for this evening came forward to politely ask Laurie if he could take his coat.

"Just mingle and smile," she murmured in his ear as she led him toward another cluster of people in the dining room. "I'll take care of the rest."

There was no point in telling his mother he didn't

want anything taken care of. She wouldn't argue with him, not in front of everyone, and she wouldn't step into the study and indulge him, either. She had him neatly trapped, because he couldn't leave without causing a new scandal, and this guest list, however accepting they might be, had to be at least partly expecting such a scene from him.

He saw it in their eyes as he clutched his champagne glass and made mindless small talk with the parade of guests who came up to poke at him and see what happened. None of their attempts worked, of course. If they were too pointed, his mother deflected them, and if they didn't take the hint, his father was drawn in to shift the subject to business or sports. She tossed out hints he might open up a chain of dance studios across the cities, which he had no intention of doing, but that hardly mattered to his mother. If he argued with her, she'd dismiss his protests as him being cagey.

Laurie told them about his Eden Prairie studio, softening his mother's descriptions, and the game went on. She embellished, he downplayed, and between the two stories his accomplishments appeared greater than they were, and he looked humble. It was the same routine she'd used since he was ten, but it still worked. By the time dinner was served, several of the guests had put business cards in his pocket, either because they wanted to invest in his franchise or because they had a niece they wanted on his waiting lists.

He supposed he should thank his mother, but all he could think of right now was how much he wanted to take her out to the stables and string her up by one of the beams.

She seated him at dinner beside Oliver, which was a small gift. Oliver Thompson was a longtime family friend and an influential member of the Hennepin Theatre Trust. He was also Laurie's godfather, though Caroline was always the first to remark how lackluster he'd been in his performance of this role until Laurie had come out to him.

Though Caroline never much cared for Laurie's "flaunting" of the few male companions he'd brought to her parties, Oliver was here with his longtime partner Christopher, and Laurie's mother treated both of them as if they were royalty deigning to pay her a favor of their attendance. This was because in addition to being heinously rich, Oliver was even more influential and manipulative than Caroline.

"I keep asking your mother when you're going to let us book your comeback show." He scrubbed his graying mustache discreetly with his napkin before returning it to his lap. "She tells me tonight I might have a decent chance at succeeding."

Laurie crushed his own napkin tightly in his hands. "I don't have any wish to return to the stage. I'm quite happy as a teacher." He reached for his wine and took a deeper drink than was polite to drown the lie. No, he wasn't happy. But he knew very well he wasn't going to be any happier returning to the stage.

As he scanned the table, he caught sight of his father. Albert Parker leaned in to listen to someone, a man whose name Laurie couldn't remember but whom he thought was a senior executive at some Minneapolis-based corporation. Albert's gray-blue eyes sparkled with interest, and a ghost of a smile played around his lips. There was joy there, real interest, and it was such a stark contrast from the removal Laurie usually knew in his father that for a moment he lost himself, watching.

Oliver nudged his arm. "You're the only one who thinks the incident still matters."

Blinking, Laurie pulled himself out of the spell watching his father had cast on him and pasted on a dry smile for Oliver's benefit. *The incident.* God, he hated when people called it that. Laurie scanned the table, taking in the speculative gazes being discreetly and overtly cast at him over wineglasses. "Oh, you think it doesn't matter, do you?"

Oliver sighed. "You're the one making it an issue. If you behaved as if it wasn't a problem, it wouldn't be one."

"I just want a quiet life."

"Quiet is overrated." Oliver lowered his voice. "At least you should come to one of *my* parties again. And this time don't leave before the entertainment begins."

On Oliver's other side, Christopher stifled a laugh with his napkin. Laurie blushed ferociously. "Thank you, but hot-tub orgies aren't quite my style."

Oliver grunted in dismissal. "My parties aren't orgies. Just a few friends having a good time."

Memory of two tipsy young men naked and clutching each other in the water while Oliver watched made Laurie shiver. It upset him that he couldn't decide if he was disgusted or aroused. "Your parties are why people are prejudiced against us."

"Better to dance with the devil and enjoy yourself than hover under the glower of nuns." He stabbed at a thin slice of veal. "Enjoy your life, Laurie. Don't squander it. Start by letting me hire you for *The Nutcracker* performance this year."

"What?" Laurie hadn't expected this turn of the conversation.

"You make a lovely Prince, and you can do the part in your sleep. And it would keep your mother happy for a few months at least."

Laurie snorted. "No. It would only encourage her." Then he frowned. "Wait. You don't have the Prince hired yet? The performance is in less than two months."

Oliver pursed his lips. "The dancer I hired cancelled on me last week. I've lined up a few replacements, but none of them are as good, and all of them want more money than they deserve plus travel. The Sugar Plum Fairy is Arietta Poychna, and her going rate makes me sweat just thinking about it. We talked about giving the part to one of the youth, and it's a possibility, but it rather ruins the spirit of the performance. It's meant to be a highlight of local talent, crowned with adult professionals as role models." He looked slightly abashed. "I admit, I asked your mother if she could convince you to do it as a favor to me. The trust is hurting this year. It would be a real boon if you did this. You'd bring in more ticket revenue, and of course, not having to pay either a salary or the travel fees would help a great deal."

Laurie took another drink. *Exquisitely done, Mother.* Laurie would look like a heel for not helping the trust when they were in trouble. *But to get back on stage after five years.* His hand shook, and he set the glass down. Yes, it was just a local performance with Twin Cities children, but it was a higher profile than Laurie wanted.

A guest watched him from farther down the table. He was young, early twenties at best. A dancer, surely, and from the way he was looking at Laurie, he'd heard the stories.

Ran off to Toronto and tried to foist same-sex dancing on the international championships. Huge scandal. Didn't perform for six months, but when he did, it was a disaster. Fell apart right there in the middle of the stage. No one could believe it. Such a bright future ahead of him, and now it's over. What a shame.

But whoever this dancer was, he'd decided it was worth risking the crazy to ride on Laurie's reputation, because he winked and smiled. When Laurie didn't turn away, he inclined his head to the French doors leading to the patio and raised his eyebrows in both question and invitation.

Laurie looked away. "Fine. I'll do it, but only because it's you and because it's the trust. Please make it clear, however, it's a one-time thing."

He'd work out later how he was going to get himself onstage without falling into a panic.

Oliver squeezed Laurie's shoulder. "Thank you. I'm more grateful than I can say. Let me know if there's a way I can repay you."

He wanted to tell Oliver he could repay him by never asking him anything like this again, but that would be rude, so he simply smiled, toasted Oliver's glass with his own, and tried to drown the realization of what he'd just agreed to.

LAURIE NEVER DID manage to call Ed and cancel, which only made his standing Laurie up on Tuesday an all-the-more-bitter pill to swallow.

He hadn't had a chance to call him on Saturday night, as by the time he got to his apartment he'd been good for nothing but sitting in front of the television with a pint of Chubby Hubby and a well-used DVD of *What's Up, Doc?* On Sunday he'd tried to work up the courage to call, but each time he'd thought about facing the class alone and found he couldn't pick up the phone. He told himself he'd call on Monday, but he didn't, and in a fit of extreme stupidity, he deleted the text from Vicky so he *couldn't* call.

Now here he was, so strung out he was ready to run across the street to the convenience store and buy a package of cigarettes, and Ed was nowhere to be seen.

A soft hand fell on his shoulder, startling him. He relaxed when he saw it was only Maggie. "Sorry, I'm a bit keyed up. I should never have agreed to take this class."

"I still don't understand why ballroom bothers you so much. Especially when it's teaching this group. It's grandmas and grandpas from First Baptist wanting to learn a little rumba. Don't make it into a federal case, because it isn't one." She smiled. "I hear you're going to dance in *The Nutcracker*. It's going to be such good publicity for the studio."

Yes, and such personal hell for me. Laurie glanced at the clock, deciding to change the subject. "I was supposed to have an assistant tonight, but it looks like he's going to stand me up, unfortunately."

"Assistant?" Maggie sounded amused, but then her smile fell. "Wait—*he*? Oh, *Laurie*. What's gotten into you? You're bent out of shape because of what happened in the past, so you're going to have your assistant be a *man*? With a bunch of Baptists?"

"It doesn't matter, because he isn't going to show. Though if you must know, yes, I'd planned to dance with him. I'm more comfortable following than leading in ballroom."

Maggie's sigh was full of exasperation. Before she could scold him again, however, the door to the studio burst open and Ed Maurer came breezing in with a wide grin on his face.

"Hey." He grinned at Maggie as he peeled out of his jacket, nodded at Laurie. "Here I am, boss." He rubbed his hands together. "Where do you want me?"

Maggie's mouth fell open as she took in Ed—big, lunky, disheveled-even-in-dress-pants Ed. It was a reaction Laurie enjoyed, he had to admit. *Not what you were expecting, sweetie?* But he wasn't in the mood for any more nonsense, so he said, "Your class is waiting, Maggie."

She gave him a scathing glance but headed for the door. "We'll talk later."

Laurie waved blithely at her, but once the door to the studio closed, he turned to Ed and glared. "You're late."

Ed looked at the clock and rolled his eyes. "Fine. I'm three minutes late by your clock, which is five minutes fast by the one in my car. I'll give you three minutes past eight to make up for it. You happy now?"

No, Laurie wanted to shoot back, but he bit his tongue and inspected his assistant's dancing attire instead. Ed wore khakis and a T-shirt, a black one that hugged his muscled body and made his shoulders bulge. His pants, though slightly wrinkled, gathered loosely at the waist and tapered all the way to his ankles. As Laurie moved around to Ed's backside, he noticed they were also nicely snug in the seat.

He had to admit, Ed had done well. Pursing his lips, Laurie pointed at Ed's feet. "Show me your shoes."

Ed arched an eyebrow and picked up his left foot like a flamingo, revealing his inch-and-a-half high-heeled black loafers. "This do, boss?"

Laurie gave him a withering glare. "Do not call me *boss.*"

"This do, Laurence?"

He came around to face Ed. "This is a beginning ballroom dancing class for husbands and wives. It's not going well, and they only have five weeks left. The men in particular are struggling. Their wives try to compensate for them, which makes everything worse. I show them the part by dancing with their partner, but they aren't getting it. And they're all from a conservative Baptist church, so when I try to dance with the men, they act like I'm trying to stick my tongue down their throat, and everything deteriorates from there."

Ed frowned. "So you want *me* to dance with them?"

"No." Laurie pursed his lips. "You'll dance with me, to demonstrate."

"But how is that going to help? And why ask me instead of some woman?"

Because the real problem isn't them, it's me. Because I keep having panic attacks, and I can't let any other dancer see that. Because the only women I know well enough to ask who aren't dancers are my mother, who is out of the question, and Vicky, who is too busy. Because, frankly, I dance the following part much better than lead, and right now I need every leg up I can get.

He crossed to the barre. "Forget it. I should have

called you and canceled, but I didn't have your number. Go ahead and leave."

Laurie saw Ed coming toward him in the mirror and braced himself against the barre as Ed bore down on him. "Listen, buddy, I came all the way across town for this. You wanted an assistant, and now you've got one."

"This is a mistake. I don't know why I asked you. You can't even dance."

This time both Ed's eyebrows came up. "Is that so?"

Oh, God, Laurie wished he could hit him. "I'm not talking about jiggling around with some bimbo at Club Drunk. I'm talking about the waltz. The foxtrot. The tango. *Ballroom* dancing."

"How about you give me some instructions and we see what happens?"

Laurie pulled the towel off his neck and dabbed at the beads of sweat on his forehead before crossing the room to get the bottle of water he kept on the shelf beside the sound system. "Fine. Stay. Go. Whatever you want."

Ed tucked his hands in his pockets. "How'd it go the other night? With the speakers?"

It had been a mess. Laurie had ended up canceling class and telling them he'd add another twenty minutes to their next session. "It went fine."

"Good." He rocked on his heels. "Never danced ballroom with a guy before. This will be interesting."

"You don't have to. I told you that."

"Didn't say I minded. Just said I hadn't." He gave Laurie a critical glance. "You okay, boss?"

"I'm fine." Laurie made a production of recapping the bottle of water. He didn't feel as sick now, which was good, but the butterflies were still wild in his stomach. These, however, he knew he could attribute fully to Ed. He hadn't known being alone in a room with him would make him feel so uncomfortable. *And now you're going to dance with him.*

"What do you do, Ed? When you aren't lifting weights and terrorizing my aerobics class?"

"I work at Best Buy headquarters. Corporate drone."

"Really? I would have pegged you for something a bit more…active."

"Oh, I used to play semipro football for the Minnesota Lumberjacks."

Football. That made more sense. "Where did you play? Somewhere up north?"

Ed laughed. "No. Here, in the Twin Cities. Semipro isn't a paying gig, only a summer football league."

"You say you used to. Why aren't you playing semi-football now?"

"Semipro. And I'm not playing because I hurt my neck." He made a vicious wrenching motion with both his hands. "Damn near twisted my head off and got a concussion to boot. Doctors said if I get hit there one more time it'd be the end of not only football but maybe walking too, and maybe even feeding myself. So football's done."

Laurie glanced at the dance floor, worried.

Ed's perpetually sunny disposition soured. "Oh, I'm all healed up now. Bouts of irritation every so often, but that's it."

Laurie'd had no idea about any of this. He felt a little bad for Ed, not because Laurie gave a damn about football, but because he knew about leaving a career you loved, and he couldn't help his empathy. "Did the class go well the other night?"

Ed gave him another smile. "Yeah. Thanks."

Laurie blushed and turned away in relief when the door opened. "The students are arriving. Wait at the barre, and I'll call you over when I'm ready for you."

The couples entered in clusters as they usually did—Laurie suspected they lingered in the parking lot until they found a buddy couple to enter with. Even if they hadn't been here for ballroom, these couples wouldn't be his favorite students. Allegedly they were going on some cruise ship where they all planned to dance. From the evidence of their collective girth, Laurie personally doubted they would venture much farther than the buffet, but he didn't voice that thought out loud. He squelched the snarky voice that wanted to tear down his clients inside his head and smiled, holding the gesture in place as he waited for the hands of the clock to edge their way to the top of the hour.

There seemed to be some benefit to having Ed in

the room, because even though he was still and silent at the back, Laurie was highly aware of his presence, and instead of having irrational upset over explaining the steps of a waltz, he was obsessed with wondering what Ed was thinking, wondering why he stayed, if he was going to make some snide comment and undermine him in front of his students. But Ed said nothing and did nothing, and the next thing Laurie knew, it was time to begin.

He started them off with the rumba.

"Quick, quick, slow. Mr. Gerisher, quick, quick, *slow*. You turn on slow. Not quick."

It was the box throwing them. They could organize their legs well enough to move backward and forward, and they could do the turns when they did them on their own, but if he made them face each other, they did nothing but stumble. Laurie had tried it with and without music, and he'd counted down so slowly turtles would have looked dapper attempting the maneuvers. He stood beside them, ghosting the steps they should take. He guided them one by one, gentling his tone until he was so calm and quiet they had to be straining to hear him. No matter what he did, they still couldn't get it.

This was just the *rumba.*

As usual, as he taught the past crept up on him. He thought about Paul, about the last time he'd done ballroom, about that ridiculous horrible night, reliving it as if it were his own personal foxhole. The panic filled him, and as had become his custom, now he fought not only their bad skill but his own ghosts.

Out of nowhere, someone tapped his shoulder. Ed stood there, expectant. "As your assistant, I thought I should offer to assist." Ed frowned as he ran his gaze over Laurie. "Anyway, you seemed kind of pale. I was worried you'd fall over."

Finding out he appeared as unhinged as he felt didn't help. Laurie shoved a hand through his hair and pursed his lips. "I don't think—"

Ed held up his arms, inviting Laurie into his space. Then he lifted an eyebrow and switched, holding his right up instead of his left. "Unless you wanted to lead?" When Laurie hesitated, Ed rolled his eyes. "Come on. You gave up your sound system to have me stand at the back of the room and watch you be over-tired and frustrated?"

"Who is this?" Mrs. Anderson asked, regarding Ed with suspicion.

"The assistant." Ed gave her a winsome grin. Mrs. Anderson blushed and smiled back, and Ed turned to Laurie once more. "So, boss? You ready?"

God, no. Laurie raised his right hand but stopped short of putting it in Ed's left, and his left hand hovered over his partner's shoulder. "Do you have any idea what you're doing?"

"Quick, quick, slow." Ed captured Laurie's raised hand, settling his other along Laurie's shoulder. "Piece of cake."

To his surprise, Laurie found himself confidently steered across the floor, perfectly executing the box turn his students had failed to grasp.

Ed winked. "Under-arm turn?"

Before Laurie could protest, he was spun expertly beneath Ed's arm and out again.

Memory, always ready with daggers on these nights, sent him briefly five years into the past to that fateful night in Toronto, and for a moment he saw the crowd, the lights, the judges, felt the strong, steady grip of Paul's hand. Then he came back, finishing the turn not in his former lover's embrace, but Ed Maurer's. He stumbled, then with a deep breath and iron will, brought himself back to the beat.

"So," Laurie said when he was recovered enough to speak. "You know how to dance."

"Nope. I was recently told by someone with authority that I don't."

Laurie blushed. "Is this some sort of game?"

"It's awfully fun to get a rise out of you. Easy too."

Ed was a little clompy, but he wasn't bad, only rough around the edges. Laurie lifted his chin and tried to recover his dignity. "Do you know more than the rumba?"

"A few other dances, but I forget the names. And probably the steps. Somebody suggested dance classes might be good rehab after my injury, so I took my mom ballroom dancing. I mean, I know I'm only okay. But I remember most of the basics." He waggled his eyebrows. "Still want me to hold up the wall?"

Laurie caught a glimpse of the wide eyes of his students in his peripheral vision, and for the first time in a long while, Laurie stumbled in a step beyond what he could recover.

Dear God. He hadn't simply forgotten Paul. He'd forgotten he even had a class.

Laurie put his hands on his hips. "So. That was the rumba. A football player did it. I think the rest of you can probably manage too."

Mr. Gerisher turned his wide eyes to Ed. "You play football?"

"Used to. Minnesota Lumberjacks. Did you play?"

Gerisher's grin widened. "Yeah. I was wide receiver in college. For Concordia."

Ed patted Mr. Gerisher on the back. "A Golden Bear shouldn't have any trouble with a box step."

The other men beamed at Ed like he was some sort of god. When Ed turned to Laurie, he barely kept the glare from his face.

"What?" Ed held out his arms and looked around, as if what had displeased Laurie might be lying on the floor.

"Nothing." Laurie turned to his class. "Try it again: and one, and two, and three, four. Quick, quick, slow. Quick, quick, slow. *Turn.*"

The students never did get it. But they were a lot happier about their failure, and a few of them had come pretty close to managing at least part of the dance. When Laurie gave them a little break at 7:30 before they switched over to the foxtrot, they were high-fiving each other and doing *quick, quick, slow* all the way to the drinking fountain in the hall.

Ed stayed behind with Laurie. "You're pissed at me. But damn, boss, what'd I do?"

Laurie pursed his lips, then reached for his water bottle. "I'm irritated *you* and your bumbling football gig got to them when my teaching couldn't."

"Oh, *that*. You're right, they're all worried you have the gay germs. God, I'd love to go out there and chat them up, casually mentioning *my boyfriend* to watch them have a coronary. Gay football player would really mess with their worldview."

Laurie choked on his water.

Ed took the bottle from him and pounded on his back. "Sorry, boss. Didn't mean to kill you."

Laurie stepped away. He coughed a few more times before turning to Ed. "Is that some kind of joke?"

"What? No, damn it, I wouldn't actually want to kill you."

"*No.*" Laurie wiped the back of his hand over his mouth. "The gay-football-player line."

"Not a line. No boyfriend, so that is a line, but gay? Yeah. I am." When Laurie stared at him, he snorted. "Oh, are *you* going to have a coronary too?"

"Obviously not."

Except it *did* bother him. He didn't know what to do with gay Ed. Gay, I-like-dancing Ed. Gay, charming

Ed. He hadn't thought about Toronto or Paul at all, not after that first turn. He felt jumbled and confused. And awkward, which was why he blurted, "I am too."

Ed's eyebrows lifted in surprise. "Huh. I would never have guessed you played football."

Laurie pursed his lips and locked his arms tighter over his chest.

Ed laughed. "Sorry. You make it too damn easy, boss."

"*Laurie,*" Laurie corrected.

Ed made a mock bow of apology. "You make it too damn easy, Laurie. But yeah. I kinda figured. Actually, to be honest, Vic told me."

And why the hell had she done that, Laurie wondered?

The couples came back into the room, and Laurie took the escape they gave him. He reviewed the steps, and when they stumbled, he had Ed demonstrate with him once more.

He waited for the memories to hit him, but they didn't. He was, though, completely distracted by the revelation that Ed was gay. Everything felt different now. He'd assumed Ed had agreed to this to jerk Laurie around some more, and somehow Laurie had been willing to accept that from a straight man. But Ed wasn't straight.

Unless he was lying after all.

"You're pissed at me," Ed said after the students had waved cheerily at him as they left. "What'd I do now?"

"Nothing." Laurie grabbed his towel and dabbed it at his hairline. "You don't have to come again, though."

"*Hey.*"

Laurie stiffened as Ed turned him around, but Ed didn't back down. He was seriously pissed off. "What is your problem?"

Panic attacks and PTSD over a catastrophic, career-ending performance. "My *problem* is you. You've done nothing but make me insane for a month solid, and now suddenly you're my big buddy? And you're gay. Am I supposed to fall for you and go to bed with you? Is that it?"

"What?" Ed's rage fell away as he blinked in confusion.

Oh, God, why the hell did I say that? Laurie lifted his chin and steeled his countenance as he flailed for recovery. "I was tired on Thursday when you asked me what I wanted, and I was worried about this class. But it was a dumb idea. You're off the hook. Go home and leave me alone."

Ed opened his mouth, abruptly closed it, and glowered. "Fine." Reaching for his coat, he tossed Laurie a salute. "See you around."

Laurie tried to let him go, he really did.

But as the former semipro football player headed for the door, Laurie saw his hips move, remembered the way he'd felt in those arms, remembered what it felt like to dance with a partner without panicking, and he called out, "Wait."

Ed stopped and turned around, still angry. "What now?"

Laurie kept his arms folded over his chest. "Did they teach you about Cuban motion in your dance class?"

Ed frowned. "Cuban what?"

Once more. Just once more, because there's no way two dances with him cured me, and if I don't dance with him now, I may never dance again.

Laurie unfolded his arms and motioned to Ed. "Get back here. There's something I need to fix."

CHAPTER THREE

*salida: exit, or start. In tango, the word for the
basic step to start a dance is also the same
word as the step which leads the dancer out of
a figure.*

I T WAS NICE to see Ed as the one thrown off his game for a change. *See how it isn't fun?* Laurie thought this but didn't say it out loud. He had some teaching to do.

"You're a little clumsy when you rumba because you're keeping your body too high."

Ed pointed to his shoes. "I thought you said—"

"It's not your shoes. It's your body. Your motion." He held up his arms in the follower's position. "Dance with me again, and I'll show you what I mean."

Still wary, Ed took Laurie into his arms and led them back into the box—quick, quick, slow, quick, quick, slow—and Laurie held his gaze as he spoke.

"Watch my shoulders. Notice how I don't rise. See how I'm swaying, moving my hips from side to side?

I'm almost squatting, and I don't let my body get any taller when I take a step. The rumba is a sensual dance. Let your body roll with it. Feel round and sexy. No, don't overdo it, or you'll stumble the way you just did. Easy does it. Like you're sliding up against a pretty girl." He remembered Ed's confession, and he missed a step.

"Pretty boy. I got it." When Laurie glared, Ed laughed. "God, *that's* what's got you in a knot? That I'm gay?"

"You aren't gay," Laurie snapped.

"Okay. I'm a straight, dumbass football player who can't dance. Gotcha. You want to tell me my underwear size too?"

"You don't act gay. You're only saying this to mess me up. You'll come in to the gym on Thursday with your goddamn football team and a herd of cheerleaders, and you'll laugh your head off at me."

Ed winced. "Shit. Vic's right, I really *did* ride you too hard."

Laurie forced his gaze to the center of Ed's chest. "Forget that. I just need to teach you the motion, because it's criminal to let you be so close and not fix it."

"I swear, I am as gay as a parade. I tried to keep my focus on women in high school, but in college I blew a guy in the locker room and never looked back. I don't advertise, no. But I don't hide it either. The guys on the team know. They're cool with it, overall. Why the hell does it make a difference to you?"

Laurie didn't know. "I need to teach you Cuban motion." Best to stick to the safer subject.

Ed sighed. "Fine. But can we have some music? I can't believe we had a whole dance class and never heard a single note of tunes."

"That's because they aren't good enough for that yet." Laurie cued the stereo to a song that would work. "But you're right. The music will help you feel the motion better."

A soft Latin beat began to pulse as Laurie returned to Ed's arms, and the music did help Ed with his Cuban motion. This was wonderful for Laurie, because he was beginning to believe he would be fine in any dance with Ed. But Ed still didn't have the moves right, and with the panic pressed down, the dancer in Laurie emerged.

"Really roll your hips. Feel it. Watch me move and mirror what I'm doing. Don't fight your hips, Ed. Use them. *Relax.*" Laurie dodged Ed's foot as he missed a step by trying too hard. "It's a natural movement. Your hips want to do it. Let them."

All of a sudden, he was. It took Ed a minute to realize he'd gotten it, and when he did, he laughed and ruined it again, but he had it back soon enough, and it wasn't long before Ed spun Laurie out into a turn, rolling his hips like an expert as Laurie came around.

"Show me something fancy to knock Mom's socks off."

Laurie hesitated. "I could teach you the Cucaracha step."

Ed beamed.

Laurie left the music going, because Ed was good enough that it wouldn't matter. "It's the same step, quick, quick, slow, but you take my hands by the palms and we move from side to side." Laurie positioned their hands together. "We're not actually stepping. We're almost moving in place. You can modify the dance between the three moves: box, turn, and Cucaracha, and your mother's socks should be in a great deal of jeopardy. But *stop rising*, Ed. Use your hips."

"Shit, sorry." Ed put his focus on his hips. It wasn't long before he had all three steps down, executing perfect Cuban motion all the while.

"You're a quick study." Laurie smiled as he came back from a turn.

Ed wasn't smiling. The music ended, but Ed didn't let Laurie go.

Laurie didn't pull away. Catching a glimpse of the clock on the wall behind him, Laurie realized he'd spent more than an hour and a half between the class and the extra lesson dancing with Ed. Ballroom dancing. No flashbacks, no ridiculous overblown reactions. No aching memories of Paul. Just dancing. And Ed.

Ed squeezed his hand. "I want to come again. I'll pay to take the class and bring my mom as a partner."

Say no. Say no. Say no. But Laurie said nothing.

"Please." Ed took a step closer, his expression

pleading. "I swear I won't tease you any more, ever."

Laurie lifted an eyebrow.

Ed grinned. "Okay. I won't tease you *much*. But seriously, what do you say, boss? Can I come back?" He sobered. "*Laurie*. Can I come, Laurie?"

Laurie gave up.

"You can, but you're not paying for anything. In exchange for helping me with the class, I'll give you any other lessons you want gratis. Your mother can stay at home."

He regretted the last because it felt like he was coming on to Ed, and then he worried part of him was, if not to the man, then to the idea of dancing with someone once more, which was dangerous and stupid.

Ed beamed. "For real? You'll teach me more stuff like this?" He did a quick rumba in place, hips rolling.

"Yes." Despite his internal turmoil, Laurie couldn't help a smile. "But not tonight. I have to get home."

"Sure, sure. You got things to do." Ed tucked his hands into his pockets, still smiling.

Laurie needed to get away from Ed and his silly grin. "So. I'll see you next week."

"Sounds great." Ed winked.

He's very handsome, Laurie thought, then tried not to think anymore. He needed to go home and soak his head. "Have a good evening, Ed."

"You too, boss."

"Laurie," Laurie corrected softly as Ed sashayed out the door.

LATER THAT NIGHT, Ed lay awake in his bed, pressing an ice pack to the side of his neck as he stared up at the ceiling.

He'd gone to bed two hours ago, and he'd slept for a little while, but he'd lain on his neck funny, and now he couldn't sleep because it hurt. Once again, a full dose of ibuprofen had at best taken the edge off, so he was trying ice. Except there wasn't anything quite like ice to wake you way the fuck up. And since to ice his neck he had to lie flat on his back, he had nothing to do but think. Which meant he thought about the dance class, and Laurie.

Ed *had* taken ballroom as therapy, and he'd enjoyed it. But Laurie's class had been different, and he didn't know why. Maybe because Laurie was so bristly? But that didn't explain why it was different. That only explained that Laurie was a headcase. And he really was a headcase. Goddamn, but twice Ed had thought Laurie was going to pass out. What the hell was he so worked up about?

And why had he seemed so much better when he was dancing with Ed?

The cold started to hurt, so Ed shifted the pack. He turned on the light beside his bed, fumbled into some boxers, and padded out into the living room to watch some TV.

He tripped over a laundry basket full of clothes, swore, and stubbed his toe on a hand weight that had fallen off the pile of junk on top of his overflowing dresser. Limping, he navigated carefully to his living room area, where he fumbled with the lamp, remembered he hadn't changed the bulb, then limped to the other lamp on top of the stereo cabinet. When that bulb also proved to be burned out, he swore again and headed over to the front door, where the light switch was easily findable on the wall.

Now that he could see, he rooted through the pile of junk on the couch, marveling briefly to see *this* was where the new package of toilet paper had ended up, found the remote, and settled in on top of probably clean laundry he hadn't gotten around to folding. He surfed aimlessly, landing on an infomercial for a memory-foam pillow and mattress set because the blond male model kind of gave him an erection.

He was too tired and too sore to jack off, though, and when the male model gave way to a female, Ed's attention drifted to dancing and Laurie.

Somehow the evening had softened Ed's feelings about him, even when Laurie kicked him out for no reason and then called him back to teach him Cuban motion like he wasn't going to sleep if he didn't. He still thought Laurie was a snot. A rich, spoiled snot. Except…well, outside being snippy, he hadn't been a snot tonight. He was a neurotic mess, but he was okay. It was nice of him to give Ed lessons. And once he got the corncob out of his ass, he was actually pretty fun. Cute too.

Laurie changed when he was teaching. He was

good with the couples—nervous, but good. He'd been amazing when he'd taught Ed about the hip thing. Better than any coach Ed had ever had on the field, and he'd had some damn good coaches. Laurie made you want to do well, not to please him but to get it *right*. Except Ed had wanted to please Laurie too. All he could think of was how he wanted to do it again.

Ed shuffled to his bed, moving the ice pack from his pillow and setting it on top of a dirty plate resting on a stack of magazines. He took a second to make sure it wasn't all going to topple over, then rolled on his side and stared out across the room into the open door of his closet where junk spilled onto the floor. His gaze fell on a pair of cleats, and he studied them for a minute.

Teaching the class at the center was good, but dancing with Laurie was better. It wasn't the same to tell other people how to lift weights as it was to lose himself in something. To fight with something and achieve it. To wrestle with his own body and convince it that it could do more than it wanted to. And dancing had been fun. Dancing with Laurie, sparring with him—all of it. When he'd got the Cuban motion right, he'd had a buzz like he hadn't since the Lumberjacks. As if he'd eaten cardboard pizza for five years and gotten used to it, and now somebody was waggling a Chicago-style deep dish under his nose. He had to have more.

So why the hell hadn't that happened when he'd

taken the class with his mom?

His eyes unfocused as he remembered the way it had felt to take Laurie in his arms, to touch him, to watch him move. Laurie made it seem so easy. But he made it beautiful too. It was different, dancing with Laurie.

Fuck, maybe it was simply that he was a guy. Ed hadn't ever done that before—danced with another man—not like he had tonight. Sure, he'd ground against a guy at a club. But he'd never *danced* with a guy before. Never held hands and put his hand on a guy's waist as he turned him around. Never had a guy tell Ed to move his hips, to be sexy, to listen to his body—not outside of a bedroom.

Laurie had pushed him so hard to get that motion right, and it had been a real rush, pushing right back. And it hadn't hurt his neck at all.

Ed wrestled the sheets into place and arranged his pillow carefully under his neck, trying to ward off further pain incidents. Maybe he could practice a little every night to make sure he didn't forget anything before the next class. He'd spend the next week gearing up, and on Thursday he'd stop by Laurie's class after to say hi, to show him he was done teasing him and being a shit. And then on Tuesday he'd get more lessons.

He'd get to hold Laurie again.

Ed rolled his eyes at himself. But that didn't stop the warm feeling he got when he thought about holding Laurie, of moving with him, of spinning him out and catching him when he came back. The feeling didn't go away, not even when he closed his eyes.

THOUGHTS OF HIS dancing lessons with Laurie lingered still on Wednesday as Ed was out with the guys. In fact, at one point he'd been about to throw a dart when he saw somebody slow dancing with a girl across the bar, and the next thing he knew the guys were waving hands in front of his face and laughing.

When Thursday came around, Ed was excited for his weight class at the center, but he was also eager to see Laurie. Which was weird. They weren't going to dance. It was that shit music and Laurie screaming. What the fuck was there to look forward to in that? But Ed was. And this time, when he heard the disco pounding its way into the hall, he didn't grumble at all. He simply smiled.

Until he got into the weight room and heard the disco in there too, louder than it had ever been.

WHEN LAURIE SAW Ed come through the door of the gym, he braced for another assault. But then he remembered dancing with Ed, of the way he'd charmed the dance class, and Laurie's inner fortifications crumbled under a sense of betrayal.

Fifteen ragtag young men followed in after Ed, and Laurie faltered mid-step, because he had no idea what was happening now.

Ed and his tribe didn't approach the stage but instead assembled in an open area by the bleachers. Laurie let his body move through the aerobic routine on autopilot while his mind tried and failed to figure out what Ed was up to.

Ed arranged the boys into a semicircle and began instructing them. Sometimes he would raise his hands above his head and make pumping motions with his arms. Sometimes he led them through some sort of movement, nodding or shaking his head while they did it. Some of them had hand weights, and some had Pilates bands or tension cords with handles.

It was too early for a break, but when the song finished, Laurie called one anyway, hopped off the stage, and wove his way through his students toward the perpetual thorn in his side.

"That's good. Good." Ed spoke to a young man with a hot-pink bandana wrapped around his dark-skinned head as Laurie approached the group. "But keep your shoulders back, Duon. Think about the muscle you're working. Set your body, then work just that muscle. If you let your shoulder roll forward, you're going to end up working something different, and you might injure yourself. The music's stopped, but you can make your own beat in your head. Keep regular. That's it. There you go. You got it."

Ed saw Laurie and smiled.

Laurie simply stood with his arms over his chest.

Ed cocked his head to the side and put his hands on his hips, showing off his broad chest. "Suppose you want to know what we're doing in here, boss."

Laurie had been about to take him to task for the "boss" comment, but he decided he'd rather know what was going on. "Yes."

Ed nodded at the door to the hallway with a grim expression. "They didn't fix anything with the sound system. If anything, it's worse. We could barely stand to be in there long enough to get equipment."

"What? But Vicky told me—" Laurie looked anew at Ed's students assembled in the corner of the gym. "Wait, this is your class?"

"Yeah, sorry. The gym is the only place left. Not even a racquetball court was open. I checked. But this works enough for tonight. I mean, ultimately I need to get them on equipment, but there are enough basics to work on that we can make do. And the beat helps, in a way. A little hard for them to hear me talk, but we're taking it slow. Unless—are we bothering you?"

Laurie still had this vague sense that Ed was putting him on, except now he wondered if that wasn't actually a fear rather than a feeling. "Could I speak to you in private?"

"Sure." Ed addressed his class. "Take a break, guys. Get a drink and stretch." He grabbed a bottle of water and headed to the alcove behind the bleachers.

Laurie followed. He wasn't exactly sure what he was going to say to Ed. All he knew was that he didn't want an audience. So he followed Ed into the corner, hoping to God inspiration struck on the way.

Wiping his wrist across his forehead, Ed let out a sigh. "I love Vic. But right now, I could string her up by her damn P.A. system." He shrugged. "I guess we disband my class until she finds me an open slot sometime when your class isn't going, because clearly they aren't going to fix the P.A., and if we're bothering you, there's nothing else to do."

Laurie faltered. "What?"

Ed's lips pressed together. "Look, what else do you want? I'm going to dismiss them when they get back from break. I'm giving up the slot."

Laurie held up his hands as if the gesture could ward off the confusion. "Ed—you mean you truly only came in here to do your class? You didn't do it to drive me crazy?"

"Okay. I was going to be all outraged that you'd think that, but I had it coming." He squared his shoulders. "What are you doing after this? After your class?"

Laurie felt like he was missing pages from the movie script, and it was starting to make him angry. "What?"

"What are you doing after this?"

"I'm going home and sticking pins in my Ed voodoo doll."

Ed grinned, and the gesture did uncomfortable things to Laurie's insides. "Can I get you to put that off for an hour so I can take you to dinner?"

Laurie stared at him.

Ed stared back.

Laurie spoke carefully. "Do you mean…you want to ask me out?"

Ed's expression became unreadable. "For dinner. To apologize for yanking your chain so often that you don't believe me when I'm serious."

Laurie felt dizzy. He steadied himself on the edge of one of the bleachers, but it didn't help.

Ed uncapped his water and held it out. "Here. You've got to be thirsty. You've been up there shouting and waving your arms. Drink up. I'll refill it after."

Laurie took the bottle, but he didn't drink. "Why are you being nice instead of driving me crazy?"

"Because I went to your dance class. Because you taught me that Cuban-motion thing. Because I liked it and want to do more, and if you're pissed, you won't let me."

Had Ed actually hit on Laurie, he'd have deflected it without thinking. Laurie would have told him no, he was not having dinner, and he'd have let Ed dismiss his class and gone on with his own. But Ed hadn't hit on Laurie. In fact, there was nothing remotely sexual about the way he regarded Laurie. There was passion, though. A spark. A light. A mirror to the one inside of Laurie himself.

Ed Maurer wanted to dance, wanted it badly enough to give up his class. This wasn't an act. This was the real thing.

Laurie was in so much trouble.

He drank, keenly aware of the pressure of the rim

of the water bottle against his lips, of the slick wet of the liquid as it slid down his parched throat. He was aware of Ed's eyes on him, watching, waiting, hoping, and the look made Laurie's pulse kick. But Laurie made no move other than to finish the water, every last drop. Then he wiped his mouth with the back of his hand, and handed the bottle over. His eyes never left Ed's.

"Don't dismiss your class. You're fine where you are. And don't cancel it, either. I'll talk to Vicky about it and find a solution."

Ed took the empty bottle and nodded, waiting for the answer to his other question.

Laurie told himself he was being ridiculous and theatrical, that he was reading far too much into this exchange, because of course a hulky, bulky jock was not standing there spellbound because he'd fallen in love with dancing after two turns with Laurie on the floor.

Play it cool. Just be careful.

"I'm not free for dinner. But if you don't mind working late—" He stopped, suddenly uncertain.

Ed perked up. "Yes?"

Laurie trembled like some stupid turn-of-the-century virgin in a nightgown telling her suitor how to work the trick latch in her bedroom, knowing full well she was going to leave the casement open and help her lover over the sill. But the truth was Laurie could have had sex with Ed right there in the open, right now, easier than he could traverse the mental line he was crossing.

"If you come by the studio after nine tomorrow night, I can show you a few more moves after my last class gets out. Or not. I mean, if you don't want—"

"I'd love to. If you don't mind giving up part of your evening."

"Not at all."

Ed nodded at the gym. "We should probably get back to our classes. You sure we're okay here?"

"Yes. I'll wrap up early. We were going to stay late tonight, but I'll tack on another session at the end to make up for all the disruptions."

"We gotta figure out what the hell the hang-up is with that P.A."

"I'll take care of it. I promise." Laurie smiled tentatively. "So I'll see you tomorrow?"

"Absolutely." Ed saluted briefly with the water bottle. "Catch you later, Laurie."

Laurie watched him go, tracking the way his body moved, remembering how it had felt surrounding him on the dance floor.

CHAPTER FOUR

*pivot: a step in any direction followed by a turn
with one foot anchored firmly to the floor.*

LAURIE'S STUDIO WAS in a tidy strip mall in Eden Prairie, sandwiched between an office for the DMV and a store called Tuesday Morning. Ed sat in his car for a few minutes, staring at the name and trying to figure it out. Was there something special about Tuesday morning? Was it only open on Tuesday mornings? Except he'd peeked at the hours, and according to them, no, they were open the standard hours of most suburban businesses. He thought maybe the name referenced what they sold somehow, but as far as he could tell it sold random department store stuff: furniture, bedding, appliances. There was no real way he could logically link it to Tuesday, let alone the morning.

It was probably one of those suburb things, one of those insider deals that people who grew up in tract houses understood and Ed never would.

Even if the parking lot hadn't been full of SUVs

and minivans, the people who came in and out of Laurie's studio were a big clue Ed was in the burbs. Last time, in addition to the Baptist couples, there had been scores of blonde girls in leotards being chased by blonde mothers in yoga pants. Tonight it was sleek, model-esque teens giggling and texting madly on their cell phones as their parents waited impatiently in idling vehicles. Everyone had been dipped in tidy and dusted with proper and nice. Everyone was polished and clean, and Ed felt too grungy and hulky to be among them.

You're here to dance, not impress people, he reminded himself as he entered the building. He pressed against the wall as another gaggle of girls came out of a dressing room. They paid no attention to Ed, and he wondered if they thought he was just another parent. Or maybe they thought he was a janitor.

Ed glanced at himself, at his dress pants and shoes. Nope. He didn't look like a janitor.

Did he?

A petite, pretty woman with her hair drawn into a bun approached him. "Can I help you?"

"Hi. I, I'm here—" He stepped aside as another wave of girls came by, this time from the lobby *into* the dressing room. "Laurie. I was supposed to meet Laurie."

The woman arched a neatly plucked auburn eyebrow. "The assistant. Yes, I remember." She extended a graceful hand. "I'm Maggie Davies."

Ed shook it firmly. "Ed Maurer." He nodded toward the room where he'd found Laurie last Tuesday. "He in there?"

"He's in the smaller studio with the pointe class. They ought to be done any minute, though. There's no one in the office, if you'd like to wait there."

Ed stuffed his hands in his jacket pockets. "I'll wait here, if that's okay."

"Of course." Maggie weaved through the chaos of the lobby, heading into the office.

A class let out. They came from the big room Ed had been in last time, and they were heading straight for the dressing room off to the left side of the hall. There was another dressing room near the classroom itself, but this one was for boys, and hardly anyone came out of it. Ed thought he'd seen two testosterone representatives slip through in one of the waves, but mostly this was an estrogen party.

The girls chattered, talking over one another, whispering, waving their hands—in short, they were being teenage girls. There were only about fifteen of them, but they felt like thirty for the space they commanded. Reminded Ed of high school, ducking swarms of girls as he wove his way through the lockers and to class. He'd spent a lot of time identifying the ones he thought he could date. Someone to call a girlfriend and someone he'd enjoy being with, maybe even occasionally necking with, and if things went well, getting sweaty with in her bedroom when her parents weren't home. An accessory.

Real attraction was for males: boys and men with sleek stomachs and tapered waists. Ed had faked it with girls, but his passion had been for hard thighs and tight asses. For cocks swinging boldly over a tender sac of balls. For tight nipples and corded necks and broad shoulders and mouths that tasted spicy, not sweet.

Somehow being here in the middle of all this teenage estrogen stirred up all those feelings of panic, of exposure. Reminding him of when he'd been the dirty kid from the wrong part of town, the guy who wanted cock when he should be happy with pussy. It was stupid, because he'd left all that years ago, but now he stood here, soaking in it as if he'd never left.

Ed peered beneath the gap in the privacy curtain in the window to the room Laurie was in, trying to see what a pointe class was. He saw another girl, this one all leg, and she leapt like a gazelle across the floor before she stopped, rose on the tips of her toes, and turned.

"No, Anna," a familiar voice said.

Ed watched, mouth dry, as Laurie crossed to the girl.

Laurie wore tights. The other night he'd worn a sleek black pair of pants that clung but still hung loosely around his body. At aerobics he wore knee-length running shorts. These were tights. These were a pair of white, *tight* tights, and they were all Laurie had on south of the border. No leotard. Nothing over it, not even a pair of Superman-style underwear. He had a T-shirt on over the top, a striking royal blue, but, goddamn. *Tights.*

They were borderline obscene. Not that Ed minded, obviously. But Jesus. Talk about a tight ass, pardon the pun. The thighs weren't bad either. Ed would have written Laurie off as scrawny, but now that he got a better view—practically an X-ray—Ed had to admit Laurie had some meat on him. Nice, toned meat. Legs, arms, abs. Laurie looked good. Laurie had a fine body.

Laurie turned, facing the door as he rose on his toes before coming down into a sort of squat. Ed's eyes fixed on the bulge of Laurie's white-clad crotch.

Really nice meat.

Feeling suddenly overheated, Ed stepped away from the door. Spying a drinking fountain along the wall by the men's dressing room, Ed took a deep drink, then leaned into the wall as he stared into the drain and collected himself.

First he'd been yanked back to adolescence, and now all he could think about was the way Laurie had filled out his tights. He wondered how he'd ever look the man in the eye again without imagining the way his thighs had strained the Lycra or remembering the way the tights had both smoothed out and defined his cock at once. Maybe because they were white? Maybe that was why the image grabbed Ed around the throat so bad?

All he knew was he'd written Laurie off as a bit of a pouf, that at best he might be a nice guy Ed could get to know, maybe have sex with for something different, but now the wires in Ed's brain had rerouted, and Laurie wasn't associated with *ridiculous idiot at the gym* or even *nice guy teaching you how to dance.* Now he was *man with tight butt, hard thighs and bulging cock.*

An image filled Ed's brain, and he saw himself kneeling in the middle of a dance floor as Laurie walked toward him wearing those tights, just those tights, and Ed stared up at the bulge at Laurie's groin as it came closer. He nuzzled it, and then, as Laurie put his hand on the back of Ed's head, Ed pulled down the waistband and groaned in pleasure as Laurie fed that bulge to his eager mouth—

Blinking, Ed bent over the fountain and aimed the icy water right at his face.

He rubbed it in with both hands as he rose and stared at the poster over the drinking fountain, only to wind up looking at Laurie yet again. It was a poster of a ballet, and Laurie was the only image in the picture. He wore tights here too, but they didn't seem as obscene as they did live and in person. Laurie was lit like a god, caught in mid-leap, his muscled thighs bulging. He was art. All arches and lines and light and shadow. The bottom of the poster said *Joffrey Ballet 2001: Light Rain.*

Laurie was beautiful. Laurie was the most fucking beautiful thing Ed had ever seen.

"Oh, don't look at that."

Startled, Ed turned, and there was the real Laurie, still wearing his white tights. Sweat beaded at his brow and ran in erotic rivulets down his throat, disappearing over his clavicle and into the neckline of his shirt. He glared at the poster. "Maggie insists on hanging it for the snob value." Laurie dabbed at his neck with a towel.

Ed couldn't stop staring at the photo. "You do ballet, huh?"

"Ballet, jazz, tap, and everything in between. Except Irish." Laurie put his hands on his hips and gave Ed a quelling look. "I suppose given the way you keep surprising me, you're going to tell me you've performed too and that you're some sort of closet Fred Astaire?"

Ed worked not to let his gaze slide to Laurie's crotch. "No. Sorry. Just the occasional ballroom dancing."

Laurie tossed his towel over his shoulder. "Speaking of, are you ready for more?"

"Sure," Ed said, trying to sound cool.

"Great. Give me a few minutes, and I'll be ready too." Laurie bent, took a long drink of water, then rose, wiping his lips. "I need to change first, though. Do you want to wait in the small studio for me?"

Change. That meant Ed wouldn't get to dance with Laurie in his tights. That was probably for the best.

Still.

The memory of Laurie's squat filled Ed's mind, and his dick plumped as he recalled the way Laurie's cock strained that tight white—

"Ed?" Laurie's frowning face appeared in front of his own. "Are you okay?"

Ed blinked. "Yeah. Fine."

"Okay." Laurie regarded him dubiously for a minute before nodding at the dressing room door. "I'm going to go in there now."

And take off his tight white tights. And free his hard thighs and bulging cock, touching them, sliding his hands over them—

"*Ed.*" This time Laurie gripped his shoulder too.

So he could push Ed to his knees—

Another group of girls came out of the dressing room, interrupting Ed's carnal thoughts, and he drew back sharply. "I'm fine. I'll wait for you inside."

As he made a beeline for the studio, he caught Maggie giving him a dirty look from across the room, but he ignored her, too intent on getting out of the hall and into a space where he was the only person there. He ducked beneath the outstretched arm of a girl demonstrating a move to her friend, shutting the door behind him with more force than was necessary. Then he shut his eyes, took deep breaths and focused on figuring out what the fuck Tuesday Morning could be about, because it was the one thing he could think of that didn't successfully support an image of Laurie and those goddamned fucking tights.

"SO WHAT DANCES do you know?"

They sat on stools opposite one another near the shelf that held the sound system and other various supplies. Laurie had debated in the dressing room over what exactly he should wear. He hadn't brought the right clothes, so focused on whether or not this would go well that clothes hadn't even been on his radar. As a result, he had his chinos and his tights. He'd gone with the chinos in the end, but now, as he sat across from Ed in his dress clothes, he felt ridiculous. He was glad he at least had the right shoes.

He took some comfort in the fact that Ed seemed uncomfortable too, shifting on his stool and huddling in a sort of protective slouch. "Well, I started with Rumba Rehab, which was supposed to help get me moving after the surgery. And that got me into the other Latin dances, but I forget all the names."

"Salsa, I assume," Laurie suggested, and Ed nodded. "Merengue? Mambo?" More nods. "Cha-Cha? Samba? What about cumbia?"

"Yes and yes, but not cumbia. Never heard of that."

"What about the more traditional dances? I know you know the foxtrot. What about the waltz?"

"Yep, I know how to waltz."

"But which waltz?"

Ed looked surprised. "There's more than one?"

"Probably the American, then." Laurie tapped his thumb against his leg. "Hustle?"

"Hustle what?"

Laurie smiled despite himself. "That's a no. Tango?"

Ed brightened. "Oh yeah. I like that one."

So did Laurie. "Do you know what kind you

learned? Ballroom? English? Argentine?" When Ed blinked at him, he had to bite back a smile. "Ah. Well, why don't we try and see? I'll put on some music, and you lead me in whatever style you know."

They rose from their stools at the same time, bringing themselves mere inches from one another. Ed's hands came up, and for a moment Laurie thought Ed would grab his shoulders. But instead he ducked around the stool to walk into the center of the dance floor.

Laurie cued the music and joined him.

"Start whenever you feel ready." Laurie stepped into position and raised his arms for the embrace.

Ed put his hands on Laurie's waist and shoulder tentatively, hesitating before leading them into a basic ballroom tango. For this being Ed's favorite dance, he was certainly awkward about it. Laurie was tempted to ask if he was feeling okay, but something held him back. Instead he reverted to instructor mode, dissecting Ed's movement, noting where he did well and where he could improve. Except it had been a long time since Laurie followed in a tango, and he found his inner teacher crowded out by his own itchy feet. All he could think of right now was how much he wanted to dance.

"What would you say," he asked after a few turns around the room, "to learning the Argentine tango?"

"What's the one I've been doing?"

"Ballroom. The Argentine tango is closer to the original. It started in the brothels."

"Oh?" Ed raised his eyebrows. "How is it different?"

"There's a lot more variation. It's more of a conversation than the ballroom tango. Lots of push and pull. The follower's part is more involved than the leader's, but the leader keeps the balance and the structure of the embrace. And, of course, he instigates the steps."

"Okay." Ed flexed his hand against Laurie's. "So what do I do?"

Laurie walked him through the adjustment of the steps between ballroom and Argentinean tango, which initially wasn't much, mostly getting him to go toe-heel instead of heel-toe. That took the better portion of a song, which didn't bother Laurie except that he was impatient. His real goal was to teach Ed ochos. And boleos. He was aching to do an arrastre, but he knew that was likely a dream, at least for tonight.

But it's been so long.

The desire—not panic, only bald, aching desire—grabbed him briefly by the throat, and he paused.

Ed stumbled as he ran into Laurie. "Did I do something wrong?"

"No. You're fine." Laurie wrenched his focus back to the lesson. "I want to teach you the ocho. Again, it's a step mostly I'll be doing, but I can't do it without you. Your job is to bear the balance, not only of our bodies but of the dance itself. The tango can be aggressive or gentle, and it's best when it's a bit of both. Some steps are a fight between the leader and the follower. You can trap my feet, or you can step in front of my leg and stop me mid-step, forcing me to change direction. You can drag my feet, and I can do the same to you. You can push my foot along, almost stepping on it. And this doesn't count turns or pitter-patter."

"Wow." Ed gave a lopsided smile. "Yeah, they didn't cover any of that in my classes."

"I could teach you."

"I'd love to learn." But Ed was still hesitant. Last week he'd been all sass, but not tonight. Laurie wondered where that Ed had gone and what his absence meant.

He pushed the thought aside and led Ed into the steps of the ocho instead.

"Your job is to lead us into a pivot. Follow your hips. Move naturally, leading with your shoulders. You'll need to use some muscle, but don't push. Let it flow with the music and the pulse of the dance."

Ed executed a passable pivot. Laurie, impatient, stepped back, behind, and went into the gather. Ed stumbled after.

Laurie caught him and righted them both. "Again. Another pivot. That was an ocho. They should come in at least sets of two."

Ed looked lost, but to his credit, he led them into another pivot, and Laurie followed.

"Your hips," he reminded Ed as he moved awkwardly into a third pivot. "Smooth, Ed. Let your body follow the music. Don't be shy."

Ed jerked, nearly stepping on Laurie's foot. "Sorry. I'm all off my game tonight."

"Do you want to stop?"

"No, no." Ed met Laurie's gaze. "No. I want to keep dancing, if you don't mind being patient with me."

"I don't mind."

Ed smiled. *Shy.* He was so shy, and it was so, so strange to see. And alluring.

Adjusting his hold, Ed counted himself into the music and led them into the dance once more. Within twenty minutes Ed had ochos down fairly well, and Laurie decided to push his luck and add boleos too.

"This is a sort of kick, and it's best done out of an ocho. Once again, the showiest part goes to the follower, but without the leader, it's not possible to do. My axis here is crucial. If you don't maintain our balance, I'll stumble and take you down with me."

"So how do I do it?"

"We'll start at the barre."

Ed was such an eager student. He paid close attention to instruction, asked questions when he didn't understand. His greatest flaw was he didn't fall naturally into a graceful motion. His rhythm was fine, but his movements tended to be too aggressive.

"This isn't a football field," Laurie scolded him. "It may be a bold dance, but the goal is to move together, not to tackle me."

Ed rubbed his cheek. "Sorry."

"It's all right." Laurie smiled and made Ed show him again.

When he was about to suggest they try and put the step to a practical test, he glanced at the clock on the wall in shock. "It's after eleven."

Ed seemed equally surprised. And disappointed. "Shit. I should probably head home. I've got a good forty-five minute drive ahead of me, and I have to get up early tomorrow."

Laurie stepped firmly on his dismay. "Of course. I'm sorry. I should have kept better track of time."

"No, no." Ed ran a hand through his hair and gave him a sheepish grin. "It was fun. Dancing with you. You're really good."

"Thank you. You aren't bad yourself, once you re-lax."

For a moment Ed looked as if he wanted to say something more. But then he shook his head and stepped back. "Yeah. I should…go."

Laurie felt flustered now too. "Do you—I mean, you don't have to come next week for the class, but—"

"I'd like to. If you still want me there."

"Oh, yes. I mean—yes, thank you." Breathless. Laurie felt flustered and breathless, and he had no idea why.

Ed nodded. "See you then?"

"Sure." Before he could stop himself, Laurie added, "If you have time, maybe we could work more on the tango, after."

A smile broke out across Ed's face. It was the sort of smile that used to annoy Laurie, a cheeky, brash sort of smile, but tonight it didn't annoy him at all. If anything, it made his heart beat faster.

Ed stuffed his hands in his pockets. "See you then."

Laurie watched him walk across the room and grab his coat. Ed went out the door, and it closed behind him.

It wasn't until he heard the engine of Ed's car start that Laurie let his shoulders fall forward. Heart beating faster than it had a right to, he leaned over the stool, bracing himself as the tango music played on.

CHAPTER FIVE

D ANCING THE PART of the Prince for Oliver's
Nutcracker was, technically, something Laurie
could have walked onto a stage cold and performed on
the spot. He had literally lost count of the number of
times he'd performed it. He'd played this role for this
production when he was eighteen, the youngest dancer
in Twin Cities history to ever do so. Though it wasn't a
complicated part. The Prince was mostly there to prop
up the ballerina and then do a bit of skip and jump to
make the boys shuffling through their bit parts want to
try a little harder. Oliver hadn't been kidding when he'd
said Laurie could do it in his sleep.

Yet as the weeks of the performance drew closer,
Laurie's unease grew, until by the first week in November it had begun to approach out-and-out panic.

"It's nothing but a mountain in your mind," Oliver
told Laurie backstage after a rehearsal. "The best way

to dispel it is to plow through and realize there's nothing in your way but yourself." With a grace and ease of movement that belied his white hair, Oliver sat on the floor opposite Laurie. "You're doing fine in the rehearsals themselves. And you dance as beautifully as ever, Laurie. Where is this coming from? Surely all this isn't for that idiot Paul."

Laurie rubbed his arms. "I just don't want to perform anymore." He cut a glance to Oliver. "This is the part where you tell me what a waste of talent my retirement is, or how I'm being silly, or that I'm letting one bad moment ruin the rest of my life."

Oliver tilted his head to the side as he studied Laurie. "Did you ever enjoy it?"

Laurie frowned. "What do you mean?"

"Did you ever enjoy performing? I know you don't want to perform now. But did you ever want to?"

Laurie had no idea how to respond to this. "You think I went through all that for years because I *didn't* like it?"

"Honestly? Sometimes I wondered. Sometimes I worried you'd gotten caught up in your mother's ambition and your burning need to turn your father's head. I worried the limelight had gotten too bright for your eyes, and I waited for you to burn up. Then I'd see you perform again, and I'd think, no, dancing is what this man's soul wants to do. What happened to that fire, Laurie? Was I only imagining it? Or did it truly go out?"

It took biting his tongue to keep from asking what

Oliver meant by *burning need to turn his father's head,* so Laurie said nothing.

Oliver sighed. "It's not my desire to force you into anything. If you need to back out—"

"No." Laurie straightened. "Good God, Oliver. Do I seem that ridiculous?"

The look on Oliver's face was answer enough.

Laurie pursed his lips. "I'll be fine. It won't be the performance it should be, but it's fifteen minutes of dancing, and despite what you and my mother say, they truly aren't going to come see me. Just a few vultures."

"I heard a rumor you've been dancing ballroom after hours. With a man."

Laurie kept his gaze carefully averted. "And where did you hear this?"

"Maggie told me in hopes I could possibly get you to stop." When Laurie glanced up sharply, Oliver chuckled. "Why are you surprised?"

"Because it's none of her business." Laurie's cheeks burned, partly in anger, partly in embarrassment. "I don't know what's worse, that she told you or that she thought you could stop me. Why would she want to?"

"She thinks you're her pet. Of course she's upset. Apparently this man is handsome too. She fears he'll whisk you away."

The amusement in Oliver's tone didn't help Laurie's temper. "It's only dancing, for heaven's sake." He smoothed imaginary lint from his trousers.

"*Is* he handsome?" Oliver pressed.

"That's completely beside the point."

"That's a yes. And does he bat for Dorothy?" When Laurie gave him a withering glare, Oliver laughed. "And another yes. Well, well. Bring him to the performance. Perhaps he'll center you."

"He isn't my boyfriend, and he's certainly not my savior. My God, he'd laugh me out of the room if I asked him to come hold my hand at *Nutcracker*." Though as soon as he said that, he felt guilty. Ed hadn't laughed at him, not in a long time.

"If you aren't sleeping with him, perhaps you should be. I'd say you should date him openly, though I suppose we should encourage you to walk before you run. But sex is a must for you, I think. How long has it been?"

"*Oliver*."

Oliver dismissed Laurie's discomfort with a wave of his hand. "It's all teenagers at this rehearsal, and I promise you, if they aren't having sex, they're thinking about it. Answer my question. How long has it been?"

"It's none of your business."

"Always a discouraging reply. Please at least tell me there has been someone since Paul."

Laurie was now beet red. "Of course."

Oliver sighed. "Let me guess. A few awkward dates, some passable but mostly mediocre sex, and long, depressing dry patches where you tell yourself you don't need such bestial pleasures in your life?"

It was so spot-on Laurie had to bite his tongue to

keep from asking how Oliver could possibly know. "Why are we having this conversation?"

"Because bestial pleasures are the stuff of life." Oliver moved to stand in front of Laurie and stared him down. "Because sex makes you feel alive. Because you're a sexual being, because you're young and attractive, and because with the right individual you'd be the most responsive partner a man could dream of. You're gracious and giving, and you have so much beauty stored up to give. But if you don't stir that beauty up every now and again, it will wither and die. Try giving it to your dancing partner and see where it gets you."

An image flashed in Laurie's mind of Ed, smiling Ed, pressing him onto his bed. It was an alarming and highly pleasurable thought. He shook it off. "Ed would never be interested in me. He's a football player. He's big and handsome and flirty."

Oliver smiled. "He sounds perfect."

"Yes. And perfect men aren't interested in skinny, uptight, neurotic messes."

Oliver's smile faded. "I wish I knew how you began thinking so poorly of yourself you stopped being able to see your own worth. I wish I had tried harder to assure you that you were fine as you were."

The conversation made Laurie downright uncomfortable. "I need to go." He turned on his heel and walked off before Oliver could reply.

But his thoughts kept drifting to their conversation all through rehearsal. He thought, too, about Ed. He knew Ed would never be interested in a man like Laurie. Flirt, yes, but date? A man who tackled football players for fun? He'd probably laugh Laurie out of the bed.

Thinking of Ed sexually put a shadow over their dancing together, which had become a bright beacon in Laurie's life. He knew Ed was doing it because he'd discovered a love of dancing, that it was giving him an outlet he missed. He knew Ed came to the class as a favor but stayed for fun. But Laurie knew it wouldn't last. Ed would move on. Laurie didn't want to sully their time together by pining after Ed, however desirable he was.

There was no denying, though, that he wished Ed *were* coming to his performance. He told himself he'd look foolish for asking, and even if Ed agreed, it might backfire and make Ed nervous. It might make their time end too quickly. It might stop the magic.

But he couldn't stop thinking about Ed coming to the performance all through the rehearsal, especially when he found the harder he wished Ed were there, the easier it became to dance.

ED HAD TO admit, right now things weren't bad.

The sound system had never been fixed in the weight room, but they'd given up and established Ed at the back of Laurie's class in the gym permanently. Eventually Vicky found him an alternate room, but by that time Ed wasn't interested, because now he kind of liked being in the gym. He'd started working with Laurie's moves too, giving the guys Pilates bands to pull in time to the beat. For the machines, he arranged to have the kids come in on Saturdays at eleven.

Duon came to every class, and every time Ed stopped by to check on something with Vicky, the kid was there. While Duon had always been a regular at the center, he had started to seem like a fixture. Ed asked Vicky about it.

"I'm looking into it," she told him, grimacing. "I have a feeling something bad is going on at home. I'm not sure he's even there anymore."

This wasn't good. "You think he got kicked out?"

"Or he removed himself. I don't think he's got a sugar daddy, but that might be wishful thinking." She sighed and sank in her chair. "I dropped the ball on him like I'm dropping everything else."

Ed frowned. "What do you mean? You're not his social worker, Vic."

"He comes to the center. He's my kid." Vicky flicked a pen across the papers littered on the desk. "I've been so busy. Funding is a special kind of hell this year. We're running out of grants, and the city is eyeing us as if we're the fat it could trim and seal up its budget. And don't bring up local sponsors. You know how I feel about them."

"Even if they're the difference between keeping the center open or having it close?"

Vicky pursed her lips and resumed sorting through

her papers. "It's not going to come to that."

Ed hoped she was right.

The center was rocky as it always was, but dancing with Laurie was great. The ballroom class had one more session before it was done, but Laurie had already hinted he'd keep giving Ed lessons after. Which was fine by Ed.

He'd managed to control himself after that one night when he'd seen Laurie in tights. It helped that he didn't leave the car until mere moments before class, and on the nights they met for bonus lessons, he made sure he lingered in the waiting area until Laurie came to get him. This meant he had to endure giggling from the teenage girls and glares from Maggie, who Ed was pretty sure didn't like him at all. But it was better than trying to figure out how he was going to hide a boner while he danced.

And he *really* loved dancing with Laurie.

What he loved most was how disciplined Laurie was and how hard he worked Ed. During the classes he let the Baptists get away with all kinds of slop so long as they remembered at least seventy-five percent of the steps and kept to the beat, but when it was the two of them, Laurie was ruthless. At first he was tentative, but the more they worked together, the more exacting Laurie became.

"Absolutely no slouching, Ed. You're the frame. You're the stem to my flower. Quit giving me crooked pictures and wilted flowers."

"Sorry." Normally Ed would have cracked a joke about Laurie being a flower, but there was something about Laurie when he got serious about teaching that made Ed ten times more eager to please than he'd been with any coach. He straightened his spine.

"I can't dance if you don't lead. Your job is to be strong and stable. Never forget you're the anchor. Your mistake will become mine."

Jesus. Ed wiped sweat from his brow and nodded. "Okay. Let's do it again."

It was work. It was fucking hard work. He went home sore most nights and usually so hungry he had to stop for two cheeseburgers on the way. He practiced the steps in his living room, clearing space enough to dance on the ragged rug in front of the TV. When he confessed this to Laurie, Laurie got a broom and showed him how to use it to perfect his balance and his frame. Unable to find his broom at home, Ed took contraband from the janitor's closet in one of the deserted offices at work over his lunch hour, dancing with an imaginary Laurie until he had to head to his one o'clock meeting.

Dancing was rough. But man, was it worth it.

Because every so often he'd do it right. Every so often the planets would line up and he could feel he was getting it even before Laurie praised him. When he got it right, it was as good as football. The world fell away, and it was only Ed, the music, and the dance.

And Laurie.

As he spun Laurie out into a turn and drew him into the embrace, he didn't just see but felt Laurie's perfect form, his control, his utter beauty in a dance. When he danced with Laurie, Ed felt ashamed at how he'd written Laurie off as a pouf. God yes, Laurie was feminine. And yet so very male, something Ed became exquisitely aware of as he held the other man in his arms. The arms that bent with such feminine grace were chiseled and muscled and strong under Ed's hands. Laurie was slight, but he was powerful.

Dancing with him made Ed want to be more graceful too. He mirrored Laurie's style, letting his body give the way Laurie's did. This earned him praise and a smile, so his mimicking became more conscious. But what he loved most was feeling he truly was Laurie's anchor, feeling the tension at their grip when Laurie turned or leaned or spun off the axis he provided. It gave him a thrill so much like sex that twice he'd fumbled to keep Laurie from sliding up against his body and finding something that would embarrass them both.

Then one day they danced the milonga, and Ed discovered a whole-new level of sexual tension.

"This is an older kind of tango," Laurie explained. "The frame is strong, and almost all the movement is in the feet. You're still an anchor, but there is more play, more pitter-patter, more traveling and turning. The key is to remember the dance's roots. It was danced by the mountain men who had come to the city to work."

He held up his arms, and Ed followed his lead, creating a frame.

Laurie took his hands and kept speaking. "You are a clumsy workman holding a prostitute in your arms. She is not pretty. Neither are you. But you make a civilization here. You are a worker. I am a whore. But we will dance before we do what is expected of us, because it is a pleasure. We will dance, and in the dance we will have the beauty life has denied us."

Ed's throat was so dry he had to clear it. "Okay."

Laurie smiled. "Ready? And forward, and step, and slide, and step-step, slide, and step…"

At first it was awkward, Laurie calling out the steps, showing Ed how to lead Laurie around the room. They moved slowly at first, Ed hulking and uncertain. But soon the dance came together. Laurie stopped calling out steps unless Ed fumbled, and then he stopped calling them out altogether. At last he broke away from the dance and went to the cabinet, where he started up some music.

"Lead in whenever you're ready." He stepped into Ed's frame and waited.

Their bodies were so close, and from the waist up they barely moved, Laurie's cheek nearly resting against Ed's. He could smell Laurie's detergent, deodorant and the sharp, sweet smell of his sweat. The music was strange. It wasn't tango at all but some electronica number with a percussive beat. It bore Ed up as he drove them around the room, as he held Laurie so close that sometimes when he inhaled through his mouth, Ed felt like he could taste him.

He had to keep his mind on the steps and on his form, but as the music wrapped around him and his feet began to learn the dance on their own, his thoughts wandered to Laurie's story. A dance from a brothel. A clumsy working man coming to dance with a whore, first on the floor, then in a bed. Well, Ed could play that role well enough. Laurie was no whore, though. Ed wondered if the mountain men ever fell in love with the beautiful prostitutes, if as they danced, they felt they danced instead with goddesses.

Ed wondered if any of those brothels had been full of men waiting for men.

A scene played out in his mind's eye. Ed came to a dark, dirty bar, gaslight flickering above. Across the room he saw Laurie standing in a line of men, painted, groomed, dressed in hand-me-down finery. He saw Laurie cross to him, saw him smile as he paced a graceful circle around Ed, toying with him, pretending he might not accept his invitation to dance. Ed imagined taking Laurie into his arms, knowing what the dance would lead to, knowing that when the songs were over they would go up the stairs, where he would dance a different dance with Laurie in bed.

Laurie, so beautiful, Laurie, so graceful, so strong, Laurie who smelled so good it was all Ed could do not to bury his face in his neck. Laurie, who Ed wanted to bury himself inside.

Dizziness hit Ed like a truck. He stumbled, tripped over his own feet and pitched backward onto the floor, bringing Laurie tumbling on top of him.

Laurie, sliding over him, Laurie's open mouth on his chest, his tongue snaking into his belly button before traveling down, down—

"Are you okay?"

Laurie loomed over him, half-sprawled across his chest, his hands braced on either side of Ed's head. The lower half of his body was draped over Ed's left leg, which was good because otherwise he'd be lying directly over the top of Ed's raging hard-on. Laurie wasn't aroused, though. He was worried.

"Ed?" He leaned in closer. "Ed?"

Ed blinked. The Laurie in front of him and the Laurie in his daydream mingled, then merged, and it was the tights all over again, except this time it was more than just nice legs. He was hot for Laurie because he looked good, yeah, but also because he was such a hard-ass teacher, because he was so beautiful, because Ed's whole body lit up when he saw him. And he realized, finally, what that meant.

When Laurie's hand cupped his cheek, Ed shut his eyes and turned his face into his palm.

"Ed." The voice was sharp, as was the grip on his face. "Stay with me, Ed."

The worry in Laurie's face registered, and Ed blushed. Laurie wasn't coming on to him. Laurie thought he'd hit his head.

"I'm fine," he murmured, shutting his eyes tighter in embarrassment.

"Your neck, is it...?"

"I'm *fine*." Ed lifted his hand and rubbed his eyes before pinching the bridge of his nose. "Just clumsy."

Ed rolled to a sitting position. Despite what he'd said to Laurie, he reached up and felt tentatively at his neck. A little tender. He'd take a pill and ice it and be fine.

Got a pill you can take to stop you from falling for Laurie?

Rattled, he pushed to his feet.

Laurie hovered, looking suspicious. "You hit your head so hard. Are you sure you're okay?"

No, but not for the reason you think. Ed felt so strange, so exposed. Like he was naked in the high school hallway with everyone giggling. "I think I should go home and rest."

Laurie looked crestfallen. "We have ice in the fridge. And I have some Tylenol in my bag."

Ed wanted to say no and get the hell out, but actually, icing now wouldn't be a bad idea. "Sure. Thanks."

"I'll be right back," Laurie promised, and hurried from the room.

Ed paced idly as he waited. He wasn't falling for Laurie. It was likely something that happened to all dancers. Laurie would laugh if he knew.

It didn't have anything to do with the fact that simply thinking about Laurie made him happy. And the fact that he hadn't so much as considered hitting a bar for a hookup in weeks was just coincidence.

Oh *fuck*.

"Here." Laurie had a cold pack in one hand and a bottle of water in the other. He handed the latter to Ed and held out his palm to reveal two white tablets tucked inside. As Ed swallowed them, Laurie dragged over a stool and made Ed sit on it. "Where do you need the ice?"

"I can do it."

Laurie wouldn't budge. "Where?"

Ed pointed at the center of his neck. "There, but—"

Grabbing a towel from the barre, Laurie wrapped up the pack and pressed it gently to Ed's neck. "You can't hold it well on your own. Relax and let me do it."

Ed submitted reluctantly. "Sorry I was so clumsy."

Laurie laughed. "This? This was nothing. Once I injured three ballerinas, brought down two backdrops and gave myself a concussion, all by lunging left instead of right because I was so nervous."

In the mirror, Ed watched their reflections. Laurie stood straight and tall while Ed slumped in his seat. Reflexively, he straightened, but he still looked like a hulking beast next to a beauty.

Laurie's reflection stared at Ed's reflection. "You're such a natural at dancing, Ed. You have such strength in your form. It's so easy to dance with you. Which is difficult to admit, because you're destroying all my stereotypes about football players."

"That was the plan. I learned how to dance to make

you mad," Ed quipped. But it was halfhearted. He couldn't look at Laurie now without part of him whispering, *You like Laurie. You want him.*

Still smiling, Laurie shook his head. "Sorry, didn't work. I'm not mad."

But he's not smitten, either.

The thought was a knife in Ed's chest. He watched Laurie's face, studied it, and what he saw drove the blade deeper. Laurie looked friendly. Concerned. Relaxed. But not turned on.

Because he didn't like Ed, not that way. As Laurie held the cold pack to Ed's neck, he chatted idly about the dance, giving Ed gentle feedback about how he could improve, praising what he'd done well, and it might as well have been him giving encouragement to Duon about his weight training. Whatever euphoria Ed had felt, whatever emotions had come in revelation, none of it was reciprocated.

Whatever. Ed wasn't going to fuck this up, wasn't going to lose dancing by being stupid and making a pass. This was some kind of puppy love for his dance partner. His *teacher.* Which was why Laurie looked at him like Ed looked at Duon. Because to Laurie he was just another student.

So why did Ed feel as if somebody had kicked him?

Ed rose. "I should get going. It's getting late."

Laurie frowned. "We've only been working for half an hour."

"Yeah, well, I got…I forgot. This meeting. In the

morning. Remembered it while I sat here. Gotta go home and get to bed."

The lie no doubt sounded as bald as it felt, but he didn't care. Well, he did, but he had to leave. He had a lot worse problems right now than his neck. He needed to stick his head in a toilet and flush until he had some sense.

He offered Laurie a weak smile. "Thanks."

"Okay." Laurie seemed bewildered. "So, I'll see you next week, I guess, at the last class."

Ed turned sharply, ignoring the twinge in his neck. "What?"

"It's the last class. Beginning Ballroom ends after next Tuesday." He smiled wanly. "I won't need you after that, sadly."

Slash, slash, slash. "A relief for you, I guess."

"We can still do private lessons, if you want."

"You're probably busy." *Tell me you're not that busy.*

Laurie laced his hands in front of himself and gave Ed a polite smile. "We'll have to see then, I guess. Let me know next week." He paused. "Do you need me to drive you home?"

The pity in his voice grated on Ed almost worse than the politeness. "I'm fine. Thanks." He tossed a salute. "See you next week, boss."

For what might be our last dance.

As the door to the studio closed behind him, Ed slumped and stuck his hands in his pockets, huddling against the wind as he hurried out to his car.

THE FOLLOWING MONDAY there was another staff cut at work.

Ed was lucky yet again and wasn't cut, but he felt lousy for it, especially when the woman with three kids in the cubicle across the hall turned out to be one on the list. He could tell she was trying not to cry as she packed up her desk under the watchful eye of security. He felt empty and morose all the way home, so much so that he only stayed in his apartment long enough to find some workout clothes and head to the center. He couldn't bear the thought of sitting in his apartment alone, thinking about how much he hated work, how much he needed work, how bad he felt for Mary.

Of course, the center made him think of Laurie, of how they were about to maybe have their last dance, about how he had a crush he couldn't seem to shake and Laurie absolutely didn't return.

He needed to work his body and shut off his mind. So he went to the weight room, put Britney in his headphones and pumped iron like he hadn't for weeks. He ran on the treadmill, did squats until his calves were on fire and worked for an hour on the Smith press. When he finally got back to his apartment, he dripped with sweat and his body ached. After a hot shower, he fell into bed, physically and mentally exhausted.

He woke in the middle of the night with his neck on fire.

Ibuprofen worked this time, sort of, with help from some ice, but he was up half the night, and when his alarm went off at five, he felt as if someone had hit him in the head with a hammer. His body ached all over, but his neck was the worst, throbbing at him in a worrying way. By the time he pulled into his parking spot at work, he was cranky and perfectly positioned to have a complete fuck of a day in an environment already rife with tension. As the day wore on, it didn't improve.

He wished to God the supervisors would figure out that when you cut the staff in half and upped the workload, it did *not* get done faster just because you yelled a lot and threatened to cut the coffee budget. The thought of slogging through to the end of the day was bad enough, but the thought of doing this until he was sixty-five was even worse.

He couldn't let himself think about seven o'clock, when he'd cap off a shit day by saying goodbye to the best thing in his life right now.

When Liam called him at four thirty and asked him to meet the guys at Matt's Bar, a few pitchers and a couple of Jucy Lucys sounded so good he agreed. It was a long way from Eden Prairie, but kicking back and hanging with the guys before dance class with Laurie was probably the best thing for him. Tease, laugh, have a drink or two—perfect.

Big. Fucking. Mistake.

Why the hell he'd thought for two minutes that it would be a good idea to sit and listen to his former teammates brag about how far they'd gotten in their training, he couldn't say. He hadn't been thinking about that when Liam called. He only thought about seeing the guys again, about sitting in the corner booth eating greasy burgers stuffed with cheese, about baskets of fries you could drown in, and about chugging cheap beer while the guys made dirty jokes. He'd told himself it didn't matter, that he'd made his peace about football and being with the guys at a bar wouldn't bother him. But one hour and one pitcher later, he realized he'd been completely wrong. He was not over football. Not at all.

It hurt. It hurt a lot to listen to them plan, to know he wasn't going to be a part of it ever again. It hurt to watch them cram as much fattening food as they wanted, knowing they'd burn it off in training and on the field. Ed had to back off unless he planned on spending the entirety of his Saturday on the treadmill.

It hurt most of all knowing he couldn't tell them how much it hurt to feel so left out, knowing he couldn't ever let them see.

So he drank. He drank until he was a fucking mess and had to lean on Liam to hold himself upright. When Liam made a joke about how he wasn't going to bed with him, no matter how he groped his thigh, Ed laughed along with the rest of them, then slurred something about Laurie in his tights, a reference no one would have understood even if he'd used consonants.

But then he remembered. Laurie. Dance class. The *last* dance class.

Last dance with Laurie.

He pulled out his phone, squinted at it, then finally asked Liam to tell him what the fuck time it was. It turned out to be a quarter to eight.

Ed stared at his phone as if it was what had betrayed him, not the pitcher of beer.

He'd missed the last dance class. Even if he were sober enough to drive to Eden Prairie, he'd never make it in time to catch Laurie. And he didn't have Laurie's number to call him and apologize.

His depression, already voluminous, became so acute he thought for a minute he was having a heart attack.

Excusing himself, he pushed back from the table and went to the jukebox at the window by the door where he had a prayer of getting reception, though it was still even odds if he'd be able to hear. At first he simply stared at the album selection in front of him, sad and lost and drunk, and then he stabbed at buttons on his phone until he managed to pull up the number he wanted.

"Vic," he said when she answered. "Vic. *Vic.* I need *help*. Please. Help."

"Ed? What happened?"

The floor listed like a ship, making it difficult for Ed to stand on it. He gripped the jukebox for support and focused on a Steely Dan album cover. "Need a favor, Vic. Need Laurie's number."

"You need lumber? What?"

"LAUR-EES NUM-BER." Ed forced his tongue into compliance with consonants.

"Ed, are you drunk?"

Ed shut his eyes to try to stop the jukebox from moving on him, but that only made things worse. "Missed class. At Matt's. Need to call him. Say sorry." His chest hurt. "Really sorry."

"You want to call *Laurie?*" Vicky sounded highly suspicious. "Why?"

Hadn't he just said? "Need to say *sorry.*"

"Ed, I'm not giving you Laurie's number so you can harass him under normal circumstances, but I'm absolutely not going to let you call him when you're hammered."

"I'm not gonna harass him. Told you, I missed *dance class*. Wanted to say *sorry!*"

"Ed, you aren't making any sense."

Vicky sounded exasperated, and Ed empathized. He pinched his nose. "Never mind."

"Ed, are you okay?"

No. He wasn't okay. Fucking around with weight classes and dancing with Laurie like it mattered. Nothing mattered. He'd never feel that high again, never feel the rush like he had once upon a time in a football game. It was monotony from now until the day he keeled over dead.

Ed didn't say goodbye. He hung up, shoved his phone into his pocket and pressed his head against the wall.

He stood there until a waitress came by and asked him, with suspicion, if he was all right. She looked ready to kick him out, but then Liam came over, and she smiled.

"Oh, if you're with the Lumberjacks, that's different."

Not a Lumberjack. Only *with* them.

But not with Laurie.

With feet like lead, Ed followed Liam to the table and vowed he would drink until he didn't know what football or dancing was anymore.

He wasn't halfway through his next beer before his phone rang. He tried to ignore it, but Butch, sitting next to him, hollered at him to make the thing shut up, so Ed pulled it out to turn it off. Except he accidentally answered it instead, so he put it to his ear with a heavy sigh. "What?"

"Ed? Is this—Ed? Ed Maurer?"

Laurie. "Hey." He felt euphoric until he remembered why he'd wanted to talk to Laurie in the first place. "So sorry."

There was a pause on the other end of the line. "Ed, are you okay?"

Ed looked at the guys around him, who were happy and laughing. "No."

"What happened? Where are you? Were you in an accident?"

"No. I'm at Matt's."

"Matt who?"

"Matt the bar." When Laurie said nothing, Ed added, "Jucy Lucy."

Another pause. "Ed, is anyone there with you? Anyone sober enough to talk to me on the phone?"

Ed glanced around the tables, drunkenly trying to assess the men around him. He turned to Liam. "Hey. Laurie wants to talk to you."

Liam raised an eyebrow at Ed, but he took the phone. Ed watched Liam's lips and his jaw, not hearing the words, just looking. Because Liam had a nice jaw. And nice lips too.

All of a sudden Liam handed him his phone. Ed picked it up and put it to his ear. "Laurie?" But the call had ended.

Liam eyed Ed skeptically. "You okay, buddy?"

Ed nodded, but man, did that make the room spin around. He frowned at the phone. "Why did Laurie hang up?"

"Who's Laurie?" Butch snickered. "You finally give up and admit pussy's the way to go?"

Ed gave him his best withering glare.

He became the butt of their jokes for a while, but that actually was good, because it was like old times. Ed tried to make his usual wisecrack that he'd be happy to show them what a real blow job was, but it was getting tough to make the words in his brain come out of his mouth. Liam noticed this too.

"I think it's time for you to switch to soda," he declared, taking Ed's beer away.

Ed wanted to protest, but it was too much work, so he gave up and sank into his chair. A can of Coke was placed in front of him, and he stared at it glumly. After awhile he decided he should brave a trip to the bathrooms downstairs, but he used the women's by accident and got lost in storage for several minutes before he found his way upstairs again. When he squeezed into his seat in the booth, somebody put a glass of water in front of him next to the Coke, and he sipped at it reluctantly.

He was tired. He caught himself nodding off twice and blinked himself into as much alertness as he could. But the third time he simply went under, and it wasn't until someone shook his arm that he woke, and he grunted and lifted his head to tell Liam to fuck off and let him sleep.

Except it wasn't Liam shaking him. It was Laurie.

CHAPTER SIX

*ocho: follower's step in tango whose name comes
from the figure eights women tango dancers
would make while doing the step. Leaders
should note that the more relaxed they are, they
better they may instigate an ocho.*

ED BLINKED. *LAURIE*. Laurie was here. He grinned. "Hi, boss."

Then he fell onto Laurie.

Laurie pushed him carefully upright, but his hands stayed on Ed's shoulder, holding him in place. Ed tried to grab Laurie's shoulder in return, but he missed and pitched forward.

Laurie caught him before he tumbled out of the booth. "What did you give him?" he asked the other guys at the table. "Grain alcohol?"

Butch gave a large belch before turning to Laurie. "You the wife?"

Laurie went rigid. Ed wanted to say this was Butch and not to mind him, and he did his best to give Butch a look that said *Knock it the fuck off, asswipe,* but mostly he swayed in his seat. It was possible, he acknowledged, he'd gotten a bit too drunk.

Where Ed had failed, Liam stepped in. "Hey, butthead, how about you be nice to Ed's friend who doesn't know you blew out all your brain cells bashing into guys on the field?"

Butch murmured an apology and retreated into his beer.

Liam extended a hand to Laurie. "Hi. I'm Liam Nelson. We spoke on the phone."

"I'm Laurie Parker." Laurie shook Liam's hand as he glanced at Ed. "Is he okay? Should I take him to a hospital?"

Ed started to object, but Liam steadied him. "Easy, big guy. He's just worried, like I am, that maybe you went a bit too heavy on the beer. How many Lucys did you pack in?"

"One." Ed made a face. "Not training. Not like you. Can't burn it off."

Understanding dawned on Liam's face, and Ed hated it. "Shit. I should have figured it out sooner."

"What," Laurie asked, "is a Lucy?"

The Lumberjacks erupted into spontaneous outbursts of disbelief and outrage, and two guys got up to hunt down a waitress. Laurie looked nervous, so Ed explained for him.

"Jucy Lucy." He held up an imaginary burger. "Hamburger with melted cheese in the middle."

"They're exclusive to Minneapolis-St. Paul, but Matt's is now verified by public contest as the best in the Cities." Liam pointed to a banner along the wall. "They're cheeseburgers, but the cheese is inside the meat. It becomes a sort of molten cheddar center. You *never* eat them right away. You have to give them a minute to cool off so you don't burn off your tongue with the liquid cheese."

Laurie relaxed. "I was a little worried, when Ed mentioned them, that I was coming to collect him at some seedy strip club."

"We meet there on Fridays," somebody called out from the other side of the table, and everyone laughed. Everyone but Laurie.

Ed didn't laugh, either. "You came to collect me?"

"Vicky called me. She was worried about you. And then when I called you—well, honestly, I didn't know what to think."

Ed sobered, as much as possible anyway. "I missed class. I got drunk. I'm sorry, Laurie."

Laurie seemed hesitant. "You didn't have to—I mean, I appreciate it, but—"

Ed sensed that his point was not being made. "I wanted to dance with you. But it was a bad day, and then…" The emotions hit him in the center of the chest, and he looked away. But that brought the Lumberjacks into his focus, the team that didn't include him anymore. Ed swore and reached for Liam's beer.

Liam deftly moved it out of his reach. "You're on

water and Coke now. And you're having another Lucy whether or not you think you can work it off. Something's got to soak up all that booze."

"We ordered some," Jared the fullback called out. "For Ed and his date."

"Oh, I wasn't going to stay. If Ed's all right—"

Ed turned to Laurie. "You can't leave, you just got here."

"You have to try a Lucy," somebody called out, and the whole team hooted out their agreement in a rough chant. *Lu-cy, Lu-cy, Lu-cy!*

Ed put his hand on Laurie's thigh. "You have to stay. Please?"

It was clear Laurie did not want to stay. But he bit his lip, then sighed. "Would someone order a Diet Pepsi for me, then?"

"Diet Coke," Butch corrected.

"I'm glad you came." Ed's whisper carried across the whole table.

"Yes. Well." Laurie patted Ed's hand, and when Ed didn't lift it from Laurie's thigh, Laurie picked it up and moved it onto the table.

"I'm sorry I wasn't at dancing. I wanted to come. A lot."

"It's all right. Don't worry about it."

But Laurie didn't understand. Ed wasn't sure he did anymore, either. He leaned forward, determined this time to actually whisper. "I missed you."

Eyes wide, Laurie stared at him. Then his gaze softened, his brow furrowed, and he opened his mouth to say something.

"Lucys are here," Jared crowed, and the next thing Ed knew somebody shoved a burger basket under his nose.

It was fun to watch Laurie try a Jucy Lucy. After poking at it dubiously, he took a bite, and the whole table hooted and cheered when the greasy cheese squirted out the side of the burger and ran down his chin. "He's a gusher!" Ed loved how easily the guys accepted Laurie. But Laurie looked nervous.

He had some cheese dangling on his chin, so Ed swiped it with his thumb. But his aim was off, and his thumb ended up brushing against Laurie's bottom lip too.

Jesus, his lip was *soft*.

Dazed, Ed picked up his burger. He wasn't hungry, but he ate it anyway, and as he did, he listened to the conversation around him. Liam kept talking to Laurie, drawing him in. Laurie leaned slightly on Ed. Or maybe Ed was leaning on him. He got confused. Anyway, he settled on Laurie's shoulder, and it felt so nice that Ed put his arm around him, letting his hand rest on Laurie's opposite hip.

The hell of the layoffs, the flare-up in his neck, and the reality of being an outcast among the guys carved a huge, hollow space inside Ed that not even a keg of beer could fill. But Laurie, simply sitting beside him, made that space feel so much less important, less like it was going to suck him down. He still didn't understand why, exactly, Laurie had come to Matt's. He only knew he was glad he had.

Ed anchored himself more firmly to Laurie's side and smiled as he reached for his glass of water, willing to believe for the first time in two days that things might actually somehow work out after all.

LAURIE FELT FOOLISH for rushing across the city only to discover Ed's crisis was that he was drunk. He wanted to blame Liam for luring him here, but it was hard to hate Liam. He was courteous and thoughtful, always trying to keep Laurie involved in the conversation. He asked what Laurie did, and he seemed pleased when he heard that Laurie was a dance instructor. Clearly he believed Laurie and Ed were some sort of item, and he approved.

Liam also looked vaguely like Brad Pitt, which Laurie found highly distracting.

But the quarterback wasn't the only one at the table who thought Laurie and Ed were a couple. At first Laurie had thought they were making fun of him, but he'd slowly come to realize their bawdy jokes were some sort of nod of acceptance. The thought baffled Laurie. Gay-friendly *football players*? Wasn't that an oxymoron? Though as the evening progressed, as the men around the table grew more intoxicated and more gregarious, and as he watched how they interacted not with Laurie but with Ed, Laurie began to understand it wasn't so much that the football players were gay advocates. They were simply Ed advocates.

The bar itself was as mystifying as the men. From the outside it looked like a real dive, and to be honest, it did from the inside too. But instead of bikers and brawlers, he'd seen mostly couples and small clutches of friends. The football crew was the largest group, and from the way the other tables rotated in and out, Laurie got the idea they were monopolizing their tables more than was generally encouraged. Of course, given the number of burgers and fries and pitchers of beer they consumed, he suspected their lingering was welcomed.

Ed turned to Laurie with a drunken, sleepy grin. "You like the Lucy?"

This was the burger with the cheese inside. The Jucy Lucy. The sandwich hardening Laurie's arteries and threatening, half-eaten, to make his leotards snug-fitting. "It's very good, but I'm full."

Ed beamed and slid his hand over Laurie's thigh. "I'm glad you're here."

This was at least the fourth time Ed had told Laurie so. While the declaration was amusing at this point, it was still disarming. Laurie put his hand on Ed's, keeping it from straying higher. "Maybe you should have some more water."

Ed frowned at him. "Are you mad at me? Because they think you're my boyfriend?"

"No, Ed. Please drink your water."

"Because I know a guy like you wouldn't go for a

guy like me."

Laurie frowned. "What do you mean, 'a guy like me'?"

"It's the tights. You look so fucking good in them."

Laurie was truly lost now. "You think I look good in my tights?"

Ed nodded. "I wanted to blow you. Right there at the drinking fountain."

"Oh." Laurie felt dizzy. The drinking fountain…at his studio? Yes, that was the only time he'd worn tights. That first night he'd come for a private lesson. The night they'd done the tango.

Ed had thought about going down on Laurie that night?

Had he thought about this often?

Ed shook his head. "Don't worry. I'll leave you alone."

It might have been a noble statement, even drunk, if Ed's hand hadn't slipped out of Laurie's to slide all the way up to Laurie's groin as he said it.

"Ed." Laurie fumbled with the roving hand, then stilled with a gasp as Ed cupped him boldly through his jeans.

"God, but I'd love to taste your cock." Ed massaged the length of Laurie through his denim.

"Get a room," somebody called across the table.

"*Ed.*" The word came out as a squeak, and Laurie's hands trembled as he tried yet again to disengage from Ed.

Liam hauled Ed closer to himself. "Buddy, you're crowding your boyfriend. How about you sit by me for a while?"

Ed shook his head in drunken exaggeration and glowered at Liam. "Not my boyfriend. Don't call him that. Make him mad again."

Laurie started to protest, but Liam winked at him and shook his head. "Ed here is not what I'd call a cooperative drunk. It's best to keep him happy and redirect him when he gets to be too much." He patted Ed's head, which was now resting on his shoulder. "Isn't that right, buddy?"

"So fucking hot in those tights."

God, but I'd love to taste your cock.

Laurie rose. "I should get going—"

Everyone at the table protested, offering him more Diet Coke and, God help him, Jucy Lucys. Ed's objection was loudest, however, and most troubled, and he fought out of Liam's hold to try to physically stop Laurie from going.

Liam caught him, whispered something, then looked at Laurie. "Can I talk to you for a second?"

A man named Casey sat with Ed while Liam drew Laurie aside, though Laurie noticed they stayed within Ed's line of sight and that Ed kept watching them with drunken suspicion, as if Laurie might dash for the door if he so much as turned his head away.

Liam leaned against the wall, nodding at Ed as he spoke to Laurie. "I think I may have misread things. I take it you two *aren't* seeing each other?"

Laurie's mouth opened and closed a few times. He wanted to tell the man it wasn't any of his business, but he could tell Liam cared for Ed and that he felt this was somehow pertinent information. "To be honest, we barely know each other. For a long time, actually, we fought every time we saw one another. And then..." He paused, trying to find the way to explain how they'd gone from adversaries to dance partners. He could come up with nothing. "Then he helped me with a dance class, and somehow I started giving him private ballroom dancing lessons."

Liam smiled knowingly. "Oh, *okay*. Now I get it."

Laurie arched an eyebrow at him. "Please explain, because I don't."

"I assume Ed told you that he used to play football. And you've figured out we're the Lumberjacks, his team? His former team, technically, though it's not as if we're going to stop hanging out with Ed because the doc told him he can't play. But it's not the same for him. And really, not for us. I know it upsets him and that sometimes coming out with us is too tough. I think for Ed we were a family. His actual family is pretty cool, but he loved hanging with us, being with us. And it's mutual. But now he's outside of us. He acts fine, but he's not. Tonight it's hitting him hard for some reason."

He acts fine, but he's not. Yes. Laurie knew all about that. "But what does this have to do with dancing with me?"

Liam seemed taken aback. "You're the one who showed him he could dance. Isn't it obvious?"

"I didn't teach him to dance. I'm more fine-tuning."

Now Liam looked lost. "So you aren't the one who taught him to dance? With his mom?"

"No, I'm the one at the center. We both volunteer there. I was teaching aerobics, and my music was too loud. And one night he said he'd do anything to get me to quit early, and I had him come to my beginning ballroom class to be my partner. Things have sort of…snowballed from there."

Liam seemed disappointed, but he rallied. "Well, here's what we were thinking, a few of the guys and I. We saw him dance once. He was good. Real good. We thought maybe he could get into it. Oh, not professional or anything. Except—well, like semipro. Maybe he could do contests or something. Shows. Something to get him out there again. He's a competitive guy. The doc said no football, ever, but dancing is fine. So I kept nudging Ed to do something with it. I thought he'd given up, and then when you showed up and said you were his dance instructor…" He looked hopefully at Laurie. "Could you? Help him get into competing somehow? Would you?"

Warning bells had sounded during most of Liam's story, but at the direct questioning, Laurie couldn't hold back anything at all. "Absolutely not. I'll have nothing to do with competitions."

Liam held up his hands. "Hey, no big deal. It was only a question."

Laurie knew he'd overreacted, but he felt ambushed. "It's not what you're thinking, competition dance. It's not fun. Competition ballroom is grueling and backstabbing and awful. I don't want any part of it."

Liam grimaced. "I'm sorry you don't think that'd be something Ed could do. Because he needs an outlet, and I can tell he likes you a great deal."

Laurie blushed. "He's just drunk."

"Not *just.*" He sighed and rubbed his neck. "Well, one thing's for sure. I gotta get the guy home. He's in no condition to drive, and drunk *and* upset is not a good combination in him without a shepherd. But I can't stay. My wife is going to be mad at me for staying out as late as I am already, and I still have to get his car back for him."

"You think something will happen if he's left alone?"

Liam patted Laurie on the shoulder. "Don't worry about it. Butch or Jared or somebody will sit with him."

It would've been easy to let it go. Laurie could say, "Sounds great. Thanks," and bolt. But that wasn't what Laurie did, or what he said.

"I can sit with him."

Liam raised his eyebrows. "Are you sure? He can be a handful. And he is clearly determined to get into your pants. Also, since it sounds like you haven't seen it, you should know his place is a real pit. I mean, it's *Hoarders*-level bad. Most of the guys won't go over there."

"I'll keep him at my house." Laurie ignored the part about Ed wanting to get into his pants. "It's not far from here, and I don't work until two tomorrow."

"He'll need to wake up and call in sick. Which, given what he said about work, isn't going to go down well. But he's going to be lucky to be functional by two. And odds are good you'll have to clean your bathroom once he's gone."

"It's fine."

"Well, okay then." Liam smiled. "You've been warned, and you're willing to make sure he doesn't hurt himself or drown in his own sick. I say we do it." He clamped a hand on Laurie's shoulder and turned toward the group of football players. "Hey, Maurer, come on, buddy, your show is over. Time to pack it in."

Ed, who had been dozing fitfully on another man's shoulder, snapped his head up, blinked, and then glared at Liam. "I'm not going home."

"No, you aren't. You're going to Laurie's."

Ed looked at Laurie in surprise. Then he rose and hurried to them in a somewhat straight line.

The table burst into hoots and catcalls. "He's gonna pack it in all right," somebody called, and Liam turned to Laurie, wincing.

Laurie, blushing, murmured, "It's all right. Let's

go."

Ed came up beside Laurie, which is to say that he ran into him. "You're taking me home?"

"Yes." Laurie tried to play it cool. "You're a bit too drunk to leave alone."

"You have to behave, Ed." Liam pulled Ed firmly away from Laurie. "Otherwise you have to go home by yourself, to your own apartment."

"I'll be good," Ed promised, but his hand claimed Laurie's, and he wouldn't let go, not even as they wove their way to the door.

He also insisted point-blank that he ride with Laurie, not Liam.

"I don't mind," Laurie said to Liam as Ed locked himself into Laurie's passenger seat and gave Liam a challenging glare. "Really."

"Suit yourself." With a salute, Liam headed to Ed's car.

ED DID BEHAVE while Laurie drove. But he talked a lot.

"So you aren't mad at me?"

Laurie glanced at him. "Why do you keep asking that?"

"Because you seem mad. Because I'm a big oaf. Because I missed dancing class."

"Ed," Laurie began wearily then remembered Liam's advice. "I'm not mad. Sit back, please, so I can drive."

"What did Liam say to you? What did he tell you? Did he say something about me? Why did you look at me all funny?"

Oh, God. He hadn't thought Ed was paying attention during that discussion. "I don't know what you're talking about." Laurie merged into another lane of traffic.

"At the bar. You looked at me weird."

"You probably had cheeseburger on your face."

"You looked at me like you were sad. The way I feel sad sometimes."

Laurie didn't say anything, only kept his eyes on the road and kept driving.

"What did Liam say to you?"

Laurie gave up. "He said you missed football and that tonight it was bothering you a lot."

"Yeah." Ed frowned at Laurie. "But why did you look at me that way?"

"It doesn't matter."

"I want to know."

Laurie's sweaty hands slipped on the wheel. "I'm trying to drive."

"Why did you look at me like that, Laurie?"

He's drunk. He's not going to remember. And so, to shut him up, Laurie told him the truth. "Because I miss dancing the way you miss football."

"That's not true, because you still dance."

"Not the way I used to." Laurie's hands flexed, then relaxed in a sort of defeat against the wheel. "I used to compete. A lot. I tried for every award and trophy, for every artist-in-residence. I was never anything but a huge success."

He kept his eyes on the road, but his mind was busy tunneling into the past. The night seemed to expand and shrink around him, making him feel strange.

"But I never felt satisfied. Nothing was ever enough, and so I kept reaching. And reaching." Laurie shut his eyes for a long blink, hating that he had to open them to look at the road. "And then I had to stop."

"Why did you stop? I don't understand. What do you mean, you were reaching? For what? What did you do?"

Laurie realized he'd never told anyone the story, because everyone already knew. He wasn't sure he wanted Ed to know, either. He wasn't sure he wanted Ed to know how awful he had been.

Which didn't explain at all why, with that decided, he told the story anyway.

"I was in a relationship with a man. Another dancer. We kept it quiet, because that was what you did. Even if people suspect you're gay, they'd rather you didn't bring it up. But we started dancing together in secret. He was into international ballroom, which I admit I dismissed at first. But Paul showed me how fun it could be. And I was good at that too, really good, especially with him. He'd tease me for being such a natural follower, but it was true. I loved performing on stage, but when I danced with Paul, it felt like I was coming home. I'd go to his competitions and watch him with his female partners and hate them. I wanted to be them. I wanted to be the one dancing with him. I wanted to be the one to win with him. And that was how it started."

Laurie took a deep breath before pressing on. "I convinced him I should be his dancing partner, that we should both come out. I told him we were so good that it wouldn't matter. People might whisper, but in the end we'd be so amazing we'd take over the international dancing world the same way I'd taken over the stage. And I convinced him. We entered as a pair, listing me as Laurie Parker, not Laurence, which was how I was always billed on stage. People assumed I was female, all the way until I stepped out with Paul onto the competition floor."

"Did it work?"

"No." Laurie fixed his gaze on the road. "We danced our first dance, and after that they kicked us out of the competition. It was a huge scandal for both of us, but it was especially bad for Paul. It made people laugh at me, but it killed his career completely and nearly destroyed him psychologically as well. He's doing all right now, relatively. A former mutual friend was kind enough to let me know last year. But he won't compete again. And it's all my fault."

The last confession hurt so much it made Laurie's

vision blur, and he slowed the car as he blinked and tried to recover. But then he felt Ed's hand on his.

Ed gazed with amazing sobriety into Laurie's eyes. "It's not your fault."

"It is. He didn't want to do it, but I pushed him."

"Then he should have said no. If he agreed, he wanted to do it too. It wasn't your fault." He pointed in the general direction of his neck. "This isn't my fault. Or the fault of the guy who landed on me. It just happened."

Laurie's vision blurred, and he blinked furiously. "Sorry, I'm being ridiculous."

Ed's hand tightened on Laurie's. "No. You're not ridiculous. Not at all."

Laurie squeezed back, and they held hands all the way off the interstate and down the street, into the parking garage beneath his condo, until Laurie absolutely had to take his hand back to navigate into his space. He was aware of Ed looking at him, conscious of the intensity of his gaze. The car shrank around him. Laurie didn't dare look at Ed, because he knew it would be over if he did.

When Ed reached for him, Laurie opened the car door and escaped.

Liam had found the visitor parking, and by some miracle he'd managed to score a spot. He approached Laurie's car, handed him Ed's keys. "You want help getting him upstairs?"

For a second, Laurie wanted to insist Liam take

him home. But he shook his head. "No. I'll be fine."

"I'm gonna go catch a cab, then." He tossed Laurie a salute. "Best of luck. I hope I see you again." He shouted toward the car. "Remember, Maurer, you promised to be good." Liam laughed, and when Laurie turned to see why, he saw Ed's hand above the roof of the car, middle finger raised and aimed in Liam's direction.

"Good night," Liam called, and then he was gone.

Laurie felt strangely out of body. He told himself this was because of his confession about dancing, but as he came around the rear bumper of his car, all the way up beside Ed's door, he knew better. He looked at the man he'd agreed to host for the evening, the man whose shirt was unbuttoned, who swayed in his seat. The man whose dark hair was a mess, whose beard was rough and visible against his flushed cheeks. The man whose dark gaze bore into Laurie with bleary but clearly sensual promise.

It wasn't his confession making Laurie feel light-headed. It was Ed.

Laurie managed to get him out of the car without incident, even got them into the elevator. Down the hall was tricky, because Ed had a penchant for navigating them into a wall, but Laurie got them to his door and propped Ed against the frame as he fumbled with his key. But once inside, he saw Ed standing in his entryway, filling the space, and Laurie faltered.

Ed gestured at himself with distaste. "I'm sorry for

this. For being drunk. For being a problem." His gaze met Laurie's. "Sorry you have to settle for a partner like me now instead of someone who made you feel like you were home."

Laurie should tell Ed he'd misheard, that it was partner dancing, not Paul, that made him feel that way. That he and Paul hadn't worked half as well together on the floor sometimes as the two of them did. That he felt more attraction to Ed, whom he'd never so much as kissed, than he ever did for his partner of several years. But he couldn't say that with Ed standing in his hallway, filling it.

Ed, stinking of beer. Ed, who had held his hand and told him the past wasn't his fault. Ed, who drove him crazy, but who never made Laurie feel alone. Those thoughts swirled around Laurie, forcing him to admit the real reason he'd been so eager to take Ed home.

But Laurie still didn't know what to say. So he stepped forward, pushed Ed to the closet door, and kissed him.

CHAPTER SEVEN

*sacada: a displacement, to move your partner's
leg out of the way gently with your own.*

E D WOKE TO sunlight streaming through a window onto a bed where he lay naked. The mattress beneath him was exceptionally soft, but it was little comfort, because Ed felt like complete crap. His head pounded, his mouth tasted like dog shit, and he had to piss so bad his teeth were floating.

Beside him, someone stirred in sleep.

Ed shut his eyes and said a silent, desperate prayer. Then he told his bladder to shut the fuck up, and he did his best to assess. He began by taking a deep breath.

He let it out with relief. He'd smelled man. Women smelled soft and fresh. Women smelled vaguely sweet. And women's bedrooms tended to smell of hairspray and fabric softener and…well, women. Men, even the fussy ones, smelled muskier. Sharper. An edge of spice or savory. Yummy, as far as Ed was concerned.

This was a man smell. This was a man's room. Which meant he'd gone home with a man. Thank fucking God.

Ed then focused his attention with some trepidation on his ass.

It felt fine. Bit of gas, maybe, but mostly his backside felt like a plain old ass. Nobody had fucked him, or if they had, they weren't anybody to write home about. But probably nothing had happened. So no condomless orgies. Ed thanked God again.

Drawing another breath, he gathered his courage and turned to ID the stranger he'd gone home with. But when he saw who was there, he nearly pissed the bed. Because the man lying next to him was no stranger. It was Laurie.

Laurie Parker lay, also naked, beside Ed in the bed, in the fancy, high-thread-count, pristine white sheets. Laurie's dark-blond hair lay beautifully mussed over his pillow, and in sleep, his features were soft and relaxed—exquisitely beautiful.

Pretty. Laurie was handsome, yes, but pretty, like a china statue. His cheeks were pale but stained pink, and his lips were flush enough to draw attention to them.

I am lying in bed with Laurie. Naked. In bed. With Laurie.

Laurie had gotten naked with him.

I fucked Laurie.

The cold, horrible reality of the situation hit Ed like a defensive tackle.

I fucked Laurie, and I don't remember doing it.

The thought drew a strangled, anguished sound out of him, and the noise woke Laurie. Now Ed stared, openmouthed, as beautiful, gorgeous, fucking lick-me-pretty Laurie regarded him blearily and smiled.

He woke up enough to read Ed's expression and withdrew.

Ed's hand shot out and stopped him, gripping his shoulder. "Laurie?"

Laurie lifted his chin. "Yes?"

Ed felt like the world was sliding out from beneath him. It had to be a mistake. How could he fuck Laurie and not know? How did they go from polite Laurie to naked Laurie? "Laurie, we… Did we?"

Laurie freed himself from Ed's grip on his shoulder, tugging the sheet up to the top of his armpits as he lay back on his pillow. "Did we what?"

This posture sent off warning bells for Ed, but he was having a hard enough time sussing out his situation, let alone finessing it. "You and me, did we…?"

"Have sex?" Laurie supplied for him patiently.

Ed nodded. He felt like he was steeling himself for the answer, but he couldn't tell what answer he was hoping for.

Laurie kept turning more and more frosty. "It depends on your definition."

Ed shut his eyes and ran a hand over his face. "What did we do?"

"Nothing that warrants the kind of horror you

seem to be experiencing." Laurie's tone was sharp and clipped. And pissed.

Ed clutched his hand to his head. "The last thing I remember is being at work. How did I get from—and you—?"

I didn't even know you liked me that way.

He stared at Laurie's naked chest, thought of his fully naked body beneath the sheet, of how he'd seen it and possibly explored it *and didn't remember.*

Ed drew the blanket over his head to hide it in his misery.

Then he realized what else was under the blanket and opened his eyes.

Laurie rolled to the side, pinning part of the sheet beneath his body and effectively shrouding himself from Ed's view. Annoyed, Ed came out from the covers and glared.

Laurie glared back. "You're welcome, by the way, for taking you home and keeping you from killing yourself in some drunken fit. And for cleaning up the bathroom floor, and putting up with your pawing at the bar—"

"We were at a bar?" Flashes of memory returned, and Ed sat up. "Matt's. We were at Matt's. We—"

The act of sitting bolt upright with a hangover caught up with him. He groaned and sank to his pillow.

"Yes. I came to Matt's after you didn't come to class and Vicky called me, frantic because you were either drunk or hurt or maybe both, and you were upset and asking for me. Your friend Liam told me how to get to where you were. I sped all the way over, worried sick."

"You were worried about me?"

"Yes, because I'm an idiot." Laurie's cheeks were flushed now. "Because there you were, not hurt, sloshed with your football buddies."

This felt familiar. Ed beamed. "Yes, I remember you showing up." *I remember you looked worried.*

"You made me eat a greasy hamburger with cheese inside it. You wouldn't let me leave, and so when Liam said someone had to sit with you to make sure you were okay, I volunteered." He flattened his lips, looking disgusted.

Ed was touched. "You did all that for me?"

"Yes."

"Thank you."

Laurie snorted and rolled onto his back.

Ed caught him before he got away. When Laurie lifted a hand to block the touch, Ed captured his hand instead. "So you took me home. And we had sex. Of sorts."

"Regretfully, yes."

"What sort of sex?" When Laurie didn't answer, Ed slid his thumb along the back of Laurie's hand, stroking encouragingly. "Since you're giving it restrictions, I'm assuming there was no penetration?"

Now Laurie looked really pissed. "You think I'd let you fuck me when you were so drunk you don't remember what happened?"

"*You* might have fucked *me*," Ed pointed out.

"I considered it, but then you started vomiting, and the urge passed."

Laurie delivered the line so drily that Ed couldn't tell if that was a barb or if he'd truly almost fucked him. But the thought of being that close to being *with* Laurie, with Laurie all the way, pierced Ed in a yearning ache, and he went still. His bladder screamed at him, its insistence he urinate exquisitely intense, but Ed shoved the need down and focused on Laurie.

"So what did we do? What happened?" When Laurie said nothing, Ed stroked his hand again, pleading now. "Please. Tell me."

Laurie withdrew his hand and lay there, staring up at the ceiling.

"You'd been touching me all night. If you weren't hanging on me, you were touching my shoulder or my neck or my hand. When I tried to leave without you, you looked at me with such betrayal I couldn't bring myself to go without bringing you along. In the car you didn't paw me, not much, but you talked to me, asking me about myself. About my past. Because I was feeling foolish, I told you, and you seemed to understand. Probably because you were so drunk. But I wasn't thinking about that, not then. I felt safe with you. And it was because of that, I suppose, that when we were both standing inside my apartment, alone, you looking at me with longing, I kissed you."

Ed tried desperately to remember this. He couldn't catch it, not even its shadow.

"I kissed you against the wall. You kissed me back. And then you dragged your mouth across my cheek, dug your hands into my hair and started to whisper. You told me you thought I was beautiful, over and over. I tried to kiss you to shut you up, but you wouldn't stop talking."

Ed did think Laurie was beautiful. He thought that all the time. But he'd never meant to say it out loud. He sure as hell never meant to say it and not remember.

Laurie kept going, but the words came out stilted and halting, like he didn't want to say them any more than Ed wanted to hear them. "You told me I was beautiful when I danced. You told me when you watched me move, it made you ache inside. You told me you wanted to move with me. You told me you wanted to move inside me. You pressed me to my knees, talking to me all the time, telling me beautiful, drunken-slurred things, and after I helped you unbutton your pants, you put your fingers in my hair and drew me close, and then, yes, you did indeed move inside me."

Ed, full of arousal and despair, shut his eyes, unable to take any more of this. But Laurie went on, merciless.

"At some point we went to the bedroom, where we kissed some more, and then you said more pretty, silly things. About how you thought about dancing with me all the time. About how alive it made you feel. You slid down my body, kissing and whispering. You pushed my legs back, and you made love to me with your mouth and your hands, sucking me, stroking me, and I gave in and let go to you. I didn't think about anything, only what you were doing to me. Like I don't think I have for a long, long time."

Stop, Ed tried to whisper, but his throat was too dry to work.

"And then you got sick."

Ed winced and shut his eyes tighter.

"You made it to the bathroom but not the toilet. You apologized. A lot. I told you not to worry, and I cleaned you up. Got your teeth brushed, your body cleaned off, and your stomach calmed. I put you in bed, then stood in the hall, trying to decide if I should sleep beside you or take the couch. You called out to me, talked me out of the pajamas I'd put on and into bed beside you. Pressed kisses to my forehead and whispered tender gibberish, and then went to sleep."

He paused, and Ed, thinking he was done, dared to open his eyes. It was a mistake, because he got to watch Laurie's face harden.

"Then you woke up and looked at me with horror, and I realized it had all been drunken lunacy, all that sex I'd mistaken for something more."

That look was a cleat right in the center of Ed's gut. He wanted to reach for Laurie, but his hand wouldn't move. Nothing about him worked. Even his bladder had given up vying for attention. He simply lay there, stunned.

The chorus of "Piece of Me" began to chirp happily from across the room, his ringtone for work.

Ed saw the clock on the nightstand and swore under his breath as he staggered out of bed toward his pants. They lay neatly folded over some kind of rack until Ed retrieved them to fumble in the pocket for his phone. "'Lo?"

"Ed?" Tracy, his supervisor, sounded harried. "Where the hell are you?"

Ed dropped the pants and rubbed the side of his face. Oh God in heaven, he had to piss. He wandered toward the door on autopilot and across the hall to the bathroom. "Sick." He flipped up the toilet lid, leaned against the sink so he could stay upright, and gave his bladder its longed-for release.

"Why didn't you call in?"

"Sick." Ed shivered at the pleasure of a bladder no longer full to the point of pain. "Threw up."

"We have the presentation to senior management today. I need you here." She paused, then added, "Are you…urinating?"

"When's the meeting?" Ed gave himself a shake before flushing.

"Two, but—"

"I can be in by twelve thirty, but you're gonna want to put me in the back."

He could feel Tracy's tension through the phone. "Ed, this isn't good."

"I gotta go. See you later." He hung up before she could launch into a scolding.

After staring at the phone for a few seconds, Ed lifted his gaze to the door. Laurie. He was there, waiting in the other room, pissed as hell. Laurie, who had wanted him. Laurie, who had blown him. Laurie, who had kissed him, whom *he* had blown. Laurie, who had cleaned Ed up when he'd been sick, who had taken him home.

Laurie. *Laurie.*

What am I supposed to do now?

Ed had no idea.

He got into the shower, hid under the warm water and wished it could send him into the drain. He washed his hair. He soaped off his body, trying not to think about Laurie's mouth moving across it as Ed pushed his fingers into that soft blond hair. He rinsed out his mouth and used one finger as a toothbrush, then all of them as a comb for his hair. Finally, he tucked his towel around his waist and left the sanctuary of the bathroom.

Laurie was in the kitchen, fully dressed, reading something on the counter. He didn't look up when Ed came in. "I don't have much for food right now, but I could probably produce some toast and coffee."

Ed clutched at the edge of his towel. "Can I take you out for breakfast?"

Laurie shrugged, still focused on the magazine he was flipping through. "I suppose."

Ed gave a curt nod. "Let me get dressed quick."

He moved as fast as his unsteady body would allow him, climbing into his pants and shirt and socks and shoes, all of which were arranged on the tidy rack. He didn't see his coat, but it had been warm the day before. He had probably left it in his car. Which he didn't know where it was.

But his car turned out to be parked in Laurie's parking garage, because Laurie drove them right past it as they headed out to the street.

And there was the Walker Art Center. He could see the entrance to the sculpture garden from here. "Wow. Good location."

Laurie nodded curtly. "Where are we going for breakfast?"

"Keys Cafe?" Ed suggested carefully. "There's one close to here, right?"

Laurie nodded again.

They drove the rest of the way in silence. They didn't say much as they waited for the hostess to seat them, either, and as they sat across from one another in their booth, the silence grew heavy.

Ed tried to take comfort in the homey atmosphere, to bask in the smell of pancakes and eggs, to revel in the acid bite of the pungent coffee warming his hands through the mug. But he was too aware of Laurie for any of this to bring him any meaningful ease. He watched Laurie's long fingers tightly gripping the handle of his own mug, watched him look everywhere but at Ed, retreating into the stony wall Ed was accustomed to seeing him hide behind. All Ed could do was stare into his mug. So they simply sat there, not saying anything, all the way until their food arrived.

"I love their pancakes here." Ed slathered the pat of butter across his stack before reaching for the syrup.

"I haven't had them. I always get eggs."

Ed gaped at him. "Are you serious?" Ed cut a generous, syrup-laden bite and aimed it across the table. "Eat," he demanded, and when Laurie tried to protest, Ed shoved it into his open mouth.

He watched Laurie's lips close around the fork, the pink flesh sliding slowly down the tines. He withdrew the utensil, but kept it suspended in the space between them as Laurie chewed. As Laurie's tongue darted out to catch the last hint of syrup that coated his lips.

And then you dragged your mouth across my cheek, dug your hands into my hair, and you started to whisper. You told me you thought I was beautiful.

"It's good." Laurie set down his fork and wiped his mouth with his napkin.

You told me I was beautiful when I danced. You told me that when you watched me move, it made you ache inside. You told me you wanted to move with me.

Ed didn't say anything else. He just ate. And it wasn't long before the meal was over and he was paying at the cash register, and then they were heading to Laurie's car.

This wasn't what Ed had planned. He didn't know

what he'd meant to happen, but it hadn't been this…this complete fucking silence. He felt angry. He felt helpless and frustrated.

Fucking hell, he felt *cheated.*

How had he fucked this up? And what exactly *was* this, while they were on the subject? Ed understood he'd gotten drunk of his own free will and that all this was the result of that. All this awkwardness and misunderstanding. Except that was the problem, wasn't it? It *wasn't* a misunderstanding. He *did* feel that way about Laurie. He hadn't quite articulated it to himself, but yeah, everything Laurie told him he'd said was how he felt.

Every beautiful thing. Every word. Every longed-for touch. All those things he'd done but couldn't remember, not even after Laurie had recounted the evening to him. It was too much. Too fucking much.

They were at the stoplight at Dunwoody and Lyndale on the back side of the art center, the grass browning and dying in the November cold. It was space, open and inviting, and Ed wanted it. So he opened the car door, jumped out and ran.

He could hear Laurie shouting, first worried, then angry, but Ed kept going. At this point he was well past being able to stop. He felt dizzy. Sick. Stupid. Really fucking stupid.

So sad, and scared.

His head pounded and his pancake bounced unhelpfully in his gut, but Ed ran deeper and deeper into the sculpture garden. He'd come here a thousand times, but he took the art in now in a blur, identifying it in a weird subconscious tour as he ran past. He heard the tree chimes and felt their surreal song cut into him, opening him up. He ran past *Spoonbridge and Cherry*, its sprinkler turned off for the winter. He ran past *Knife Edge* and *Standing Frame*, running until his lungs burned and the soles of his feet sent needles through his legs with every step.

He didn't know where he was going. *My car is at his place, just through this hedge.* Yes. He could get his car and get out of here and end this. No goodbye, no more Laurie looking at him with daggers.

Except he'd screwed up, and instead of hitting the path that would have taken him out to the street, he ended up at the *Two-Way Mirror Punched Steel Hedge Labyrinth*—dead end. Wheezing, he bent over, bracing his hands against his knees. He stared into that fucked-up vision of himself, blurred and morphed and darkened, and he knew despite all the cheerfulness he projected every day, this was the way he felt inside. It wasn't simply screwing up with Laurie. Everything was wrong. Everything about him was fake and disjointed.

He pined for a man he thought would never want him, and when he managed to find out the attraction was reciprocated, he was too drunk to remember. He held on to a job he hated by the skin of his teeth and had to be grateful he still had it. He taught weightlifting classes and hung out with the guys, but it was all fake, all empty, all for nothing.

He was nothing. All he'd ever really had was football, but even that had been a joke. Only a hobby, a parking space for old dreams. He could fake it all he wanted, but this fucked-up reflection was more real than he'd ever been.

Ed stared at it, shivering and weary and sick and hurting, hating himself, hating his life.

"Ed."

He heard the call distantly, and at first he thought he'd imagined it, that he was losing his mind on top of everything else. But then he heard his name, and he turned in a daze toward the sound.

Laurie stood across the grass near the sidewalk. He looked seriously pissed off. But worried, too, and uncertain.

Ed's eyes burned. "What did you tell me last night in the car? About your past? What did you tell me that I said I understood?"

Laurie put his hands in his coat pockets and hugged the panels protectively to himself. "I said I'd lost the ability to do something I love. I said that I knew that part of my life had to end, but it hurt, and part of me died with it. I don't know if the pain of losing it is ever going to go away." He wrapped his arms around himself. "I said it was my fault, too, but you insisted it wasn't, that it was simply something that happened to me. You made me feel better than I've felt in years. It was a nice moment."

"Sounds like it. I'm sorry I missed it." Ed tried to laugh, but he choked instead and looked down.

When had he gotten so lonely?

Despair made him turn away. But he was surrounded by mirrors, and he couldn't hide, couldn't keep Laurie from seeing his tears. When he felt the soft, warm touch of Laurie's hand on his arm, the despair caught up with him.

"I do think all those things about you." Ed's voice was rough and broken. "It wasn't only that I was drunk. I'm so sorry I fucked this up so bad."

The hand on his arm was hard enough, but the soft brush of lips against his cheek undid him. He went like a baby into the warm strength of Laurie. He waited for Laurie to say something, to tell him he hadn't fucked it up, that it was okay, but Laurie didn't say anything. Only held him.

Did that mean they were okay?

Ed let out a ragged sigh. "You make me crazy, Laurie. You fucking turn me inside out."

The arms holding Ed up drew tighter to his body, pulling him closer into the embrace. "The feeling is mutual."

This time the silence wasn't a tension, only a continuation of the release. Ed let it float up around him, easing him. Supporting him. "Where did you park?"

"In a no-parking zone. I saw you through the trees and left my car there, not wanting to miss you in case you took off again." Laurie nuzzled the side of Ed's neck. "It's probably towed."

The breath from Laurie's nose tickled Ed's skin. He slid his hands down Laurie's back, toward his butt. "I'll pay to get it out."

"Forget my car. It doesn't matter."

The sorrow which had been so heavy moments ago was gone like rain clouds burned away by the sun. But even as Ed reveled in the feel of being in Laurie's arms, of touching him, he was aware, too, of the impending future. "What do we do now?"

When Laurie spoke, his lips brushed Ed's skin with every word. "We go to my apartment. You get your car. You go home, get dressed, and you go to work. I get my car from wherever it is, and then I do the same thing."

"Then what?" *Can I make love to you, this time when I can remember?*

"Then you call me, or I call you. And if we feel like it, we go to dinner. We talk." He stroked Ed's skin. "We take it slow, and we see what happens."

"Okay. But I want to dance with you again."

Laurie slid his nose along the length of Ed's jaw, and when he pulled back, Ed saw his smile. "Me too."

His gaze fell to Ed's lips, and his eyes went dusky. The world fell away, and all Ed saw was Laurie. "How about Saturday? You want to get together Saturday?"

"Saturday sounds perfect."

Laurie ran a finger along Ed's cheek. "Try to remember this, will you?"

Ed shut his eyes and opened for him, letting Laurie deep inside. He shivered at the feel of Laurie's tongue alongside his own, stilled at the sharp-sweet taste of him. He turned his head to let the kiss go deeper, pulling Laurie harder to him, moving his lips until they had a seal. Laurie yielded, and Ed took him, gladly welcoming him into that place where neither of them was alone.

CHAPTER EIGHT

*dosado (also dos-y-dos): circular movement
where two people, who are initially facing each
other, walk around each other without turning.*

ED GOT IN less trouble for coming into work five hours late and hung over than he thought he would, but he still got into trouble. Tracy was too busy to read him the riot act until after the meeting, but at the first available opportunity, she dragged him into her office.

"You don't seem to understand how intense upper management is about streamlining the next round of layoffs. I can't pretend you didn't come in here looking like someone recovering from a bender. This is your chance to tell me otherwise."

Ed stared at the top of her desk. "It was a bad night." He rubbed absently at his neck.

Tracy leaned forward over her desk, suddenly eager. "Oh it was your injury? You should have said. That could help, because I can put you on medical leave.

The compensation is less, but it looks bad to can somebody with a disability, so this might actually be—"

"*Hey*. I am *not* disabled. I have a muscle that spasms in my neck. I'm fine. I can't play football, is all."

"But that doesn't matter. We can still use it. I can protect you this way, Ed."

"I'm not disabled. You're not putting me on medical leave."

Tracy's smile died. "So I should put you on the top of my cut list, then?"

Ed let his forehead fall forward to the top of the desk. "I'm *not disabled.*"

"Fine. You're not disabled, and I won't put you on med leave. But I want a doctor's note from you, Maurer, by the first week in December. Have them write up your 'difficulty' adjusting to the neck, or give a new report of your neck. Something, Ed. Give me something to put in your file besides *came in to work smelling like cheap beer.*"

The vision of Tracy slumped in her seat, staring at a stack of personnel files, haunted him all the way home. It lingered especially as he sat in his car on the street beside his apartment. He thought about the heavy silence and the mess that awaited him up there. He thought about the long weekend ahead of living in it.

He thought about Laurie and the kiss in the Sculpture Garden, and he thought about the date they were supposed to have on Saturday night.

He thought about heading to Matt's and having another few pitchers of beer.

In the end, Ed plopped onto a pile of clothes on the couch, used the phone to order a pizza, then turned on the television and stopped thinking entirely.

THE FIRST OFFICIAL date with Ed went better than Laurie thought it would.

He'd worried it would be awkward, but if anything, things felt more the way they used to. Ed cajoled and teased him, and Laurie alternated between flustered and flattered, which seemed to be where Ed liked to keep him. As they walked to the car after dinner, Ed captured Laurie's hand then held the door for him.

Laurie was acutely aware of how many men and women flirted with Ed. Sometimes Ed seemed to notice, and sometimes he didn't. When Ed charmed the waitress, it was kind of cute, but when he winked at the busboy, Laurie felt a stab of jealousy so hot he had to drown it in water. It was a silly reaction, though, because the casual attention Ed gave to strangers was nothing on what he gave to Laurie. He smiled, he laughed, he teased, and he held Laurie's hand.

But Ed would never want for romantic company. And it made Laurie realize what an odd choice he was for a man like that.

Laurie was still brooding over this as he strapped himself into the passenger seat of Ed's car, until a somewhat familiar pop vocalist began to sing over the stereo. He turned to Ed in disbelief. "Britney Spears?"

"I don't want to hear any crap about Britney from somebody who plays La Bouche in aerobics class and goes to Barbra Streisand concerts with Vicky."

Laurie started to object to any comparison of Britney Spears and Streisand in the same sentence, remembered how many smiles other men had given Ed, and simply said, "Hmm."

It was a full Spears album, apparently, and each song was as ridiculous as the one before. They were catchy, yes, but so was the plague. Ed, however, clearly loved the music, which baffled Laurie. How many other secrets did Ed have?

He was so distracted by watching Ed groove along that he didn't get back to sorting out his earlier dilemma at all, and the next thing he knew, they were pulling into the parking garage beneath his condo. Ed put the car in park, turned the music down and bumped it a few songs forward, then turned to Laurie. His face was shadowed, but there was no mistaking the passion there.

Ed's fingers brushed Laurie's wrist. "No classes this week, with Thanksgiving. I suppose you'll be with your family?"

Laurie had forgotten all about Thanksgiving. He nodded. "You?"

"Helping Dad deep-fry a turkey, as usual." His fingers never stopped on Laurie's wrist. "Can I call you later in the week?"

"Yes." Laurie tried to keep his arm from twitching

as Ed's fingers tickled his skin. Then he remembered. "Oh, actually, next weekend I'll be out quite a bit." His stomach knotted. "For a performance. Two of them, in fact."

Ed brightened. "You're performing? Why didn't you say? Can I come?"

"It's only a local performance of *The Nutcracker*."

"You wearing tights?"

Laurie's cheeks heated. "Yes."

"I'll be there." Ed resumed his hypnotic massage of Laurie's wrist, squeezing it briefly. "Where do I get tickets?"

The goose bumps Ed's stroking had given Laurie turned into a low-grade heat. *Ed will be at the show.* "I have tickets I can give away. Let me give you one."

"Excellent." The fingers traced circles over his palm. "Maybe I can call you sooner than the weekend."

Laurie's fingers flexed—nervous, eager? He didn't know. "Sure."

Ed's hand slid to Laurie's thigh. "Maybe I could walk you upstairs right now."

Wait. Laurie's panic rose. *Wait, we were going to go slow.*

Ed's fingers tightened, and he leaned over and nuzzled Laurie's ear.

He wants you. Right now, he wants you.

Laurie closed his eyes, and all thoughts shut off.

He could hear Spears singing, something about not remembering what she did last night, the music sultry, a perfect complement to Ed's determined assault. He was kissing the rim of Laurie's ear, nibbling gently on the skin, making Laurie shiver. He gasped when Ed's tongue stole inside, his hand sliding high on Laurie's thigh at the same time.

His tongue dipped in again, bolder this time, and Laurie sighed, opened his thighs, and gave in. One hand tangled in Ed's hair, and his other hand closed over Ed's, placing it squarely over Laurie's rising erection. Now Ed groaned, and Laurie thrilled as they fumbled toward each another in the dark, mouths seeking, hands clutching—

Ed drew back, breathing heavily, but in a different way. He was also clutching at his neck.

"Are you okay?" Laurie asked.

Ed grimaced and gave a careful nod. "Turned wrong I guess." He rubbed at the cord of muscle. "Fuck." He looked at the clock on the dashboard. "I should probably go home."

For all his earlier hesitation to take this further, Laurie now found he was disappointed. "Do you need me to drive you? Or do you want to come upstairs and rest?"

"I'm fine. I have to get up early in the morning." He seemed to realize he'd been too curt and turned to try to smile—then winced. He swore under his breath and rubbed at his neck some more.

"Ed," Laurie began, but Ed reached over and squeezed his hand.

"I'm fine." He sounded tired and resigned. "It just does this."

"Okay. If you say so." Laurie squeezed back. "Talk to you soon?"

"Sure."

Ed turned the music off, keeping his gaze on the dashboard.

Laurie leaned over and brushed a kiss against Ed's cheek.

Letting out a sigh, Ed turned his head carefully and caught Laurie's mouth for a quick kiss. "Thanks."

Laurie wanted to kiss him, to offer to drive him, to try to convince him to come upstairs. But he didn't. He simply smiled, crawled out of the car, then waved as he headed for the door to his elevator, where he went upstairs to his silent apartment and went to bed alone.

DESPITE LAURIE'S BEST efforts to shelve thoughts of Ed, however, they lingered. As promised, Ed did call on Monday and even Wednesday, but both times Laurie thought he sounded down. He talked a lot about his job at Best Buy, frustrated with his department and the volume of work they had to do, about more possible layoffs looming.

"I hate this job, but I need it. At the very least for the insurance."

"What would you do, if you could have any career in the world?"

Ed laughed bitterly. "I'd play football for a living.

That's what I'd do."

"Have you ever thought about coaching? You're so good with the boys at the center."

"That's not a job."

"But it could be, couldn't it?" Laurie sank into the couch, tucking his feet up beside him. "What about at a school?"

"Have to be a teacher to do that."

"Ah. Well, you'd be a good teacher too."

"My mother would love you. I looked into that sort of thing once upon a time. There was even an assistant director job open at Halcyon Center once. But the pay is terrible. I can't live on the salary those places can pay, and few come with insurance."

Laurie chewed his lip thoughtfully. "Well, it's a shame."

"It's life." Ed cleared his throat. "What about you? Do you enjoy being a teacher? Or do you want to get back to the stage?"

"Stage? No."

Ed laughed. "But you're performing next weekend."

The thought made Laurie queasy. "This is a special exception. It won't happen again. Just teaching for me."

"You've done it all, I guess. Teaching is a sort of retirement? Resting on your laurels?"

The picture Ed painted seemed so hollow. Was that what Ed thought of him?

They made idle small talk after that, steering clear of all potential landmine conversations. Laurie wanted to ask if Ed's neck was bothering him, but he knew that would only upset him, so he didn't.

His mind stayed on Ed all week, most prominently when he was at his parents' house. He kept wondering what would happen if he brought Ed along to dinner. He wondered if Ed would be able to charm his mother or if they would fight. His father would probably look down his nose and go back to his paper. But it would be nice, Laurie thought, to have someone to talk to besides his mother.

She, of course, launched into her campaign to get Laurie back onto the stage, dropping hints all through dinner. He got a brief respite when he took a ride with her afterward. But he hadn't been on a horse in a long time, and his seat, never exactly stellar to begin with, had degenerated significantly, which meant by the time they finished he was quite sore.

"You should come out here more often," Caroline chided him. "You used to have such promise at riding."

Laurie grimaced as he rubbed at his backside. "Horses are your ambition, not mine."

"And what *is* your ambition now, Laurie?"

Laurie sighed. "Leave it alone, Mother."

She hung her horse's bridle on its peg outside the stall and turned to Laurie, hands on her hips. "You're doing nothing but moping around that studio, letting Maggie run you like a surrogate wife. When you're not there, you're brooding at home. Or at that center. Honestly, what on earth are you trying to prove?"

"I'm not trying to prove anything. I volunteer at the center because it helps Vicky and because my mother raised me to believe charity was important."

Caroline folded her arms lightly over her chest and lifted an eyebrow. "I want to know when you're going to reclaim your life. Dancing for Oliver is a good start, but it's only dipping your toe. You need to get back out there. You need to reclaim your place."

Laurie snorted. "I lost my place a long time ago."

"Then make a new place. Start small. There's a benefit coming up this spring. Headline it. Show everyone how good you are. Remind them. *Beat* them, Laurie."

"*I don't want to perform.*"

"You have so much talent. So much promise. You could do anything you wanted, but you do nothing. You're better than that. You deserve better than that."

Usually by this point Laurie was exasperated too, but today he was simply tired. "Can you continue this harangue over pumpkin pie? I'm starving."

To his relief, that was the last they discussed the subject that day. He ate his pie in relative silence, the only sound the noise of his father's football game on the television in the den. But later, Laurie rehashed the conversation with his mother. What had she meant, Maggie ran him like a surrogate wife? *Wife?* That was ridiculous, and he should have said so. He and Maggie were business partners, and that was all. They weren't married in any way, literally or metaphorically, and they never would be. He knew what his mother thought he deserved, and there was no way to convince her of that, but…

Later that night as he lay in bed staring at the ceiling, her words echoed in his head. What, he wondered, *did* he deserve?

Oliver's comments about his father lingered in Laurie's thoughts at rehearsal. He wasn't trying to turn his father's head. He'd given that up long ago. There were times he seriously wondered if the man *was* his father. And yet he knew that wasn't the case. He had his mother's build and temperament, but he had his father's face, his nose, and even his jawline. Besides, he wasn't sure Oliver could get drunk enough to have sex with Caroline Parker.

He thought of Ed, drunk and insisting Laurie was blameless. Of Ed assuring him there was nothing wrong with him at all. Laurie found he wanted desperately for Ed to be right. He was tired of feeling guilty. Tired of licking his wounds and huddling in his studio.

He didn't want to dance anymore, not like he used to. Not in flashy shows in New York and Toronto and wherever the top billings were. He wondered if this, more than guilt, was what had been holding him back. It wasn't that he was punishing himself as much as it was that he didn't want anything anymore. But was that true? Did he really not want anything? What did he want to do? What did he want, period?

A vision of Ed's mouth sliding down his chest in the dark cut across his mind.

Ed, taking him in his arms as they prepared to dance.

Ed smiling.

Ed leaning toward him, eyes closing for a kiss.

Ed vulnerable and sad, looking like he needed someone to hold him and whisper that everything was going to be okay.

Laurie turned to his side and hugged his pillow to his body. He did want Ed. He wanted to dance with him. To be with him. To go to bed with him.

But that wasn't a life goal. That wasn't a career. That wasn't the sort of thing his mother had meant, wasn't what he was supposed to want.

Except it *was* what he wanted. It was, honestly, all he wanted.

And what will you do when he gets bored with you? What happens when the sexy football player gets tired of playing around with the dancer? What happens when the right man flirts with him? What will wanting him get you then? Better to want to work. Better to want something else, something you can control. Something you know you can achieve.

But no matter how he tried, all Laurie could think was that he wanted Ed.

Clutching tighter at the pillow, Laurie closed his eyes and tried in vain to sleep.

ED'S THANKSGIVING WAS good, but too quiet. He wished his sister had come back. It didn't feel like a holiday with just him and his parents, like it could be any night of the week. The food was good, but he couldn't help feeling lonely.

He wished he'd invited Laurie along.

On Friday, he called him. He was nervous that maybe he was calling too much, but Laurie didn't seem to mind.

"Did you have a good day with your family?" Ed asked.

"Well enough." Laurie sounded too polite about it to Ed. He kicked himself for not issuing an invite.

"I'm looking forward to tomorrow. I have my ticket."

"Oh. Yes."

Uh-oh. Ed clutched at the phone. "Is it still okay that I come?"

"Yes, it's fine. It's just…I'm nervous to perform."

Ed laughed. "But why? You did all those fancy shows."

"Not for a long time. Honestly, I wish I hadn't let myself get railroaded into this."

"You'll be great. I have no doubt."

"Well. It will be nice to know you're—" He broke off. "I hope you're right. And I hope you don't find it a waste of an evening."

Ed would bet a million dollars Laurie had been about to say, *"It will be nice to know you're there."* The thought warmed him. "I can't imagine I'll think that at all. Anyway, you'll be wearing tights. You could simply stand there and I'd be happy."

"It's a children's performance. Nothing lewd at all."

"I'll save lewd for after."

"Hmm." Laurie's voice was soft now. God, Ed wished he were there with him. Or that Laurie was here.

Ed looked around his cluttered, dirty apartment and frowned. Well, not *here*. Not yet.

"Speaking of after," Laurie went on, "go ahead and come backstage once the performance is over. Ask one of the hands the way to my dressing room. It might be awhile before I can get away, and I don't want you to have to wait out in the lobby. I mean, I guess I was assuming you wanted to do something afterward."

"Sure. Your place, maybe?"

"Parking is hell on the weekends, I'm afraid. I have a spot, but you might have trouble. Would it be okay if we came to your apartment?" When Ed hesitated, he added, "Or not. We could go for a drink or something."

"We'll play it by ear. I only want to be with you."

Ed could hear Laurie's smile. "I want to be with you too." There was a bustle in the background. "I should go, though. I'm actually in the middle of the grocery store. But I'll see you tomorrow?"

"See you tomorrow."

They hung up, but Ed held on to the phone for a

few minutes, staring out at his disaster of an apartment. He thought about how good he had felt simply hearing Laurie's voice in his ear. He imagined how good it would feel to have him here. All night long.

He thought about Laurie's impossibly neat apartment and how he would react to seeing Ed's.

The worry was prominent in his mind Saturday morning when his mother stopped by. She started fussing as soon as she saw him. "You look terrible. Did you not sleep well? Is it your neck?"

He hadn't slept well, but for once it'd been because of worry, not his neck. He grunted.

Annette clucked at him and breezed into his apartment. "You need some coffee." She scanned the kitchen counter and frowned. "Of course, first we need to *find* the coffee."

Ed started to help her look, but she ushered him onto a stool as she bustled around his kitchen. She shoved the garbage higher on the counter and fussed in the cupboards, searching for the filters and the coffee tin.

Ed rubbed at a stiff spot in his neck. "Where's Dad?"

Annette waved the filters she'd found in the back of the spice cupboard and used them to dismiss her husband. "Bill called and dragged him out to poke at some engine." She caught Ed massaging his neck, and her expression shifted from irritated to concerned. "Have you taken your pills? Should we call the doctor?"

Ed pulled his mom toward him and kissed the top of her head. "I don't want to talk about my neck." He turned back to the coffee. "Who came in to the salon this week? Anybody I know?"

She considered this a moment while Ed tried to make room in the garbage can for the dead filter and grounds. When this didn't happen, he emptied it into a pizza box. "Monica Graber," Annette said at last.

Ed paused with the clean filter halfway in the tray and frowned. "Do I know her from church or school?"

"Both. She was a lunch lady at Farnsworth Elementary and your catechism teacher at St. Casimir."

"Ah." Ed recalled a severe, slightly stooped woman with gray upswept hair and a permanent frown. He scooped coffee into the filter and withdrew the pot to give it a rinse and a refill. "How is she?"

"Her arthritis is acting up something terrible. But her great-grandchildren are coming this weekend, so that will help take her mind off things. I gave her a shampoo and a set. Oh, and Ellen Rudawski was in. Lord bless her, but she tans too much. Face like old shoe leather, but she thinks she's beautiful. I did talk her into fewer highlights this time, so at least she doesn't look like the bride of Frankenstein. She of course asked why she hadn't seen you in church."

"She mention what Aaron is up to lately?" Ed kept the question casual, but he needn't have bothered. This was one of his mother's favorite outrages.

"No, and I wouldn't ask." Annette made several disapproving clucks before she could bring herself to go on. "And it isn't funny, so stop smiling. I don't mind who you sleep with, of course, but Ellen is a fussy thing, and no, she didn't take kindly to finding you in bed with her son. And I didn't like being the scandal of the neighborhood, thank you."

In bed and with Aaron's lovely cock halfway down his throat, Ed amended to himself, smiling at the memory. To his mother, he said, "It was twelve years ago, Mom."

"He's married now, God save that poor woman. Anyway, you're too good for Aaron Rudawski."

Ed turned the coffee on before leaning against the counter in front of it. "So what are we doing today?"

Annette gave the apartment a distasteful glance. "We *should* clean this pigsty you call home. Honestly, Ed, how do you live in this?"

"Do you want to go shopping?" Ed asked, ignoring the commentary on his apartment. "We haven't been to the Mall of America or IKEA in forever. It'll be busy, but they'll have good sales. And I wouldn't mind stopping by REI." He glanced at the time on the microwave and frowned. "Though I need to be home by five or so."

"Oh?" Annette brightened. "Do you have a date?"

Ed opened his mouth, then shut it and turned to the coffeepot, willing it to brew faster.

Annette slid off the stool and hurried over to Ed.

"What's his name? What's he like? When do I get to meet him?"

The coffeepot handle jiggled under Ed's nervous hold, and he let it go. "Laurie. His name is Laurie Parker. He's a dancer."

Annette drew back, a sour expression on her face. "One of those tarts in the dirty bars?"

"No, Mom. Ballet and stuff. He teaches over in Eden Prairie. He used to be big time too. They have posters of him. Now he has a studio, and he does the aerobics class at the center. That's where I met him. But we're…I don't know. Just, you know, if you do meet him, play it cool."

Ed's attempts to downplay Laurie were somehow only making his mother more excited. "Is he handsome? Is he nice?"

"Yes, he's handsome." Ed considered the second question. "He's a little wry. He definitely does not take my shit."

Annette was getting more excited all the time. "Is he Catholic?"

Ed gave her a withering glare. "*Mom.*"

"What? It's wrong to want a good Catholic boy for my boy?"

The coffee wasn't done, but it was close enough Ed could steal a cup. He rattled through the cupboard, searching for a clean mug. There was one. He pulled it out, filled it and handed it to his mother.

She accepted it, glancing dubiously at the fridge.

"How old is your milk?" When Ed looked at her blank-ly, she put down the mug and took Ed's arm. "Honey. I don't mean to nag. But your apartment? To be hon-est, I'm standing here trying not to gag. I'm *afraid* to open that refrigerator. You were never clean, but since you had to leave the team, you've gone from bad to qualifying for the watch list of public health."

Ed shook free of her grip and busied himself with washing a mug in the sink. Which was a trick not only because the sink was full but because he'd apparently run out of dish soap. He wanted to deflect her or tell her to leave him alone, but he thought how he'd prob-ably have to turn Laurie down after the show, because he knew better than to bring a guy like Laurie to his dump. It all stewed inside him, and he found he couldn't say anything in his own defense, not this time. So he said nothing, only dried his mug on his T-shirt and poured himself a cup of joe.

Which to Annette was nothing more than an invita-tion to carry on. "You're not happy, honey. You tell me you are, but I can tell that you aren't. You're trying, I know. Teaching that class was a good idea, and maybe it will help, but you need *something.* You've always been that way. You need a focus. A passion. You can put up a good front for other people, but I know you're dying inside, one little piece at a time. Your apartment used to be messy because you were busy and untidy, but now it's a disaster because you don't care. And you should care about your life, Ed. It's the only one you get. If you could get a job that paid decent and had good insurance and gave you your passion, that'd be one thing, but you don't love your job, and without football—" She shook her head. "I worry about you, sweetheart. I worry so much."

Ed listened to this whole speech with his back to his mother as he stared into the depths of his coffee, and he continued to do so for a few heavy seconds after she'd finished. He remembered that morning in the sculpture gardens with Laurie and the despair which had driven him there, and how funky he'd been after that.

Then he thought of Laurie and the way he'd felt whenever he kissed him.

Passion.

He looked out his apartment and admitted, finally, that no passion with Laurie was ever going to happen here. Not like this. Which meant not tonight. Which depressed the hell out of him.

Ed took a fortifying sip of coffee. "I'll clean my apartment. I'll clean it all up and make it a gleaming palace. Happy?"

He waited for the explosion of joy, but his mother didn't say anything, so he glanced at her. Her eyes were wide, and she looked like she might drop her coffee cup.

Ed frowned. "Mom?"

"Did you…did you just say you'd clean your apartment?"

"Is that a problem?"

"Never." Her hand shook now. "Not when you were little, not when you were grown. Never. You never cleaned your room for me. Not when I asked you. Not when I told you. Not one time. You did it when you felt like it, and never very well." She took Ed's face in her hands and kissed him hard on the mouth. "I don't care that this Lars isn't a Catholic. I love him already."

"Laurie," Ed corrected absently, still thinking about what she'd said about his cleaning habits. He'd cleaned up when she'd told him to. Hadn't he?

From the look on his mom's face, clearly not.

"I want to be able to bring him over, is all."

"And you will." Annette kissed him again, then let him go. "Tonight, if you want, after your date. Because we're cleaning right now."

"*What?*"

She held up a hand to still his objections as she punched in numbers on her cell phone and held it up to her ear. "Dick? Honey? Come over to Ed's place right away, and bring the truck, and all the garbage bags we have. Bring Bill too. Ed's cleaning his place up for a boy."

"*Mom.*" Ed tried to take the phone from her, but his mother turned away, gave a few more instructions to his father and hung up.

"You can be mad all you want, sweetheart." She picked up the bag of garbage sitting beside the full can without a liner in it. "But this is happening."

Ed started to protest, then thought of bringing Laurie here tonight and making love to him in his own bed—with clean sheets—and reached for the trash can. He was out of trash bags, he remembered now. And dish soap. And laundry detergent. And milk. And everything.

He swore under his breath and tossed the can down.

His mother took his face in her hands. "We'll get it done, honey. We'll have this place gleaming by five o'clock." She winked and patted his cheek. "If Aaron Rudawski didn't live in Rochester, I'd drag his sorry butt in to help too."

Ed smiled despite himself. "Thought he wasn't good enough for me?"

Annette shrugged. "He's good enough to take out your garbage."

Ed laughed and hugged his mom close, loving every soft, round inch of her. "Thanks, Mom."

She hugged him back, then swatted his butt. "Get to work," she scolded, and hauled her bag of garbage off toward the door.

CHAPTER NINE

drift apart: an adjustment from a partner to a position where partners are separated but still have close contact.

THE SATURDAY CLASSES were Laurie's least favorites. He didn't mind working on Saturday itself so much. He enjoyed having more time off during the week to run errands or rehearse or be at home. The classes themselves were what annoyed him. They were all classes for younger children, and as such were overpopulated by students who had no real interest in being in dance but whose parents wished to believe they did. If Laurie had taught the very young dancers, it might have been more bearable, but Maggie handled all the "little cherubs", as she liked to call them. In addition to the teenagers, who were often more serious, Laurie also ended up with the third through sixth graders who largely fell into two camps: the whiners and the frightening, miniature adults.

Some of them had real talent, yes. But almost none

of them had personality. He knew on some level that assessment was cruel, but God help him, he couldn't stand them. They all had cell phones, to start. Why? Why did a ten-year-old need a cell phone? Who were they calling? Of course, they weren't calling, were they. They were texting each other, sometimes from across the room. When they weren't punching on keypads, they were chattering about Taylor Swift or a new game or movie. He never heard them speaking about toys unless it was to catalog how many of a hot item they had. One girl had seventeen American Girl dolls, and she liked to hold court discussing the new outfits she'd purchased that week. The boys were equally unbearable. There were rarely many in dance, but there were certainly no little Lauries here. The male dancer conversations were all about Xboxes and their prowess in their local soccer league.

Laurie wanted to believe it hadn't been that bad when he was ten, but on some level he knew it was. The eighties weren't exactly known for their openness of spirit and sharing, especially in the suburbs. Laurie had flaunted having the best dance gear and the most state-of-the-art everything in his rehearsal room. Maybe it wasn't different at all and this was simply what it looked like from the other side. Maybe his teachers had stood in front of his classes and wrinkled their noses in the same sort of disgust.

Or maybe, he acknowledged as he dismissed the giggling masses of Advanced Junior Tap, he was getting old.

By the time Laurie finished at noon, he felt listless. He didn't need to be at the theater until four. He could go early, certainly, and since their studio was in charge of keeping their students who were in the chorus in line during warm-ups, he should probably be a gentleman and help Maggie. But he didn't want to go there at all. Not to work, not to perform. He fantasized about simply driving west, not stopping until he hit the ocean.

He drove to a deli instead, grabbed some lunch and headed for his apartment. But he didn't get off at his exit. He kept going toward St. Paul. He wished he knew where Ed's house was so he could stop by. But he didn't know, and he wasn't going to call and ask.

He ended up at Halcyon Center.

"Laurie." Vicky beamed when he stuck his head into the doorway of her office. "What in the world are you doing here? You have a performance today."

"Not until later." He wasn't sure how to explain why he'd stopped by, since he didn't know himself.

"I was hoping to take some of the kids, but my alternator died, and I had to replace it instead."

This shook Laurie out of his awkwardness. "Why on earth didn't you tell me? I'd have gotten you tickets. I still could, if you thought it wasn't too late to round up the kids." He pulled out his cell phone. "How many tickets do you want?"

Vicky looked flustered. "Laurie, you don't have to do that."

"Vicky, you're being ridiculous. The profits from this event go to charity, some of it likely back to the kids at your center. I have a wad of tickets they gave me as a thank you for the donation of my performance. If you don't use them, they're going to waste."

"Fine. But you know how I feel about the center owing anybody."

Laurie felt refusing tickets to an amateur ballet was taking principle well past too far, but he kept this opinion to himself. He punched the theater's number into the keypad and turned away to make the call.

A young man leaned against the wall. Laurie recognized him vaguely from the group of Ed's young men who came to his aerobics class, but then the boy was clothed in the usual gym uniform. He was not so now.

The boy drowned in more clothes than Laurie would have ever thought one person could wear. An oversized red jersey bunched at the youth's waist and spilled over onto his thighs. He wore athletic pants of an iridescent material with a reflective stripe along the side, but he also wore a pair of shorts over them as well. Beneath the jersey there was a hoodie, but also a T-shirt. On his feet were unlaced high-top athletic shoes, gleaming silver and white even in the industrial-issue fluorescent glow of Vicky's office. Topping the boy's look off was a bright green ball cap that had BITCH stitched across the crown in neon pink letters.

Catching Laurie staring at him, the boy lifted a defiant gaze and stared back.

The automated greeting for the theater ended, and Laurie wrenched his focus to the phone in time to enter his code. He spoke to the receptionist, arranged for Vicky to collect as many tickets as she needed, and hung up.

"There. That's settled," he told her. "Go straight to the will-call booth, and you'll be taken care of. You can take up to twenty-five students."

"Thanks." Vicky blushed but seemed pleased. "I'll round up some kids and bring as many as I can stuff into the center's van."

Laurie pocketed his phone. "Outside of your alternator, how are things going?"

Vicky looked grim. "Hectic. I'll tell you about it later. Did you ever get a hold of Ed?"

"Oh—yes." He blushed. "Yes. Thank you."

"Seeing him anytime soon?"

"Tonight, actually. He'll be at the performance too. Your seats will be next to his."

He fished for a redirection of the conversation, but the boy was oddly distracting. Laurie felt self-conscious around the young man in a way he couldn't identify. It was a sort of aggression that filled the small office and pushed against him at the door. It made Laurie want to leave, and so he did, murmuring a goodbye and thanks to Vicky.

Once in the hall, however, the same restlessness which had driven him to the center returned. It was still too early to go to the theater unless he wanted to get roped into helping. Even if he escaped that, Maggie would parade him in front of the parents, and he'd end up spending an hour pasting a plastic smile on his face as he pretended to enjoy listening to other people embellish his past. That wasn't going to help him burn off his restlessness.

Only one thing he knew of could do that. But he couldn't work out how, exactly, to explain to Ed that he needed him to come to the center and dance with him so he could calm down.

It was a measure of his desperation that he tried to make the call, but in the end he went to Ed's voicemail. Feeling ridiculous, Laurie faltered through a message saying what he'd already told Ed, that his tickets were at the will-call booth, and hung up.

Now what?

You could always dance by yourself.

The thought arrested Laurie. Dance by himself. Not rehearse. That wasn't the problem. Dancing, though. Dancing for fun. Freeform. An improv, the way it was when he danced with Ed. Could that possibly work?

He didn't know, but he found he was eager to try.

Laurie stuck his head in the doorway of Vicky's office. "Sorry, but I wondered—is there a room upstairs free? The regular aerobics room, maybe? Not the gym?"

Vicky paused, thinking. "The aerobics room is in use, but 3B is clear. Will that do?"

"Yes. Thank you."

After a quick trip out to his car to grab his iPod and dig a portable speaker out of his trunk, Laurie headed to 3B. The room was stale and stuffy and bordering on too small, but after Laurie pushed the boxes of yoga equipment to the side, he had adequate space.

He was eager for this in a way which, if anyone else were watching, would make him self-conscious. He almost laughed. Good God, how the mighty had fallen. He who had once performed at the Met was now worried someone might see him cutting loose in a storeroom.

Yet he felt very serious, each action weighted as he set the player up in the ledge by the window. He was more meticulous now arranging this improv for no one than he had ever felt preparing for a performance before thousands. He took a moment to center himself. He did a few stretches. He made himself feel the space of the room, absorb the energy of it, let its boundaries, its weight, its feel become part of him.

He put on his favorite playlist, took a centering breath and let himself go.

It was clumsy at first. He hadn't danced like this in a while, not by himself, not *for* himself. This was something he'd done a great deal of when he was young, so young the memory was washed to sepia with age. Instruction had burned improv out of him. He couldn't quite shake the background notation of what he was doing. This was a slide. That was a leap. An arabesque, tweaked into something that would have cost him points in a competition but onstage would have been considered brilliant. But soon this faded too, and he lost himself and simply danced.

He didn't compose, didn't demonstrate and didn't perform. He let the music move him across the room as it would, let it slide under his skin and into his blood, taking his body. He did not think. He did not plan. He only moved. And in that movement he found an ease he hadn't known he needed, a peace he'd forgotten he should seek. The soulless routine of his morning classes, the sadness of the past, the fear of the future fell away, leaving only the dance. Leaving him whole and strong and sure.

Like a slow tide, he felt the yearning come in. It mixed with memory, of the feel of Ed's hands on his body as he taught him to dance, the smell of him that had lingered in Laurie's bed and in the taste of his kiss. It was a terrifying want, and it should have slowed him down, but Laurie was an artist, so he used the terror as fuel instead, pushing it into the dance, exposing himself in a way he would never in life. His longing for Ed filled him, put an edge on every turn and a sharp ache in every extension of his arms. Thinking of the possible encounter to come this evening, Laurie let himself imagine. Let himself want.

When he stopped, he dripped with sweat. Breathing hard, chest burning, arms and legs aching, he felt renewed all the way to his core, and he wasn't listless anymore. Smiling, he snapped off the music and wiped his face with the hem of his shirt as he leaned into the wall.

As he reached for the bottle of water he'd set beside the player, the door, which had been cracked open, slammed quickly shut. But before it did, Laurie thought he caught a flash of bright green.

Self-consciousness tried to rise at being caught, but it gained no real purchase. The dance had done its job. He felt good. He felt released and energized. He thought of the performance ahead, and he didn't so much as flinch.

He thought of the night with Ed to come, and his blood hummed.

Draining the bottle of water, Laurie wiped his lips and pushed away from the wall.

It was time to dance.

ED HAD GONE to the State to see a show two years ago, but other than that, he really hadn't gone to the theaters in downtown Minneapolis for much. The State was a nice place, and the seats were comfortable. It was elegant and ornate, the walls all gilded and scrolled, and the lights dripped with bits of crystal. It had made him feel underdressed the last time, though, and he'd forgotten that part until tonight.

Worst part was, he'd made a real effort with his clothes. It wasn't like Ed didn't own nice duds. He worked in an office, for crying out loud. And thanks to that afternoon's cleaning spree, he'd rediscovered how many nice outfits he had. He'd arrived in a suit coat his mom had rushed out for one-hour cleaning after rescuing it from the bottom of the closet. But Ed wasn't naturally a dress-up kind of guy, and this place had been built, it was clear, for those who didn't know anything *but* dressing up. And it reminded him Laurie *was* that kind of guy.

What plagued his thoughts as he settled into his seat and waited for the show to start was why suddenly he cared. The haunting thought of Laurie seeing his place was what had stirred him to clean. Because Laurie mattered. What Laurie thought mattered. What Laurie did mattered, which was why he was here, but it weirded Ed out. A month and a half ago he was baiting Laurie on a regular basis and had a difficult time remembering his name. Now he acted like a besotted lover. Which he supposed he was. Or wanted to be. Or something.

Ed slouched in his seat and rubbed his forehead, shutting his eyes as confusion swam inside him. How the fuck did he get here? They hadn't even had sex, except for that drunken bit he couldn't remember. They'd had just that one kiss. Well, two kisses.

But they'd danced. And as Ed sat there marinating in longing and confusion, he admitted it was the dancing that had done him in.

Ed swore and shifted in his seat. Goddamn, but this was the biggest fucking cocktease ever, and the worst part was he couldn't figure out which one of them was doing the teasing.

Thinking of cocks made him wonder if he'd get to taste Laurie's tonight.

He hoped to hell he got to see him in tights again, at least.

"Put your feet down, Maurer, and let me get to my damn seat."

Ed sat up abruptly, blinking at the familiar face glaring playfully at him. "Duon?" He blinked as he saw Vicky and several other kids from the center. "What are you guys doing here?"

"We're here to mow the lawn. What the hell you think we're here to do?" Duon nudged Ed's feet. "Seriously, man. We had to park a fucking mile away. Let me sit my ass down."

Ed stood, letting the crew pass. There were ten kids total, plus Vicky. She moved through and placed herself in the center of the kids. Duon sat next to Ed.

"Laurie gave us tickets," Vicky explained. "Just this afternoon."

Ed nodded, still slightly bewildered. To Duon he said, "Didn't think you'd come to the ballet."

"Same to you." Duon looked like he was fighting to keep from being impressed. And losing. "Man. I feel like I'm in a queen's palace or something."

"Yeah," Ed agreed. That was about all the eloquence he had. But it made him feel better to sit there with Duon, who was as fish out of water as he was.

The houselights flickered and dimmed, and Ed set-tled in to watch the show.

It wasn't bad. Ed vaguely knew the story, but it was a mystery enough that he got caught up. Yeah, the kids were definitely amateur, but they were cute. It made him feel good to see all the families and aunts and uncles and grandparents in the audience—because, honestly, outside of him and a few other anomalies, it was clear that everyone was here for a kid—and made him think of his own youth, of his mom coming to all his games and his dad teaching him to throw. It made him yearn in a way he'd never expected to, for a family of his own. He'd never really decided for or against kids, but he wasn't doing it without a partner, so he figured he should start there.

He wondered what it would be like to have kids with Laurie.

Beside him, Duon shifted, and Ed glanced at him as surreptitiously as he could. Duon's expression was softer than it usually was. It remained that way even when the curtain came down for intermission. They left to file into the hallway with the others. After a visit to the restroom, they held up the same part of the wall as Vicky took the few who had brought money to buy some refreshments.

"So all those kids been taking dance since they was little." Duon snorted. "Hell. Some of them still *are* little."

Ed shifted on his feet to get out of the way of

someone trying to weave through the crush. "My sister took dance for a few years, but she had to quit because it was too expensive. The weekly fees weren't so bad, but the shoes and the costumes and the performance fees were brutal."

They stood together silently and watched the crowd go by.

"I wonder what that's like," Duon said after a while.

"To take dance?"

"To have family that would pay that kind of money out on you for something you wanted. That could pay. Even for a few years."

It was a bald confession for anyone, but from Duon it was especially resonant. Ed felt he should say something, but he didn't know what he could offer in reply.

The lights flickered, and they had to make their way to their seats. Duon buried himself in his program, signaling that he was done talking. Ed picked up his own and flipped through it absently as he waited for the show to start up.

When it did, he saw Laurie.

At first Ed didn't recognize him. He came out on the arm of a ballerina wearing a seriously intense tutu, but Laurie had his hair slicked back and wore something around his eyes—liner, but glitter too. He'd dressed all in silver, and his costume was much simpler than his partner's, but he glistened in the stage lights.

And oh yeah, he was wearing tights. His muscular legs were defined by the smooth silk, and the bulge in his crotch was like a magnet to Ed's eye.

God.

Laurie left the stage, and Ed sat through parade after parade of other people's kids dancing to all different kinds of music in a rainbow array of costumes. Each time they came out he was disappointed they weren't Laurie. But when he was about to give up hope, there Laurie was with the tutu lady again. To Ed's disappointment, Laurie mostly propped her up while she did all manner of tricky dances. It was nice, but he wanted to see Laurie move. He supposed this was it, and he tried to enjoy, but mostly he felt disappointed.

Then the tutu lady left, and Laurie remained. And he danced.

Leaping. Arcing. He'd move his arms and slide his leg up his other leg, and he'd kick and leap some more. It was beautiful. It was like watching light. It was like…God, it was like Laurie was finding something inside Ed and pulling it out. Not because Ed was attracted to him. It was a lot more than that. He'd have been moved by this even if he'd never met the man. As Laurie danced and the audience gasped in wonder, something in Ed opened like a lotus, and he knew.

It was that Laurie was beautiful. That Laurie was male, and beautiful, and when he danced he made male beauty come alive. Laurie wasn't simply good. Laurie was a fucking *artist.* As far as Ed was concerned, he was a legend.

And I've kissed him. A soft, startled thrill rushed through Ed, the kind he hadn't had since he was twelve.

I've kissed him, and I have good odds on kissing him again. Soon.

And then, without warning, Laurie fell.

It was a brief stumble, a turn that didn't quite pan out, and he was on his feet almost instantly, but Ed could tell it had been a mistake. The crowd erupted in whispers, and onstage, Laurie's expression went glassy as he attempted to hide his mortification. But the spell was broken now, the grace gone. The rest of the dance seemed jerky and stiff, and when it was time for Laurie to exit, he all but bolted into the wings.

Ed ached for Laurie, and his absence left Ed feeling bereft. The tutu chick was back, and yeah, she was fine, but who cared? How could anybody care about anybody else dancing after watching Laurie? Ed wanted to see him dance more, wanted to dance *with* Laurie. He wanted to feel that beauty in his arms.

When the show was over, all the dancers crowded onto the stage, the leads coming up to take their bows, including Laurie. Eventually the dancers all disappeared behind the curtain, and the houselights came up in full.

Vicky beamed. "What a show. Did you guys enjoy it?"

The kids murmured varying degrees of interest. Most of the guys pretended to be bored, which gave the girls a great outlet to tease them. Duon remained quiet, as did Ed.

Vicky glanced over the throng at Ed as they shuffled toward the door. "You want to come with us? We're going for sundaes at the center before I take everybody home."

"Ah, no. I'm—" He glanced at the stage door, then jerked his head at it, blushing.

Vicky grinned. "Tell Laurie hi. Tell him he did great. Don't let him focus on that flub, either. Come on, guys. Stick together, and nobody wander off."

Ed stepped back to let them pass.

Once they were gone, he headed for the stage.

He felt out of place now that the magic of the performance had been spent, and by the time he was on the stairs, ducking little girls in angel costumes, wrapped in the din of parents and children greeting one another, it felt so surreal, and not in a good way anymore. He wished the center kids were with him, because at least they'd feel out of place together.

A stagehand in a headset looked as if he wanted to expel him for daring to be where he shouldn't. Ed hurried to explain he was there for Laurie, that he was expecting Ed. He felt like an idiot, but he followed the stagehand down the hall, nodding thanks as he saw the door. He dodged mothers and grandmothers and giggling teenage girls—and then he was at the door, watching his own hand knock. Sick with nerves, he might as well have stood there buck naked.

The door opened, and there was Laurie.

He was still in his costume, still glinting and glistening, his eyes still lined and his face spackled with glitter. His hair was mussed, like he'd been shoving his hand in it. He looked like a fairy prince, more surreal up close than he had on the stage.

He still wore the tights.

Laurie's glitter twinkled in the dim light of the hall. He was upset, Ed could tell. Ed wanted to make him feel better. "You did great. Amazing. So beautiful."

Laurie forced another smile. "Do you want to come in?"

Ed did. Laurie shut the door, clearly nervous. Ed searched for the words to reassure him, to get him to glow again. But Ed couldn't think of anything to say, couldn't imagine how in the world he could turn the chaos inside him into mere words. Couldn't think of how he could ever explain what watching Laurie onstage had done to him.

So he didn't say anything at all. He slid a hand behind Laurie's neck and kissed him.

WHEN THE KISS began, Laurie's eyes were still open.

If he'd seen it coming, he might have closed his eyes and sank into it right away. But it was the last thing he'd figured Ed would do, so he stood there for a few heavy seconds, stunned. He stared into Ed's face, so close to his own it was out of focus. But he saw too how soft and tender Ed was, lost inside the kiss, and it undid Laurie.

Shutting his eyes, Laurie slid his hand to Ed's neck, tilting his head to the side and deepening the kiss. He dove into that spice, into the wet softness of him, taking in deep draughts of Ed, woodsy and sharp. The terror and then the thrill and the ultimate shame of the performance warred with his yearning for Ed. This was real, here, now, with Ed.

When Ed pushed Laurie against the door, pinning him with his body, Laurie went pliant, letting his body bend to Ed's will. When Ed drew Laurie's bottom lip into his mouth and sucked on it, Laurie gasped and dug his fingers into Ed's shoulders, then offered him his tongue as well. His erection strained the Lycra of his tights as Ed rubbed him with the buckle of his belt, catching the tip in a friction that edged toward but did not cross over into discomfort. The kiss had begun tenderly, but now it was raw.

Ed's mouth slid along Laurie's throat, his chest, all the way over his stomach to the hem of his tights, which Ed gripped and tugged insistently down as he went to his knees on the floor.

When Laurie felt the wet heat of Ed's mouth on his cock, he gasped and reached for Ed's hair. He didn't care that his students were on the other side of the door. He didn't care that if he ruined these tights, he was seriously screwed for the Sunday matinee performance. He didn't care, he didn't care, *he didn't care*. Because Ed was blowing him. He looked down, ready to watch, and he shivered as Ed took him deep, his tongue circling—

Laurie cried out, then bit his lip to stifle the sound. He gripped Ed's hair, tipped his head back and started to thrust. Outside the door he could hear kids giggling and mothers chattering on and on and on, but inside this room he was fucking Ed's mouth. He sank into the pleasure of the moment, the wickedness of what he was doing, and without warning it was too much. He cried out with a cascading shout that probably carried through the door and absolutely sounded like someone having sex. His balls drew tight and spilled out, flooding Ed's mouth as he thrust.

When he was spent, he wilted against the door. Ed rose and took Laurie's face in his hands. This time the kiss was slow and sensual, and it was salty too.

"I want to fuck you," Ed whispered.

Yes, Laurie thought, opening to him, trying to spread his knees to invite him there, but the tights trapped his legs. So he kissed Ed back, tasting himself, letting Ed's words roll deliciously inside his head. *I want to fuck you. I want to fuck you. I want to fuck you.*

A sharp rap on the door startled them both. "Mr. Parker? Ms. Davies is looking for you."

"Yes," Laurie called out, his voice breaking. He felt Ed's hand close over his fading erection, and he shut his eyes and leaned into his lover. "Yes. Thank you."

"Is everything all right in there? This door was shaking."

Ed snorted a laugh, and Laurie couldn't help a grin. "I'm fine." *So very fine.* He tipped his head to the side as Ed kissed his way up his shoulder.

"That you are." Ed licked a long muscle down the slope of his neck.

"Ed." Laurie fought the urge to beg Ed to push him onto the floor and take him right here, right now.

Ed nipped at Laurie's clavicle. Laurie clutched Ed's shoulders as hands found their way to Laurie's ass. "I cleaned my apartment." Ed trailed kisses along Laurie's jaw. "And bought new condoms."

Laurie couldn't think, or speak, only make a *hngh* noise. He sagged forward, letting his backside part.

"You are fucking hot in tights." Ed teased the edge of Laurie's hole. "You're even fucking hotter out of them."

The fingertip pushed partly inside Laurie, and he moaned.

The pounding on the door resumed, but this time all Laurie managed was a twitch, and most of that was because Ed had wedged himself a little deeper.

"Laurie?" This time the person pounding on the door was Maggie. "Laurie?"

Laurie's reply strangled in his throat as Ed stretched him. It burned, more all the time, and he needed lube, but he couldn't bear to make it stop.

"Laurie, are you all right?"

No. I'm trying to have sex, and people keep getting in the way. He bit Ed's shoulder for a second before composing himself enough to say, "Yes."

"People are looking for you." Maggie's nag cut through the muffle of the door.

Laurie shivered as Ed's finger fucked gently into him. He buried his cries in Ed's jacket.

"Laurie?"

"Give us a minute," Ed barked.

There was a heavy pause on the other side of the door. Laurie's hands tightened on Ed's sleeves, and he held his breath.

"Okay." Maggie sounded dazed. Laurie heard her heels clicking as she went away.

He sagged into Ed. And laughed.

Ed did, too, trailing his finger up Laurie's cleft and resting his hand on Laurie's hip. Laurie nuzzled his way to Ed's mouth. He hadn't known how wound up he was, not until now when he felt like a limp noodle in sequins and glitter. The dance this afternoon alone in the room at the center had been freeing. This was centering. It was probably blasphemous to feel centered by a blow job given in a *Nutcracker* dressing room, but then, Laurie had never been much for religion. He felt like the genie let out of the bottle, and he did not want to go back in.

"I should probably let you get changed. And you probably have stuff to do here that I'm keeping you from." Ed kept stroking Laurie's backside. "Do you still want to come over?"

He nodded. "Wait for me out front. I won't be

long." Laurie shut his eyes at the pleasure of Ed's touch. "They want to see me. Maggie brags."

"She should. You're amazing, Laurie. I didn't know anybody could dance like that."

I want to dance with you. Naked. In your bed. "I'm glad you enjoyed it." He lifted his head, but it felt so heavy, and it seemed easier to rest. To press his half-naked body against Ed.

What had become of the walls he'd so carefully built? What was this with Ed?

Everything had happened so fast, and yet they'd actually been dancing around this for a month, with a few false starts. It was more that this relationship had crept up on them like a shadow, and now suddenly they were drowning in it. At least Laurie was.

He couldn't seem to make himself move. He needed to get changed, to go see Maggie and smooth her ruffled feathers. He needed to figure out why he'd lost himself so badly during the performance. He needed to do a thousand things, but all he wanted to do was grab Ed and kiss him again. He was so full of feeling and had been, he realized, ever since Ed.

Ed touched his cheek tenderly.

Laurie gave up. "Hold on." He grabbed the hem of his tights and pushed them the rest of the way down, stepping out of them as carefully as he could while still hurrying. He tossed them onto the counter and fumbled with the fastenings of his costume top. But his fingers shook, and in the end he looked up at Ed in desperation. "Help me."

Ed's fingers weren't a lot better, and his gaze was hooded. "Fucking hell, Laurie."

"Just get me out of this." Laurie fought the buttons from the top as Ed tackled the ones at the bottom. He kept faltering, though, because Ed was so close, and so…Ed. And fully clothed. In a suit. Ed in a suit. It looked good but strange. *I want to see him naked.* "Hurry."

The last of the buttons fell away, and Laurie wrenched the costume off. Tossing it on the counter, he locked the door.

Then he pushed Ed into the nearest chair and straddled him.

It was all mouths and hands and thrusting hips and murmured endearments too bald and nonsensical, but they were both past everything now but release. Laurie knew he had no hope in coming a second time so soon, but that wasn't what this was about. He wanted Ed to come. He wanted Ed to come as he slid over him, naked, while Ed was fully clothed. And that's exactly what happened. With Ed's mouth attached to Laurie's nipple and their naked cocks trapped together in Ed's hand, Laurie rode him, pressing on Ed's shoulders, dancing their own private dance together. When Ed came, Laurie cried out, letting his heart release even though his balls were still trying to get themselves organized.

I want him so much. I need him.

It was a beautiful, terrible desire, one he'd sworn he'd never let himself feel again. It was the door that led to heartache, and he had sealed himself off, yet somehow here he was.

What frightened him most was that he didn't care.

Ed kissed Laurie's chest weakly as he tried to catch his breath. "I need to get out of here and let you get dressed. Because clearly it's not going to happen if I stay."

Laurie nuzzled the top of his head, smiling as he shut his eyes. "I think you're right."

They kissed at the door, little nibbling kisses that tasted of longing and nervousness. When Ed slipped out, Laurie lingered at the door, his cheek pressed to the wood as he shut his eyes, swimming in sensation.

When he emerged from his dressing room, most of the parents had gone, and Maggie was upset. She didn't lecture him because too many people were around, but her lips pressed together far too much for Laurie's liking, and she kept glaring.

It irritated him.

"I have to get going." He squeezed her shoulder before smiling to the bigwigs she'd gathered to show him off to. "See you tomorrow."

"Laurie," she began, her voice sharp with disapproval, but he ignored her, hurrying down the aisle of the theater, searching for a tall man in a gray suit with untidy black hair. He found him in the lobby, leaning against the wall out of the way in a corner. But when he saw Laurie, he pushed upright and smiled. Laurie wanted to run up to him and throw himself in his arms. Instead, he stood before him, feeling giddy.

Ed grinned. "Ready to go?" He held out his arm.

On the way out the door, Laurie caught a glimpse of his mother and father, but thankfully they were speaking to another couple and didn't see him. Oliver saw him though, and he smiled and tried to call Laurie over. But Ed was still moving, so Laurie waved as he was pulled out of the building, out onto the street.

He didn't look back.

CHAPTER TEN

*pecho (chest): a close-embrace tango with more
of a chest-to-chest position than other tangos.*

AS THEY HEADED to St. Paul after dropping Laurie's car off at his apartment, Laurie had to resist the urge to rest his head against Ed's shoulder. He had a duffel in the backseat with a toothbrush and a change of clothes. He was going to have sex. With Ed.

There was a bit of worry on that point, a distant cloud. It had been a long, long time since he'd let anyone fuck him, and he wasn't yet sure he was ready to go from zero to anal in one night, even with Ed.

Laurie studied Ed as he drove, and when Ed caught him, he gave Laurie a wry smile. "What are you thinking about there, beautiful?"

Laurie blushed. "You don't have to flatter me. I'm already going home with you."

"You are, Laurie. So fucking beautiful you make me ache." Keeping his eyes on the road, Ed rested his hand on Laurie's thigh. It was a sensual, eager touch, but almost reverential. "I love watching you dance. I'm going to be at every performance you give from now on, right in the fucking front row."

Laurie put his hand over Ed's and threaded their fingers together. "I don't perform that often anymore."

"Why not?"

Because it hurts too much. Laurie's thumb stroked absently over Ed's. "I just don't."

"Maybe teaching is more rewarding for you right now?"

"To be honest, I hate it. I mean, I don't *hate* teaching, but it's not…it isn't…" He sighed. "Ignore me. I think I've turned into a crotchety old queen, and nothing makes me happy."

"You seem okay when we're dancing together. Maybe you should teach more ballroom dancing."

It's not the ballroom dancing making me okay. It's you. But it was absolutely not the time to confess *that*. "I wish my students cared about the dance more. Some seem glad to be there, but sometimes I think the eight-year-olds are more jaded than I am. Which is depressing."

"You should work with kids at the center," Ed suggested. "They enjoyed watching tonight. I bet they'd love to learn."

That made Laurie laugh. "I can't imagine they want to learn ballet." But then he remembered his observer from earlier in the day, and he wondered. "Though maybe that's me being elitist."

"Kids want attention. The ones at the center have

had to buck up and put up with a lot in life, and they pretend they don't need it, but they're as hungry for it as anybody else. Your suburban kids are too, I bet. They're caught in the same rat race that will kill their souls the same way it killed their parents'." He withdrew his hand from Laurie's and shook his head. "Sorry. That was uncalled for."

The absence of Ed's hand made Laurie's thigh feel cold. "What was uncalled for?"

"The crack about suburban kids. I mean, you work in the burbs."

Laurie snorted. "That wasn't a crack. That was an astute observation. The students at my studio *are* caught up in the game. I am, too, or at least I was. Maybe that's what I'm seeing, my own failures reflected in them. Maybe I'm looking at them and seeing how I went so wrong."

"Went wrong?"

This wasn't at all where Laurie had wanted this conversation to go, but perhaps it was best to get this out now. "I had quite a career, before. I've performed all over the world: in ballets, in dancing companies, as an artist-in-residence. I danced with partners and alone. They were starting to bill me as 'the next Mikhail Baryshnikov,' which was fine with me, since my goal was that in twenty years they'd be calling the next up-and-comer 'the next Laurence Parker.'" He smiled sadly, still staring out the front window, seeing not the night and the street but his old life whiz by. "But that's over now. Now I simply teach in a private studio in Eden Prairie."

Silence spread out between them. Laurie let it wrap around him for a while, but eventually he continued confessing, looking at his hands as he spoke.

"Sometimes I think two parts of me warred with each other, and they took down the whole of me in a civil war. I loved Paul, and I wanted to be with him, but I feared him, feared my affection, feared what both would do to my career. Sometimes I wonder if I didn't subconsciously sabotage myself. And him, and his career." His hands tightened in his lap. "But once he was gone, I didn't have him as an excuse anymore. I wasn't happy, period. Everyone kept telling me I could go back. They've been telling me for years. But I can't figure out how to explain that I don't want my old life anymore. That maybe I never did." Laurie let out a shaky breath, feeling suddenly exposed. "I didn't mean to say all that."

Ed caught his hand, squeezing gently. He didn't say anything, only held Laurie's hand and kept driving.

They were in St. Paul now, off the highway and on city streets, heading toward Dayton's Bluff. It was a neighborhood Laurie's mother would cringe at and call *colorful* in a way that made you want to paint the world beige. Ed parked on a side street so narrow and full of shadows it would have had Carolyn Parker's mouth puckering.

Ed climbed out of the car and reached for Laurie's

duffel before Laurie had his door cracked.

"I can carry my bag," Laurie pointed out, but Ed shifted it to the arm farthest away from Laurie and touched his elbow as he nodded toward a building half a block down.

"That's me. Third floor. Do you mind if we take the stairs? There's an elevator, but you go gray waiting for it."

"The stairs are fine," Laurie assured him, and soon he followed Ed up an industrial set of stairs in a not-well-lit hallway that would also have set his mother tittering. Laurie was having a hard time with it himself.

He wondered why he was thinking so much about his mother.

Ed caught the look on his face and winced. "Sorry. I don't live in a nice place like you. But my apartment, I can assure you, is spic and span."

Yes, but were there bars on the windows? "It doesn't seem terribly safe, this neighborhood."

Ed shrugged. "If you're smart and careful, it's manageable." He fumbled with a key in the lock before pushing open the heavy metal door. "And the rent is fantastic, especially for the space."

It was a loft space, the kind Laurie had considered in downtown Minneapolis and had decided he couldn't afford. Except Ed's space wasn't polished and sleek and modern. Ed's loft had the look of something that still had the original industrial ambiance, not manufactured by the developer. It was all one room—the kitchen was set off a bit by cupboards and shelving that once again had come straight from the warehouse floor. A metal table broke up the space between the food prep area and the living room, and off to the side Laurie saw what he suspected to be a bathroom door. Bookshelves held about three books and a hodgepodge of everything else, and nearby stood twenty or so plastic storage containers, neatly stacked and labeled. Beyond that a large piece of burlap fabric hung from the ceiling like a curtain, and behind that Laurie saw a bed on box springs and a frame, and a solitary bedstand that screamed IKEA. A side area housed more storage containers and some weight equipment.

"Sorry about the tubs. My parents and I spent the day cleaning." Ed gestured to the stack by the weight equipment. "That's all the stuff I have to get rid of, store or sell. Or something."

Laurie stood in the center of the loft, taking it in. "Ed, this space is amazing."

"Well, it wasn't earlier today."

Laurie turned to Ed, bemused. "Why do you keep telling me how messy your place was?"

He didn't expect to see Ed blush and duck his head, and he didn't quite catch whatever it was Ed murmured under his breath as he stared at the floor and shuffled his feet. But Laurie finally caught the subtext, and it made his heart flutter a bit.

He cleaned for me.

Laurie wanted to kiss him then, and he nearly did.

But he was afraid once they started down that road they might explode, and now that he'd had the thrill of a spontaneous encounter in his dressing room, he wanted to do this right. At least he wanted to wash the gel and hairspray from his hair and do a better job of removing the glitter from his face. He nodded toward the bathroom. "Would you mind if I cleaned up a bit?"

"Go right ahead. That's clean too. Towels are on the shelf. Soap and stuff is in the window behind the curtain. Washcloths are in the blue fabric drawer in that shelf thingy." Ed held open the door and passed over Laurie's bag. "Take all the time you need."

Laurie accepted the bag, smiled shyly and closed himself into the bathroom.

It was the same industrial decor as the rest of the loft, but yes, it was quite clean. And homey. When Laurie saw the clawfoot tub, he nearly swooned, and after a few minutes of deliberation, he went for a bath instead of a shower. He filled the tub with hot water and soaked in it, letting the bath soothe his nerves.

Before he got out, he took the washcloth and cleaned himself well.

Everywhere.

Music played when he finally came out of the bath-room, and Ed appeared from behind an open cupboard. "Can I get you anything to eat? Something to drink?"

"Do you have wine?"

Ed winced. "Sorry. Beer?"

No, he didn't want beer. "Tea?"

"I have coffee," Ed said, a little desperately.

Laurie felt like he was kicking a puppy. "Water?"

Ed sighed. "Sorry." He ducked into the kitchen.

Laurie thought about going after him, then decided he had enough of a job dealing with his own nervousness. He couldn't take on Ed's as well. So he went the rest of the way over to the player. It housed an older generation iPod, and the readout declared they were listening to "Boom Boom Pow" by The Black Eyed Peas. Well, at least it wasn't Britney Spears.

"Here's your water." Ed emerged from the kitchen bearing a bottle of beer in one hand and a glass of water in the other. "Sorry I didn't have anything else."

"Water is fine. It's what I should have asked for anyway, after dancing." Laurie took the water and sipped at it, watching Ed. He was nervous, which was so odd on easy, breezy Ed. It touched Laurie even as it frustrated him. Someone had to lead this dance.

An idea struck him, and he smiled to himself before heading to his duffel. He rooted around in a side pocket, pulled out his own iPod and crossed to the player. He held his breath, hoping the speakers would be compatible with his, and thank God, they were. After removing Ed's iPod and stopping the pulsing thump of The Black Eyed Peas, he replaced it with his own and started scrolling through the album art.

Ed watched over his shoulder. "Don't like BEP?"

"It's fine," Laurie lied, "but I had something else in

mind. If that's okay." He glanced at Ed with a sly smile. "Would you care to dance, Mr. Maurer?"

Grinning, Ed set his beer on the coffee table. "Thought you'd have had enough of that for one night."

"But I haven't danced with you yet." Laurie selected a song and put it on repeat. "Are you up for a tango?"

He liked the way Ed's gaze darkened and went soft at once. "Sure. But I'm still pretty clumsy."

Laurie slid into position in front of Ed. "We'll take it slow."

Ed backed them out into the middle of the room, and as the music played, they danced. No, it wasn't the most artful tango in the world. But none had ever made Laurie's heart pound and his body go soft as this one did.

"This song keeps repeating," Ed remarked as he led Laurie into an ocho.

Laurie let his body revel in the sensuality of the dance. When he was in front of Ed again and moving into the standard pattern, he looked him in the eye. "Do you want me to change it?"

"No."

Ed started to lose his focus, and Laurie gently nudged him into form. "Bear the balance, Ed. When you're ready, why don't you try a boleo?"

Ed did try, but he still needed coaching on those. They spent the next few minutes perfecting the step, and all the while the female singer sang that she didn't need a parachute so long as she had her lover, that she wouldn't fall out of love but would fall into him.

I want to fall into Ed. Laurie closed his eyes and let himself merge with the dance, trusting Ed to bear his balance through the sensual moves.

Laurie lost count of how many times the song had played. All he knew was Ed. The strength of his arms, the sureness of his step. Part of Laurie could have kept dancing forever.

But as Ed drew him back into the tango embrace, as the music filled him, Laurie closed the distance between them, sliding not into an ocho but up against Ed's strong, beautiful chest. He put his hand behind Ed's neck and pulled Ed's lips toward his own.

The kiss began in a jolt, with Ed still focused on the dance and Laurie so thrown over into his desire he knew nothing else, but it was only a moment, a hesitation. Laurie opened for him, letting him in, tasting the beer on his tongue, tasting Ed.

As abruptly as it started, it was over. Laurie swooned into him, unbalanced, lost. But Ed kept hold of him, leading him to the bookshelf near the sofa. He grabbed a remote, pushed a button, and the music stopped. Silence rang in Laurie's ears a moment, and then Ed took him in his arms, aiming his mouth for Laurie's as he eased him onto the couch.

The panic Laurie had worked so hard to keep at bay rose, making him brace his hands against Ed's chest. "I'm a little rusty at this."

Ed's hands skimmed Laurie's back as his lips trailed their way down Laurie's face. "We'll go slow."

He took Laurie's mouth once more, and Laurie gave it to him, gave everything to Ed as he let himself fall.

ED HAD NEVER wanted to get anything right more in his life than making love to Laurie.

He wanted Laurie so desperately that a part of him wanted to plow through and take him, strip him bare and suck him and fuck him until the man couldn't move, couldn't leave Ed's arms. He felt possessive and hot and full of fire—but he also felt tenderness. He was aware that even though part of Laurie wanted that kind of claiming, he was scared of it.

Ed wanted *all* of Laurie. He wanted to possess him not only in body, but in that twisted, sometimes bitter mind he had.

He pressed Laurie into the leather of his couch and kissed him, so forcefully he had to watch to make sure Laurie could still breathe. They humped against one another, Laurie pushing up and Ed grinding down. Laurie shuddered and made the sexiest moans in the back of his throat Ed had ever heard. Laurie wore high-quality wool trousers, and Ed could feel his cock through them, hard and ready. The cool, almost aristo-cratic Laurie was coming apart in Ed's arms.

When Ed came too close to coming apart as well,

he pulled away to sit on the end of the couch and think about nuns.

Laurie sat up, gasping for air. He regarded Ed with a hooded but uncertain gaze.

"Just didn't want to come in my shorts, babe." Stroking Laurie's soft, smooth cheek wasn't helping with that goal, either, but Ed couldn't stop. "You make me so crazy."

A host of emotions played over Laurie's features. Desire, lust, but fear too. "I'm sorry. I'm so ridiculous. But it's been…"

Been so long. What Ed didn't understand was why Laurie had been living like a monk. He tried to figure out how to help Laurie feel more at ease. "Do you want to move to the bed?"

Laurie nodded. As Ed led him around the couch to the rough curtain separating the living room from the bedroom, he felt like a pasha leading a virgin to his tent. Normally he'd crack the joke, but he didn't think Laurie was going to appreciate that now. He had never seen Laurie so vulnerable.

He'd never thought he'd find vulnerable so arousing.

Ed led, this time without Laurie coaching him. He drew Laurie up to the platform that housed his bed, kissed him lingeringly, then undid the buttons to his shirt. While he slid Laurie out of it, Ed kissed his shoulders, his neck, the divots of his clavicle. Ed's gaze lingered on dusky, hardened nipples, but he made himself wait for them, kept fueling the fire until Laurie melted once more. Then and only then did Ed pause to remove his own shirt.

He repeated the same maneuver with Laurie's pants and briefs and even socks, kissing his way down his stomach and around the tops of Laurie's thighs until he was bare. Standing, Ed divested himself of his own clothes. He put Laurie's hand on his erection and swallowed the urge to say, "All for you, baby," because he was afraid it sounded silly.

But it was. God in heaven, it was all for Laurie. And oh, but he loved the way Laurie kept hold of his dick as Ed lay them on the bed, side by side, naked bodies quivering with anticipation and desire.

"What do you want, Laurie?" Ed whispered as he made love to Laurie's chin. "Tell me what turns you on. Tell me what you want. Top? Bottom? If you want to fuck me, hon, you so can."

Laurie sank into Ed and laughed nervously. "Sorry. I think I gave you the wrong impression at the theater. I was so pent up I couldn't think. I should have—" He stopped talking as Ed stuck his tongue in his ear. "*Oh.*"

"I liked the theater. That or a variation of would work for me."

"You'd be okay with only frottage?"

Ed lifted his head and laughed. "*Frottage?*"

Laurie got huffy. "You liked it well enough then, and you said—"

"The name, Laur, not the act." He grinned. "Frottage. Makes it sound like a textbook. Do you want me to touch your penis and penetrate your anus too?" *Oh, stupid, stupid,* Ed scolded himself as Laurie stiffened. Ed tried to gentle him with a stroke of his shoulder. "Hey. I'm teasing. Which was dumb. I'm sorry. I take it all back."

"No, it's me." Laurie closed his eyes. "I'm ridiculous. And appalled at myself."

Ed nuzzled Laurie's cheek with his nose. "You're not ridiculous. What's got you spooked, baby? Am I coming on too strong? Too boorish?"

Laurie opened his eyes. "No."

Ed stared into those eyes, held that gaze. "Is it that you're nervous about fucking?"

Laurie's eyes shuttered. *Bingo.*

Ed kissed Laurie's forehead. "It's okay. We don't have to."

Laurie covered his face with his hands. "I'm sorry. God, I'm so sorry."

Ed bent and pressed a kiss in the center of Laurie's chest. "Will you let me make love to you, Laurie? Will you trust me to lead? Play with me? It'll be like a dance. There's a line we won't cross. I'm not going to fuck you tonight, Laurie. So stop worrying about it."

Laurie kept his hands over his face. "I'm such an idiot."

Ed pulled his hands away. "You're not. Stop acting like this is a bad thing. It gives us something more to look forward to later. The tension, the anticipation, will make it sweeter." He kissed the tips of Laurie's fingers. "Because I want to make love to you any way you'll let me." He drew the fingers into his mouth, holding Laurie's rapidly softening gaze. "Dance with me, Laurie."

There was touching, and a lot of kissing, and Ed did finally get his mouth on one of those nipples. Ed was a licker, and he licked those peaks until Laurie clutched at his shoulders and cried out. Then he drew their cocks together and gave Laurie his frottage. But when he was close to coming and he thought Laurie must be too, he stopped and slowed them down, kissing his way along Laurie's hip, turning him over onto his stomach. Laurie quivered, but he yielded, even when Ed pulled Laurie's legs open and gave himself a beautiful view. He glanced up at Laurie, head buried in the comforter, hands clutching at it, ass taut.

Then Ed bent his head, spread Laurie's cheeks and licked his taint.

He made sweet, lingering love to that taint—perineum, he corrected himself with a smile. He gave it more attention than he'd ever given that anatomy in his life, and he didn't exactly shy away from that lovely little patch of skin in any circumstance. Why he fixated so much on it now he wasn't sure, but it felt right, so he did.

Maybe it was because it was such a tease. Close to Laurie's ass, but not in it. There was only the barest hint of sweat there, too, which Ed never minded and kind of liked, but mostly Laurie's taint tasted like soap and clean and Laurie. Ed loved it. He loved it up and down and sideways and in circles until Laurie wept. All the while he held Laurie open, letting his pink pucker take in the air, letting it ache. Sometimes he lifted his head enough to watch it convulse, begging him, but Ed simply smiled and went back to his patch of skin until he heard the word he'd been waiting for.

"Please." Laurie's hands rucked up the comforter around him in his desperation. "*Please.*"

"Yes, sir." Ed laid his tongue flat, slid it up the now glistening and quivering bit of flesh, into the shallow valley that flexed for him. Ed licked Laurie's asshole as thoroughly as he had his taint, reveling at the incoherent noises Laurie made. He loved the way Laurie had forgotten his hesitation entirely and humped the bed, frotting against the comforter on his own, pushing himself harder at Ed's mouth.

Ed took firm hold of Laurie's cheeks, pulled them open wide and shoved his tongue inside.

Oh, God help him, but it was almost better than fucking him. Laurie went from begging and pleading to grunting and bucking, animal now, rutting so roughly Ed had to dig his fingers in and really push into him or risk being thrown off. He imagined what it would be like to ride Laurie with his cock, to feel him pulsing and fucking back as his dick was in that velvet heat, and Ed moaned and wiggled his tongue inside Laurie.

Laurie made a sort of cascading yelp, and Ed felt

him drawing up, ready to come.

But Ed withdrew, purring at the cry of frustration that tore from Laurie's throat. He was being vicious now, but he wasn't breaking the rules. He was only leaning on them pretty heavily.

Turning Laurie to face him, he ran a finger along his crack. "I want to put my finger inside you."

He about came right then and there as Laurie shut his eyes, lifted his leg to rest his knee on Ed's hip and opened himself, nodding.

Ed pushed the leg down gently and sat up to reach into his drawer. He was generous with the lube, kissing Laurie as he snaked his slick finger around Laurie's body, but to his surprise, Laurie turned away from the kiss.

Oh, right. Ed had recently had that mouth all over Laurie's ass, and yeah, Laurie would be fussy about that.

"Sorry," Laurie whispered, still half lost to his lust.

"No worries." Ed reached for a tissue.

Then he thought, *no, do it right,* and wiped his finger off instead.

"Gimme one minute."

He hurried to the bathroom, where he washed his hands and face. Then, because he'd come this far, he brushed his teeth too. When he returned, Laurie was sitting up and hugging his knees. He didn't say anything until Ed crawled up beside him and brushed a minty kiss across his lips.

Laurie kissed him back. "Thank you."

Ed eased him onto his side, passing the lube to one hand before lifting Laurie's knee high on his hip, giving himself access. "You know, you could tell me this stuff."

"I know. I'm sorry." Laurie slid his hands up Ed's chest. "I—*Oh*."

Ed nudged his way into Laurie's hole. "Open for me, baby. Relax and let me in." He nipped at Laurie's bottom lip. "Let me in your hot little hole, sweet thing. Let me slide around inside you and make you moan."

Laurie's eyes were shut now, and he breathed heavily but easily. Relaxing. Ed was still working on entry, but his mind ran ahead to imagine the slick heat he'd felt the edge of with his tongue.

Let go to me, baby. He urged him with his mouth and his finger, his hand on the back of Laurie's neck, until at last, with a sigh, Laurie opened and sucked Ed inside. Ed moaned too, because it felt so, so good.

He hadn't planned on the dirty talk, but he fell into it, whispering into Laurie's ear how good and tight he felt, how hot, how just fucking him with his finger made Ed's balls ache. He explained to him how it was his middle finger, and though Laurie certainly couldn't be missing this part, he told him he was shoving it all the way in, so hard, going faster and faster and faster. He told Laurie he felt so good inside, that he loved fucking him with his finger and his tongue, that he was so hot and sweet and amazing.

Laurie moaned and cried through it all, clutching at Ed's chest, his shoulders, his cock, wherever his hands could reach. Ed wished he dared put two fingers in, or three. He had a brief fantasy of his whole hand, but holy shit, was Laurie not ready for anything like that. Maybe never would be.

But it was okay, because this, even in its dialed-back form, was nothing like anything Ed had ever done in bed. He'd never felt this wound up. He'd never wound anybody else up like this either. And so he fucked on, moving his finger in and out of Laurie, faster and faster until Laurie shouted and dug his fingernails into Ed's shoulders before he tensed, shrieked and came all over Ed's chest.

Ed kept his finger inside as Laurie came down, fucking him slower and slower until Laurie went limp beside him. Ed withdrew and lay there, watching the flush of Laurie's cheeks spread over his body, a flush not of embarrassment but contentment. He watched those eyes open, and he stared into them.

But then Laurie took hold of Ed's cock, gave him a wicked smile, and the game changed.

He shoved Ed up against the pillows and wrenched his legs around in one movement. He knelt between them and with no preamble took Ed deep into his throat. Ed drew his knees up, spread them open, and watched, so horny he thought he'd blow out all his insides. Laurie stared up at him with those sultry eyes— and Ed snapped. Roaring, he took hold of Laurie's hair with both hands and fucked his mouth, mindless, eight hard thrusts. He came like a geyser, felt it leaking out of Laurie's mouth and onto his own sac.

Spent, he realized what he'd done and gazed at Laurie in horror.

But Laurie only wiped his mouth on the back of his hand and slid up Ed's body, semen on his lips as he aimed for Ed's. Half an inch away he paused, uncertain.

Ed grabbed his hair and took him roughly, licking the semen away and then simply licking for good measure until they rolled together on the bed, weak and sated and yet full of energy and joy.

Eventually they both went to the bathroom, cleaned up and brushed their teeth. Laurie put on knit pants as he headed back to the bed, and following his lead, Ed put on a pair of boxers. They lay together beneath the sheets, pressed close, nuzzling gently, bathing in the aftermath of great sex. Ed was glad for the softness but mostly glad for the quiet, because he needed the space.

Because he was in love with Laurie. He understood that now. Hopelessly, completely, ridiculously in love. And he knew loving this man was going to be one hell of a ride.

But right now it was soft and sweet, and Ed clung to it, glad for the first time in his life to be taking things slow.

CHAPTER ELEVEN

*free spin: a general freestyle dance term used to
describe a turn without a handhold and with
no set landing position.*

LAURIE WOKE TANGLED in Ed's arms.

He faced the gym equipment and the end table, Ed pressed to his back, arm wrapped tight around Laurie's waist and knee over Laurie's hip. He nuzzled Laurie's hair, and if he concentrated, he could feel the warmth of Ed's breath on his nape.

He didn't have to focus to feel the pressure of Ed's erect cock along his backside.

Shutting his eyes, Laurie soaked in all the sensations: Ed's body, the weight of him, the smell of his pillow, the muffled sound of traffic from the street below. Sunlight streamed in through the industrial window above their heads. Laurie's body hummed with release, wrung out from coming not once but twice, and as he lay there basking, it was a perfect, crystalline moment.

Then Ed nuzzled Laurie's neck, purred, and slid his hand into the front of Laurie's pants.

Laurie gasped as Ed fumbled beneath the waistband with no preamble whatsoever. When Laurie made soft, breathless sounds, Ed…well, he *growled,* which made Laurie whimper.

Ed shoved down Laurie's pants, licked a long trail up the line of Laurie's spine from his shoulders to his hairline, pulled himself out of his boxers, and thrust his cock between Laurie's legs.

It felt like fucking. It was the same motion they'd be making if Ed had pushed inside of Laurie and taken him, except he wasn't inside, and somehow that was more arresting than if Ed had plowed him raw. Laurie cried out as Ed continued to fondle his cock and whispered incoherent, wicked endearments into Laurie's neck, and Laurie reached back to grab hold of Ed's hair, anchoring him in place. It was torture—so much friction, so much shock and raw, pumping sex, but no penetration, just the whisper of Ed's pubic hair as he spread Laurie's ass and ground into him.

"You like this, baby?" Ed licked Laurie's ear, huffing his breath into it as he thrust. "Feel good to you?"

"Yes." Laurie's eyes were closed, his mouth open, and he thrashed, chasing something. Not release, not yet, but there was something, something he couldn't find but something he needed—

Ed pushed at Laurie's shoulder, slowing but not stopping his thrusts. "Roll on your belly, baby, and lift your ass."

Laurie did as he was told, aching, needing, fearing too, but not Ed and not this. He felt all jumbled inside, which made him upset, because he'd been so happy a minute ago, and this was so good, what was wrong with him?

He gasped as his cheeks were pulled apart. Ed's cock slid beneath his. Laurie jolted as his own legs were slammed together around it, and then Ed was fucking. Laurie shut his eyes and let go to sensation once more.

Then he heard Ed spit, and something wet landed on his cheeks.

His eyes opened wide and stared at the comforter.

The sound and the wet of spit came again. And again.

Ed's split-slick finger pushed into his hole.

Laurie resisted for a few seconds, jolted out of the moment, but Ed stroked his backside, slapped it lightly and pushed his finger a little more. Laurie convulsed, but his anus relaxed enough that Ed's finger slipped deeper.

Ed withdrew, returning cold and slick with lube.

Ed wedged himself into place, meshing their bodies, thrusting with his hips to slide his cock beneath Laurie's as his finger worked insistently inside.

Laurie didn't fight him. He let go, more than he had before, letting Ed take him. The finger was all the way in now, buried inside him as Ed pistoned his cock. Laurie felt full, but it wasn't enough. He needed—he needed—

"Fuck me," he cried weakly, then lifted his head. "Fuck me, Ed. Fuck me. Fuck me—"

He moaned as Ed did, thrusting his finger in time to his cock, giving Laurie the sensation that he really was being fucked, that this was Ed's cock inside him, pushing into him, filling him, taking him—

He cried out, a strangled scream, and came all over the bed.

But Ed didn't stop. "So hot, baby. You're so hot, so fucking hot. So beautiful. So fucking beautiful." He withdrew his finger, gripped Laurie's ass again, and Laurie shut his eyes, shaking, knowing Ed was looking at him, wanting him.

When he had the courage, Laurie bent forward, spreading himself, a silent invitation.

Yes, Ed. Look at me. Have me.

Ed swore under his breath, and for a few moments the bed shook as Ed jerked himself. Hot ejaculate sprayed all over Laurie's back, some making it all the way up to his hair. It should have been as jarring as the spit, and on some level it was. But he was coming down from an intense orgasm, and he was quite sated, and all he could think of was how much he loved that Ed wanted him so much.

A tiny part of him liked the wicked feeling of being covered in cum…so long as it was Ed's.

All of him loved it when Ed sank against him, gluing his chest to Laurie's back as he rolled them to their sides, out of range of the puddle Laurie had made on the comforter. Drawing Laurie tight to his body, Ed kissed Laurie roughly on the shoulder. "Good morning."

Laurie smiled. "Yes, it is."

"Sorry I went everywhere." Ed kept tasting Laurie's skin. "You had me so wound up. Fucking hell, Laur. That was seriously hot."

Laurie's smile was going to break his face. "You're the only one who's ever told me that."

"You are. You're a fucking wildcat in bed, baby." He stroked Laurie's arm. "Can you come over tonight?"

"I have another performance this afternoon and a reception after I can't skip." He slid his fingers through the hair on Ed's arm. "But after, sure."

"I don't care what we do while you're here. Or what we don't do. I just want to be with you."

Laurie was quite certain they'd end up in bed, doing this and more, but it made his heart warm to hear Ed say sex wasn't essential. It made him feel…wanted. Which was an odd thing to cherish, because Laurie had been wanted a lot in his life. But it had been professional or for sex. This was different.

Don't break this, he urged himself and rolled over for a kiss.

Ed tried to take him out for breakfast, but they'd lingered so long in bed that Laurie was edging toward running late. So after another shower, Ed fed him coffee and toast before he drove Laurie to where he'd left his car downtown. They had a lingering goodbye inside the car, and Laurie promised to call once he was free for the evening.

He felt buoyant until he got to the theater and had to worry about his performance. He made no missteps this time, but he was more careful too. A critic might say his heart wasn't in it, and several likely would. He didn't care.

As he waited in the wings for the curtain call, he thought about Ed, the memories making his blood hum. The way Ed regarded him, with open affection and his heart in his eyes, made Laurie feel warm and safe. Sex wasn't too difficult to come by, if one was determined to go and get it. The way Ed looked at him…well, no one had ever looked at him like that. Laurie decided he deserved to feel a little giddy.

Especially when he came to his dressing room after the show to find a ridiculously huge bouquet of red roses waiting for him. He tried to temper his heart as it leapt at the sight of them, tried to warn it that the flowers might not be from Ed, but Laurie saw the two-letter signature before he read the note.

Figured I shouldn't come backstage, because you know how I get when you're in tights. Sent these instead. I wrote this card before the show, but I know you were amazing as always. Looking forward to seeing you later. —Ed

Laurie's heart moved well beyond his throat and hovered somewhere near the ceiling. Ed had come to the performance? Again? And he'd sent flowers? Laurie clutched the card to his chest, smiling so hard his face hurt. With reluctance, he set the card down and got dressed, though he had to stop frequently to reread the card or stare at the bouquet and grin.

He was fingering the edge of a rose and trying to work out how he could skip the reception when a knock came on the door. Leaving the roses, Laurie crossed to open it.

Caroline Parker smiled her thin, abstracted smile. "Good. I was hoping to catch you before you left. I wanted to talk to you about the charity benefit." When he didn't move right away, she patted his arm and nudged him gently aside so she could come into his dressing room. Her eyes lit up as she saw the flowers. "Are these from the children? That's lovely." She reached for the card.

Laurie snatched it out of her hand before she could read it. She blinked at him, surprised and clearly a little affronted. Laurie pretended not to notice and tucked the card into his trouser pocket, his thumb rubbing the edge of the cardboard for comfort. "What about the charity benefit?"

"I want you to agree to perform, sweetheart. Now that you've done so well for Oliver, surely you're ready for more?"

Laurie didn't physically withdraw, but the warm

glow inside him was superseded by the emptiness this argument always inspired. "I'm not performing."

"I was thinking it could be something unconventional. Even if you were to do something with Maggie, that would do. It'll draw people any way you do it, if they think they'll be seeing Laurence Parker perform after all these years."

"I'm not performing. If you advertise otherwise, you'll be the one explaining why you misled them, and if you make it purposefully awkward for me, I simply won't come."

"Stop being so petulant, Laurence. It doesn't become you. You performed half an hour ago, and you performed yesterday as well. And it went well, as we told you it would. Now it's time to take the next step forward." She glanced at the roses, then at Laurie's pocket, where he'd stowed the card. "Who *are* the flowers from?"

"From my boyfriend."

The confession shocked them both, and they stood there reeling for a few seconds.

Caroline fingered the petals of one of the roses, staring at it intently as she spoke. "I see. I take it this is someone you're seeing…publicly?"

Laurie's chest hurt, his heart and belly open and vulnerable. But he thought of Oliver and all his talk about raw sex, about what he had done that morning with Ed, about how good it had felt, and he made himself say, "Yes."

"I see." She gave him a polite, distant smile. "I won't be coming to the reception, so I'll say goodbye to you now. But while all these people greet you and tell you how wonderful you were, think of what it would be like to perform for real. To be normal again."

She pressed close in a formal, polite embrace, put her hands on his shoulders and her cheek to his, her lips grazing his skin with little more than a brush of breath as she withdrew. "I'll call you later in the week once you've had a chance to think things over."

Once the door closed behind her, he turned to the flowers. He didn't touch them, didn't smell them, just stood there with his hands in his pockets, clutching the card as everything jumbled inside him. When it became clear it wasn't going to settle, he slipped into his coat, pulled out his keys and grabbed the vase, bracing it as gracefully as he could against his side as he carried it out of the dressing room.

It garnered him plenty of stares. At first that unsettled him, but the floral scent kept wrapping around him. Roses didn't really smell that wonderful to him, but the arrangement collectively did. It was more earthy and grassy than floral, associating the bouquet more strongly with Ed. By the time Laurie was on the back stairs, he was smiling and enjoying carrying a ridiculously large vase of flowers out to his car. He didn't care that it took him ten minutes to get it arranged on the seat so that the flowers wouldn't get crushed and wouldn't tip over as he drove, and he glanced over to smile at the bouquet every time he was at a stoplight.

There were at least three dozen flowers in there. He was late to the reception because he'd tried to count them. Laurie pressed his hand over his lips to stay his ridiculous grin, heart swelling as he imagined Ed picking them out. He could just see him standing there, overseeing the stuffing of the horribly gaudy vase, rejecting roses he didn't think were good enough, not caring about how many were in there but how it *looked*.

Laurie tried to think of the last time someone had done something like this for him. He couldn't come up with anything that remotely compared.

The reception was at a country club in the wealthier part of St. Paul. Ostensibly it was a thank you to some of the sponsors of the performance, but mostly it was a chance for Maggie and the other studio instructors who organized it to brag up their studios. Laurie had never liked these things, but he especially disliked them tonight. All he wanted to do was go to Ed and thank him for the flowers, kiss him, touch him, make love to him. Be with him. Instead he was pasting on a smile and staying the urge to dull the edges of the event with too much champagne.

Especially when he found out his mother had already begun her campaign to get him to perform at her benefit. Everyone at the reception kept telling him how excited they were to see him perform again.

It was this that ultimately led him to leave early. He'd planned to cut it short as it was, but he left before they brought out dessert, not bothering to excuse himself to Maggie. He would hear about it the next day at the studio, but he didn't care. The longer he stayed, the angrier he would be at the donors, at Maggie, and most of all at his mother. And he didn't want to be angry. He wanted the giddy feeling back that he had when he was with Ed.

Normal, his mother had said. Laurie didn't know what that was. He didn't think he'd ever known. He might not be meant for normal. All he knew was he was tired of feeling guilty and sleepy. He needed something. Something more.

Ed. He needed Ed.

He hoped Ed needed him too. He feared he'd had an emotional, ridiculous day and had imagined all this. He feared this would end somehow, that it would end and hurt more than he could bear. But right now all he knew was that he needed Ed. *Needed* him. Now.

As he climbed the stairs, his heart beat in his ears and his stomach flipped over with every step. By the time he knocked on Ed's door he was a wreck, and as he waited in the endless seconds before it opened, he had to remind himself to breathe.

Then Ed was there, disheveled and messy and wearing a dark gray muscle T-shirt stained with sweat. He was surprised, and then his face changed, and Laurie realized this was what he'd needed to see, why he couldn't call to warn him, why he had to simply arrive. Because there it was, Ed's joy at the sight of

Laurie. The same eagerness and giddiness that had wrapped Laurie up since he'd woke this morning in Ed's arms.

"Hi." Breathless, Laurie couldn't stay his smile. "Did I come at a bad time?"

"Oh, of course not." Ed blushed. "Come on in. Did you get…?"

Laurie could not have stopped his smile if his life had depended on it. "Yes. I got the flowers. Thank you. They're beautiful."

"Good." He rubbed at his hair. "I hoped they weren't out of line. I mean, we hadn't… We haven't said if we…" He swore under his breath. "Fuck. I'm no good at this, Laurie. Are we dating?"

Oh, Laurie could have flown to the moon, he felt so high. "I'd like to be. If *you* want to."

"Yes, I do." Ed smiled now too, a beautiful, ridiculous grin. He started for Laurie, glanced at his sweaty shirt, then jerked his thumb at the bathroom. "I'm gonna go shower up quick."

Laurie stepped forward and took Ed's face in his hands. Giddiness bounced crazily inside him as he watched Ed's eyes hood.

"I've been working out," Ed murmured, but his eyes were on Laurie's mouth. "I'm kind of smelly."

There was some line here Laurie could have given, some flip reply about how he could use a workout too, but he wasn't deft at this sort of game. So he pulled Ed's face to his own, shut his eyes, and kissed him softly on the mouth.

When they came up for air, Ed pressed his forehead to Laurie's and ran his hands down Laurie's back.

Laurie kept his eyes shut. "Make love to me. Please."

Ed kissed him like a sigh, a man coming home, and the last of Laurie's tension left him. When Ed swept him up into his arms, he laughed, but then Ed's hands started to move on him, and he was too lost in sensation to laugh.

All thoughts of his mother, the studio, the benefit, and anything that wasn't making love to Ed Maurer sailed away as Ed lowered him into the mattress. Laurie opened his mouth, his legs, his body and took Ed all the way into his soul.

IT STARTED WHEN Ed woke up on Monday morning with a nagging pull down the side of his neck.

He didn't consciously notice it until he was in the shower, when he caught himself massaging the spot. It had bugged him off and on the whole weekend, acting up something nasty after they'd done all that cleaning, but he'd doubled up on painkillers, and the pain had gone away. He hadn't thought about it much after that. But now the pain was back, louder and angrier than it had been in a long time. He stopped, and for a moment he stood under the spray, panic blooming up from the place it always lurked. Then he pursed his lips and resumed scrubbing his chest with the bar of soap. It was probably nothing. He'd slept on it wrong. He'd done that before, and he'd do it again.

Even so, he popped a few ibuprofen before he shaved, in case. He'd done too much on Saturday. It wasn't a big deal. It'd be fine in a day or so.

He made himself focus on good things, like how nice it was to get ready for work in a place that was clean, of how the pillow Laurie had clutched while Ed made him come his brains out still carried the echo of his scent. He lingered over his coffee and cereal, thinking of Laurie while he stared at but didn't watch a morning news program. Laurie worked late, but Ed was going to go over and meet him at his place at 8:30. Which meant they were going to have sex again.

Ed smiled around the rim of his coffee cup and hummed to himself as he finished getting ready for work. Before he headed out the door, he went back and took two more ibuprofen, finishing out the maximum dose. Nothing wrong with hedging his bets.

Even with the painkillers, though, he rubbed at his neck a lot during the day, and by lunchtime it started to worry him. He must have hurt himself on Saturday. That was the only explanation. And it timed out about right. It had hurt Sunday, but he'd ignored it and had some…well, the sex hadn't been rough exactly, but it had been intense. It was too fun, thinking up ways to fuck Laurie without literally fucking him, and he hadn't thought about being careful of his neck. And that was the way it went. Once he woke it up, every little thing sent it screaming. Normally that would have depressed him, but not today. Not now. He wasn't going to get down about this. He'd take it easy the next few days, and he'd be fine.

But by three in the afternoon his neck hurt so much he could barely focus. He'd borrowed Aleve from a woman in the cubicle next to him when it was safe to re-dose—okay, a bit sooner than that, but it was close enough—and he might as well have taken Tic Tacs for all the good it did him. At four he had to duck out of a meeting and put his head on his desk while the colors exploded in his head.

At four thirty he gave up and called his mom.

She was upset. She came over with his father so they could take both him and his car, and as they went she told him six different times about how she'd already made him an emergency appointment at the clinic. Thankfully, his father overrode her when they got to the parking garage and insisted on driving Ed, leaving her to bring along their vehicle. Ed climbed into the passenger seat and hunkered down as his father ferried him silently back across the city.

Dick Maurer was as taciturn as his partner was exuberant, and simply being with him had long been a restorative for Ed. But today not even that was enough, and when they got caught in a traffic snarl and slowed to a crawl, Ed filled the silence with the thoughts gnawing at the edges of his mind.

"It's never been like this." He hunched forward

and stared at the dashboard. "I've screwed it up before, but never over so little. It never got this hot this fast."

"You don't normally work it all day long the way you did on Saturday." His father patted Ed's thigh. "You were a man possessed."

Because he'd wanted to impress Laurie. And wasn't that a good thing? But his reward for cleaning up his place for the first man he'd cared about in a long time was to have this damn thing act up. It wasn't fucking fair.

"Put some music on, son. Something fun to distract you. Don't go making this into something big before Dr. Linnet tells you it is."

Yes, but what was the doctor going to tell him? What could he? What was wrong with his stupid neck now? What was the treatment going to be this time?

What else was he going to have to give up?

He plugged in his iPod, and the song "Nothing Matters When We're Dancing" by The Magnetic Fields came on. That was when Ed realized what worried him most. What if he had to quit dancing too?

Shutting off the stereo, Ed stared into traffic and hated the whole damn world all the way to the clinic.

By some miracle they didn't wait long in the lobby, and before he knew it he was in an exam room. His mom came with him. His dad tried to dissuade her, but she wasn't having any of it. She was going with her baby because he was hurting. Though Ed grumbled on the outside, secretly he was glad. Ed didn't protest when his mother took his hand in hers, running her thumb over the back of it soothingly.

Dr. Linnet's diagnosis wasn't as bad as it could have been, but it wasn't great either. "You've strained it. Working all day the way you described when you aren't used to doing that is going to cost you. This happened, Ed, because that muscle and the ones surrounding it are so weak. You didn't come to your therapy the way I wanted you to, and you aren't treating your body as if it's been injured."

Ed grumbled, not able to look the doctor or his mother in the eye.

Linnet made a disapproving sound. "I've already given you my opinion on keeping a desk job. You'd do better with something with moderate movement. Have you been taking breaks like we discussed?"

Ed had not. It was a nice idea, getting up to stretch every thirty minutes, but even with a doctor's note, somebody taking breaks that regularly in a department constantly downsizing didn't stay to take breaks long. "I've been doing some ballroom dancing." He decided not to mention the athletic sex.

Linnet brightened. "That's good. Be smart about it, because yes, you can injure yourself dancing, but I'm for anything that keeps you moving. Is there any prayer you've kept up with the exercises PT gave you before you quit?"

"I've moved a bit beyond them."

"I know they're not what you're used to doing from

training for football, but lifting weights is not rebuilding the muscles of your neck. You need to keep to their schedule for your recovery. I want you back on a regular PT schedule for the next month. Mrs. Maurer, if you have any sway with him, I suggest you use it. And, Ed, I want you off all physical activity outside of what they assign you for a few weeks. That includes weight-lifting, dancing and sex. And work."

Ed looked up sharply at him, raising his gaze only, because his neck was fucking killing him. "I can't be off work for two weeks." *And the hell I'm telling Laurie we can't fuck for fourteen days.*

He couldn't let himself think about the dancing.

"Then you can look forward to having this kind of pain at frequent intervals, and probably with increasing degrees of pain as well." The doctor braced his elbows on his knees. "I know dealing with this is rough for you, but this isn't a usual injury. If you'd hit a few millimeters over, we'd be having this conversation as you sat in your wheelchair. This isn't something you're going to recover from. This is something you're living with. You'll get better at it, but it's not leaving you." He paused, then added, "Have you given any further thought to my suggestion that you see someone to talk about what that's going to mean to you long term?"

Linnet was talking about a therapist. For his head. And yes, Ed had thought about it. He'd thought about how it wasn't fucking going to happen. "I'll be fine."

The doctor handed him several scripts. "Here.

You're going back on some higher dose painkillers until this calms down. I've included something for anxiety too, because that helped you last time. And I want you making an appointment with physical therapy before you leave the clinic."

Ed scanned the papers and saw his old friends Voltaren, Ativan, Skelaxin and Vicodin. He grimaced.

"And once you get back on your feet, keep up the dancing." Linnet shook Ed's hand when he rose to go. "Be sure to mention it to PT. They can work it into your plan."

They swung by the pharmacy on the way home, where Ed picked up all the meds and a Diet Mountain Dew to wash them all down. By the time he hit the stairs to his apartment, he was so high he was practically floating up them. He ate the soup and sandwich his mom put in front of him with only the barest acknowledgment that he was doing so. But when she put him into bed, he remembered, and he sat up, pushing the covers away.

"Laurie." The room pulsed in and out of focus, but Ed was determined to get to his phone. "Have to call Laurie."

Annette fought him, and when she couldn't take him, roped Dick into the act as well. "I'll call him, honey. Is his number on your phone?"

I want to call him, he tried to say, but his lips felt numb. *I want to hear his voice.* But it was all he could do to keep himself conscious enough to get into bed. He sank into sleep before his mother had finished pulling up the covers, and he dreamed sharp-edged narcotic dreams where he lay numb and broken on the ground, reaching out helplessly to Laurie as he danced into purple-tinted fog.

And then Laurie was there, touching his face, talking quietly. He sounded like he was underwater, so at first Ed assumed he was still dreaming. But then he felt the dull ache of his neck, and he knew this was real. Laurie really was here. He reached for him, thrilling when Laurie's cool hands closed over his own.

I was supposed to make love to you tonight. He watched Laurie swim in and out of focus, and out of nowhere depression swamped him. He didn't realize he was crying until the tears ran into his nose, and then he was alarmed, because that was definitely not something he was ready for Laurie to see.

Someone pushed something small and hard and round into his mouth, and he tasted the bitter tang of a pill before a straw appeared to draw up water and chase it down. Then another pill came, and another, and another, and another. The full monty, which meant he'd gotten an Ativan too. He'd said no earlier, but his mother apparently had seen the tears. Well, Vicodin and Ativan would iron those out. No pain, anxiety, no depression. No nothing.

He lost track of dreams and reality once the meds took hold of him. For a while he floated naked on a cloud while Laurie kissed his way along his spine, but mostly there was nothing. Sometimes he thought maybe someone was petting his hair. Sometimes he thought he smelled Laurie, but he might well have imagined it.

They're going to fire me, he thought dispassionately as the Ativan bore him away like a Lotos-Eater. *They're going to fire me, and then I won't have health insurance.*

The dream-Laurie started kissing him again, and Ed smiled. *Wouldn't it be nice if that meant I could spend all day dancing with Laurie?*

Sometime in the middle of the night his full bladder woke him up, and before he could finish letting the queasiness settle he felt hands sliding over his shoulders and Laurie's whisper in his ear. "Are you okay?"

"Bathroom," Ed slurred, fumbling to find Laurie's hand and hold it tight.

Laurie helped him to the toilet, sitting him on it so he didn't fall over while he pissed. "Your mom said you might be queasy, and that if you were, I was supposed to make you toast. Do you want some toast?"

Ed nodded, then sat there on the toilet swaying. He took a few moments to rise when he was done, and Laurie helped him get his pants up. He also made Ed wash his hands, which Ed found kind of funny, but he'd do about anything to keep Laurie touching him like this. When they were through in the bathroom, he let Laurie lead him into the kitchen, where he listed on a stool and gnawed on toast.

"I took tomorrow off." Laurie wiped crumbs away

from Ed's cheek with a napkin. "I'll call Vicky for you in the morning. Your mom is calling your office for you, since they know her better than me."

At first Ed didn't know what Laurie was talking about, and then he remembered. His class on Thursday. He wanted to argue he'd be okay by then, but he didn't know. Probably not. He wondered if he was going to get to teach it at all now.

Laurie kept stroking his face, this time with his thumb. "Your mom said you hate the painkillers but that you needed to take them regularly for now. She told me how to taper them off in the morning so I can get you to your therapy appointment in the afternoon. Will you tell me, though, if you're hurting? Because she said you can be obstinate about that too." He paused and bit his lip. "Sorry, you're not awake enough for this conversation, are you?"

Ed blinked at Laurie for several minutes, everything swimming. He thought about what Laurie had told him, how tenderly he was caring for him. What he'd given up for Ed, to be with him, to help him.

"I love you." He shouldn't have said it, but he was so high he hardly cared.

Laurie's face softened, and his thumb slipped to the corner of Ed's mouth. Then he rose from his stool, leaned forward and kissed him sweetly. "Let's get you to bed."

Ed went, sinking gladly into Laurie's arms, nestling into his shoulder and the ice pack Laurie tucked into his sore neck. As he drifted to sleep, he thought he heard Laurie whisper, "I love you too."

He might have been dreaming already. But Ed decided that either way, it was the best medicine he'd had all day.

IT UPSET LAURIE to see Ed in the condition he was in.

The first night, Ed had been so drugged nothing registered, but by the next day he was less groggy and more clearly hurting. He slept a lot, but when he was awake, his eyes were hazy with drugs and pain. Annette came to take Ed to his doctor appointment the day after that. Laurie should have gone to the studio, but he cleaned up Ed's apartment instead, then ran to his own place to do laundry. When he came back, he brought over some more of his own things.

He hoped that was all right. Ed didn't seem like he should be left alone. And honestly, Laurie wouldn't do anything but worry about him if he wasn't there. There wasn't much he could do, but it felt better when he was there to help. He looked for signs to see if this upset Ed. He couldn't tell. Laurie decided perhaps his staying over *was* unwelcome, so he went back to his place at night and began "popping by" in the mornings and afternoons. He wasn't even sure Ed noticed the change.

Nothing engaged him. He didn't respond to gentle teasing, and he didn't want to do much beyond sit on the couch and stare absently at the TV. On Wednesday he'd roused himself briefly, but it was to try to go to work. Until he keeled over sideways when he put his leg in his dress pants, right over the top of the sweatpants he'd slept in. After that, he'd gone quietly to the couch, and he hadn't spoken much after that.

Annette said he didn't usually hurt this much, but yes, this sort of spasm came and went. She'd confided, too, that the doctor had told Ed the desk job wasn't good for him. "All kinds of data entry." She hunched over an invisible keyboard and mimed typing with a look of distaste. "Strains the injury. The doctors all say it's movement he needs, but controlled." She'd smiled hopefully at Laurie. "He mentioned that dancing was good."

Laurie acknowledged this was part of why he felt so unsettled. He hadn't gotten around to worrying that dancing might have caused this, but it was like finding out you'd nearly had a car accident. He still needed a few minutes to feel the hot terror of what might have been. *Had* dancing caused this in any way, despite what she'd said? What about the sex? The thought of losing either was equally hollowing.

He couldn't let himself think about losing Ed, period.

Laurie was completely overreacting, making mountains out of molehills, and he absolutely wasn't helping Ed. Clearly *he* needed help. So instead of calling Vicky to tell her about Ed, Laurie drove himself to the center.

She was in a meeting with the door closed tight.

Laurie, pumped up on anxiety over Ed's condition, angry at the universe in general, didn't feel Vicky's closed door applied to him right now.

"She don't want to be bugged when that door is shut, man."

It was the boy from Vicky's office the other day, the one with the BITCH cap, which he wore again today. He stood halfway down the hall, arranged as if he had worked hard to look casual but slightly tough as well. And perhaps a little bigger than he actually was.

Laurie straightened, putting on an awkward, uncomfortable smile. "Were you waiting to see her? Sorry if I budged in line."

"Shit, no. Don't you tell her I'm here, neither. I'm ditching." He jerked his chin at Laurie. "I saw you dancing and shit in that room the other day. Saw your show the other night too. You're good, man. Real good."

Laurie had no idea what to say to that, so he went with a slightly awkward, "Thank you," and worked to keep from glancing at the door. Something about the boy was making him self-conscious, though he knew he shouldn't feel that way.

But if the boy had picked up on Laurie's discomfort, he ignored it. "What was that? The dancing, I mean. Some modern shit? 'Cause it didn't look like no ballet, but nothin' else I seen, either."

"I wasn't dancing any particular style. Improvising, I suppose you could say. But I know a number of different styles, so I was probably flitting between ballet and jazz and—" He was likely giving more information than the young man wanted. "Just a bit of this and that, which was why it may have seemed odd. Free form."

"Didn't look odd. It was wicked cool, man." Now the young man was the awkward one, his posture artificially aggressive as he regarded Laurie with a guarded intensity that made his heart pound. "Don't suppose you ever teach classes or nothin'."

"Actually, I do. In Eden Prairie. I teach aerobics here on Thursdays, but I teach dance too, at my studio. Which I suppose you knew already, from Ed's class."

"Why aren't you teaching us that shit? I ain't taking no aerobics, but I'd take *that* class."

Laurie couldn't help a smile. "Vicky never mentioned there was a call for dance, or I'd have offered that too."

"Depends on what you try and teach. None of that fancy shit gonna fly here. But you dance cool like that night, hell yeah, people will come."

"The truth is, everyone has to start with the 'fancy shit' before they get to 'cool'. Anything else is like trying to read without learning the alphabet first. You might be able to fake it to a degree, but you won't really know how."

The boy stuffed his hands deeper into his pockets. "Well, when Ms. Vic gets out of her meeting and you go in, tell her Duon says she needs to knock off that aerobics and get you teachin' dancing." He held up a hand. "But you tell her I told you couple of days ago, yeah?"

Laurie smiled. "I'll do that."

Duon lingered. "So what you all agitated about? You look like you're about to climb the door and go in through that window above it. What'd Ms. Vic do? Or what'd *you* do?"

Laurie ran a hand briefly through his hair. "My—" He stumbled, glancing at Duon as he waffled between a series of nouns and pronouns. His eyes flicked up to the BITCH hat. Taking a chance, he pushed on. "My boyfriend had an injury flare-up. I need to…talk to Vicky about it. I guess. She should know. And I thought…well. I don't know why I'm here."

Duon straightened. "This Ed, this boyfriend?"

Laurie tensed, worried that he'd shared what he shouldn't have or that Duon would turn up his nose at their relationship. "Yes."

"Shit." Duon grimaced. "I mean, glad you two are dating and all, but damn that his neck got bad again. That's what it is, right?"

Laurie nodded, rubbing at his own neck as he eased the last of his awkwardness away. "Yes."

"He gonna be okay?"

"I think so. Right now he's mostly tripped out on painkillers." *And ignoring me. And everything. And I don't know what to do.*

"Do *not* tell him I cut, man. He will kick my sorry ass into next week if he finds out."

Laurie couldn't help being amused at Duon's sudden panic. "With as much effort as you have to put into hiding the fact that you're skipping school, has it ever occurred to you it might be easier to simply attend?" Duon's face turned dark, and Laurie immediately regretted his teasing. Too late, it occurred to him why a young black man who wore a BITCH cap and came easily to empathy for a gay man and his boyfriend might be ditching school.

"Bunch of shit anyway. I'm doin' time till I can go get my GED." Duon adjusted his position at the wall, hefting his shoulder higher. "So Maurer is gonna be okay?"

Laurie paused a moment as he tried to decide how to frame his answer, and before he could settle on anything, the door to Vicky's office opened. Duon was gone before Vicky appeared in the doorway, but she wouldn't have seen him anyway, because she was completely engaged in a heated conversation with a man in a suit.

"You've got to give me until the end of the year at least. Through the holidays."

"I can get you to the middle of December if I lie like hell, Victoria, and that's the best I can do." He saw Laurie, nodded curtly at him, then hefted a briefcase higher in his grip as he wedged his way past Vicky into the hall. "Who knows. Maybe we'll have some sort of miracle and this discussion will have been nothing more than a waste of both our afternoons."

He hurried down the hall toward the stairs. Vicky turned to Laurie with grim determination and motioned him inside. "Come on in. I hope you've come to tell me you want to give the center fifty thousand dollars."

"What?" Laurie said automatically, but he hadn't needed to hear any more of Vicky's conversation than he'd already heard to glean that the center had a lot greater problems just now than his.

CHAPTER TWELVE

*outside partner step: a step taken with one's
partner beside the moving foot. During this step
the tracks of the partners do not overlap.*

IN HER OFFICE, Vicky sank into her desk chair and shut her eyes. "The city is cutting funding for the center by fifty thousand dollars a year. And they assure me this is the first of many cuts to come."

Laurie shook his head. "That's a lot of money. How can they cut so much at once?"

Vicky's smile was macabre. "It's carefully done. It's enough to be a cut without killing, not outright. It looks like 'trimming' to those who need to defend themselves as budget conscious. We can apply to sponsors for the difference or try for more grants."

"You're going to, right?" Laurie asked.

"There aren't any more grants. I already do my best to keep us as funded on grants as I can."

"And what about finding local sponsors?" When Vicky looked ready to protest, he held up a hand.

"Victoria. *Honestly.* You're going to keep being unreasonable about that *now?*"

"Yes. And do you want to know why? Because as soon as you let other people into the process, you're at their mercy. They tell you what kind of kids you can have. They tell you what sort of programs you should be having. I get offers all the time from a megachurch in Bloomington. All I have to do to get twenty thousand dollars, which they assure me is a mere down payment, is let them present an abstinence-only program."

"They can't all be like that."

"No, they're not. But I can't know which will be like that and which won't. No one gives away anything for free, Laurie. Everyone always has an agenda. I don't want any agendas here that aren't set by the board."

"Let me ask my mother. She knows a lot of people. And they really do give their money away. Sometimes for the tax write-off. Sometimes because they care about kids. You might have to put a plaque over a door at best."

"I can't do that, Laurie."

"But why not? You asked me when I came in the door if I had fifty thousand dollars. I might be able to get it to you, and more."

"It's not only me, Laurie. The whole Halcyon board feels this way. They'd rather take city funding and grants they hand-pick. And until now, that's worked fine. Normally we'd solve this with a fundraiser. But this time we need three times as much money as usual—fast—and that's only the beginning."

"So…you mean it's over? But it's always so busy in here. There are never any spare rooms. If it's not a Lamaze class, it's an A.A. meeting or a Moms Off Meth or Parents as Teachers." He pointed to the hallway. "And now your kids are telling me they want dance classes. There's a need for this place. You have to fight, Vic."

"I'm *going* to fight, damn it. But it's going to be a lousy Christmas. I'm going to have to let people go. A lot of people." She leaned back in her chair, and they sat in silence for a few minutes, cloaked in doom. Eventually she looked up at him, forcing cheerfulness. "Anyway. You caught me at the onset of bad news. I'm sure I'll figure it out. What did you need, hon?"

Laurie, still letting his mind race for solutions for the center, took another moment to respond. "Ed…isn't well. I'm taking care of him."

Vicky sat up. "Is he sick?"

"His neck is bothering him. His mom said it was something about cleaning his apartment."

"Ed cleaned his apartment?" She whistled low. "He really did fall for you, didn't he?"

Laurie tried to take heart in that comment, but he remembered the Ed he had left and couldn't quite manage it. "He's in some sort of depressive funk."

"He's been in a depressive funk ever since they told him he couldn't play football. He just hid it underneath a smile and his sudden zeal to work here. That and in the three feet of garbage in his apartment." She gave Laurie a careful look. "He cleaned his *whole* place?"

Laurie felt defensive on Ed's behalf. "It was very nice."

"If you want it to stay that way, I suggest you hire him a cleaning service. Or move in and do it yourself." She sighed. "I've been hoping I could hire him to work here full-time. He's so good with the kids. But that dream's gone now. Nobody's going to help a bunch of kids from the east side. Not *in this economy*." Her fist came down like an anvil on top of her desk. "I am so *fucking* sick of hearing that. Nobody was in here waving checks at me or letting us in on tax increases when times were good. They still bitched, making excuses for why they didn't have to care about these kids. Now those same people want to take away what little this population has. God*damn* it, but I wish I were one of those fucking millionaires in the fucking burbs sitting on a pile of cash. I wouldn't even blink."

Laurie, the son of one of those "fucking millionaires in the fucking burbs," chose his next words carefully. "What if I came in and did classes more often? Not just aerobics. Dance too. Kids, older people, everything. That would bring in some more money, right?"

"But you told me you had a full schedule at your own academy. You said Thursday was the only night that worked for you."

"I can give some of my courses to another instructor. And my Tuesday night class is over. That's one night free already."

Vicky shook her head. "It's nice of you to offer, but it won't generate enough money. That aerobics class works because it's something people think they need. Dance classes are a luxury people in this neighborhood can't afford."

"Then we'll bring in people from outside the area." When Vicky raised an eyebrow at him, he raised both of his at her. "You don't think I can bring them in? I'll show you the waitlist for my classes. They'll drive across the Cities to come to me."

"And they won't mind coming into this neighborhood to take them?"

"Oh, they'll mind. But they'll still come."

"Let me get this straight. You're volunteering to give up classes that make you money in your established institution and do them here, probably in less than ideal surroundings, and give me the money?"

Put like that, it sounded ridiculous. But he thought of Duon in the hallway, with hungry eyes as he asked why Laurie didn't teach them how to dance. "I'll give the center the money, yes. And I want local kids to be able to come for free. Or, if you think they'll find that insulting, have it be a graduated fee. Or tell them they're working it off by cleaning the bathrooms or something, since you'll probably have to let go of the janitors."

Vicky looked intrigued, but she was still wary. "Why are you doing this?"

Laurie shrugged. "I told you before. I like it here. And because I want to help. Please, let me dig around a bit and see if I can find you some local funding that might be palatable. Can I at least try?"

Vicky shrugged. "I suppose. You said Tuesday nights? What time?"

"Eight."

She scribbled a note on a pad beside her desk. "I'll do what I can about a room and get in touch with you."

"We can work anywhere. And if you need another night, let me know."

"I'll call you."

Laurie ducked out of her office. He felt excited, and anxious, and even a little fearful. Why, did he want to do this so badly? Vicky was right: it was like holding a hurricane off with an umbrella. And yet, all he could think about was running to the beach to get wet.

He thought he saw Duon's shadow down the hall, but Vicky came out after Laurie, thanking him as she headed for the women's restroom, and the shadow was quickly gone.

THE WORST PART for Ed when his neck flared up wasn't the pain. It was that sitting still all the goddamned time so he could heal gave him too much opportunity to think about what the pain might mean.

All the fear got buried in some weird sub-basement inside him when things were good, because until the pain hit, he honestly thought he was okay. People would say, "How are you doing?" in that worried, head-tilt way, and he'd smile and say, "Great," and he would mean it. But when the pain came back, he knew he hadn't ever been okay. He'd built his whole sense of well-being on the top of that basement door, and for some reason the pain always broke the lock. Then it swamped him, and he had all the misery, all at once. It didn't simply make him depressed. It turned all the good times to ash too, because now he knew he'd believed his own bullshit. When the pain came back, he knew everything was going to fuck up, that everything he loved was going to go away, and the unfairness and the despair of it tore at him until he felt like all his arteries had opened inside and were bleeding him out behind his skin, sucking him drop by drop into that black hole his pain made.

He'd told his mom that once, and she'd said he was being dramatic, so he'd never made that comment again. But that was what it felt like. The pain was so sharp sometimes it made him crazy. As it radiated up his neck and into his head, sometimes he had to tell himself repeatedly that banging his head into the wall wouldn't help, because the urge was so strong. That or his fist. Something, anything, some different pain. A pain that didn't suck at his teeth or run icy fire through the veins at the back of his head or down his shoulder.

He knew, too, part of the problem was that except for the glazed look in his eye, he appeared fine. If you did an MRI of his neck, he'd look like fucking Frankenstein, but on the outside, it all seemed okay. And mostly he was. But he was also fragile. So fucking fragile that cleaning out his apartment and making love to his boyfriend and sitting at a fucking desk did him in. And it was getting worse.

Was this what his life was going to be like? Was he going to have to stand there and let somebody else do everything for him from now on? As he stood there, six-foot-three, built for muscle but unable to lift a box?

Of course, if the doctor had his way, he wouldn't lift weights, either.

Fuck that.

But it was difficult to keep up his rage and determination as he lay there all day, staring at the television without seeing it, leaning on the ice pack he now had permanently propped at his neck. *Was* it the weights? He was always so careful. That was the *point* of weightlifting: you had to be exact. You had to think about your form, and you couldn't be sloppy. And Ed was. *Always.* And he'd done it because he thought that was the way to keep himself in shape.

"It's not that simple," Tim, his physical therapist, had told him. "It's not that you shouldn't do weights or shouldn't do anything. It's that it's easier for you to injure yourself now. We've gone over this. This isn't something you're going to shake. This is who you are now. This injury is yours. It's you."

"I don't want it." Ed yanked on the exercise band. Then he swore as pain ratcheted down his spine.

Tim put his hand on the band and met Ed's gaze. "You could be dead. The way those guys landed on you could have killed you."

"I *know*."

"No, you don't seem to get it. You are *lucky to be alive*. You are lucky you can walk at all. You're lucky that all you have is a neck that gets angry at you when you treat it badly. We could be sitting at a table trying to teach you how to grab a pencil again, not making sure you remember how to do rows exactly right."

"But what *for*?" Ed threw the band on the floor. "Why the hell am I doing this, if I can't lift weights, can't work my desk job, can't clean my fucking place. What the fuck am I supposed to do, once I learn how to pull your fucking rubber band?"

The little old ladies on the NuStep machines gasped and gave Ed scolding looks. He didn't care.

Tim regarded Ed with the patience of Job and a will of iron. "I'm sensing it's time to review your pain goals." He paused, then feigned surprise. "Oh. That's right. You haven't *made* any pain goals. Not ever. I've been waiting over a year for your pain goals, in fact."

Ed glared at Tim until he couldn't take it anymore. Then he stared at the wooden board full of pegs, one of which his green exercise band was tied to. "Give me my damn band so I can finish my set."

Ed didn't need pain goals. He'd ride this out like he'd ridden the other times the pain had flared up, trying not to think about how it happened faster every time, about how recovery took longer, dodging therapists and doctors and family and wondering if this was going to be the time they fired him from work. At least now Tracy had her doctor's note.

He'd never had a boyfriend during a pain cycle before, though. Hell, he'd never had a boyfriend like Laurie, period. He'd dated guys a couple of times, but they'd never felt like Laurie did. Before the pain at least. Right now it seemed like too much work to be with him. The doctor had said no sex, which was a relief. Ed was scared to do it now. Scared to try. What if it happened again? What if it *was* the sex? What if when he did anything beyond a quick hello-and-goodbye fuck every few weeks this was what would happen?

Ed had felt like shit before he'd gone to his PT appointment, but he felt like complete hell now. He let his mother drive him to his apartment to watch more TV until Laurie came by to hover.

What were the odds a boyfriend like Laurie, official for one week, would be the boyfriend of a cranky, moody headcase for very long?

Popping an Ativan, Ed hunched into the passenger seat, stared out the window, and waited for the drug to let him stop giving a shit about anything.

TWO WEEKS BEFORE Christmas, Laurie excused himself from his noon classes and headed to downtown Minneapolis, hoping he would find Oliver in his office. He did.

"Laurence, what a lovely surprise. You're catching me between meetings. What can I do for you?"

"I need to ask your advice on something."

"Certainly." Oliver sounded pleased. "I'm free at twelve thirty. Can you wait that long?"

It would mean he would have to bail on the two o'clock class he taught with a junior teacher. "Sure."

"Excellent. Have a seat out in reception and tell Bobby to get you anything you need." He winked at Laurie. "Feel free to ask him for a tour of the storeroom too."

Laurie ducked out of the office and went to reception, where, after calling to arrange for someone to cover his class, he allowed the flirtatious and modelesque Bobby the assistant to get him nothing more than a cup of coffee. He checked his phone a few times for messages from Ed, debated calling him to say hello, then decided it would be better to stop by tonight like always. But thinking of Ed made him worry, and by the time Oliver came out, he felt more than a little gloomy.

"What is it you wanted to talk about?" Oliver asked him as they rode the elevator. "You seem upset. Did something happen with your football boyfriend?"

Before Laurie could stop himself, Ed's entire story tumbled out. Laurie explained the injury, the flare-up, and Ed's increasing detachment.

"He's due to go to work next week, so I suppose that's a good thing. But he's gone so quiet. I can't tell if I should stay or go most of the time. I feel like an idiot." He stopped at the bumper of Oliver's sleek Mercedes and grimaced. "Sorry. I didn't meet you to talk about all this."

Oliver looked grave. "Is he talking to anyone? His mother? One of his doctors? A therapist?"

"I don't know. Not his mother, I know that." He considered a minute. "I doubt he says much to anyone. I think he's angry. Not at me, I don't think. He apologizes a lot that I have to deal with him. I never know what to say in reply."

"Have the two of you gone out at all, or is it only you stopping by?"

"Well…no. I mean, I bring dinner, usually, or I cook something. I clean up when I can, but he gets upset if I do too much. Usually we sit and watch television."

"Sex?"

"Ah. Well, the doctor told him he had to hold off at first." Laurie averted his eyes. "I never heard that he got permission. He said two weeks, but it's been longer. I don't know if that got extended or what."

Oliver sighed. "Get in. I'm hungry."

They drove in relative silence, Oliver doing nothing more than making random commentary about handsome men he spied on the street.

"We brought home this delightful young man the other day for a third. Very vigorous. Made me think of you and your football player."

"I don't think Ed is up for duo, let alone a trio," Laurie replied. But the comment made him wonder if Ed was into that sort of thing. He'd always found it distasteful before, and he wasn't sure about it now. Maybe he should reconsider?

God, he was losing his mind.

"No, likely not," Oliver agreed. "But what I meant is that it's amazing what sex can do for you. I was all upset that night about something at the office, and the next thing I knew, Christopher was showing me Grindr profiles. I thought he was joking, but he wasn't. It ended up being delightful. We had fantastic sex, the three of us, and the next morning I was late to a meeting because I was reminding Christopher how much I adore his body. And I didn't care at all about that idiot in charge of the account." He winked at Laurie's blush. "Sex can heal a lot of things, Laurie. That's all I'm saying."

The conversation ended there, thankfully, as by some miracle there was a free parking spot outside of the restaurant and Oliver gave the tricky parallel parking job his full attention. All he could talk about from the sidewalk to the door was how lucky he'd been to score the space, and by the time the hostess seated them, Laurie was relieved at what he thought was a change of subject.

"So how are things otherwise?" Oliver asked once the waitress had brought them their drinks. "I know you're driving your mother up a wall, so you must be doing something interesting."

"Well, it could be my refusal to perform for her gala, or it could be the fact that I'm dating. Take your pick. It could be either or both."

Oliver nudged Laurie's glass with his finger. "You should bring your boy by. Christopher and I will host a little party. We can hunt up dating sites together, if you're up for it." When Laurie's blush became so acute he had to touch his cheeks to be sure they weren't literally flaming, Oliver laughed and eased in his chair.

"Oliver, you're supposed to be a benevolent philanthropist, not a dirty old man," Laurie whispered, then drained his water.

"Why can't I be both?"

"Because you're my godfather. It's…unseemly."

"Bah." Oliver waved this away. "It'd be inappropriate if you found it uncomfortable, but you don't. You're mostly scared to see yourself as a sexual being. If I'd ever behaved as your uncle or father figure it would be wrong too, but at best I've been Santa Claus, occasionally descending into your life for presents, fun and a saucy wink. I tease you because the job I take most seriously as your godfather is getting you to accept yourself as a gay man."

Laurie blinked at him. *That* was why he teased Laurie so mercilessly about three-ways and sex?

Oliver rested his arm on the table. "I doubt you called me to lunch so I could lecture you about accepting your orientation. What's on your mind?"

Relieved to leave the subject of *accepting himself as a gay man,* Laurie dove into the explanation about the center, of what it was and what had happened to the funding and what he wanted to do to help. Oliver nodded sagely at him as he digested everything, but when Laurie explained how he wanted to have some of his classes move there, he shook his head.

"You can't save the center with ballet classes, Laurence. What they need are sponsors."

"But they're set against sponsors. They worry about outside influence."

"They're going to have to decide if they'd rather worry or think about the center that used to be. It's the sort of place that will never make money, and it's always going to need support. If they want to keep control, they need to have the center's profile raised as public service. Help people see this is a place that helps, not drains. These nice boys and girls and little old ladies and families it services need to be highlighted and propped up on posters and pushed in front of people with money. And there, Laurie, you can help. You can give it a profile. What grants are they using currently?"

"I don't know. The city, I think. I thought…"

"You thought you could come in and save it. And you can, but not the way you're thinking. *Do* teach. And plan for a benefit in…oh, let's say April. It's a bit fast, but it can be done. See if you can put together some sort of showcase. Local people performing. Kids would be wonderful. Having it at the center itself would be best, but I'll have to tour it to be sure. We'll want you to perform though. That will draw people, and you'll move them to donate. The show is a distraction, a focal point. The real goal is harvesting interested donors." When Laurie protested, Oliver smiled and spoke over him. "I'll guide you through it, Laurence. We'll discuss it, perhaps in a hot-tub meeting with your boyfriend along to relax your nerves."

The latter was meant to tease him, Laurie knew, but he wasn't in the mood for it now. "Oliver, I don't want to perform."

Oliver sighed. "I know. But you'll need to. That will be the draw. Right now you appear to be tucking your tail between your legs, working at a suburban center, not performing. Volunteering at a center, teaching the kids how to dance, performing with them, for them—that has panache."

"I don't have my tail between my legs."

Oliver raised an eyebrow at him but said nothing more on that point. "You're right about doing less in Eden Prairie. We've all been waiting for you to move on from that little studio. Do you need the income from teaching?"

Laurie shook his head. "I own the studio. I get a cut of all classes taught there. And this is to say nothing of my investments or savings. I haven't done much but let money pile up for years. I could make no income for a long time and still be quite comfortable."

"You should consider your mother's franchise idea, you know. And have Maggie be the director. As you said, they'd lease to use your name. You could make the center a branch of your operation, if you wanted to teach classes from there. Though you'd almost do better to have a designated space, something you can control. We could make it nonprofit, funneling money to the center on a permanent basis."

Laurie snorted a laugh. "Maggie would have a coronary, and they'd hospitalize her next to my mother."

"Excellent. They'll have each other for company." Oliver sipped at his drink. "I'll hook you up with a friend of mine who has a great deal of property in St. Paul. I'll convince him to give you a deal. Could you meet him tomorrow?"

Laurie blinked. "Tomorrow?"

"Yes. Tomorrow. No time to waste. I haven't seen you this lit up about something in years. I'd like to capitalize on it."

Laurie sighed. "Maggie will hate this."

"Of course she will. But she's had you longer than she should. And you aren't married to her. You're business partners and nothing more."

"My mother called me Maggie's wife." And Oliver had practically accused him of being sexless. Good God, did everyone in his life see him this way?

Laurie felt dizzy. He'd come to Oliver hoping to

hear how to inflate a bake sale, and now he was considering leaving the studio. What frightened him was, though it was all crazy, he was eager to do it.

"Very productive lunch," Oliver declared, "and we haven't even eaten yet. Let's skip dessert, though. After, we'll head over to LaSalle and visit Candyland. I'm in the mood for some caramel corn." Oliver winked. "You can take some home to your football player. Let him eat it off your chest."

"Ed." Laurie blushed, determined not to deflect Oliver's sexual teasing this time. "His name is Ed Maurer."

"Can't wait to meet him." Oliver signaled to the waitress they were ready to order.

CHAPTER THIRTEEN

jazz split: a split executed on the floor with the back leg bent up from the knee. The knee may be held and/or head arched toward it.

ED SAT ON the couch with an ice pack propped behind his neck, staring at his stupid pain-goal sheet.

If he could, he'd crumple it into a ball and toss it into the garbage like he'd done all the other sheets Tim had given him in the past twelve months. But after his last burst of temper in the therapy room, Dr. Linnet "happened" to stop by to see how he was doing. After a few minutes of watching Ed's frustration, Linnet pulled him off to the side and gave Ed an ultimatum: He either turned in his pain-goals sheet to Tim by the next session, or he was going to go on antidepressants. Ed could take his pick.

The declaration upset Ed. Linnet had talked about using antidepressants before, and it wasn't entirely about being depressed, he knew that. There was something about how chronic-pain patients could get side effects from the drugs, taking the edge off some of the lower-level aggravation to the nerves. At the time they'd ruled it out, and Ed had thought they were over that, but apparently not.

He knew, too, that this time Linnet wasn't only after the side effects. He was after the main effects too.

Ironically, the news that he was a hairsbreadth from going on antidepressants made Ed more depressed than he'd been yet. He wasn't that bad. And he wasn't in *chronic pain*, either. Occasional pain. More frequent than occasional lately, yeah, but if they'd leave him alone, he knew it would go away.

Except it wasn't going away. He'd done jack shit for two weeks. Linnet had cleared him for work but with great reluctance and had brought up going on disability.

Disability.

Ed took out fucking three-hundred-pound guys. He could still bench one-seventy-five. Sometimes one-ninety.

Disability.

And antidepressants.

Ed glowered at the paper in front of him, ready to fill the thing out simply to get this over with.

What are your physical activity goals for one month? For one year?

Ed tapped his pencil against the paper and glanced over at the clock. It was almost six. Laurie stopped by about now on Fridays. Something must have come up with one of his classes. Or traffic was bad. But he usually called to let Ed know when he was leaving. Or that he would be late.

Had Ed been a shit to him too, like Tim said he'd been to all the staff lately? Was Laurie sick of putting up with a banged-up, cranky boyfriend? Had he found something better to do?

Someone better to do, who wasn't making up reasons not to make love to him because he was afraid his neck would give out mid-stroke?

Ed gripped his pencil more tightly and returned to the form.

What are your physical activity goals for one month? For one year?

His eyes darted around the room as he tried to think of something to write down that would get Tim off his case. He spied a pile of laundry on the edge of the counter, neatly pressed and folded. Laurie had done that. Twice, in one week, he'd taken Ed's dirty clothes and brought them back clean. It both touched Ed and embarrassed him. His eyes passed beyond the laundry to the sink where the dishes had begun to overflow onto the counter. Laurie washed those too, when he came over. And he made dinner, or he ordered it. Ed's mom was going to the store for him lately, because Ed never did anything but sit around.

Did that mean he was depressed?

Ed pushed the paper aside and rose, moving stiffly

to the kitchen. He'd do the dishes, in case Laurie still came by.

But thinking it was only *in case*, that Laurie probably *should* find someone less of a loser to date, Ed backtracked and cued the stereo to Britney.

He hummed under his breath as he worked, but his heart wasn't in it. When he finished his chore, his neck hurt, and it was almost seven. Turning Britney up a little louder, Ed went to the couch and pulled the notebook into his lap.

What are your physical activity goals for one month? For one year?

What were his goals? To be normal. To play football. To not think about his neck all the damn time. That was what he'd told Tim, and Tim had given him "To not think about his neck all the time" as a fair start, but that was the answer to *Where do you want your pain management to be in one month? In one year?* not physical activity goals. He didn't know what to put there, and so he usually didn't look at the sheet at all, let alone try to fill it out.

What were his physical activity goals? *To be normal enough for Laurie.* But like hell he was writing that down.

Another half hour went by, form still blank, and Laurie didn't arrive. Ed shoved the paper away, got up, paced. When his head began to pound, he fished the gel pack for his neck brace out of the freezer and strapped it on before lying on the couch to stare up at the ceiling.

What are your physical activity goals for one month? For one year?

When the door opened, Ed bolted upright, then swore because that hurt his neck.

Laurie dropped his duffel and shopping bags and hurried over. "Are you okay?"

"Yes." This came out as a snap, which was a shitty start. He ripped off the neck brace and rubbed at his hairline, feeling like one big jagged edge. "You scared me is all. I forgot you had a key."

"Sorry. Your mom gave it to me, to make things easier. Do…you want me to give it back?"

Oh, fuck. "No." Ed found Laurie's hand. "Sorry. I'm just…"

Cranky.

Depressed.

Because of my chronic pain.

Laurie squeezed his hand and smiled. It was a shy smile, and it made him look alluring. He also, Ed noticed, seemed breathless. Happy.

"Hungry?" Laurie rose. "I brought things to make a steak salad, unless that doesn't sound good to you."

God, but Ed hated it when Laurie was careful around him. "It's fine."

Laurie frowned at the papers strewn about the coffee table. "What's that?"

Ed scooped up the pain-goal sheet. "Nothing. Just this thing I have to fill out for PT."

"I'll put dinner together while you finish it."

Laurie disappeared into the kitchen. But Ed knew there was no way he'd be able to focus on the sheet with Laurie in the room. He made a pretense for a few minutes, balancing the sheet on his knees as he tracked Laurie through the kitchen out of the corner of his eye. He could tell Laurie was forcing himself to appear relaxed, like he had every other day he'd been over the past few weeks. Sometimes he'd glance over at the couch, and Ed knew Laurie was waiting for a clue as to what they were supposed to do now.

That was the problem. Ed had no idea.

Eventually Ed shoved the paper away, rose and went to stand at the edge of the kitchen. "I'm sorry."

Laurie set down the bowl he was holding. "For what?"

"For this. For me. For—" He gave up and leaned his head against the cupboard.

Some of Laurie's guard went down, and he looked relieved. "I thought maybe I'd done something."

"Fucking hell, Laurie, it's not you. It's nothing to do with you at all."

"Then what's wrong?"

"What's *wrong*?" Ed gestured angrily at his neck. "This. *This* is what wrong. I don't want to be like this. I especially don't want to be like this with you."

Laurie frowned. "What do you mean, with me?"

Ed swore and pushed away from the counter. "I don't know why the hell you're here. I mean, what the hell is good about this, Laur? Even when my neck settles, it'll just happen again." He glared at the pain-goal sheet. *Chronic pain.* Rage swelled inside him, and he stormed over to the table, picked up the worksheet and wadded it up before hurling it across the room. "It's fucking worthless. There's no fucking point." He wiped a hand over his face and turned away. "And you deserve better than this."

Ed wanted to call the words back as soon as he said them. He meant them, but he didn't want to say them. He was so confused, so miserable. He watched, rigid, terrified, as Laurie crossed to the paper, picked it up and un-crumpled it.

"What does it mean, 'physical activity goal'? What you'd like to be doing in a month?"

"I'm supposed to write something I can't do now because of the pain but want to do. But it's worthless, because I don't know when it's going to hit or what it's going to do, so I don't know—" He stopped, because Laurie had sat on the couch, picked up the notebook and pen Ed had discarded, and now was writing something down. Ed peered closer to see, but his neck got mad at him, and then he swore. Which made Laurie glance up at the clock.

"Have you taken your meds?"

"What did you write?" Ed tried to take the notebook from him.

Laurie pulled it out of his reach. "*Did you take your meds?*"

"No, dammit. Now give me my notebook."

Laurie went to the counter and poured out the pills. "Do you want a Vicodin?"

"It's not that bad. And I didn't eat enough. I'll feel sick."

"What about your TENS unit?"

Ed's jaw tightened, and he wanted to tell Laurie to fucking leave it alone, but then he thought, *Depression.*

He forced himself to relax and sank into the couch in defeat. "I'll take a Vicodin."

"Juice or soda?"

"How about a beer?" Ed asked, his tone mocking despite his resolve to be good, but to his surprise, Laurie came back with one, and a plate of wicked-good-looking salad with a piece of whole grain bread on the side. When Ed glanced at him in surprise, Laurie just smiled.

"You're actually talking to me, telling me what's wrong for a change. I thought it was reason enough to celebrate."

Ed took the beer, but it was heavy, weighed down by the pain-goal sheet. "You know, I'm Catholic, so I should know about guilt, but Jesus God, nobody does it quite like you, Laur."

"Wait until you meet my mother." Laurie picked up the notebook. "So what does the 'social goal' mean?"

"What'd you put for the first one?" Ed demanded. When Laurie ignored him, he popped the pills and took a long sip of his beer. "I'm supposed to have a social goal. It's dumb, because I'm not one of those sad sacks who are so wrapped up in their pain that they don't get out. You can cross that one off. Even Tim said so. I swear."

But Laurie kept scribbling. "What is ADL?"

"Active daily life goal. Like, be able to do my laundry or something. Something the pain keeps me from. These aren't for me, Laurie. They're stupid. They're for fucked-up people who are so down about their pain they never leave the house, not for me."

Laurie ignored him and wrote anyway. It was starting to piss Ed off. He ate, but he watched Laurie like a hawk while he did so. How the fuck would Laurie know what his goals should be? But he didn't want to be cranky, since that got everybody's underwear in a wad. He sat there, ate, drank his beer and waited.

Eventually Laurie spoke. "Pain management. Is that as self-explanatory as it seems?"

"It's supposed to be what kind of pain I want to be feeling in a month and in a year. How I want it to affect me, how I want it to have diminished. But I can't predict it, so—Damn it, Laurie, quit writing. What the fuck is this?"

Laurie didn't look up. "I'm almost done."

"*Laurie.*" Ed slammed his beer bottle down. "What—?"

But then Laurie set his pen aside, and his notebook too. "I know why you don't want to fill it out. I understand. But it doesn't help."

"What do you understand?" Ed felt edgy and

shaky, like someone was about to pull the blanket off his head and show him the monster.

"I understand you don't want to fill this out because it means your injury is real. That it isn't going to get better. That you truly do have to live with it."

Ed opened his mouth to contradict him, but he couldn't speak.

Laurie leaned closer and caught his hand. "Ed, the way out isn't denial. The way out is figuring out a new set of goals. A new normal."

Why did Ed feel like he was suffocating? "I can't play football." His voice cracked on the whisper.

Laurie squeezed his hand. "I know. But there are other things you can do. Other things you can enjoy." He reached for the notebook and passed it over. "I wrote a few things down. Just ideas. Obviously you don't have to keep any of them, but I thought it was somewhere to start."

He let go of Ed's hand, sat back and waited.

Ed turned over the notebook and looked at what Laurie had written.

Physical goal, one month: Dance the basic steps of the Argentine tango with evenness and precision. (Alternate goal: Learn the entirety of a decent rumba.)

Physical goal, one year: Master at least four ballroom basic dances. (Alternate: Learn the advanced steps of the Argentine tango.)

Social goal, one month: Attend game or practice or event

where football is happening. (Not necessary to feel okay with it. Just need to be there.)

Social goal, one year: Attend game of former team and cheer them on, knowing you are participating still and that they still value you as a team member.

Active daily life goal, one month: Regularly take breaks at work as Tim has said you should and do the stretches for your neck like you're supposed to.

Active daily life goal, one year: Find job better suited to both your injury and your talent.

Pain goal, one month: Be good about exercise and therapy so that in one month the pain is in remission.

Pain goal, one year: Learn to listen to your injury so that when flare-ups happen you know how to take care of them. Learn what exercise helps and hurts, and be honest about it. Learn to find the way to do the activities you want to do but in a way that respects your injury.

Ed hadn't realized he was still staring at the paper until Laurie put his hand on his leg.

"Ed?"

Ed couldn't speak. He felt overwhelmed—moved, sad, angry, terrified, grateful. He felt like he was dying and being reborn all at once. Nothing about football at all on there. Nothing. Just the hanging out with the team, which was hell.

But there was so much dancing.

All of it with Laurie.

For weeks he'd pushed Laurie away, trying to make this easier on himself. On Laurie too. He sat there now, staring at his pain-goal sheet, filled out at last, filled out by Laurie—Laurie, who hadn't left him, no matter what kind of asshat he'd been.

He picked up the pen and held it, hand shaking, over the paper. On the line beneath the pain goals Laurie had written, he added a goal of his own.

Goal, four hours: Make love to Laurie.

He loved the way Laurie laughed—quiet, soft, but open. He also liked the way Laurie's hand slid over his thigh.

"Are you cleared?" Laurie asked, his hand brushing Ed's groin.

Ed hated how nervous he was. "He said I should play it by ear."

"And?"

Ed hesitated. "It's coming that's the trouble. You tighten up like all fuck before you orgasm, and you get full of adrenaline and think you're Superman. And then later you pay the piper. I'm probably okay." He grimaced. "But I don't want to find out I'm not."

Laurie took his hand, lacing his fingers through it. He kissed Ed's cheek.

Ed closed his eyes.

"We could take it slow. Easy," Laurie whispered. "We're good at that."

"I don't want easy." Ed's voice was rough. Laurie's breath on his ear was doing interesting things to his dick.

Laurie nipped gently at Ed's ear. "I want you."

Ed turned carefully and kissed him. Then kissed him a little deeper.

Laurie's stomach growled loudly.

Ed laughed, and Laurie blushed. "Sorry. I guess it's been too long since lunch."

"Eat, then." Ed sat back so Laurie could get up. But he watched Laurie's ass as he strode to the kitchen, and he thought of all the things he wanted to do to it.

Maybe I can. Maybe it's okay.

Ed shifted against a sudden discomfort in his pants. "What were you doing, anyway? I thought you'd be by earlier."

He worried that sounded pathetic, but if it did, Laurie ignored it. In fact, he grinned at Ed as he served salad onto his own plate in a generous heap. "In point of fact, I was negotiating for dancing space in St. Paul." When Ed's eyebrows went up, Laurie laughed, a soft, pretty sound that did strange things to Ed's insides.

"I didn't know you were looking for dancing space in St. Paul."

"Neither did I." Laurie settled beside Ed on the couch and paused to eat a bite of salad before speaking. "Oliver started the idea in my head and hooked me up with one of his contacts. It's a nice space. Honestly? I think I might do it. It will need all kinds of work, but…yes.”

Ed didn't know what to say. Laurie was opening a studio in St. Paul? Would he still work in Eden Prairie?

Did this have anything to do with Ed?

Who was Oliver?

He watched Laurie eat in silence. But thoughts kept rolling around in his head, and eventually one of them fell out of his mouth. "So you're going to be busy, huh, with two studios?" The lump in Ed's chest got a little bigger. "Probably not a lot of time for teaching a big goofy football player ballroom dancing."

Laurie put down his fork, caught Ed's chin and held it. Ed was surprised by the intensity in Laurie's face. "I will always have time to dance with you."

The confession should have eased Ed, but there was too much doubt inside him, and it spilled out. "Me and all my pain bullshit will get in your way."

"You're not in my way, Ed. You will never be in my way." He stroked Ed's skin. "Please, don't shut me out anymore. Unless that's your way of telling me you'd rather do this alone."

Ed turned his head carefully and kissed Laurie's palm. "No."

Laurie's hand lingered, and Ed kissed his palm, his wrist. He made his way up Laurie's forearm, but then he saw the plate of salad about to fall off his lap and remembered himself. He sat up, picked up the plate and gathered another bite before holding it up to Laurie's mouth. Laurie tried to protest, but Ed shoved the food inside.

"Eat, so I can take you to bed." The declaration made him nervous, though, so he gathered another bite and fed it to Laurie. "So what are you gonna teach in St. Paul? Same stuff?"

"Yes, but hopefully to a different mix of clientele." He took the next bite Ed gave him and chewed quickly so he could keep talking, then gave up and spoke around the food. "I want to have kids from the center come too. For no charge."

Ed raised his eyebrows. "Oh?"

Laurie nodded. "This was Oliver's idea, to make it nonprofit. It changes what funds we can use and our tax system, and if it works out, I can align myself with the center. But that's still up in the air."

Ed fed Laurie another bite and watched his lips slide over the tines. "Didn't know you wanted to do that sort of thing."

"Neither did I." Laurie's eyes were dancing. *So beautiful.* Ed tried to feed him another bite, wanting to move on to dessert.

Laurie pushed it away and shook his head.

"You're hungry," Ed reminded him.

Laurie swallowed and leaned forward. "Not for salad."

They moved to the bed, nuzzling all the way, but Ed's mind raced ahead. His neck was better, but it was still really fucking tender. He undressed carefully, leaving his boxers on.

When Laurie gave him a questioning glance, Ed stroked Laurie's arm. "How about tonight we make this all about you?"

Laurie stripped down all the way. When his cock sprang free, it was already bobbing at half-mast. Ed wished he could grab him, turn him over and lick him into submission before he fucked him into next week.

Don't focus on what the pain is taking from you. Focus on what you have.

He did his best to hold Tim's advice in his mind as he lay back on the bed and watched Laurie climb over to him.

Laurie was here. Ed had quite a lot.

"Straddle me." Ed motioned to the tented area of his boxers. "Let's have more of your frottage."

Laurie hesitated and glanced at Ed's neck.

Ed ran his hand down the pelt of his chest and grinned. "Come all over me, babe. I want to watch."

Laurie gave Ed a wicked smile as well. "That all?"

Ed lifted his eyebrows. "You have something else in mind?"

Laurie climbed over Ed, and that's when Ed realized, God bless him, that Laurie had a tube of lube. He picked up Ed's free hand and placed it on his thigh.

Ed's blood hummed. He stroked Laurie's thigh as he turned silently around, presenting his ass to Ed's face.

Oh, it was fucking hot to watch naked Laurie straddle him, to have that prim little ass backing up toward him, and wasn't it heaven itself to pull Laurie's hips closer until he could run his tongue over that butt, fondling his balls and stroking his taint and pushing his tongue into that hole. God, but the noises Laurie made were heaven.

Ed lay like a fucking sultan and pushed lube-slick fingers into that ass as it quivered over Ed's chest, to listen to Laurie gasp and moan. As Ed watched Laurie's ass open to take first one, then two, then three of his fingers, his own cock swelled, brushing Laurie's chest.

When it became too much for Ed to thrust, he slapped Laurie's ass and repositioned him so Laurie could do all the work himself, which was actually so fucking hot Ed almost came. He might have tried, except pain took care of his erection pretty quickly. So he watched, turned on as all hell as Laurie gripped the metal frame of the headboard with one hand while he leaned into Ed's body and fucked himself. Eyes shut, head back, body slick with sweat, erect cock bobbing until he shot all over Ed's chest, his neck, his mouth and his hair.

Laurie melted into a puddle beside Ed. But when Ed started to rise, Laurie shook his head. "Stay here." He stumbled to the bathroom, coming back with a warm washcloth, which he used to clean Ed's face, chest, hair, and, finally, fingers. Just when he thought he was done, he found more semen in a tuft of hair by Ed's ear.

Laurie grimaced and tried to get it out with a washcloth. "Sorry. I made a mess."

"I like your mess." Ed caught Laurie's hands, intending to say something playful, but somehow when he looked up into his lover's eyes, everything overwhelmed him.

Laurie kissed him sweetly. "What's wrong?"

"Why do you stay with me?"

Laurie touched Ed's face. "Because I don't want to dance by myself."

Ed shut his eyes and turned his head away, but Laurie kissed the tears, and when that only made them come faster, he curled up beside Ed and hugged him close, pressing his naked body to Ed's side, stroking the hair of Ed's chest and whispering against his shoulder, so softly Ed couldn't hear.

Before long the tightness in his chest eased, and soon he was sleeping, wrapped safe in Laurie's arms.

CHAPTER FOURTEEN

*enchufla: dance movement common in salsa
dancing where two partners facing each other
change positions, keeping constant contact with
one or both hands while rotating one hundred
and eighty degrees around the same point in
opposite directions.*

LAURIE STAYED THAT night after the pain-goals sheet with Ed, and he spent most of the weekend with him too. Ed came with him to tour the new studio space, and they'd gone over to see Vicky afterward. Unsurprisingly, they'd run into Duon, who volunteered to help clean things up at the studio in exchange for lessons.

The new space wasn't anything fantastic. For dressing rooms Laurie would have to use two undersized offices, and for his own office he had to set up a cubicle off to the side. The carpenter's price for a new floor made him want to drink heavily. After dipping so much into his savings already to buy the building, he was starting to feel less confident about this investment. This was before he'd priced the mirrors. But he felt good every time he went there, even though the neighborhood was depressed and he still hadn't quite gotten over the urge to run to his car with his keys ready in his hand to gouge out the eyes of any approaching attacker.

He'd arranged a meeting for Vicky and Oliver. Vicky was even more bristly about outside funding than he'd thought she'd be, but Oliver was Oliver, and it wasn't long before he had her charmed. He introduced her to a few short-term grant possibilities she hadn't known about, but he also convinced her to let him throw a benefit for her in the spring. They'd see how the benefit went, and if the board liked it, Oliver would be happy to help them look for more stable local funding.

For his own studio's future, Laurie had his advertisements ready for printing, announcing he was opening a new center, but he hadn't posted them because he hadn't talked to Maggie yet. The only preparation he'd done was to turn over his Monday and Friday classes to other teachers so he could focus more on getting the St. Paul center ready. Maggie had given him several confused glances, but he'd done his best to avoid her.

His mother, however, was far more difficult to dodge.

"You seem tired," Caroline remarked as Laurie slid

into his seat across from her. They were at a quiet restaurant downtown that she favored. "What has you working so hard?"

Laurie forced a benign smile. "Nothing. I'm only tired. And a little busy."

"I heard a rumor you're giving up some of your classes." She gave Laurie a sly look. "New project?"

Laurie put down his glass. "You heard about that?"

This seemed to amuse his mother. "One of the adjunct instructors' mothers is on my benefit committee. She's excited about the opportunity, and her mother wanted to thank me." Her eyes danced. "Maggie doesn't know yet, does she?"

No, she didn't. But did his mother know, or was she guessing? She couldn't possibly know the truth. She hadn't tried to strangle him.

His mother let the subject shift, talking of mundane things and detailing the planning of a party she was throwing. But then during dessert she asked, "Have you given any thought as to what you'll be performing?"

Laurie looked up sharply. "Performing?"

"For the benefit." She smiled encouragingly.

Laurie clutched at his napkin. "I hadn't agreed formally with Oliver that I'd perform." His grip went slack. "Though I suppose he's right. I have to."

His mother frowned. "Oliver?"

Now it was Laurie who was confused, until realization dawned. "Oh—you meant *your* benefit."

"There's more than one benefit? Laurie, how wonderful." She took his hand across the table, and for a horrible moment Laurie thought she would cry.

It was clear she didn't understand what he'd done, and Laurie couldn't take it anymore. He told her the truth. About the studio, about the center. About everything.

It wasn't pleasant to watch her smile fade and then to see her entire face crumble as she moved from euphoria to confusion to shock and finally to quiet, cold anger. When Laurie finished telling her his plans, for several seconds she simply stared at him.

"Please tell me you're joking."

"I'm not joking. I want to do this. You asked me what it was I wanted. This is it. This is what I want."

"No it isn't what you want. This is some sort of nonsense, some delusion." Her nostrils flared. "Did this *boyfriend* put you up to it?"

Laurie's expression became as cold as his mother's. "Because my decision to see someone publicly is as ridiculous as my desire to start a nonprofit studio? Is that what you're trying to say?"

Caroline threw her napkin on her plate and rose, fumbling through her purse for cash, but it was difficult with her fingers trembling in rage. "This is nonsense, all of it. I don't know why you persist in it. Except of course to torture me."

"If I'm so much torture to you, I won't trouble you any more with luncheon dates."

His mother glanced at him, briefly wounded. Then she threw her money on the table, turned on her heel and left.

It was a Friday, and Laurie had planned to spend the afternoon at the St. Paul studio painting so it would be ready when the carpenters started the next week, but he was full of residual anger from lunch, and it was difficult to focus as he cracked open a can of paint and poured it into a tray. He thrust the roller angrily back and forth over the surface of the walls, replaying the conversation with his mother in his head.

Delusion. She was the one with delusions, full of idiot ideas of who Laurie should be, of how he should behave, of who he should be attracted to. Never mind that he was more excited about this project than anything else he'd done. Never mind that everyone else kept telling him how happy he looked. Never mind that Annette had kissed him and told him he was *such a good boy* when he'd told her his plan over her tuna casserole. Never mind that his mother would have fixated on the fact that he'd eaten tuna casserole.

Never mind that Ed's father had promised to help him sort out the dodgy water heater and the hole in the ceiling at his studio and had started calling him *son.* Never mind Laurie's own father hadn't promised him anything, hadn't even said a word to Laurie in the past four months that hadn't been "pass the salt" or "where has your mother gone off to?"

Never mind that neither of them had so much as

asked when they were going to meet Ed, apparently waiting for him to fade away.

Jaw set against his building fury, Laurie turned around to dip his roller in the tray, only to find it was dry. He'd used up the last of that gallon, so he sorted through the others on the floor, looking for the second gallon of that color. When he couldn't find it, he went out to the trunk of his car, thinking he must not have brought it in, but it wasn't there either. He sifted through the remaining cans, sure he must not be seeing it, because he *knew* he'd bought two of Perfect Peach.

Then he remembered, as he saw the two gallons of Right White, that he'd changed his mind. Perfect Peach was the trim, and Right White was supposed to be for the main walls. Which meant he'd spent an hour and a half painting half the room the wrong color.

With a rage that came out of nowhere, sweeping over him like a Minnesota wind, he threw the can and then the roller at the wall. He tossed the paint tray too, and the newspaper underneath it, and then the paint can opener and the stir stick and the unused brush, and then he ran around the room, kicking them all, swearing and shouting until he wore himself out and collapsed in a heap in the middle of the disaster.

After a few moments, a quiet voice said, "Bad day?"

Ed at the front door. Laurie hadn't even heard it open, but Ed leaned against it, hands in the pockets of his dress pants, shirtsleeves rolled up, tie pulled loose and top button undone to give his neck some breathing room.

Laurie fixated briefly on the neckwear. "You weren't wearing a tie when I left this morning," he observed, trying to keep his voice level and calm, as if he hadn't been pitching a tantrum.

"Had a meeting with mucky-mucks this afternoon. Didn't put it on until lunch but haven't taken it off yet." He pushed off the door and came forward slowly, carefully, hands still tucked away. He looked tired, but his eyes were a brighter than usual, making him seem more like himself than he had lately. Ed nodded at the mess. "Need some help cleaning up?"

Laurie surveyed the carnage he'd wrought. "I suppose I've done all the damage I can for one day." He glanced at Ed's nice clothes. "I don't want to get you full of paint."

"I could help you naked."

Laurie smiled. "That'd be fine, but with no shades yet on the windows, I think we'd get arrested."

Ed winked as he undid his tie. "Well, they're not my best clothes or my favorites. If they get ruined, they get ruined." He tossed the tie over a folding chair and reached for a wad of newspaper in front of him on the floor. "So, I got a story for you. Do you remember when I told you about the guy in marketing who we all think is an ass? Well, we found out what he's been up to."

As they cleaned up Laurie's mess, Ed kept talking,

telling a story right out of the *National Enquirer* about secret mistresses and Brazilian vacations and highly unethical use of the corporate credit card. By the time the story was winding down, the paint was cleaned up, and Laurie was feeling much less like a jagged piece of glass.

"He's fired, of course. Which I wish meant better job security for the rest of us, but it's the wrong department. More layoffs are coming, a few before Christmas, a few after." He grimaced, then shook his head and smiled at Laurie gently. "Feeling better?"

Laurie nodded, letting out a breath. "My mother wound me up a bit is all."

Ed glanced across the room. "Do you have a music player here still?"

"In the back. Why?"

Ed disappeared into the storeroom, returning with the player. After plugging it into the wall, he cued up a song. As he approached Laurie, the opening notes to Streisand's "My Melancholy Baby" began to echo through the room. Ed held up his arms in an open dancing embrace and smiled a crooked, slightly shy smile.

"Dance with me?"

Laurie's heart melted more than a little, but the roughed-up parts of him had to push back anyway. "Am I your melancholy baby?"

Ed shrugged. "There wasn't one on there about a pissed-off and stressed-out baby, so I did the best I could."

"You don't like Barbra," Laurie pointed out.

"You do." Ed motioned to him with his hand. "Come on, babe. You need to dance."

Laurie did, he acknowledged, and stepped forward tentatively into Ed's arms. "What are we dancing?"

"Well, I've been trying to figure that out. I was gonna say the waltz, but it's the wrong beat, isn't it." He wrinkled his nose. "Rumba?"

"Night club two-step," Laurie suggested.

It only took half a minute to teach Ed the dance, since technically he already knew it from half a dozen other dances, but of course Laurie had to give him the correct carriage and fuss over turns. It was an easy dance, and soon they were turning graceful circles around the room.

"You're not trying to make it easy on poor injured me, are you, with a dance this simple?"

Laurie let Ed spin him out for a turn before he returned to the embrace. "I'm in the mood for simple, and it suits this song. Besides, done correctly, it's a romantic dance. Very soft and open."

Ed's fingers kneaded gently at Laurie's side. "Are you feeling soft and open, Laurie?"

Yes, Laurie thought, but said nothing. He felt as if he were floating across the floor. Ed held him in a perfect frame, strong and sure and smooth, making Laurie feel totally safe, and eventually he gave in and shut his eyes, surrendering to the feeling.

Ed shifted his grip slightly to get a firmer hold. "Do they have any competitions for men to dance? With each other?"

"No. I mean, they do, but those…well, it's not the same as an opposite-sex competition. It felt like the Special Olympics, to be honest." He opened his eyes and stared at Ed's chest. "It hardly matters. Ballroom dancing isn't the same as the sort of dancing I did professionally anyway. Performance ballroom is a bit more polished, but really, it will never be true art." He realized Ed was looking at him oddly, and he blushed. "What?"

"You're such a snob, Laur." Ed smiled, and when Laurie started to sputter, he silenced him with a kiss. "I'd dance with you anywhere. For anything." He drew him in a little closer than was correct for form and nuzzled the side of Laurie's head with his cheek. "You look so beautiful when we dance."

"I like the part of the follower." Laurie shut his eyes and let the dance and the music and the strength of Ed's arms overtake him. "With the right partner, it's like I'm anchored, and I can do anything."

Ed's lips brushed Laurie's ear, sending electricity through his body, but his words burrowed into Laurie's soul. "I want to be your right partner."

Laurie gave in and broke the form, resting his head on Ed's shoulder as the dance became more of a high school dance sway, a pair of lovers using music as an excuse to embrace. Laurie opened his eyes and stared at the thick cords of Ed's neck, then reached up to run his fingers gently over the invisible injury. "How is it tonight?'

"Hurts, but nothing serious." His hands skimmed over Laurie's back. "Linnet said I should try hydrotherapy."

There was an odd note of wariness to Ed's voice that Laurie didn't understand. "You mean like PT but in water? Is it bad?"

"No. Supposed to be really good, actually." Ed's hands kept skimming. "Except I'm going to have to leave work half an hour early every day to get there, whenever I go. Their hours are only during the day. Once I get established I can go anywhere, but for now I'd have to get to the clinic to see the therapist." Ed sighed and rested his lips on the top of Laurie's head before he spoke. "Part of me wants to quit work and get it over with. Except I don't know what the fuck I'm going to do without a job." He sighed. "Sorry. This is not the mood I was going for."

Laurie wanted to reassure him that he would help him, no matter what happened, wanted to explain to him how very much money he'd made when he'd toured professionally, how he had money of his own from his grandparents. He wanted to promise Ed that it would all be okay, that he'd make sure it was. But he said nothing, only lifted his head and kissed Ed gently on the lips. Ed tipped his head down and opened his mouth to kiss him back, and Laurie welcomed him inside, tasting the familiar soft spice of him as Barbra sang on.

Ed kissed Laurie's ear. "I want to make love to you. I want to be inside you, Laurie."

Laurie went still. The song had ended, and "Just in Time" began to play, but he could barely hear it for the blood pounding inside him. His hand slid up Ed's shoulder to his neck and stroked it gently. "You're ready, are you?"

"Did a test run in the shower the other day. Okay then and no pain after. Probably we should stay off the trapeze, but I think we're good for the basics." This time Ed's lips ran along the length of Laurie's ear. "Are *you* ready?"

Barbra's voice climbed to the top of a phrase, sending a shiver down Laurie's spine. Or perhaps it was Ed's breath against his skin. Or the thought of Ed being inside of him.

"Yes."

Ed squeezed Laurie's waist. "Let's go home."

TWENTY MINUTES LATER Ed was pressing Laurie into the mattress.

Laurie had grown accustomed to Ed's penchant for licking and sucking and biting, but tonight as Ed stripped him bare and tongued his way down Laurie's chest, every touch felt especially charged. His belly danced and quivered as Ed kissed his way across it, and he gasped when Ed sucked the inside of this thigh. He drew Laurie into his mouth, taking him to the root, and for a moment Laurie thought he would come there on the spot. But then Ed moved to the bedstand and opened a drawer. When he came back to the bed, he arranged Laurie's feet flat on the mattress before lying beside him. He held Laurie's gaze with his own, his eyes darkening as Laurie quivered when a cool, lube-slick finger pressed against him.

Ed brushed a kiss across Laurie's lips as his finger nudged carefully inside. "I'm going to put my cock inside you, Laurie." His finger twisted gently. "That still okay?"

Laurie nodded, blushing. He wasn't a virgin, but damned if he didn't feel like one. So vulnerable, so exposed, like Ed's probing finger could reach all the way to his soul.

Ed liked this too, Laurie could tell. All his self-doubt, all his worry fled as he regarded Laurie with heavy-lidded, loving possession. *Mine,* his eyes said, and as Ed pushed a second finger inside, Laurie's body surrendered in answer.

Yes. Yours.

"You're so hot and tight." He bent and kissed Laurie's nipple, and when Laurie arched up toward him, he nipped at it too, making him cry out. "You make me ache, baby. I want to be so dirty with you. I want to make you blush and gasp and do things you wouldn't do, except with me. I love watching you come undone. I want to come undone inside you, Laurie. I wish I could come all over your insides so you'd carry me with you, so you'd feel me as I slid out of you."

Only Ed could make the thought of semen oozing out of his ass turn Laurie on, and it did. It made him want to be ridiculous and say, "Oh, don't use a condom," though part of his brain was still not sure this was a brilliant idea *with* a raincoat. But another part of him, a lower, baser part of him, wanted that brand. Five years ago he'd stood at a dinner party with a bit too much wine in him, snidely carrying on about anal sex being a feminization of gay men, and now here he was, fantasizing about coating his insides with Ed's fluids, of feeling Ed shudder as he thrust his cock inside of Laurie's body. The motion of Ed's fingers, already erotic, became an acute sensation, promising what was to come, and Laurie moaned.

But Ed was in no rush. He pushed Laurie's legs back with his free hand, urging Laurie to hold them before he settled between them, crouching on the floor beside the bed as his fingers continued to work. Laurie looked down at him, across his own chest, at his spread legs, and heat pooled inside him.

Ed grinned from between Laurie's thighs. "Spreads you open when you hold your legs back like that." He pushed his fingers inside Laurie, stretching the tight ring of muscle, and then he withdrew, his slicked fingers tracing the skin around Laurie's hole. "You're open now. Just a little." His thumb pressed into Laurie, making him contract. "Clench, baby. Clench hard, baby. Let me watch you open and close."

Laurie's face flamed, but he did it, his breath coming in shallow gasps as he worked the muscle of his rectum so that Ed could watch. Why was he doing this? But he only had to look at Ed's face to have his answer. Because it turned Ed on. Because Ed had asked. Because Ed was leading, and he was a strong, sure partner.

Because this was what Oliver had meant, about accepting himself sexually. This was celebration. This was liberation.

Ed kissed the inside of Laurie's thigh. "Do I make you feel dirty, baby?"

Laurie had to swallow twice before he could reply. "Yes."

Ed's smile was slow and wicked. "Do you like it when I make you feel dirty?"

"Yes."

Ed's tongue stole out and ran down a vein in Laurie's thigh. Their eyes were still locked. "Tell me what you want, Laurie. Tell me the dirty things you want."

Laurie held the gaze. "Put your fingers in me." His eyes rolled back briefly as Ed breached him with two, then, carefully, three fingers. But they didn't move, only held there, stretching him.

"Anything else?" Ed asked lazily, but his voice was husky too.

Laurie gripped his shins tighter and fought for breath. "Ed. Please."

Ed kissed Laurie's thigh, still looking him dead in the eye. "Please what? Kiss you?"

"Fuck me," Laurie whispered. "Fuck me, Ed." He cried out when the fingers began to move, deeper and deeper inside him, but it only took a minute of this to drive him crazy. Enough. Enough teasing. Enough chasing, enough everything. He let his feet fall to the mattress.

"Fuck me with your cock." He watched, thrilled and terrified, as Ed's eyes went dark and he pulled his fingers away.

Ed shed his clothes, his erection bobbing into view. Laurie's penis quivered, hard and aching and red with the blood of arousal, jerking with the flexing of his groin muscles as Ed sheathed himself in latex and smeared the condom with lube. His lover's cock suddenly seemed so big, so fat, so full, but Laurie thought about that fat fullness spreading him, filling him, moving inside his heat, and his elbows wouldn't support him anymore.

Inside me. Ed, Ed's cock inside me.

Ed arranged Laurie's feet on his own shoulders, joining them in an entirely new way. Laurie had always taken it up the ass on all fours or with his face buried in a pillow, enduring. But yes, Ed would want to watch. Ed would want him to watch too.

And so he did. He lifted his head and looked down as Ed lined himself up, guiding the head to Laurie's hole. Laurie watched Ed's face, his focus zeroed on breaching Laurie, and then Laurie gasped and bore down as Ed's cockhead thrust against his muscle.

It was dancing, and Laurie followed once more. It was his body, his muscles straining and stretching, his tightness, his bowels turned host to Ed's cock, but it was Ed who led, Ed who squeezed his calves and held him in place as he gasped and arched against the mattress, Ed who kept on pushing in until Laurie's body swallowed him. It was Ed who led with shallow thrusts until Laurie moaned and tried to draw him deeper. It was Ed who buried himself to the hilt, filling him, Ed who grazed his prostate, Ed whose full balls nestled behind the flesh of Laurie's backside, Ed who stroked Laurie's cock gently as he clenched around the welcome invader.

Ed began to move. Slow, smooth, steady, his thrusts long and deep, but he moved his hips in a way that drove Laurie out of his mind, rubbing against his balls, his perineum, his insides. When he looked up at Ed with passion-glazed eyes, Ed grinned.

"Cuban motion," he said, and continued his thrusts.

Laurie had never made so much noise during sex. He watched Ed thrust, and he moaned, shut his eyes and focused on the feeling inside himself, on the ache of his own erection, and he made a high sound, like a whine, like dirty porn on the Internet, his call broken by the increasing thrusts of Ed's fucking. He undulated with Ed's movements, dancing the oldest dance of all.

When Ed withdrew, Laurie felt bereft, but when Ed turned him over onto his stomach, drawing him to his knees, he went quickly, compliant. Laurie accepted him easily, pushing back to take him deeper. As Ed wrapped his arm around Laurie's waist and leaned forward to growl at Laurie's neck, Laurie gave over. He mewed, he keened, he purred, he shouted, urging him harder, faster, *harder* with words and with sound and with his soul. And he might as well have been a virgin, because this was sex, sex he had never had, had never even dreamed of.

In Ed's arms, Laurie let go, and he flew. He sailed across the Mississippi River, across the hills and plains, over oceans and mountains and up to the stars and comets, and then came back. He thrust into the sleeve of Ed's hand and cried out as he came, convulsing and milking Ed's cock inside him until Ed too was shouting and bucking, and then, except for breathing hot and heavy at Laurie's neck, he fell silent.

After several minutes, Ed said, his voice raspy and spent, "You okay, Laur?"

Laurie, his bones melted, his muscles slack, his heart pounding like a happy caged beast against the wall of his chest, his backside throbbing and still half-full of Ed, let out his breath. With great effort, he nodded.

Ed kissed his ear, then moved higher so he could give another to Laurie's cheek. "Be right back."

Laurie lay palms pressed to the quilt in the sticky mess of his own semen as the hot fire of his backside, swollen and still open, leaked lube. This was the part he resented. The mess. The slight squickiness of sex, the sometimes serious squickiness. The awkward part where everyone cleaned up, where he'd stand and find himself involuntarily expelling the air that had gone in with his partner's cock which then, inevitably, had to come out. His first time with anal sex had seen him padding across the plush carpet of another dancer's bedroom floor, face flaming as he farted his way to the toilet. This was the messy part of sex, and it was, he admitted, the reason he'd worked to avoid it.

Except he didn't care about it so much as he lay there now. He felt the pressure inside him, but he barely glanced to see where Ed was before he let the air out with a gentle *pop*. His face flamed, but he was so sated he couldn't do much else.

He felt Ed's hand on his lower back, felt the soft, warm touch of a washcloth on his skin, and he slid under Ed all over again.

Ed cleaned him carefully, thoroughly. He bathed Laurie's cheeks, his hole, the sides of his thighs where lube had spread. He turned Laurie over and wiped up the semen that had sprayed over his stomach, then dabbed at the congealing pool of white on the quilt itself. His gaze met Laurie's, and he smiled.

I love you.

Ed bent and brushed a kiss on his lips. "Still okay?"

I love you. Laurie nodded.

Ed lifted an eyebrow. "Can you still speak?"

Laurie opened his mouth, faltered on a breath, then gave up. "I love you."

His face full of emotion, Ed nuzzled Laurie's ear. "Love you too."

That night Laurie slept naked in Ed's arms, and he dreamed they danced across the clouds, dressed in glittering suits that glinted as they spun across the heavens. As they passed by, all the angels clapped and cried out in joy.

CHAPTER FIFTEEN

*drop and recover: a modern dance step where a
dancer drops to the floor in a controlled fall
from a dance position.*

D URING ED'S CHECKUP three days before Christmas, Dr. Linnet turned Ed's head to one side, then the other. He ran his hand over the length of Ed's damaged muscle, paying special attention to the area around the spine. "Swelling's way down. That's good. How's the pain? Scale of one to ten?"

"Nothing more than a four for the past few days." Ed kept his eyes fixed on the Ansel Adams portrait across from the exam table, losing himself in the black-and-white mountains. "Just a little sore."

"And you've done your exercises?" When Ed nodded, the doctor kept his fingers on the muscle, testing it as Ed moved his head. "How's day-to-day pain? Have you been able to resume all normal activity?"

Having lots of sex, yeah. "Far as I can tell."

The doctor smiled and pulled his hand away. "Very

good. Are you still considering the hydrotherapy?"

Tim had been telling tales. "It doesn't fit with my schedule well."

"Then you should consider changing your schedule. And you need to get away from that desk job. Keep moving. Get up as much as you can. If you need a note, I'll get you a note. I'm telling you, it's the desk job doing you in, not the Saturday cleaning or the dancing. You're really not that far from disability-level injury, Ed. You say the word, and I'll get the papers started."

Ed chose to ignore that. "So am I off the hook now for appointments with you, or what?"

Linnet grinned. "For now. Go with your body. If you listen, it'll let you know." He patted Ed on the shoulder as he moved back so he could rise. "Wean yourself off the pain meds. Take the Vicodin only when you need to, but the rest is up to you. Nothing wrong with feeling it a little, though, as you get moving. That'll help you know when to ease up. And you still have the TENS unit. That will help you get off the meds as well."

Ed saluted. "Okay."

"Take it easy at work so I don't have to see you until your next physical."

Hydrotherapy turned out to be not so bad. Ed had his first session on Christmas Eve, and when he came out of the locker room and saw the incredible collection of old ladies gabbing at the rope, he'd been leery, but he wasn't ten minutes in the water with the therapist before he realized while those women were gossiping, they were also working out as hard as he did in the weight room. He couldn't believe how much it wore him out to push and pull a foam paddle back and forth under the water, or how his calves would hurt once he got done bicycling in the deep water with a float belt on.

"Water has three times the resistance of air," the therapist told him when he expressed his surprise. "And it displaces gravity, so there's no strain. You'll be wanting some pasta and red meat for supper, as much as you worked today."

"And this is helping my neck? I mean, I don't feel it at all there or anything."

"You're dealing with more subtle tissue here. No, the pool isn't going to give you guns and flat abs. But it will strengthen your core and the smaller, connective muscles. Just because they're small and don't turn heads when they're pumped doesn't mean they aren't important. For you, Ed, these are your lifelines, especially now. Treat them accordingly."

"Are you telling me I can't even do weights anymore? But I teach a class."

"So teach, but lay off them personally awhile. You can do them, but I want you to work with Tim on what and how and when."

"Tim said I could dance." When she looked at him in confusion, he went on. "Ballroom dancing. My boyfriend is an instructor. I mean, he's teaching me, and…" He crossed his arms over his chest. "I'm not giving it up."

"You can dance. Just tell your boyfriend no head snaps. And I'd like you to not lift him over your head or anything until middle of January or so. Let's give you a chance to heal up well this time, huh?" Sandy smiled at him. "So do you guys compete?"

Ed blinked. "What? God no." But then he paused. He remembered that Laurie said there *were* same-sex competitions. "I mean, we haven't."

"You should consider it." She motioned to the water. "Let's do another set."

WHEN ED FINALLY got to Laurie's studio that night, he was feeling good but kind of jumbled. He kept thinking of what Sandy had told him about the little muscles, and he was thinking about dancing, and he was oddly hung up on the idea of dancing in a competition with Laurie. If he trained, if he worked hard, he knew they would win. And that would kick *ass*.

The thought of bending Laurie in a dip while people cheered and judges held up "10" signs like in the movies filled Ed's head, and that was why he was grinning when he rounded the corner to the front door of the building and ran into Laurie's teaching partner, Maggie.

Who absolutely did not grin back.

She walked right up to him, her heels clicking on the concrete and her coat swinging.

"*You.*" Her face was twisted up in fury, and she aimed a gloved finger at him. "It's all *your* fault."

Ed took a few steps toward the curb as he held up his hands. "Hey, Maggie, I don't know what's going on, but—"

Her nostrils flared as she cut him off, her breath making bursts of cloud in the cold air. "First he dumped the classes on me because you were sick, or hurt, or whatever. Which was fine. I didn't like it, but that I understood. But now, this *nonsense* about quitting our studio to work in this hellhole, this is *your* doing." She stormed up to Ed and shoved at his chest, nearly pushing him into traffic. "He's throwing away his career. His *work*. He has talent, real talent, and he's wasting it on those stupid *hoodlums*."

Ed cast a sidelong glance at the door as he aimed himself toward it. "Right. I'm going to go wait in the studio for Laurie."

"Maggie? Ed?"

Laurie's voice cut across the cold air from farther down the sidewalk, his long coat drifting around him as he hurried forward. A shopping bag hung from his hand and a cardboard coffee cup from a local gas station in the other, though it had a tea bag hanging off the side.

Maggie aimed her finger at him. "You didn't tell me you opened another studio. You let me find out from your *mother*."

Ed waited for Laurie to shout back, but if anything,

he shrank. "I know. I'm sorry."

When Maggie glowered, looking ready to do battle, Ed stepped toward him, but Laurie shook his head. "It's okay, Ed. I need to talk to her. I should have talked to her before." He held up the shopping bag in his hand. "Would you take this inside for me?"

Ed took the bag with a nod before fishing in his pocket for his key to the studio and letting himself inside. He set the bag on the counter, but he didn't turn on the lights. Instead he positioned himself in the corner near the window, where the dark-shrouded figures on the street couldn't see him but where he could see them.

He tucked his cold fingers into the pockets of his jacket, leaned against the wall and watched.

LAURIE'S FINGERS WERE threatening to fall off inside his gloves because of the cold, but the air temperature was nothing to the frigidity he saw on his teaching partner's face.

"I'm sorry you had to find out secondhand. You deserve better than that."

"I don't understand. Is it something I did? Something I said? I thought…" Her eyes were glassy for a second, and she blinked rapidly before wiping them with the finger of her glove. "I thought you liked the way I managed things. You never said otherwise."

"This isn't about your management. This isn't about you at all. It's about me. I want a change. I want to do something different. So I am."

"What about the spring recital? What about the specialized classes? You can't leave us in the lurch."

"I'm not. I'm not giving up all my classes, and I'm not bailing out on the recital."

"But why do you want to leave at all?" She pointed at the door Ed had gone through. "It's *him*. Isn't it. It's that big oaf you dance with. This is all his doing, I know it."

"I'm leaving because it's time. Where I'm going and what I'm doing don't figure into this discussion. I won't leave you in the lurch, despite what your dramatics are suggesting, but neither will I stand here and listen to you insult Ed and make ridiculous accusations about this being his fault."

"But it *is* his fault. You've been different since the first time you came home from the center. Even when you hated him, you were different." Her rage bubbled over, and now the tears flowed freely. "I thought we were partners, Laurie. I thought we were *partners*."

For a moment Laurie didn't know what to say. He was still angry, but—well, he was stunned. He realized, finally, exactly what she meant by *partner*. No, she didn't want to date him. That wasn't it. But she wanted to own him. Until this second, she'd thought she had. She'd assumed they had a kind of sexless marriage.

God, his mother was right. He was her trophy wife after all.

She rallied. "This is only a phase. When the sex

wears out, you'll come back."

"It's not a phase." Laurie held out a hand. "Come see the studio. Let me explain."

She recoiled. "No. No, I'm not going in there." She started walking toward the parking lot. "You'll be back. I know you will. You'll be back."

"Maggie," Laurie called, but she shook her head and turned away as she hurried down the sidewalk.

Laurie let out a sigh, lowered his hand and headed inside.

Ed hadn't turned on the light, so Laurie did as he entered, and he took a moment to enjoy the scene in front of him. The floor gleamed red-gold in its new polish. The walls were painted, the mirrors in place, as well as the barre. A counter had been installed to the side as part of the reception area, and two benches flanked the space by a coat rack Ed's father had hung.

The lights were secondhand, and they blinked a little. The walls were patched in places. It was small, and the ceiling was lower than Laurie liked. It was in no way the Eden Prairie studio. But it was right for this place. He already had three local dancers lined up as teachers, and he had a small list of local students. Less of the more well-to-do students had signed up than he'd have liked. But that was okay.

Ed stepped out of the corner and came forward cautiously. "You all right?"

Laurie grimaced. "I didn't tell her about this studio. I kept meaning to, but I knew it would go badly, so I put it off." He sighed. "I should have told her."

"Well, she knows now." Ed ran his hand down Laurie's arm. "Ready to go home?"

Home. To Ed's apartment. He hadn't officially moved in, but he might as well have. And he would stay there tonight and wake up with Ed for Christmas. His smile widened. "Just let me get my bag."

Ed peered at it curiously, like a little boy. "What's in there?"

"Your present."

When Ed took the bag from him and peeked inside, Laurie let him. Ed gave him an odd look. "Glitter and eyelash glue?"

Laurie winked. "Take me home, and I'll explain. Or more accurately, I'll show you."

Since the studio was only a few blocks from Ed's apartment, and since Ed was right, it really wasn't an awful neighborhood, especially once you knew people, Laurie had taken to walking. But he was glad for the ride now, tired and cold as he was.

"You sure it's okay to go to my parents' house tomorrow?" Ed fumbled with the key in the ignition. "Because we could head over your folks' way too, if you want."

"No, it's fine the way we've arranged it," Laurie replied, trying to be breezy.

The loft had gotten a little messy again, which was what usually happened when Laurie didn't stay over for a while. He noticed the dishes were undone, three days of newspapers were spread across the table, and a pile of dirty clothes sat next to the empty hamper. But a glance at the weight equipment revealed the bright red therapy band tied to one of the posts, and a few of the small hand weights were out. Laurie smiled.

"You relax in the bedroom for a few minutes," he told Ed. "I have to get a few things, take a shower and get ready, and then I'll give you your present."

Ed's eyebrows rose. He said nothing, but he looked intrigued as he headed back with the newest paper toward the bed. Laurie waited until he was well out of sight, then prepared the stereo, grabbed his things from the broom closet where he'd hidden them and hurried into the bathroom.

He made Ed stay in the bedroom until he'd arranged the furniture, lit the candles and cued the music. He double-checked his makeup in the bathroom, and his hair, and he took a deep breath to center himself. Then he called out for Ed to come and sit on the couch, and when the music began, he came out into the room.

For Christmas, Laurie gave Ed a dance.

He danced to a soft, sweeping arrangement from a movie soundtrack, one he was almost certain Ed would never have heard of before so that the only thing Ed would associate the sound with was his dance. It was a bit of ballet, a bit of modern, a bit of Laurie. He put in all the beauty and skill and perfection he had been taught and which he had honed, but he put in something more too, edges and colors and accents that were, he knew, gifts from Ed. Courage, wonder, enthusiasm, hope. This was not only a dance for Ed. This dance, to Laurie, *was* Ed.

He lost himself in the movement, in the music. He forgot about Maggie, forgot about the fight with his mother, forgot about everything but this time, this space. Too soon, though, it was over. When it ended, Laurie held his final form, heart beating faster as he waited to see how his gift was received.

He'd burned the song to a single CD so that it would be silent once he finished, so that nothing would break the moment if he managed to create one. Now he wished he hadn't done that. The magic that had come during the song left him, and now he simply stood there, nervous, worried he'd looked ridiculous. He used to always know when he was done with a performance if he had nailed it or not. But this—this he didn't know. In his heart, in his soul, it was the best he had ever done. But he couldn't be sure.

Was it because the dance was for Ed? Or because that was what he'd become now? Would this always happen if he danced from his soul?

He heard the murmur of the crowd in Toronto, saw their angry faces—

"Laurie."

Ed appeared fragile, like someone had opened him up too. Laurie smiled tentatively and tried to ease them into emotions a little more manageable. "I wore tights," he pointed out.

"*Just* tights." Ed's voice was thick, his eyes shiny. He took a few hesitant steps forward. "Laurie…my God."

"It was for you." Laurie's voice felt so soft in his throat. "I think, from now on, it will always be for you."

Ed looked at Laurie like he was some angel descended. And with love. With so much love.

Laurie held out his arms. "Come here."

They made love on the floor, Ed kissing and touching Laurie as if he were the most precious, beautiful thing in the world, until Laurie whispered, "Make love to me, Ed." After that the tights began to tear.

This dance ended with Ed flat on his back on the bed, with Laurie sliding over him, taking their cocks together in his hand, guiding them, leading them until Ed pushed up on his elbows and tipped them over the edge into pleasure. All worries of the studio, of Maggie, of his mother, of the dance, of the future were gone. Laurie went with Ed gladly, knowing his partner would never let him fall.

CHAPTER SIXTEEN

chassé: gallop where one foot chases the other; a traveling step.

ED WAS LATE for his therapy appointment and tried to brush off his supervisor at Best Buy when she called him into her office. It wasn't until Tracy asked him to sit and Ed got a good look at her face that he realized what was about to happen.

"No." Ed rose out of his chair as if there had been a spring in the seat. "*No.* You cannot fire me. Not now."

"You're not fired. You're being laid off. Come on, man. You've known this was coming."

No. Not now. *Not now.* "I told you, I have health issues. That's why I have to take the breaks. I got you the doctor's note like you asked."

"They reduced positions. It wasn't my decision."

Ed shoved his hand in his hair. His neck strained at the motion, making him feel sicker. "I can stay later. I can work for less. But I have to keep this job."

"I'm sorry." She looked glassy, utterly wrung out, and it dawned on Ed she'd been doing this all afternoon.

Ed had no empathy for her. He was too busy staving off raw panic. "I have to keep my insurance. I can't keep up all this PT if I have to pay for it out of pocket, especially without a job. Come on. There's got to be someone else."

"It's based on seniority. I'm sorry, Ed. There's nothing I can do." She handed Ed a manila envelope. "The severance package is outlined inside. Your insurance will continue for three months, and after that you can apply for COBRA."

Except he'd never be able to afford COBRA with no job. Ed clutched the envelope impotently in his hands. He wanted to keep arguing, wanted to fight this, but the wall of Tracy's expression told him that not only would that get him nowhere, it might end up bringing security. For a few minutes he stood there anyway, thinking there had to be some way out, some clause, some something, but of course there wasn't. By the time he gave up and turned to leave, he felt as glassy as Tracy.

Security waited for him at his desk with three empty copy paper boxes. A few people waved awkward goodbyes at him as he left, but mostly the building was empty, and Ed was able to make the journey to his car in dizzy silence, the security officers behind him. Once he was in his car, he wanted to sit there a moment and get his bearings, but the guards lingered, so he put the car in gear and drove out of the parking ramp.

The street, though, overwhelmed him, and he had to pull into an empty parking lot and put his head against the steering wheel for several minutes before he felt composed enough to drive some more. Even then he weaved around side streets for a good ten minutes before he finally remembered he needed to head to his appointment.

He tried to play along with Tim's small talk, to not let on that anything was wrong, but Tim, no dummy, picked up on his odd mood and asked him point-blank what was wrong.

And that was when it hit him. He'd been laid off. He could schedule his Monday appointment for any time because he had nowhere else to go. He'd have to tell his mother, and she would worry him into a nub. He'd have to look for work, but there weren't any comparable jobs to be had. He only had enough money in savings to get through the end of January at best, and that didn't count all the oddball stuff caring for his stupid *condition* brought into the mix.

He'd have to tell Laurie. He'd become not only the inferior boyfriend with a trick neck but the unemployed boyfriend as well.

A hand rested on his shoulder. Tim, looking worried. "Are you okay?"

No. Not even close. Ed forced a smile and shrugged. "Just tired. Long day."

Tim regarded him suspiciously a minute, then nodded. "Okay. You ready to do some therapy, or should we give you a pass today?"

Ed thought of how soon he wouldn't be able to afford this at all and forced his smile a little more. "Naw. Let's do it."

Tim smiled. "Good man. Maybe it will perk you up."

"Maybe." Ed kept his smile in place until Tim left the room to go and get the equipment he would need for their session.

THE TRANSITION FROM working at Eden Prairie to working at the St. Paul studio did not go as smoothly as Laurie had planned, which bothered him largely because he hadn't anticipated it going very smoothly to start with.

His first mistake had been how he got rid of his Eden Prairie classes. He assumed removing himself from all but the most advanced classes wouldn't cause much of a ripple, but parents kept storming in, angry. They kept him late at the studio arguing over whether or not matters were fair even as they tried to cram their children into his remaining classes. When he told them he was starting more classes at the St. Paul studio, however, they weren't interested.

"I don't understand it," he confessed to Vicky as he helped her sort through Oliver's latest batch of grant applications. "If they feel that strongly about having their students continue with me, they can bring them here."

"You're screwing with their worldview. With the social contract they believed they had with you. And I warned you about people coming to St. Paul. They won't like coming to what they see as a slum."

Laurie pursed his lips and shook his head. "Well, good riddance to them. I'm eager to work with people here instead."

But that had been the second surprise.

It wasn't that no one signed up for the classes Laurie offered. It was that so few of them did, and not for the courses he expected. Duon and his crew were still loyal, but Laurie had expected *all* the center kids to be that way, and they weren't.

Had he made a mistake? Was this going to be a disaster of titanic proportions?

"Calm down," Oliver told him when he stopped by to see his progress and Laurie had unloaded his panic onto him. "This is not a disaster. This is a startup business. Rome was not built in a day."

"But it's not *enough*." Laurie tapped the paper in his hand in irritation. "I could have twice these numbers for ballet. I *should* have twice these numbers. I don't know what I was thinking. This will never help Vicky. Never. I'll be lucky if it doesn't beggar *me*."

"Don't worry about Vicky. I have a possible donor lined up."

"Oh? Who?"

Oliver waved a dismissive hand. "Not saying anything until things are final. Though I do need to ask you to do something. I need you to come to dinner with Christopher and me. And bring Ed too. I'd like to meet him. Last weekend in February." He paused, then added, "At your mother's house." Laurie stiffened automatically, and Oliver sighed and put a hand on his arm. "Make peace with her, please. If only for my sake?"

Laurie hesitated but nodded.

Oliver released his arm with a satisfied pat. "Excellent. I'll give you further details as the date gets closer. In the meantime, try not to worry."

Duon stopped by that afternoon as well, as he had become wont to do. He had signed up for every one of Laurie's classes and did odd jobs as his method of paying for them. He was doing well, too, in every kind of dance. He liked to con Laurie into showing him "extra fancy stuff" when the studio was slow, and Laurie often did exactly that.

He was showing Duon how to do a cross-over high kick and slide when Ed came through the door, looking more weary than usual. Laurie went over and gave him a kiss.

"Doing okay?" He cast a worried glance at his lover's neck.

Ed pasted on a smile when he saw Duon. "*There's* trouble."

"Whatever, bitch." Duon bumped his hip playfully

against Ed's as he slipped past him to get his coat. "You two lovebirds have fun. I gotta get home. Shit to do."

Laurie did his best to sound stern. "I'm serious. I won't teach you next week if you don't show me the note from your counselor saying you're passing at least three classes."

"Yeah, yeah, yeah," Duon grumbled as he left the studio.

As the door closed, Ed kissed Laurie soundly on the mouth. "You're very good for him. You're good for all of them."

"I just wish I had more students."

Ed slid his hands over Laurie's shoulders and kneaded gently. "Come on, babe. Leave this for now. I came here to practice with you. People will come when they come. You said yourself the money doesn't mat-ter." Laurie started to object, and Ed stopped him with a kiss. "Dance." He nipped Laurie's lower lip. "With me. Now."

Something was wrong with Ed, but instinct told Laurie not to press right now. He waited patiently as Ed cued the music, then led Laurie into the center of the open space and took him into his arms as a tango began.

"You shouldn't leave any stereo equipment in here," Ed scolded as he led them into the opening steps and then into a baldosa. "Hide it in the back room in that spot I showed you at the end of the day."

"I lock the cabinet."

"Yes. That shows them right where to break in."

Laurie stepped out of Ed's cazas and began a molinete. As he spun through the windmill pattern around Ed, he thought of what a huge pain it was going to be to haul the equipment around all the time. He also couldn't help noting he'd never had to do such a thing in Eden Prairie. Shutting his eyes, he followed Ed into an ocho, but the worries that had plagued him in his office caught up with him, bringing their dark cloud into this space that was normally such a relief.

But then he felt Ed's leg slide against his, stepping between Laurie's own in time to turn Laurie's startled backstep into a perfect gancho. It should have knocked him over, except Ed's frame was sturdy and strong, so well-set that when he bent Laurie back, he didn't falter even then, simply arched his spine with such form it was a shame there wasn't a judge there to see them and give them a perfect score.

So perfect that when Ed righted him, for a moment Laurie leaned into him as his dizziness went away. But he felt the tension lurking inside his partner and re-membered he wasn't the only one in the room with problems. "Sorry. I'm self-involved today."

"I like you self-involved." Ed brushed a kiss on his temple. "Everything is going to be fine."

Ed had a natural affinity for the Argentine tango, and as soon as he'd discovered how much Laurie enjoyed it too, he'd demanded to be shown all the steps. He'd gone through a phase where he was a little too fond of displacing Laurie's step with a sacada or halting him with a parade, ruining the flow. This had led to Laurie having to explain while the tango might be about improvisation, it was at heart a conversation. "You don't simply feel the rhythm. You must feel the soul, both of the dance and of your partner. The tango isn't something you dance. It's a story you create with another."

It was a lecture Ed had taken to heart, and the result was beneficial not only to Ed's performance but for their mutual enjoyment. Ed had learned weeks ago that the best way to undo Laurie's foulest mood was to turn on the stereo and pull Laurie into a tango embrace.

It worked as well now as it always did. Within a minute of the dance's beginning, Laurie was lost in the steps, doing his best to anticipate Ed's lead, taking opportunities for more advanced steps and, now that Ed had a firm footing, indulging in amagues and golpecitos, and when he was lulled into a very good mood, he would rub his thigh or foot along Ed's in a caricias. When Laurie turned an ocho into a boleo and lingered with an extra rub of his knee against Ed's thigh, Ed grinned and bent to steal a quick kiss.

"That's better." He led them into another round with a salida.

It was indeed better when they danced, and that night they danced for almost an hour. But once they finished and headed to the car, all Laurie's agitation came back. Ed gave him a long look, and Laurie braced for another scolding on how he was taking things too seriously. But Ed turned on the stereo and backed the car out of its parking space.

"Britney Spears?" Laurie asked as he recognized the song. "Again?"

"He who makes me listen to Barbra Streisand shall not complain about Britney."

"You will not link that abomination in the same sentence as Streisand." Laurie frowned. "Why did you skip our turn?"

"Because we're not going home yet." Ed turned on the wipers to displace the snow that had started to fall. "Liam called while you were locking up. We're going to meet the guys."

He said this so casually only someone who knew how many answering machine messages Ed ignored from his former team captain would understand what a watershed this was. Laurie waited for Ed to expand on the announcement, but he only tapped his thumb along to the beat of "Radar". So Laurie nudged him carefully for more details. "Where are we headed? Back to Matt's?"

"Gopher Hole. It's not far from here. I figured we might as well swing by. Otherwise I'll have to watch you mope around the apartment."

That felt like a cheap shot, and Laurie wanted to call him on it at least to point out that usually Ed ended his moodiness by instigating increasingly epic sex, but he kept quiet. Ed was going out with the guys. This was victory enough.

The Gopher Hole was much like Matt's except it had more room and served less food. Liam and the other Lumberjacks had commandeered the back half of the bar between the bathrooms and an antiquated jukebox, the latter which several of the football players were huddled around as they argued over what they would play next. A few others were grouped around the pool table to the left of the jukebox, and the rest were littered around the tables, drinking and talking and checking out the women as they went by to use the ladies' room.

When Liam saw Ed and Laurie come in, he rose and came over to greet them.

"Hey there. Long time no see." He shook Laurie's hand in a beefy grip, then grinned as he turned to Ed, whom he high-fived before gripping around the shoulders in a manly half-hug. "Maurer, you dog. What the hell, man? You never come out anymore."

"I'm here now." Ed nodded at the tables. "Where should we sit?"

"Wherever you like. We're over in the corner." He pointed to the area by the jukebox. "I'm heading to the bar for another pitcher. Can I get you anything in particular?"

"Just a couple of glasses." Ed produced a twenty from his wallet. "And here's our part of the next round."

Ed looked nervous, Laurie thought, but then he was too. He wasn't sure how to behave around these men. A few players flirted with some women who had come over near the pool table, but no one other than Ed had brought a date. Laurie felt, as he had the last time, out of place within the group. He'd intended to stay sober so he could drive, leaving Ed free to drink and relax with his friends, but when Ed passed him a tall, pale glass of cheap beer from the tap, Laurie took it, rationalizing that one wouldn't hurt him and might help him relax.

He sipped frequently at it as he settled in between Ed and a broad-chested man Ed had introduced as "Casey, the best damn halfback in Minnesota," smiling and nodding along with the two men without quite paying attention. Mostly he let his eyes wander around the bar, taking in the noise, the lights. He hadn't spent much time in bars since the smoking ban had gone into place, and it was nice. When he commented on that, Ed laughed and pointed out the law had been in effect for almost five years. Feeling self-conscious and slightly unnerved at how much of a hermit he'd become, Laurie retreated once more into his glass.

That was when he realized he'd sipped at it for an hour and it hadn't gone down but an inch.

"Been takin' care of ya," Casey said with a wink when Laurie commented on this. He held up a pitcher, then poured the remainder of it into Laurie's glass.

"You're Ed's man, and Ed's man is always one of ours."

This both warmed Laurie and got his hackles up at once. "His man is always one of yours, is he?" He looked accusingly at Ed, who suddenly became very interested in his own glass. "How *many* men?"

"There have been *two*. You and one other."

"One?" Somehow that seemed worse. Laurie knew he'd had too much beer and was being ridiculous, but he now wondered what old flame was going to appear and wreck everything.

"That was that guy from your work, right? The suit?" Casey laughed and slapped the table. "God, what a fish."

"Arnie was a mistake." Ed smiled. "It was Liam's barbeque I took him to. Remember? And he got drunk and fell in the pool?"

"And then called us all a bunch of meathead idiots when we laughed at him." Casey shook his head as he tipped back his glass.

Ed squeezed Laurie's arm before rising. "I need to take a leak."

Casey toasted Laurie's glass as he started to lift it for another drink. "To you, buddy, for bringing Ed back. And for being so good for him."

Laurie met the toast hesitantly and took his refuge in his beer. He was still uncertain about all these athletes taking in a homosexual couple with such grace.

"So you're the dancer, huh?" Casey grinned. "You

gonna show us your moves?"

That made Laurie laugh. "What, here?"

"Fuck yeah, here." He nodded to the player now dancing with one of the ladies by the jukebox. "We got tunes. We got space. What else you need?" He nudged Laurie's glass. "More to drink?"

Laurie had drank enough his head was spinning slightly, and it made him cheeky enough that he deflected with teasing. "Tell you what. I'll dance if you dance with me."

"All right then." Casey pushed up from the table.

"Wait." Laurie grabbed his arm and tugged him frantically into his chair. "I was kidding."

"I'm not. Come on. Let's go dance."

Laurie eyed him suspiciously. "Is this some sort of setup?" He glanced around the room. "You can't be *that* accepting that you'd get up in a bar and dance with a man."

"Do it every time I get on the field." When Laurie didn't relent, Casey braced his elbows on the table. "Look. I won't lie to you. Some of the guys aren't cool. But you know, it's not like just because we play football we're idiots. And Ed's one of us. He made it clear long ago he is who he is, and that's that. And it's cool." He shrugged. "My older brother is gay. I watched him marry a woman and be miserable, but when he got out of that and started dating men, he turned into a whole new person. He was happy for the first time in his life. Who's gonna argue with that? He went to Iowa and got married. He lives in Des Moines now. So yeah, I'm cool dancing with a gay dancing instructor." He lifted his eyebrows. "You cool with dancing with an overweight semipro halfback? Or you all prissy and proud like Ed's other guy?"

Laurie smiled. "I'm not."

Casey rose and held out his arm. "So we're dancing, right?"

Laurie rose as well, giving himself a second to let the room stop spinning before he followed Casey onto the floor.

BLONDIE WAS PLAYING when Ed came back from the bathroom. Someone had turned the jukebox up too, which normally would have had everyone complaining, but nobody was this time. In fact, everyone was gathered around it, intermittently applauding and shouting, "*Woot.*" and "Get down, Casey."

Grinning, Ed swiped his beer from the table and hurried over to see what was going on. But when he saw, he stopped, arrested. Casey was dancing with Laurie.

Like, dancing *with* him. There wasn't much you could do to "Hanging on the Telephone", but Casey probably couldn't have done much to anything, so they were doing some sort of jitterbug thing that Ed, budding ballroom snob, noted didn't even really have a form. And Casey was a shitty lead. He could see Laurie trying to execute more advanced moves, but then

Casey would yank him into a poorly supported dip, and Laurie would shriek and laugh and clutch his arms to keep from hitting the floor. Then they'd get up and do it all over again.

Part of Ed was jealous, but not much. He did, though, check out the other players around the edges of the room. Most of the guys were laughing, and only a few seemed uncomfortable. The women actually looked more upset than anyone else, like they'd lost their leverage over their best chances for free drinks and maybe something lucky later.

Laurie caught sight of Ed and stumbled. Casey turned him away in a spin, but Laurie's gaze kept following to Ed. They were bright from fun and fuzzy from drink, but Ed read the question there too. *Is this okay?*

He grinned and raised his glass. "Show 'em how it's done, babe."

Relief washed over Laurie before he yelped at Casey's crude jerking of him into a turn, and Ed felt warm, loving that Laurie had worried what he'd think.

When the song finished, everyone applauded, including Ed. Liam turned to him and said, "What about you, Maurer? Gonna show us what you've got?"

The crowd parted for him as he came forward, and Casey winked at him before relinquishing a flushed and breathless Laurie. The setup Ed had suspected was now pretty much confirmed, but he didn't mind. To be honest, he was grateful. He'd come out of the bathroom thinking he couldn't put off telling Laurie the news any longer, only to find Laurie dancing. Hell yes, he'd rather dance right now.

Laurie, though, still looked uncertain. "I didn't know so many people would watch."

"Even more are gonna once we start." When Ed saw the flicker of unease in Laurie's face, he brushed a subtle kiss across his hair. "Hey, it's cool. It's just us. With extra people."

"I know. I'm sorry. I don't mean to be ridiculous." Laurie listed into him. "It doesn't help that somehow I managed to get drunk."

Ed squeezed Laurie's shoulder. "It's okay, babe. I got you. So, what do you say? Want to show these bozos how two guys really dance together?"

Laurie nodded. "Not a tango, though. I'm not sober enough."

"How about a nice, easy rumba?" Ed could feel Laurie's nervousness and gave his back a gentle caress as he took him into the embrace. "I got you, babe. I promise."

Laurie nodded and stared at the center of Ed's chest. Then the opening notes of "Man Overboard" drifted above their heads, and they danced.

It felt so fucking good. Not only to be dancing with Laurie, but to be dancing with him in front of other people. And yeah, it helped that it was the guys, the guys before whom Ed had been so spectacularly unmanned by his injury. There was an extra edge to looking, he knew, very suave and sexy while he danced with a *guy*. It made him bold, and he pushed their form a little, sending Laurie out into spins and turns until Laurie tightened his hands on Ed as he finally pulled him back into the embrace.

"I'm going to throw up on you," Laurie warned, "if you don't dial it down."

"Sorry," Ed said, except he wasn't. They'd laughed and wooted for Casey, but they were *applauding* for Ed and Laurie. He stroked Laurie's back. "Got carried away."

Laurie smiled. "It would be okay if I weren't drunk."

The fact that Laurie wouldn't have done this at all sober hung between them, unspoken.

Laurie sighed. "Okay, I'll admit, I'm having fun. And I wouldn't mind shaking it up, so long as it isn't literal." His fingers tickled lightly along Ed's neck. "I have a few ideas. We could borrow some things from tango and other dances, and some…" He bit his lip. "Or not."

"No, let's do it. Just tell me what to do."

As Blondie sang on, Laurie whispered moves, and Ed executed them, dipping into every reservoir of dancing knowledge Laurie had given him and learning a few there on the spot. His favorite was when Laurie had Ed spin him around and they did some sort of backward rumba. When Ed nuzzled Laurie's neck, the crowd went wild. Laurie, though, nearly lost his step.

"Sorry," Ed murmured.

"No, it's good." Laurie recovered himself and fell back into the rumba. "Just don't *actually* nuzzle me. Accents like that are good staging, and they help draw the audience in, but they need to be near, not spot on, because if they surprise me, they distract me." He reached up and ran his hand up and over Ed's hair, then over his ear before resting his palm on Ed's neck. The crowd went wild, but Ed's skin was prickling, because Laurie had barely touched him. Laurie smiled. "You want to invite them into the embrace, and you do that by leaving space."

"Got it." Ed raised his eyebrows. "Okay. You ready to wow them?"

"Yes."

The crowd loved them. The song helped. The music was bouncy, and Debbie Harry was as sexy as ever. Ed spun Laurie out and drew him back in time to move him through another form. When the song was over, everyone cheered, and Ed gripped Laurie's hand and grinned like an idiot as they took a bow.

God, it was almost as much fun as a game.

"How's your neck?" Laurie whispered as they came together for a hug after.

The reminder that he had to think of that was like a knife cut, but Ed acknowledged that he probably should have been worrying about that himself. He did a quick tip in either direction and nodded gruffly. "It's fine."

Laurie brushed a kiss on his cheek in reply, standing back as Liam approached them. "Holy shit, man, you're gonna have to give me lessons. If I dance like that with my wife, I could come home late from the bar for a week."

Ed put a proud arm around his partner. "Laurie teaches classes at the center."

"I might have to take him up on those."

They tried to go back to their table, but the crowd wouldn't let them. Someone put a new song on the jukebox, and the next thing Ed knew, both he and Laurie were giving impromptu dancing lessons on the spot. For some reason they kept playing Blondie, working their way through the entire *Platinum Collection*. Laurie taught them some sort of line dance to "Heart of Glass" and somehow he managed to lead four couples in some half-rumba, two-step to "One Way or Another".

He seemed so happy. They had him laughing, had him spinning in ten directions at once. Ed had never seen Laurie like this. He'd never seen *anybody* like this. It was beautiful, but it hurt too, because he realized that outside of Laurie, he didn't even come close to these kinds of moments.

Eventually Laurie came back into Ed's arms, with "Maria" playing on the jukebox at full blast. Laurie was flushed now with excitement, not alcohol, and Ed made him giggle by trying to tango to a song with the wrong beat.

Laurie laughed and fell into his arms. "You make me so happy." Laurie smiled up at him, full of life and love and wonder.

Ed looked at him and said, "I lost my job today."

Laurie stopped short and tried to draw back, but Ed held him as close as he could. He hadn't meant to say that, and he felt so exposed now, but maybe this was better. He didn't think he'd have the strength to confess without so many people around, so much energy and chaos to hide his failure. So he gripped Laurie's arms, knowing his fear that this would make Laurie leave him was misplaced, but he still couldn't stop it. He held his breath and waited.

Laurie leaned into Ed's cheek as they continued to sway. "It's okay."

"It's not okay."

"No, it's not." Laurie stroked him, the opposite of the staging—this was a caress few could see and only Ed could feel. All around them people danced on, carried away on the fun Ed and Laurie had brought them, not noticing Ed and Laurie themselves were now quiet and serious. "Go insane and out of your mind," Debbie Harry sang, and Ed frankly wished he could, because it would be a welcome escape.

Laurie pulled Ed's head down so he could kiss him right between the eyes. "It *will* be okay."

The music rose around them, peppered with laughter and unbounded joy. Ed pulled Laurie to his chest, hugged him so tight he could feel the breath catching in his lungs, then buried his face in the side of Laurie's head and tried like hell not to cry.

CHAPTER SEVENTEEN

*contract: basic movement where dancer contracts
the midsection of the body and pulls back
against a movement for emphasis.*

I F LAURIE HAD thought negotiating Ed fighting his injury was difficult, he quickly learned it was nothing compared to managing out-of-work Ed.

For a week or so he did sit around the house, and Laurie had unpleasant flashbacks to December. Then one day he stopped by Ed's apartment and found him cleaning. Shortly after that he frequently had to call Ed to find where he was because he was never at home. If he wasn't visiting his mother, he was at the center. He kept all his therapy appointments too, and he hadn't stopped any of his exercises.

The want ads were always open on his kitchen counter, but few things were circled, and nothing ever worked out.

Even with all this activity, however, Ed was still down, and that was the problem. It would have been easy to let things slide, to believe him when he said things were fine. But there were tense moments, and they usually had to do with money. Ed never suggested they go out, and if Laurie did, Ed didn't let him pay more than half the time, but he kept trying to keep the outings less expensive.

Ed fought with him over groceries too. Before he'd been content to let Laurie bring over things for dinner and fix them, but now if Laurie did it "too often", at least by Ed's standards, he'd object and try to pay for things. It drove Laurie crazy.

"It makes no sense," he complained to Oliver after they'd met with Vicky about the April fundraiser. "I have so much money, and I don't mind helping him. I *like* helping him. It's something that I can actually do this time. Why won't he let me?"

"Because he's a man," Oliver replied, not looking up from the notebook he was poring over.

Laurie glared at him. "Oh, and I'm a woman?"

When Oliver glanced up, his eyes twinkled. "No. You're both men. It makes things very interesting, doesn't it? Now tell me what you think of this lineup. I know Vicky wants it to be only people from the neighborhood, but that's obviously impractical. Do you think she'd accept these performers?"

"But what am I supposed to do to help him?"

"Be creative and clever. And incredibly careful."

It was exhausting, and sometimes Laurie hated it because it felt manipulative, but he soon discovered

Oliver was right. The way to handle Ed's pride over not having a job was to be subtle. He took Ed grocery shopping, and he let Ed pay a significant amount, but he made him buy items that could make meals, not instant noodles and meals in a can, which in the long run of course was more economical. He dialed down the gourmet as well and did much of the cooking. They went out rarely, staying in to watch television or make love.

He recruited Ed to help him at the studio, sometimes with clerical work, sometimes with teaching. Ed had balked at the latter, but Laurie had insisted, because Ed was quite good. And the students loved him, especially the locals. For special treats, they would dance tango for the classes.

"You guys should totally perform at Vicky's big show," Duon remarked one day after class. "You'd show all of us up."

"Oh, I don't think so," Laurie had replied quickly before Ed could say anything else.

Laurie still wasn't speaking to his mother, but he did have the promised dinner with Oliver and his mystery donor coming up. Thankfully it had been moved to March, but he knew there would be no getting out of it. The studio was beginning to come together a little, Maggie had gone from cold rage to stony silence, and the benefit for the center was shaping up nicely. And he was navigating the waters of Ed Maurer's pride quite well, he thought. Things were good. Very good.

Of course, that couldn't last.

It began with cooking. Laurie had set Ed up at the cutting board while he ducked in to take a shower after a long night at the studio. To his surprise, when he came out of the bathroom, Barbra Streisand played on the stereo.

"Barbra again?" Laurie asked as he tucked his robe tighter around his body and accepted the glass of white wine Ed held out for him.

Ed waggled his eyebrows. "I'm trying to get you in the mood."

Laurie couldn't stop the ridiculous grin from breaking out across his face, so he hid it as best he could by taking a sip of the wine. He glanced at the onions and carrots Ed had cut up, however, and frowned.

Ed turned back to his handiwork. "What? Did I do it wrong?"

Laurie took in the variety of onion hunks and minces, the carrots so fat they'd take up half a mouth. "Yes." Then he gasped as Ed grabbed him and pulled him into a rough hug, nearly spilling the wine, but when hands slid over Laurie's naked hips, breaking the robe open, Laurie's knees threatened to buckle. "*Ed.*"

Ed nuzzled the side of Laurie's head. "I want to be inside you."

On the other side of the room, Barbra hit a high note, but Laurie barely heard her for the pounding of blood in his ears. A protest formed in his throat, but it got trapped as Ed's hand found his ass, and Laurie was ready to drop the wine and bend over the counter then and there.

But Ed only pinched his check and withdrew with a wicked grin. "So, I thought you were going to cook dinner?"

Laurie stood there a moment, shaking as Ed slipped away. In fact, Laurie had to put the wine down and grip the counter for several seconds before he remembered to breathe.

"Of course," Ed called from the couch, sounding self-satisfied, "we could order in. Later."

But that smugness was all Laurie needed. He straightened, tightened his robe and cleared his throat. "No. I'm cooking. Right after I get dressed."

He was glad he had, he decided an hour later, as he watched Ed scooping up the last of his soup with the last of the bread. "This is so fucking good," Ed said for what had to be the eighth time. "Jesus, but you can cook."

"Thank you." Laurie ran his finger along Ed's arm languidly, but his heart raced. There was a conversation he'd meant to have with him for a long time, but he kept putting it off, waiting for the right time. Full of food, relaxed and with Barbra Streisand playing in the background, he decided it was time. He took a deep breath, held it a moment to center himself and dove in.

"I want us to move in together."

Ed blinked. "Move in?"

Laurie's finger continued tracing on Ed's arm, belying his nerves. "We practically are living together already. I feel like I'm wasting money paying for the downtown apartment when my whole life is over here." Even with his careful framing, though, he could tell Ed was going to object, so he rushed on with the rest. "We could do it as a trial, if you wanted. I could lease my apartment to someone for a few months if it would make you feel better. But it would be so convenient. And it would make it easier too because you could keep doing what you're doing, working with me and for the center. And maybe when the funding comes through for the grants, maybe Vicky can hire you. Or I can hire you."

"What do you mean, you would hire me?"

"Just that. I would hire you. I thought you could work with the kids. Oliver found this grant. They've had to cut the after-school programs, and I think we should bring them back. You can teach them football. Or run leagues. There's no program like that in St. Paul. Or you could work directly at the center with the grant. You could be the program director for the after-school things, maybe. Or whatever you want. You miss football. You like the kids. This would be the way to have both."

Laurie waited for Ed to say something, but he didn't, and Laurie began to get nervous. "I'm sorry. I should have waited. I hadn't meant to spring all that on you now." He reached for his fork and scraped the dregs of his dinner across his plate. "Forget I said anything."

Ed reached across the table and stilled Laurie's hand. Laurie held his breath, waiting for Ed to agree or to say that he'd try.

Ed didn't. "Laurie, I'm glad you're helping Vicky. And I can tell you're excited about it. But I have to have health insurance."

"But what about the COBRA? With me sharing living expenses, and money from the grant—"

"It won't last forever. And if they don't repeal health care legislation, eventually I can get on a high-risk insurance pool, but it won't be great, and it will be expensive."

Laurie hesitated a moment, then rushed on. "We could register as partners too. Domestic partners. You could use my health insurance. I already checked."

Ed shook his head. "I have to keep looking for a job." He forced a smile. "Anyway. There's something I need to ask you too. I want you to dance with me at Vicky's show."

Now it was Laurie's turn to blink and go rigid. "No. I'm sorry, but no."

"Something simple. Something I won't screw up. I know I suck compared to you and that I'm an embarrassment, but—"

"It's not you. You're not an embarrassment. And you don't suck. It's not you."

"Then why?"

"Can we talk about something else?"

"Sure." Ed picked up his fork.

But the rest of the meal was awkward, and the next few days were worse. Laurie didn't bring up living together or Ed working for him or the center, and Ed didn't bring up the show. But the argument hung like an iron curtain between them, even when they made love. Laurie was frustrated and angry, and he knew Ed was too.

One night they came back to the apartment barely speaking to one another. Once they were inside, Ed tossed his coat onto a chair, grabbed something from the fridge and headed for the bathroom. It was an innocent enough action, but Laurie called out, some censure in his voice, "What are you doing?"

"Getting a beer and taking a bath," Ed declared without turning around, then went into the bathroom and shut the door.

Laurie stared at the closed door for several seconds, fuming as he listened to the water run. He poured himself a glass of wine and slammed pans around as he prepared to cook, making sure the sounds could be heard in the bathroom. It did no good, of course, not for him and not for Ed. He did his best to put his mind on cooking, tried turning on news on the radio and thinking of the world's problems and not his own, but twenty minutes later, when he'd burned the onions and overcooked the pasta, he turned it all off, took a deep breath and headed into the bathroom.

Ed, neck-deep in bubbles, his beer dangling from a hand hanging over the side, didn't even open his eyes. "You're letting out all the warm air."

Laurie shut the door and leaned against it. He did his best to hold on to his rage, to find his anger, but it was difficult, staring at Ed's long, wet body, so strong, so beautiful. So male.

Proud, strong Ed, who didn't want to take help, because that was who he was. At once, Laurie understood, truly understood.

And it depressed and deflated him.

"I'm sorry." Laurie came forward and sat on the closed toilet seat, shoulders slumping.

Ed deflated too. "No, you have nothing to be sorry for. This is all me and my damn pig head." He ran his big toe along the side of the spout, staring at it intently as it slid across the chrome.

"I don't want you to be angry with me."

Ed poked his toe into the square space of the spout's opening. "I don't get why you won't go dancing with me out in public, if it's not that I suck. I mean, you get me all excited about it, say we're going to do it for therapy, and then you won't go out where we can show off?"

Laurie blinked, then frowned. "Wait. You think I'm upset about the show?"

Ed glanced at him, toe still stuck inside the spout like a sort of flesh plug. "You aren't? What the hell *are* you mad about then?"

Exasperation came rushing back. "Living together, obviously. You working with me and Vicky."

"Oh fucking hell." Ed tried to sit up—and discovered his toe was stuck fast. "Shit."

Laurie pressed a hand to Ed's chest and kept him pinned in place, staring at him with intent. He didn't let himself get distracted by how sexy Ed looked all sleek and soaped. "I want to move in with you."

"My toe's stuck, Laur."

"I want to dance with you. I want to dance for your friends, with the students, even your mom. But I don't want to compete anymore." His fingers curled gently over Ed's wet skin. "I don't want to sully dancing with you the way I know competing will."

"What the hell kind of shit were you into, Laurie? Some sort of dancing mafia?"

"Maybe. Or maybe it was me. I took it too seriously. I let it wreck everything." His chest grew tight. "I don't want to wreck this."

Ed stared at Laurie for a long moment. Then he sighed, set aside his bottle of beer, and pulled Laurie into the tub.

Laurie squealed. "Ed, put me *down*."

Ed's toe eventually came out of the tap as Laurie struggled against him, and they sloshed water and bubbles recklessly over the sides of the tub as they fought each other, Laurie shrieking and insisting that this *was not funny,* while Ed laughed and yanked Laurie's shirt over his head. When Ed undid Laurie's jeans and slid his hands under the waistband, though, Laurie began to struggle in a very different way.

"Ed," he rasped, gripping the sides of the tub as he lifted his ass so Ed could pry the soaked denim off his body. "Ed, you're insane."

"Crazy for you, baby," Ed whispered at his ear.

When he had the wet jeans off, Ed tossed them over the side, but when Laurie tried to take off his socks, Ed hauled him to his body and trapped him in place as he reached for the soap. Laurie felt outrage morph quickly into arousal.

"I think you're kind of dirty." Ed nipped at Laurie's ear as he ran the soap down his chest toward his groin. "Let me scrub you clean."

Laurie arched as Ed's soapy hand traveled behind to push between the cleft of his cheeks, and he cried out when Ed worked his way inside. "Oh *God.*"

Ed's finger was slowly fucking him now. "I like watching you come apart, baby. Like to be inside you." He curled his finger and smiled as Laurie moaned. "Yeah. Let me hear you. Let me hear how good this feels to you."

Laurie writhed above his hand as the water lapped over their bodies as first one and then two fingers thrust. He looked down at his chest, seeing the hickey Ed had left the night before on Laurie's left breast.

Ed whispered in Laurie's ear. "Come dance with me, Laurie. Dance at Vic's show with me. We aren't going to fuck this up. We're just going to fuck each other." When Laurie cried out, he bit his ear. "Say yes."

"*Yes.*" Laurie threw his head back and gripped the sides of the tub, undulating against Ed's hand as he began to lose control. "Damn it, yes—"

Ed growled and started to fuck him faster, but before he could lose himself completely, Laurie pushed off of him, flipped over and straddled Ed, wedging him sideways so one knee could have purchase on the bottom of the tub. He braced a hand on Ed's chest and looked him dead in the eye.

"I'm moving in with you, and you're coming to the studio. You're going to help me with the dancing classes, and you're teaching football at the center. Not playing. Teaching. Volunteering for now. Keeping your mind open about a job later if it works out. And you're letting me pay you or at least cover expenses for helping me out." His thumb grazed Ed's nipple. "I'll do what you want, if you do what I want."

Ed looked as if he was struggling to argue against this, but he was also, Laurie noticed, succumbing to sexual torture the same way Laurie had. Eventually he nodded and let his hands slide up Laurie's sides. "Okay."

Laurie took Ed's cock in hand. "Okay, then. That's settled."

Ed hissed as Laurie's wet hand moved over him. "Yeah. All settled."

Laurie tried to line up their cocks and fuck, but there wasn't enough room. After a few minutes of driving each other crazy, they climbed out and took the show to the rug.

They hurried, rasping and giggling to the bed. But Laurie could feel Ed's panic, and he felt the same tension within himself. The feelings didn't go away even once they were both sexually spent.

Still so wet his hair was dripping, Ed pulled a panting Laurie to his chest and arranged them against the pillow.

"I want to dance with you," he whispered into his neck, "because I feel so sexy when I do. So strong. And I want everyone to see. I want everyone to see how amazing I feel with you."

Laurie shook his head and pressed his face into Ed's chest. "I want to move in with you because I want to help take care of you. Because I love you."

Ed sighed and kissed the center of Laurie's forehead. Then he kissed his nose, then his mouth, and Laurie kissed him back. He told him—and himself—without words that it was going to be okay.

DICK AND ANNETTE Maurer lived in the same Cape Cod bungalow they'd lived in since 1972. In many ways the house was a living time capsule, and to be honest, that was the way Ed liked it.

It was especially comforting on days like today, as he came through the narrow entrance of the back door, tossed his coat onto the top stair to the basement and trudged up the five stairs into the tiny kitchen where he could smell dinner simmering on the stove. In the living room, his father sat as always in the sagging recliner, reading the paper, which he put down as Ed's shadow fell over him.

"Look what the cat dragged in. Smelled your mother's sausage from eight blocks away, did you?" He glanced around hopefully. "Where's Laurie?"

"Working late. Where's Mom?" Ed sank onto the arm of the couch and surveyed the room. "Hey, you got a new TV."

"Yep. Old one had a strip of color missing in the middle. I got tired of seeing the Cardinals wearing magenta whenever they passed through. Your mother was messing with something in the bedroom last I heard." He lifted his head and squinted in the direction of the hallway. "Annie, sweetheart, Ed's here."

"Oh, good." Her reply came back muffled. "Ed, honey, help me with this, would you?"

Ed's mother was buried in the closet, trying to reach a bag of clothing on the top shelf. She gave Ed a quick smile before motioning to it. "Could you get that for me? I can't quite grab it. And you know your father and his back."

"Sure." Ed leaned over her for the bag, shifting to the left in an attempt to get a better grip. His mother pressed into the clothes hanging from the hangers, and Ed leaned farther in. He pulled on the plastic of the bag.

He fell sideways into the closet with a sharp gasp as

pain shot down his neck, his arm, his spine, all the way to his right toe.

"*Ed.*" His mother put her hands on his shoulder. "Ed, are you okay?"

"Yeah." But Ed had to shut his eyes and brace his hands on the wall for a minute as the pain subsided. He shook in a sort of aftershock, a tremor he couldn't stop. The fall was over now, but he felt like someone had shot him with a lightning bolt.

"Oh no. Is it your neck? Oh, baby, I'm sorry. I shouldn't have asked you to reach for it."

He righted himself. "I'm fine. I lost my balance, is all."

"Have you been doing your exercises? Laurie?" Annette called toward the living room. "Laurie, honey? Has he been doing his exercises?"

"Laurie's not here," Ed snapped, his temper shorter than he meant it to be. He stuffed his hands into his jean pockets, which hid most of the shaking. "I'm fine, Mom."

She didn't look like she believed him, but she nodded. "I shouldn't have asked you to reach for anything, and I'm sorry."

"*Mom.*"

She waved a hand. "I know, I know. Stop fussing. Well, tell me something good, then. Any news on a new job?"

His father appeared in the doorway. "Annette, stop badgering the boy. You go lay an extra plate for dinner, and we'll clean this up in here."

Annette gave Ed one last look of concern, then kissed both him and her husband on the cheek before disappearing into the hall.

Dick patted Ed on the arm, then groaned as he got on his knees and started piling up the once-folded clothes strewn all over the closet floor. "Come on then. Your bones are younger than mine. Get down here and help an old man."

"You're not old." Ed knelt carefully beside him. "You're only sixty-four."

"Well, I've got the body of an eighty-year-old, feels like." Dick nodded to the plastic bag, which was now almost empty. Ed passed it over without being asked and held it open as his father half-heartedly folded a faded polo and put it inside. "Mother wants these to go to the church auction. She wants to go through the upstairs too."

"I'll come and help tomorrow."

"That'd be welcome." Dick paused. "So long as you're up to it."

Ed hesitated too. His mother's concern had made him indignant, but his father's made him feel hollow. "I am up to it."

"Good. Good. Maybe Laurie can come too."

Reaching for his neck, Ed pushed on the tender muscle. He caught his father watching him, met his eye for a moment, then turned away, lowering his hand.

Dick kept his focus on folding the clothes. "So.

You and the boy are moving in together, are you?"

"I guess so."

"Need any help getting him settled?"

"Laurie insisted on hiring movers. Said he doesn't do heavy lifting. And said I shouldn't either." He sighed. "I don't know, Dad."

"Second thoughts? But I thought you and Laurie did so well together."

"It's not that. It's just—damn it, Dad. He keeps trying to take care of me."

Dick paused with a load of neckties in his hand. "That's what we do for people we love, son."

"But, Dad. I mean, he wants to pay for everything. I know he has the money, but God, I'm already a mess because of my neck. And now I'm unemployed. And he wants to keep me, like I'm some big loser who can't do anything."

His dad put the wad of ties into the top of the bag and rose, groaning a little as he made his way up from his knees. Ed reached for the bag, but his dad's hand came out and caught his arm, staying him.

"I got this old man's body by abusing it for thirty years. They told me a long time ago to stop lifting things, but I was too obstinate and too proud to listen. I wouldn't let friends help. Wouldn't let your mother help. Wouldn't listen to her when she begged me to get a different job. Ignored her when she said she didn't care about the money, that we'd make do. I had my pride, I thought. And I clung to it. You know what that bought me, son? A permanent backache and an indus-trial-sized bottle of Aleve that frankly doesn't do me much good."

Ed thought of his assortment of painkillers and grimaced.

Dick's hand tightened on Ed's arm. "If you need to slow down, you slow down. If you need to let someone help you, if someone is offering, you let them. And if you got to swallow your pride to do it, you swallow. You swallow hard, boy. Because I want better for you than I got. It's too late for me. It isn't for you."

Ed stared at the black garbage bag full of clothes. Damn if he didn't feel shaky all over again. "I don't like it, Dad."

"Oh hell no, you won't like it. Not now, anyway. But you'll learn, son. You'll learn."

"Boys," Annette called from the kitchen. "Dinner's ready."

For a minute, neither of them moved. But eventual-ly Dick sighed and patted Ed on the back. "Come on, son."

Ed waited until his dad was in the hall before he moved. With one eye on the door, he touched his neck tentatively. He held his breath a little as he tilted his head first to one side, then another. Emboldened, he did a small rotation.

He thought of Laurie doing the shopping and the cooking for him. Of Laurie paying for everything. He thought of cleaning out a closet like this someday with

Laurie, of sorting through clothes and odds and ends and things they'd collected together through their lives.

As he followed his father into the hall, his hand remained at his neck, massaging the cord of muscle absently until he came to the kitchen, where he quickly lowered his hand and pasted on a wide, cheerful smile.

WHEN THE DAY finally came to have dinner with his parents and Oliver, Laurie was so worked up he thought he might explode.

They headed over in Laurie's car, but Laurie was nervous, and Ed picked up on it and offered to drive. Halfway across town, Ed slid his hand over Laurie's thigh before claiming his hand. "We don't have to do this."

"We do. Just please don't take my mother personally. She does mean well." He sighed and sank deeper into the seat, but his hand tightened on Ed's.

Oliver was already there when they arrived, and he greeted them on the porch. "Your mother is in the kitchen, slamming around her china. She's already broken three plates." He winked when Laurie blanched. "It will be fine, boy. Why don't the two of you come inside? It's brutally cold out here."

Laurie was pretty sure it was colder in the kitchen, but he came in anyway, tugging Ed along behind him. He didn't see the mystery donor anywhere.

Ed was quiet. He had a decidedly deer-in-the-headlights look about him. Laurie thought of the eight million ways this could all go bad, and he considered, quite seriously, grabbing Ed's hand and pulling him out the door. But Oliver had taken their coats, leading them to the den, where Laurie's father and Oliver's partner sat in a pair of easy chairs, not talking to one another. Albert Parker read the paper, and Christopher studied his fingernails, but when Oliver came in, Chris smiled and reached over his chair to slide his hand up his leg as Oliver came forward. He rose to shake Ed's hand warmly as the two of them were introduced.

Albert rose too and stared at Ed with astonishment. "Maurer. You're Ed Maurer. You played for the Lumberjacks."

Laurie stared, dumbfounded. "You know Ed?"

"Know him? Hell, no. But I was there when he went down. Jesus, I can't believe you're standing here in front of me." He stuck out his hand. "Al Parker."

Ed, surprised but recovering quicker than Laurie, shook Al's hand. "It's a pleasure to meet you, sir."

"I only get to the games occasionally, but I love football. Always have. Went to yours with an old business associate who got us right on the fifty-yard line. You play mean, boy. If I remember, you even tried to get up and play before they tied you onto that stretcher." Laurie's father chuckled and patted Ed enthusiastically on the back. He looked as if he'd opened a fortune cookie and found a hundred dollar bill instead of the trite advice he'd been expecting. "Long drive over here from the city, and it's cold.

You'll want something to drink, I expect. Let's go raid my cabinet."

Al tugged on him, and Ed gave a bemused smile and wave before disappearing toward the study. Laurie turned to Oliver, blinking.

Oliver laughed and settled beside Christopher. "That's one introduction over with."

Laurie felt oddly betrayed but did his best to shake it off. "Where's the donor, Oliver?"

Oliver's smile was strained. "It's only us today, actually." He put his hands in his pockets, looking sheepish. "Christopher and I are the donors. But I wanted you to make peace with your mother."

Laurie couldn't believe this. "You set me up?"

Christopher offered a glass of wine to Laurie. "Have a drink, hon."

A setup. This had all been a setup. Laurie did have a drink—one glass of wine, and then another, and another.

He didn't see Ed again until his mother called them to the table, which was also the first time he saw her at all. She had on her extra-polite face, which meant she was furious.

Laurie's father was still chatting Ed up as they came into the dining room. Why Laurie was so surprised they were getting along, he couldn't say. He hadn't dreamed his father would be so welcoming to his boyfriend. His father was the man who read the newspaper, watched sports and drove the car to dance rehearsal. The man who had never outright shown Laurie his dislike but who had never embraced him, either. Literally. Laurie shook his hand whenever he left the house, and he thought the last time he'd received a hug was when he'd left for resident dance school. Even that had been awkward and forced by his mother.

Now here was Al Parker, bright-eyed and engaged in a way that was almost frightening to Laurie, it was so foreign. He was reliving famous football plays with Ed, apparently, and he couldn't be sure, but he thought he'd heard them making plans to watch football together. Strangest of all, and the most painful, was the way his father touched Ed. Oh, it was casual. Occasional. But it was there, and it was deliberate. Al was enjoying his houseguest for a change, and in a way Laurie wasn't sure he had before. But then, when had they had a sports figure of any stamp for dinner, let alone one who had performed a heroic feat like nearly becoming a quadriplegic?

They sat down to eat. His mother tried to bait Laurie to anger, asking pointed questions about the center and his job and wanting to know how Maggie had taken the news, but he gave her short, flat replies, too busy watching Ed and his father to let her engage him.

Light. There was actually light in his father's eyes. His disinterested, wet noodle of a father wasn't a wet noodle right now. And when Laurie's mother turned the discussion onto Ed, to ask him about his work and make him feel bad for being unemployed, Al embraced this too. Joked about the office environment and all the "damn politics," like the two of them were the only ones in their club.

Did his father not realize this was not Laurie's friend come home from school? That Ed was his boyfriend? His gay boyfriend? He wanted to say, *You know, Dad, I let him fuck me up the ass, and he sucks my cock too. Sometimes we suck each other's cocks at the same time. Were you aware of this?*

But no. His father knew Ed was his boyfriend. His mother would have made sure of that. Which meant it had never been, as Laurie had always quietly assumed, his orientation his father had a problem with. It was Laurie's masculinity—or rather, his lack of it.

"So have you come to your senses and decided you will perform for the benefit?" Caroline asked, and before Laurie could spit a "no" at her, Ed cut off Al and spoke for Laurie, beaming.

"Yeah, we are. So far I think we're doing a tango, but I'm hoping to talk him into doing a few other dances too."

"We?" Caroline repeated, ice dripping from her voice.

Ed frowned at her, confused. "Yeah, we. Laurie and I. For the benefit show for Halcyon Center."

Oliver and Laurie winced in unison as Caroline repeated, "Halcyon Center?"

"Yeah. The benefit Oliver and Laurie are having for Halcyon Center." He glanced at Oliver and then at

Laurie. "Isn't that what you're talking about?"

Caroline let her fork hit the table with a thud and turned to Laurie. "You're performing for that *center*, and you won't perform for me?"

Laurie pushed the food around his plate and didn't meet her gaze.

"I think you should do both, Laur." Ed nudged him gently with his elbow. "What's your mom's benefit for? Is it like ours?"

Laurie swore he could hear the ice hitting the floor around his mother's chair. "The International Children's Benefit Gala, I'm sure, isn't anything like whatever you're doing for the center."

Ed leaned forward to peer around Laurie at Caroline, bracing his forearms on the table. "So how do we get him to agree to these, Caroline? I keep thinking maybe I can get him to do something with me, but I'd rather watch him do one of his solo dances."

Across from Laurie, Oliver covered his mouth with his napkin to hide a smile, but his shoulders shook with his chuckle. Christopher sat back in his chair, dangling his wineglass and enjoying it all.

At the other end of the table, Al stopped cutting his ham and glanced at Ed. "You dance too?"

There was no mistaking the disappointment in his tone.

Ed didn't seem to hear it, though. "Oh, nothing like your son. Jesus, no. But I like the ballroom stuff a lot. I'd do the other, but I don't think I have the grace for it. Not like Laur."

Now they had Oliver's attention. "That would be something to see, the two of you performing. I didn't realize you'd progressed that far. I assumed it was simply flirting."

Ed grinned. "Well, maybe that too. But I think we do okay. I want him to enter a contest with me, but that's going to take some doing. Right now I want to get us somewhere we can show off."

Laurie felt dizzy. He'd come ready to battle his mother, but so far she was the least of his worries. He wanted to go out to the car and lie down until all this went away.

"What about here? Now?" Christopher suggested. "I'd love to see you dance."

"Certainly not," Caroline said in the same moment Laurie replied, "No."

"Not until we've had dessert, at the very least." Oliver turned to Laurie's father. "Albert, Caroline tells me you shifted your investments around. Care to give a few tips?"

Albert, mellowed into business bland, began to explain the complexities of his portfolio, and the rest of the table went back to eating. Except Laurie couldn't. He was so angry, and so…hurt. He didn't know why, and it was making him crazy.

Beneath the table, Ed rested a hand on Laurie's thigh as he leaned over to whisper in his ear. "You're mad. Did I do something?"

Laurie shook his head. "I'm fine."

Ed kept his hand on Laurie's leg and stroked him reassuringly through the rest of the meal.

Afterward, Oliver brought up a dance performance again, and to Laurie's surprise, this time it was Ed who objected.

"Nah, let's save it for later. Not really room in here anyway."

Christopher looked disappointed. "But there's a studio out back. Come on. You have us all curious now."

"Can't." Ed rubbed at his neck and gave an apologetic shrug.

Laurie started to get up. "I'll get your pills. We left them in the car, right?"

Ed stayed him with a hand. "It's okay."

Laurie was ready to argue, because if the pain was bad enough that Ed couldn't dance, it had to be very bad. But when he met his lover's gaze, he read the silent message there and stilled. Ed wasn't in pain, he was lying.

For Laurie.

For whatever reason, that realization tipped Laurie back over the edge. "We'll do it." When Ed started to protest, he squeezed his arm. "Ed's right. People should see how good we are."

Laurie was still nervous, though, and he held Ed's hand all the way out to the studio. He wasn't sure why, exactly, he was doing this. He thought it might be to show up his father, to make him watch his big burly football player dance. He thought he might be thumbing his nose at his mother as well.

But when the others settled along the far wall and he and Ed went out onto the floor together, he realized mostly he was out of sorts and wanted to dance with his partner.

He'd cued up a tango, and after a whispered suggestion to Ed, he simply let go and followed. He heard their audience's gasps—he'd urged a showy start—but after that all he heard was the music. All he felt was the beating of his heart and the heat of Ed's body, the power behind his embrace.

All he knew was the dance.

Only four people watched, but Laurie was glad. When he'd gone down in flames in Toronto, it had been such a mighty, incredible fall, but somehow he knew so much as a slight tumble now would bruise him to the bone. He had no ego left to cage him, no grit or anger at the world, no arrogance to blind him, not anymore. Even this, dancing for his parents, for Oliver and for Christopher, felt too much, too loud, too dangerous, and the fear pushed on him with every step.

But with every step, Ed was there to catch him. Ed led him, Ed bore him up, and no matter how quick the turn or steep the slide, Ed always brought him home.

When the song finished, for a second there was only silence, and Laurie clung to Ed, who clung right back. Then Oliver started to clap, and then Christopher, and then they all were.

Laurie dared to look at them. They were all wide-eyed. They were all moved. Even his mother.

He wasn't sure if that made him feel better or not.

The remainder of the evening was subdued. They made small talk through drinks, and Laurie's mother kissed his cheek as he left with Ed to go home, but not much of their tension had gone despite Oliver's attempt to heal them. He wasn't angry with *her* anymore, exactly, but he was still angry, or at least agitated. If anything, he was worse, and to add insult to injury, he didn't know why.

When they were halfway across town Ed said, "I'm sorry."

Laurie glanced at him, surprised. "For what?"

Ed shrugged. "I don't know. But I can tell I did something."

"You didn't do anything." Laurie stared out the window. "I shouldn't have let Oliver trick me into going. It's him I'm angry at. I think."

"I guess I don't get why you're so mad. I mean, yeah, your mom is kind of intense. But she loves you. I can tell."

"My father certainly loved you." Laurie winced. "I'm sorry. That was uncalled for."

"Is *that* what's wrong? You're mad because your dad liked me? I don't get it. That's not good?"

"He doesn't like *me*. He never has more than two seconds for me. He's embarrassed of me. But he hears you play football, and it doesn't matter that you're gay. You're a god. And as usual, I'm nothing. Just my family's disappointment." Laurie tipped his head back and shut his eyes. "Forget it. I'm being ridiculous. I'm tired and need to go to bed."

But Ed pulled off the road onto the shoulder. He stopped the car, put the hazards on.

Laurie looked around at the cars whizzing by them. "Ed, we can't stop here."

Ed gently caught his chin. The intensity of Ed's gaze made Laurie go still. Ed stroked the sides of Laurie's face as he spoke, never letting his eyes move away. "You aren't a disappointment, Laurie. Not to me."

Emotion filled him without warning, and Laurie turned away. "It's okay," he whispered, but his voice broke.

Ed drew him back. "Listen to me. You aren't a disappointment. Not to me, and not to Oliver. I'm sorry about your dad. I wish I had figured that out. I'm sorry. But, Laurie—God, you have no idea. Here I've been all bent out of shape, feeling like a big heel because you're always having to take care of me."

That made Laurie look up. "But I *like* taking care of you."

"I know, baby. I know." He let his lips rest on Laurie's forehead, then pulled back reluctantly. "You're right. I can't sit here too long."

They drove the rest of the way in silence, but the

atmosphere in the car had changed somehow. Laurie felt agitated, but less hollow. He was more centered as he opened the door to the loft and saw not just Ed's things but his own. *My home,* he thought, trying out the idea. He wasn't set up yet, so it was mostly his mess, but it was real now. He was living here. With Ed.

He sat beside Ed on his own couch as they watched Ed's television, drinking tea from one of his own mugs. He relaxed as Ed's hand stroked his side, but he didn't pay any attention to the program, only thought of dancing with Ed at his parents' house.

You aren't a disappointment to me.

When he lay beside Ed that night, as he curled up beside Ed beneath the blanket—his own blankets, his good, clean sheets—he shut his eyes and let his forehead rest on Ed's chest.

I don't ever want to disappoint you. I want to stay here, like this. Always. I don't want to just take care of you. I want you to take care of me too.

It was less of a plea and more of a revelation. Small, quiet and terrible. He drew a deep breath and let it out on a shudder, sliding his arms around Ed.

Ed kissed his hair. "You okay?"

Laurie nodded. *So long as I'm with you. I'm okay, so long as I'm with you.*

CHAPTER EIGHTEEN

seguir: to follow.

THE WEEKEND BEFORE the benefit at the center, Oliver had Ed and Laurie over for dinner.

Everything for the program was arranged, and at Oliver's insistence, everything would be held at the center. Dinner, catered by a St. Paul restaurant donating both the food and services, would be first, held in the same gymnasium where Laurie led aerobics classes. While volunteers cleared this away and rearranged the seating, Vicky and Laurie would give tours of the center itself and hand out folders containing the propaganda and the financial nitty-gritty of the center's needs, now and in the future. Then would come the program, composed largely of center youth and their families and some of Laurie's classes from both studios, and at the end, the board would work the room over cocktails, trying to secure donations and sponsorships. It was all set up. All arranged. All they had to do was arrive on Saturday afternoon and follow the script.

The dinner, Oliver said, was to congratulate Laurie on his first job well done.

"I'll turn you into a professional philanthropist yet." Oliver poured Laurie a second glass of wine as Christopher put the finishing touches on dinner.

"Now you just need to convince him to perform solo," Christopher called from the kitchen.

"Working on it," Ed replied from the den.

Oliver laughed and clapped Laurie gently on the back as he sighed into his wine. Then he leaned closer.

"A fine, fine young man you have there, Laurence. And I will be doing my damnedest to get the pair of you into the hot tub later."

"*Oliver.*" Laurie blushed like an astonished virgin.

"Oh, come now. I'm not talking about a foursome. But I wouldn't mind seeing your partner's fine form lit by lanterns and glistening with hot, foamy water either."

Laurie took a deeper drink of his wine and went to find solace in Ed.

Ed put an arm around Laurie as he sidled up to him. "Nice place."

Laurie leaned in close to whisper, "Oliver wants to see you naked."

Ed laughed. "Okay, didn't see that coming."

"He wants us to hot tub with them later." Laurie drank more. "He's always been after me to loosen up. I think he sees this as his big chance."

"Well, I surely won't mind." Ed cupped Laurie's ass

and kissed him on the cheek.

Dinner was exquisite, as it always was when Christopher cooked. Christopher was vegetarian, but he promised they wouldn't miss the meat. After snacking on vegetarian tapenade, they had caprese salad and rosemary focaccia, followed by lasagna florentine. They finished with sweet cream over fresh berries for dessert, with some ice wine on the side. By the time it was over, Laurie was full, happy and more than a little tipsy. He accepted the glass of port Oliver handed him but frowned when he noticed Ed refused. And when he thought back on it, he realized Ed hadn't had anything to drink all evening—not alcoholic, anyway.

"Had to take two Vicodin already tonight," Ed confessed when Laurie asked him about it.

Two? It was hell to get Ed to take one, but *two*? And he wasn't giddy and acting drunk, only slightly foggy. Which meant he'd been taking enough narcotics to build up a tolerance. Which meant he'd been hurting. And hadn't said anything.

Laurie put his wine down and gave Ed a severe look.

"It's fine." Ed flattened his lips. "I mean, it's not. I have an appointment with a massage therapist tomorrow and PT the day after. It's nothing though. A bad patch."

"We should take it easy at rehearsals. And you should have told me."

He squeezed Laurie's hand. "I'll be fine. Relax and

enjoy the evening."

He slid his arm around Laurie's shoulders. On the couch opposite, Christopher and Oliver were paired much the same, except Christopher wasn't leaning quite as hard into Oliver, and Oliver's hold was much more slack. Drifting on a haze of alcohol, Laurie watched them idly stroking one another, aware that he and Ed were doing much the same.

Will we be like that when we're their age? Laurie hoped so. He hoped they were even better. He hoped they were together that long. He let his mind drift ahead, imagining wild and crazy things like children and mortgages and vacations. He imagined having a Christmas tree filled with ornaments, each with a story from the year they'd picked it out.

He tried to imagine his professional future, to see himself back on stage, but to be honest, he couldn't see it clearly one way or another. He wanted to be with Ed. However that worked out. If his taking jobs would help make that future more secure, he'd do it. If he had to open another studio, he would. After five months of trying to arrange the perfect benefit for the center, after seeing how little he could personally effect, after realizing that Oliver was right, what mattered was that they had solid backing—for the first time, he acknowledged the center could fail, and he would still be okay. That had simply been a dream to chase. A way to find safekeeping for his happiness.

The real safety was here, in Ed's arms. In the future

they had together. In the love they had for one another.

In the man he'd found within himself, by loving Ed.

Ed's hand strayed down his back to rub Laurie's hip. Across the room, Christopher had assumed a mirror position, and Oliver's hand draped over him in a similar fashion. After a while Laurie noticed if Ed stroked him a certain way, Oliver did the same to his partner. A few beats later it would be Oliver instigating a move that Ed followed. A touch across the hip, up the arm. Cupping the backside. Sliding wickedly close to the groin.

They were playing a game. Oh, Ed and Oliver were still chatting idly, about his work, about the center, about football, which was the real tell because if Oliver could name three positions on a team, Laurie would eat his tap shoes.

Laurie wasn't exactly sure he was ready for this. He wasn't sure he would *ever* be ready, and it was odd to have it happening with Oliver and Christopher. Though he had to admit it felt *especially* thrilling because it was Oliver. It was true, he'd been a rather lackluster godfather when Laurie was a child. Most of his attention had come once Laurie came out to him, and then it had always been teasing him, urging him to embrace his sexuality.

He certainly was embracing it right now.

He made eye contact with Christopher, whose lids were heavy, who was the very appearance of sated sensuality. They smiled quietly at one another. Christopher trailed his hand up Oliver's thigh. Laurie, after a moment's hesitation, did the same. Christopher nuzzled lightly against Oliver's chest. So did Laurie.

Christopher lifted his head and looked up at Oliver, who reached down and stroked his chin. Laurie copied Christopher, and Ed copied Oliver.

Laurie had known it was coming, and he didn't know who had led and who had followed, but the next thing he knew, Ed's mouth came down on his own. Without checking to see what Christopher was doing, Laurie opened his mouth and accepted his lover's kiss.

Part of him panicked. Part of him wanted to back out, and part of him wanted to thank Oliver and Christopher for a lovely evening and go home and finish this in private. But a larger part of him didn't.

He was tired of always performing in the dark.

Laurie shut his eyes and turned into Ed's arms, opening for another drugging kiss, letting Ed taste the wine from his lips. He let Ed's hand stray down his chest, opening a few buttons. His lover's hand brushed the fastenings of his trousers, not undoing, but not hesitating at all as he boldly cupped Laurie's hard and ready cock through the material.

Laurie spread his legs wider and tipped his hips farther into Ed's hand.

Ed never took him any further than a few buttons on his shirt and the unfastening of his fly. He pulled open the panel of his trousers, stroked him through his briefs. His hand splayed against his chest, staying over the top of the material.

Ed made all the love he normally bestowed to Laurie's whole body just to Laurie's mouth. Laurie became less and less aware Oliver and Christopher were watching. The fever built inside him, inside them all. But it never crested, and so Laurie floated further and further away until he wasn't sure where he was, and he certainly didn't care what happened to him.

From far away he heard Oliver say in a husky voice, "Let's take this out to the deck."

Still half in a dream, Laurie followed Ed by the hand across the room and to the sliding doors, his clothes still only half done. The urge to panic fluttered up, but he was so relaxed, so emptied out and calm that the panic wouldn't stick. Yes, this was a little bit scary. But Ed was here. Right then, nothing else seemed to matter.

Oliver and Christopher had turned their deck into what was essentially another room. It had a roof and a carpeted floor and furniture nicer than many people would have in their living rooms. But all three walls were at least half screen, and in the farthest corner stood a large wood-framed hot tub. Lights hung above it, soft lanterns casting a yellow glow over the water. A gauzy curtain had been drawn back and clipped to the side, inviting them to the water. The air out here was cool but not cold. The water steamed, and the lights beneath the surface rippled with the waves, beckoning.

Nerves came on strong as everyone began to undress, implying Laurie should too. He looked at the tub again. All of them? Naked? In there?

I'm not talking about a foursome, Oliver had teased him. Except now the words felt like a lifeline. Because while maybe Laurie could hot tub naked when he was a little drunk, he was quite sure he couldn't ever do ménage, and certainly not with Oliver.

Ed's warm hand slid over his shoulder. "Want to go home?"

Yes. Yes, yes. Except, also… "No."

He undressed. He followed Ed into the water, trying not to see Oliver's half-naked body on the other side of the room, trying not to see Christopher, who was completely undressed. He did notice Ed, who looked wonderful. Beautiful. So strong, so…so Ed. He took in his cock bobbing just above the surface of the water as he stood on the ledge, disappearing as he descended into the center. He ducked down, submerging his chest, and when he came up…

Well. Oliver had been right. Ed, naked and wet and glistening underneath the light, was something to be enjoyed.

Then Ed smiled and held out his hand. Laurie sank gratefully into the water and let Ed pull him to his side.

Oliver was fit for a man of his age, but not well-defined like Ed. Christopher looked almost frail naked, but he had an elegance about him that gave him a delicate beauty all his own. Beneath the water, Ed anchored Laurie's leg over his and stroked his cock, and Laurie stroked him back. There was something freeing about the water, something delicious and wicked about being completely naked with other men all around him. It made him think of the stories of bathhouses in the seventies.

Maybe that was why, despite the vague sense of weirdness of Oliver being present, Laurie enjoyed this. All these years, all this time, he had been so good. Even in New York, he hadn't gone wild. He'd had affairs, but they'd been fraught with difficulty. And the one time he'd tried to let go and be wild with Paul had ended in disaster.

But years of restricting himself further had done nothing to make him happy.

Was he happy right now?

His life had come so unglued in so many ways since he'd met Ed. He thought of Maggie's accusation that this was "all because of Ed." And yet, hadn't he been the one to volunteer at the center? Hadn't he finally said yes to Vicky because he was so tired of his life that almost anything new was worth grasping? Hadn't he gone to that first class nervous and terrified and yet desperate, so desperate to make something, anything work, to find even a shred of happiness and meaning somewhere, anywhere…

Dancing with Ed, moving in with him, giving up the studio to essentially volunteer at the center—it was Toronto all over again, wasn't it? The thought terrified

Laurie, made him feel he was destined for another fall. But then he thought of how lonely he had been before and after Toronto, of how empty he felt when he wasn't leaping into the abyss.

Were those his choices, then? Hollow and empty or fleeting freedom before he crashed and burned?

He trembled, and Ed nuzzled his neck, hands stilling below. "Seriously. We can leave. You don't have to prove anything to me."

Emotion filled him, feelings too primal and complicated to name, and Laurie had to shut his eyes. He was aware of Ed's arms around him, aware of Ed's warmth, his strength and his love. And it struck him—this was the difference. *Ed.* Ed was the difference.

Yes, his choices were to withhold himself or try to fly. Yes, it was wither or burn. Except when he was carried. Except when Ed was there to hold him, to encourage him, to catch him. It was still Laurie's work to do, Laurie's leap. He would have to do it with or without Ed.

There in the dark, naked in Oliver's hot tub, trembling and wrapped in Ed's loving arms, Laurie vowed silently to work as hard as he could for as long as he could to make sure that he leaped with Ed from this day forward.

I don't have to prove anything to Ed. But I have plenty to prove to myself.

"Laurie?" Ed called again.

Laurie turned his head and kissed him. He kissed

him long and fast and deep. When Ed groaned, he thrust into his hand, kissing him with all the gratitude and love and desperation and determination he had inside him, hurling it at Ed. Ed gripped him, aroused, eager, fueling him with his own tidal wave of emotions. Laurie climbed atop of him, and they were thrusting, hot and slick in the water, trying to merge with one another, trying—

Laurie came without warning, a jerk and a cry, and Ed came shortly after.

And then, because of physics, so did their spunk.

It came to the surface in a delay, appearing in little white blobs that merged together and then separated on the surface. As the foam hit it, it merged, breaking up further before being carried away on the bubbles. Though when the foam hit Laurie's chest, he could see the globs of cum were still in some ways quite intact. Glancing at Ed, he saw flecks and globs of white tangling in his chest hair.

"Oh shit," Laurie whispered. The foam kept coming. God, it was a huge, huge mess. And it was in Oliver's hot tub. At this point, the way the foam was rolling, it was probably on Oliver. Laurie winced, blushing as he settled beside Ed. "I'm so sorry."

"Doesn't bother me." Ed kissed him. "I told you. I like your mess."

Christopher, however, looked weary. "It's so hard to clean," he murmured, but Oliver grabbed his chin and kissed him deep.

Laurie thought of flight and fall, of hiding from life and letting it burn, of how different it was with someone to catch you. And as yet more semen-fuzzed bubbles swirled around him, Laurie settled into the mess and into Ed's sheltering arms.

THEY'D REHEARSED THEIR dance for the center benefit for three months.

Despite Ed's insistence it wasn't necessary, Laurie had come with him to several therapy sessions and grilled Tim on what moves were acceptable and what moves were out of bounds as far as Ed's neck was concerned. Ed had grumbled at first, but as he listened to the two of them fire questions back and forth, as they moved his body around like a puppet and discussed physiology and weight and pressure points— well, in some ways he knew more about his injury than he ever had before. He understood, finally, why he could be in so much pain and yet still function up until a certain point, why he could carry anything but lift nothing when his injury was too fired up. He understood some of the oddball pains in his arm too, and why so many of Tim's exercises had been about upper back strengthening.

He had been better about caring for his injury since that session. He had been a fucking angel over it. He'd iced every night after practice. Sometimes he found if he used the TENS unit before he had better movement, so he stocked up on pads and gave the muscles on his neck and up high on his shoulder a good buzzing before they went through their routine.

He'd found some other fun things to do with clips he'd ordered online instead of pads, but that was another story altogether.

The bottom line was he worked extra hard to take care of himself. And in the week before the recital when things had started to turn south, he got aggressive. He rested whenever he could. He had Duon come in and do most of the lifting as he got things set up for the show. While the others worked, he went upstairs and hung out with Vicky, who was, as always, poring over her ledgers.

Ed settled into a chair opposite her desk. "You could hold off until the benefit. Maybe it will take care of everything."

Vicky grimaced and rubbed at her cheek. "Yes, well, I still keep thinking that if I move things around, I wouldn't need their help."

"I thought the board approved everything."

"They did," Vicky admitted. "But we're going to have to accept outside help. And I swore I was never going to do that. I know it's Laurie, and I know Laurie would never betray us, not on purpose but…well, I hate it. That's all. I hate that I need it."

Ed smiled ruefully. "Hear you there."

He did get it, because despite letting Laurie take care of him to a degree, he kept trying to be as independent as possible. And as his savings began to dry up and no other job materialized, Ed tried to take care of his injury instead, to make sure that it at least didn't get in the way.

Ed medicated, and he stretched. He saw a massage therapist three times a week. He did the pool every day. The day before the event he stopped all activity and lay in bed as much as he could. He didn't want anything to go wrong.

Skipping the dress rehearsal, though, had worried Laurie. "Is everything okay?"

"Just making sure I'm rested. So nothing goes wrong."

It had been a good plan. A foolproof plan. Which was why it was so fucking unfair when the day of the benefit came and Ed woke in sharp, screaming pain.

There was no reason for it, none at all. He'd done everything right, fucking babied the neck like crazy, and still this. He told himself it was a fluke, that he could work through it. He took every one of his drugs. But they barely registered. He used cold compresses. Hot compresses. He used the TENS for an hour. Nothing.

He tried ignoring it. He tried pretending nothing was wrong, tried soldiering on as he helped Laurie set up, fought the bite of pain as he sat with Laurie through a rushed and nervous lunch. Laurie was a mess, a ball of nervous energy, and Ed tried to put his own pain aside and steady him.

At six, the guests began to arrive at the center. Ed was backstage with the other performers, swimming in pain. It shafted across his brain, cut across his entire consciousness. And he realized what he had known, deep down, since he'd gotten up that morning.

He was not going to be able to dance today.

The denial, the refusal he'd clung to all day, the determination that he would be bigger than this, that it would not claim him, that pain would not take away his life. As he stood there, watching the able bodies whirr around him, his facade cracked. The truth he had been dodging for almost two years now came home.

The pain wasn't trying to take away his life. The pain was his life.

It was a ridiculous moment in which to mourn. The time to come to terms with his injury was not backstage at a gala event surrounded by family and friends and community members and kids who looked up to him like he was God. This was not a public moment. This was something for the dark. This was for the middle of the night, alone in the cocoon of a bed. This was for a bathtub or a shower, or for the quiet of a chair with the television in the background.

But Ed had run from those opportunities. His pain had tried to talk to him then, but he had run away, had slammed all the doors, had put his fingers in his ears and sung. He'd even manufactured a false sense of acceptance. He'd told himself he was okay.

Though he wondered if there ever was a golden moment of crossover. If the journey of a life with chronic pain was simply finding more and more layers of acceptance, that at best the most constant tether would be that he would never find the bottom, that the bottom had different levels, and no matter how good he tried to be, sometimes he would sink into a hole.

He wanted to shout. He wanted to scream, wanted to make all these happy, well people stop being so fucking happy and try to make them ache with him, to let them know, to show them how fucking unfair it was that this was his day, his big day with Laurie, and now it was going to be gone. He wanted to show them how lucky they were, to make them feel his sorrow too.

More than this, though, he wanted this loss to go away. He wanted his old life back, his life when he could have lifted Laurie up and bench-pressed him over his head with barely a thought. He didn't want the life where he was so weak and unstable he couldn't dance with Laurie, despite working so hard and being so good so this wouldn't happen. He wanted to scream this was unfair, to appeal to God, to anything and anyone, to say he didn't deserve this, to demand a recount, a refund. To get someone to tell him that, yes, this had been a mistake.

But it wasn't a punishment. It wasn't a gift. It simply was. His pain was his life. It wasn't all his life was, not always. But today, despite his best efforts to keep it from being so, was going to be about pain. It was rain on a picnic. It was the blizzard that kept you at home. It was the hailstorm that took out your roof.

It was the pain that would keep him from dancing

his routine with Laurie today. It wasn't about fair or how good or bad he had been. It simply was.

Acceptance, sad and bittersweet and yet oddly calming, wrapped around him. He felt heavy, though. Heavy and tired and sad.

He felt the hands of others on him as they saw his distress, felt their fingers brushing at his tears. He felt Laurie's hand before he saw him, felt his concern. Felt his love.

Ed squeezed his hand and fought through the pain enough to speak. "I'm sorry."

Laurie kissed him and drew him close. "It's okay. It's going to be okay."

No, it wasn't okay yet. But with Laurie beside him, eventually it would be.

CHAPTER NINETEEN

*enganche: hooking, coupling. Follower wraps
leg around the other's leg; leader displaces
follower's feet from inside.*

LAURIE TOOK ED to the emergency room.
Annette fussed, saying she wasn't quite sure that was necessary, but the fact that Ed wasn't arguing with him scared the pants off of Laurie, and so he took him anyway. As he suspected, it came to nothing. There was nothing wrong with Ed's neck, nothing new, anyway. They gave him some heavier painkillers and a steroid because of some swelling, and they sent him home.

Laurie missed the entire benefit, and to be honest, he didn't look back. He assumed they had cancelled the show and that Vicky had run the rest of it. He had no idea, not until the next day when she and Oliver came by the apartment to visit.

Vicky was beaming. "It was a huge success, and the show was great. Probably a bit less polished than if you'd been there, but I think in the end that became part of the charm." She let out an unsteady breath. "And you were right. The donors were wonderful. I really liked them."

"It was quite a success," Oliver agreed. "Without anyone specifically intending it, the quaint clumsiness drove home the need for the funding and for the center itself. Everyone left feeling warm and positive. And the kids were fantastic. When they came out for their performance, they said, 'This one is for Laurie and Ed,' and they gave it their all. Everyone was charmed."

Laurie smiled, but it was weak. "Good."

Vicky glanced toward the bedroom. "How is he?"

Quiet. "Better."

Oliver squeezed his shoulder. "Give him our best."

Ed was up later in the day. They had lunch with his mother, and a few times he even smiled. But he was still tired and very drugged, and before long he went to lie down again.

For Laurie, the time after the center benefit went by in a blur. Ed, though tired, wasn't half as down as he had been, but he still seemed removed, and Laurie couldn't shake the feeling that something in him had broken somehow, that this time there would be no way to fix it.

Vicky's center was saved. Laurie had a new studio, and it was finally doing well. He didn't care about any of it. All he wanted was Ed. He would trade it all, everything he had, to have Ed back.

Then one day he came home and Ed was sitting up in a chair, looking serious. "Hey. I've been waiting for you. There's something I need to say." He motioned to the sofa next to him. "Come and sit."

Laurie moved as if through a fog. *I don't want it to be over. I don't want it to be over.* "How are you feeling?"

Ed shrugged. "To tell you the truth, it's been pretty good all week. Wish it would have gone that way a few Saturdays ago, but what are you gonna do, huh?"

Laurie drew back in surprise. "You haven't hurt all this week?"

Then why are you leaving me?

Ed ran his hand sadly over Laurie's. "I've done a lot of thinking lately. And talking with Linnet and with Tim. I applied for the disability, and I went on the antidepressant a few days ago. About the time I stopped hurting, in fact. They're why I've felt better, I'm sure. And I guess I needed the depression part too, because I feel a lot more myself ever since I started. I look back at the past few months, and I realize…" He sighed. "Well, I realize I've screwed up."

He doesn't need you. That's what he's realized. "You haven't screwed up. You're fine. You've worked so hard, Ed." *So have I. Please don't go.*

"I should have gone on the drug a long time ago. But I was in denial. I wanted something I couldn't have."

"But you *can* have it. *We* can—"

Ed held up his hand. "No, Laur. I know you mean

well, but I have to accept I'm not getting my old body back. That my new body could get worse. That's what I've done the last few weeks, I think. I've been mourning the fact that things have changed. Mourning that I'm not the man I want to be."

"I like the man you are."

"I know. And I love you for that. But I have to do this. And I'm probably not done yet, either. It's just going to take some time."

"You make it sound as if your life is over, and it's not. You can do so much. And Tim said you can get stronger. *Don't give up.*"

"It's not giving up. It's being realistic. You need to understand. I'm not saying I'm done trying to strengthen myself or that I'm going to spend the rest of my life on this couch. Not at all. But what I am done with is waiting for when things are better. I'm done waiting for the pain to be all gone. I'm done trying to keep it at bay."

"But—" Laurie cut himself off this time, too afraid he might cry if he kept going. He didn't even know what to plead for anymore.

Ed went on, still calm and cool. "Tim had a new idea this week. He thinks I'm developing something like fibromyalgia, though he also says that's too simplistic. It's something to do with nerves, though. There isn't technically anything wrong in my neck, not beyond what is already known. But the nerves are misfiring, reading all sensation as pain. When they get ramped up, the more I try to calm them, the more upset they get. I wanted so badly to perform at the benefit, and I fixated on it, and I ramped all the way up to eleven, and my nerves came with me."

"But what does that mean?"

"It explains why the painkillers didn't really work and neither did the steroids, but yet Sunday I was pretty much fine. We're still working on the theory, and he has some weird body awareness technique he's showing me." He shrugged. "But the truth is, he might be wrong. I might have to try this nerve-blocking drug. Or something else entirely. The point is, I think I've finally figured out what it is I need to do with this. I need to make peace with it. Some days I'll accept it and others I'll hate it. Sometimes it's going to get in the way. But sometimes it won't. It is what it is. It's *my life*. I have to accept it as it is." Ed sat in front of Laurie and took his hands. "You need to accept it too, if you're going to be with me."

"Of course I accept it. You think I'm going to leave you because you hurt?"

"No. But you do have to accept my reality. It will probably take us both a while to get there fully. And you might need to mourn too. You're right, it might get better. But what I do know is I need things to change between us."

"What do you need? Whatever you want. I'll do, give you. Ed, I just want to be with you. I promise."

"I'm going to need something a little more solid

than that."

Ed reached into the pocket of his sweatpants, pulled out a small dark box, and Laurie's whole world began to spin.

"Will you make this kind of promise?" Ed opened the box and revealed a pair of slim silver wedding bands. "Will you marry me, Laurie?"

The world spun around and around and around, but in the center of it all was Ed, focused and beautiful. Strong, no matter what his body was doing to him.

Laurie smiled, half-laughed, half-sobbed, and took Ed in his arms. "Yes."

"I want to make it real. I want to go to Iowa, where it's legal. And if we have to, we'll do it again up here when they finally come to their senses in our state. But I need this, Laurie. I don't want to be your roommate. I don't want to be your boyfriend. I don't just want your insurance. I want to be your partner, not for what I can get out of you, but because I want to be with you. I want to be your partner not only in dancing but in life." He took Laurie's face in his hands. "I want to be your husband."

Weeping, Laurie couldn't speak at all. So he answered with a kiss.

THEY TOLD THEIR parents at dinner on Tuesday night.

Laurie cleaned the apartment, made a simple but elegant dinner and invited both sets of parents to come. Annette and Dick were thrilled at the news, as was

Laurie's father in his own way. His mother, as he expected, was polite but cool. But Laurie didn't let it get him down, choosing to focus on the joy of the moment instead.

The next day his mother called him at the studio and insisted he meet her for coffee that afternoon. Laurie agreed reluctantly. This would be her trying to talk him out of it, he supposed. He thought about skipping, but he decided to get it over with. He had her meet him at a coffee shop in St. Paul, though, because he was short on time.

But when he slid into the chair across from his mother at the table, she looked at him and said, without preamble, "I want you to perform at my benefit."

Laurie groaned. "Mother, we've been over this—"

She put her hand over his. "I want you and your fiancé to perform."

This he hadn't seen coming. "It's three days away. You already have a full docket of hired performers." *You hate the idea of me dancing with my partner onstage in front of your friends.*

She waved a hand as if this were all immaterial. "One more act won't be a trouble. And I know for a fact you have something prepared. Something you never got to perform." She lifted her chin. "I want to see it."

Laurie shook his head. "Who are you, and what have you done with my mother?"

She gave him a thin smile. "It *is* odd to see you

dance with a man. It's disarming to see you hold his hand and ease into his body without realizing you're doing it. And yes, I had a vision of how I thought your life would go, and this wasn't it. But I'm not a monster, and despite what you may think, I do love you. All I ever wanted was for you to be happy.

"You were always such a fussy child. Always so exact. You knew what you wanted, and I admired that. I tried to help you. Tried to give you the advantages you deserved. Maybe I pushed you too hard. Maybe I didn't push you enough. Maybe if I had raised you today when being homosexual wasn't so taboo, I would have been more sensitive. I don't know. I honestly thought I was better than most, but I suppose I wasn't, saying that you could be gay but not act on it."

No, that hadn't helped at all. But Laurie kept silent and let her finish.

She fiddled with her napkin as she spoke. "You used to have a light in your eyes, Laurie. You used to tell me how amazing a dancer you would be, and I was so proud of you, of how strong and determined you were. At some point you lost that. And despite what you might think, everything I've done has only been to try and help you get that light back." She sighed, wiped briefly at her eyes. "In the end it turns out the only one who could do that was Ed."

"Mom," Laurie whispered, but then he broke off, too overwhelmed to say more.

She reached across the table and took his hand, giving him a small, almost defeated smile. "Dance at the gala with your partner. Dance and show them. Show them all. Show them none of them beat you. Show them, Laurie." She squeezed his hand. "Show *me*."

The rest of their coffee went by in a sort of daze, and when he went home, Ed asked Laurie what was wrong. Laurie told him what his mother had asked and that he had agreed.

Ed's eyebrows shot up into his hairline. "Holy shit. I mean, that's cool as hell, but, Laur, it's in three days."

"We can do it," Laurie said, convincing himself as much as Ed. Then he glanced at him. "Unless…"

"No. I'm good, I swear. This new treatment Tim has me on is weird, but I think it works." But even as he said this, there was worry in his eyes.

"We can always back out if something goes wrong," Laurie suggested.

Ed kissed his cheek. "Okay."

They rehearsed that night in the apartment as much as they could, and they spent much of the next day revisiting the routine in full. Laurie made a few adjustments in case, keeping the impact on Ed as low as possible.

But on Friday night, once Ed had gone to bed, Laurie lay awake, staring at the ceiling. He was excited to perform with Ed. He really was. But something nagged at him, like there was more he should do. He went over the routine in his head, trying to see what was missing, but he couldn't think of anything.

He drifted into sleep, and he dreamed. Of the routine, rehearsing in his mind. It took on the surreal oddness all dreams did. He and Ed danced on rooftops, on ceilings, across Lake Minnetonka, across fields beside his parents' estate. As the dream came to a close, Ed faded away, and Laurie danced alone, across the sky, up into the stars, out across the whole universe. Danced until his soul flew free, with a fervor that could take him on until the end of time. Dancing with joy. Dancing with his heart.

Dancing alone. Just dancing.

He woke in the center of the bed, drenched in sweat, staring at the ceiling. In the other room Ed hummed softly along to The Black Eyed Peas as he did his physical therapy. But part of Laurie lingered in the dream, and in that moment, alone in the bed with Ed humming in the distance, Laurie knew, finally, what he had to do.

CHAPTER TWENTY

resolucion (resolution): the ending of a set of
tango steps. Does not necessarily end the dance.

ED THOUGHT THERE was something funny about
Laurie as they got ready for his mother's benefit.
For one, he'd disappeared for three hours that morn-
ing. And he seemed out of breath when he returned.

"You're up to something," Ed accused.

Laurie laughed. "Yes." Then he kissed Ed on the
cheek. "Wait and see."

For the center recital they'd had simple costumes,
but for the gala, Laurie had given them both an up-
grade, though to Ed's delight Laurie still wore tights.
Instead of the white T-shirts they'd picked out before,
they were wearing fancy tops with glitter and sequins in
a sassy little dash across the front in colors that com-
plemented one another. They also had glitter streaks
across their faces. Ed had thought it would look like
war paint, and it kind of did, but it was something else
too. It felt like magic.

When they got to the venue—a fancy hotel ballroom with a massive stage constructed at one end—Ed got nervous. Could he really do this? In front of all these people?

Laurie came up behind him and wrapped his arms around his waist before kissing his neck. "You'll be fine."

"It's just…that's a lot of people."

"Two thousand," Laurie said, not sounding concerned.

"You're not nervous at all? You're okay with this?"

"Yes." He nodded across the stage. "Ah. Here comes my mother."

Ed steadied himself. Okay. He could do this. Caroline would introduce them, and then they would go out and take their position, and the music would start…

Oh God.

The room burst into applause, and Ed clutched Laurie's hand, ready to go onto the stage. But then Laurie stood in front of him, blocking his path and smiling.

"We'll dance together in a minute. But first I'm going to dance on my own."

Ed blinked at him. "What?" Laurie's words sank in. "On your *own*? Like, a *performance?*"

Laurie's smile turned into a grin. "Yes."

"There are *two thousand people out there.*"

"I've danced for ten." He squeezed Ed's hand, his eyes lit, his expression eager. "I want to do this. I *need* to do this." He kissed Ed on the cheek. "Wait here. Though if you want to go out front and watch, I'd like that very much."

He stripped out of his shirt, revealing more glitter stripes across his bare chest, and then he strode out onto the stage.

Laurie took the mic from his mother and explained the switch in programming. The crowd burst into applause, and most of them got to their feet. Laurie shooed his mother away and struck a pose in the center of the stage as the lights went down.

Ed hurried out into the audience so he could watch.

The music started. The lights came up. And Laurie danced.

Ed didn't know the song, but it was no Barbra Streisand. It was some kind of pop music, loud and rich, full of swells and synthesizers. But the music didn't matter. It was simply there to fill the air as Laurie performed.

He leaped across the stage. He spun. He danced as Ed had never seen him dance before. He saw hints of all the styles he'd ever seen Laurie teach—ballet, jazz, and some moves from the tango. He saw the moves Laurie taught the kids at the studio. He saw the moves Laurie had done in the dance he'd done for Ed at Christmas. They were all part of the dance now. And they were beautiful.

Laurie was beautiful. He was lithe and graceful and

strong, so strong. His muscles rippled across his naked back and in his tight-clad legs as he sailed through the dance as if it were nothing to him, as if his body had been made for this. And maybe it had. Even without the glitter, there was something magical about watching Laurie dance. The same magic Ed felt when he danced with him, but to watch him this way, to see him perform…

It was more than seeing into Laurie's soul. It was as if, by watching Laurie dance, he could see into all souls. Into the power of the body. Into the aching beauty and thrill of movement. Into the grace and wonder of the human form. When he watched Laurie dance, he believed. In everything.

When the dance ended, the crowd roared. They rose to their feet as one body, and they shouted and cheered and clapped so loud the din hurt Ed's ears. Ed became aware of Caroline standing there, cool and composed as ever, but tears streamed down her face.

In the center of the stage, Laurie stood tall and proud.

"Go to him," Caroline whispered, and pushed Ed forward. He went. He didn't go backstage, took the stairs on the side and went forward to the middle, to where Laurie had turned to greet him, beaming like the sun.

The crowd took their seats and the lights lowered, shifting to the soft tones they'd agreed on for their dance together.

"Ready?" Laurie asked, still smiling.

The opening strains of a tango began, and Ed smiled back as he took Laurie into his embrace. "Ready."

And they danced.

ON THIS DAY

the eleventh of October, in the year twenty eleven
in the beautiful city of Des Moines, Iowa at four
o'clock in the afternoon at the First Unitarian Church
of Des Moines,

Laurence Albert Parker,

son of Albert and Caroline Parker,

and

Edward Howard Maurer,

son of Richard and Annette Maurer,

were joined forever in marriage.
May their future be filled with happiness, and may they
never forget that above all
they should enjoy the dance and always dance together.

Want more Ed and Laurie?

They have cameos in *Lonely Hearts* (see the Love Lessons series below) and will get their own novella in late 2015/early 2016.

Want to make sure you never miss a new release? Sign up for Heidi's newsletter at heidicullinan.com.

Want to check out some of Heidi's other titles? Keep reading!

Thank you for purchasing this title. Your support means a great deal to me, especially in this independent publishing endeavor. If you choose to recommend this to a friend or leave a review, thank you yet again, as this is the most sincere compliment you can give my work.

The Love Lessons Series

Love doesn't come with a syllabus.
College-set new adult LGBT romance

Love Lessons

When virginal, shy Kelly arrives at Hope University, he lands Walter, the charming gay campus Casanova, as a roommate. As Walter sets out to lure Kelly out of his shell, he discovers love is a crash course. To make the grade, he'll have to overcome his own private fear that love was never meant to last.

Also available in audio

Fever Pitch

Giles can't wait to get the hell out of his homophobic hometown, but when his popular, straight-boy summer dalliance appears on campus, memories of hazing threaten his haven. As the semester wears on, their attraction crescendos. But if controlling parents have their way, the music of their love could come to a shattering end.

Also available in audio

Lonely Hearts

As college ends, Baz is at a standstill as his friends are moving on. With loneliness looming, he hooks up with a fellow lonely soul. Elijah isn't used to good things happening to him, much less being the object of a playboy's affections. Yet all signs seem to point toward happily ever after. At least, until the media hounds drag their pasts into the light, and they must find out if they're stronger together…or apart.

Audio coming soon

Cullinan reached inside and pulled out ALL the feelings: fear, guilt, sadness, anticipation, happiness, love, lust, bitterness, loneliness, togetherness, and coming of age.
—The Book Pushers

**More titles coming soon.
Free short on Heidi's website.**

The Minnesota Christmas Series

Falling in love can be snow much fun.

Holiday-themed, small town gay romance

Let It Snow

Frankie's malfunctioning GPS sends him into a blizzard…and the arms of a sexy North Woods lumberjack. Once a high-powered lawyer, Marcus has no interest in a sassy city twink who might as well have stepped directly out of his past. Yet as the snow falls, the deeper they fall in love. Though all they want for Christmas is each other, the gift of forever may be too much to ask.

German translation coming soon

Sleigh Ride

Arthur wants nothing to do with romance, and he certainly doesn't want to play Santa in his mother's library fundraising scheme, or let her set him up with the town's lanky, prissy librarian. Gabriel doesn't want him, either—as a Santa, as a boyfriend, as anyone at all. But as their arguments strike sparks, the sleigh they're trying not to board could jingle them all the way to happily ever after.

Winter Wonderland (*coming soon*)

Paul can't find a boyfriend in Logan—no one except too-young, too-twinky Kyle, who sends him suggestive texts and leaves X-rated snow sculptures on his front porch. Kyle's loved Paul since forever, but Paul comes with baggage. When his family's anti-LGBT crusade spills beyond managing Paul's love life, Kyle and Paul must fight for *everyone's* happily ever after, including their own.

This is a great book for any season, but for Christmas it's truly special. Highly recommended with extra heart.
—USA Today

New series in this story universe coming soon!

The Special Delivery Series

Ride cross-country. Take the casino. Own the stage. Fall in love.

Erotic Gay Contemporary Romance with BDSM Elements

Special Delivery

When a long-haul trucker offers to take Sam out of his small town on a road trip west, he jumps at the chance. Mitch is the star of Sam's X-rated fantasies…but he's not a porn star, he's a real man, with real problems, and a seriously broken heart. On the road, Sam grapples with the meaning of letting go, growing up, and the meaning of love—and that no matter how far he travels, eventually all paths lead home.

German translation coming soon

Double Blind

Down and out in a seedy Las Vegas casino, Ethan has no idea what he's going to do with himself once his last dollar is gone—until Randy whirls into his life with a heart-stealing smile and a poker player's gaze that sees too much. Soon they're both taking risks that not only play fast and loose with the law, but with the biggest prize of all: their hearts.

Tough Love

Chenco Ortiz harbors fierce dreams of being a drag star on a glittering stage, but when leatherman Steve Vance introduces him to the intoxicating world of sadomasochism, he finds a strength in body and mind he's never dreamed to seek—strength enough maybe to save his tortured Papi too.

So romantic that the ending is like a fairy tale…so sexy that your e-reader might catch on fire.
—Joyfully Jay

Two free novellas in this series on Heidi's website

The Roosevelt Series

Normal is just a setting on the dryer.

**Contemporary New Adult LGBT Romance Series
Featuring Characters With Disability**

Carry the Ocean

Jeremey doesn't judge Emmet for his autism. He's too busy judging himself, as are his parents, who don't believe in clinical depression. When his illness reaches a breaking point, Emmet rescues him and brings him to The Roosevelt, a quirky assisted living facility. But before they can trust each other enough to let their friendship turn to love, they must trust that their bond is a healing force, and that love can overcome any obstacle.

Heidi Cullinan continues to amaze with vivid characters who leap from the page into my heart.
—K.A. Mitchell

More books in this series coming soon!

Clockwork Love Series

(coming soon)

Love, adventure and a steaming *good time.*

Alternate History/Steampunk LGBT Romance Series

Clockwork Heart

Cornelius saves an enemy soldier using clockwork parts, knowing he risks hanging for treason. More worrisome, though, is the realization he's falling in love with his patient. Johann never expected to survive his regiment's suicide attack on Calais, much less wake up with mechanical parts. To avoid discovery, he's forced to hide in plain sight as Cornelius's lover—a role Johann finds himself taking to surprisingly well. When a threat is made on Cornelius's life, Johann learns the secret of the device implanted in his chest—a mythical weapon both warring countries would kill to obtain.

The Tucker Springs Series

What you see isn't always what you get.

Contemporary, Small-Town, Multi-Author Romance Series

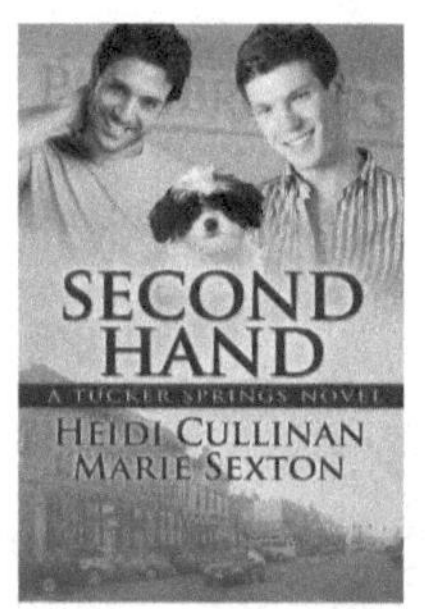

Second Hand (with Marie Sexton)

When Paul tries to find a present to win back his girlfriend, he meets El Rozal, pawnshop owner, and starts to wonder if he truly wants his girlfriend back at all. El doesn't do relationships, but he can't stop inventing excuses to be with Paul, up to and including adopting a dog. Together El and Paul discover that, when it comes to love, second hand doesn't always mean second best.

French translation coming soon

Dirty Laundry

After Denver rescues Adam from frat boys at the Tucker Springs laundromat, thanking Denver turns to hot, hot public sex. Adam loves playing Denver's sexy games but worries how he'll accept Adam's pile of personal neuroses. Funny, because Denver's busy worrying a sexy geek like Adam won't ever want more than a quick fling with a dumb lug like him. The course of true love doesn't always run clean, but sometimes getting dirty is half the fun.

Sizzling hot with that touch of vulnerability
—Under the Covers

Check out the other residents of Tucker Springs.

Contemporary Romance Standalone Titles

Nowhere Ranch

Love will grow through the cracks you leave open.

Roving ranch hand Roe Davis never mixes business with pleasure, but his new boss, Travis Loving, lines up with Roe's kinks like a custom-set rail and makes it clear Roe's days of running away from love are over.

Also available in audio and Italian.
French translation coming soon.

Heidi Cullinan is one of the undisputed queens of scorching gay romance. Long may she reign!
—Christopher Rice, *New York Times* bestselling author

Family Man (with Marie Sexton)

Sometimes family chooses you.

When maybe-I'm-gay Vince ventures into Chicago's Boystown to test the waters, naturally he runs into someone from the neighborhood. Trey has no time to take on anyone else's troubles, but he agrees to help Vinnie figure things out: no promises, and no sex. It seems like a simple plan—until their "no-sex" night turns into the best date of their lives.

Cullinan and Sexton's second collaboration…takes the traditional romantic trope of older experienced man/younger inexperienced woman and turns it on its ear.

—Library Journal

Historical Romance Standalone Titles

A Private Gentleman

To seal their bond, they must break the ties that bind.

It's difficult enough for a stammering noble recluse and a bookish male prostitute to fall in love, but when Lord George Albert Westin finds out his father is the one who sent Michael down his road to ruin, their road to happily ever after becomes even rockier than ever.

Fantasy Standalone Titles

Hero

Heroes don't always come in the shapes you expect.

Los Angeles construction worker Hal Porter doesn't consider himself special, but that doesn't seem to stop anyone from thinking he's the one who can break shifter Morgan's curse.

Miles and the Magic Flute

The forest is full of danger…and delight.

Unemployed Miles Larson returns to his Minnesota hometown to lick his wounds and ends up lost in love and danger in an erotic fairy kingdom that lies just beyond the edge of the door of his friend's pawnshop.

The Devil Will Do

Everyone has a destiny, however humble. Everyone has worth.

In a land unforgiving of indulgent sex, merchantman Eryn does his best to keep his desires in the dark…until the plight of a beautiful prince leads him into dark, dangerous, and sensual adventures. Before Eryn can embrace the affections of his true love, he must conquer the self-loathing he carries in his heart.

About the Author

Heidi Cullinan has always enjoyed a good love story, provided it has a happy ending. Proud to be from the first Midwestern state with full marriage equality, Heidi is a vocal advocate for LGBT rights. She writes positive-outcome romances for LGBT characters struggling against insurmountable odds because she believes there's no such thing as too much happy ever after. When Heidi isn't writing, she enjoys cooking, reading, playing with her cats, and watching television with her family. Find out more about Heidi and sign up for her newsletter at www.heidicullinan.com.